Catherine Fer[illegible]

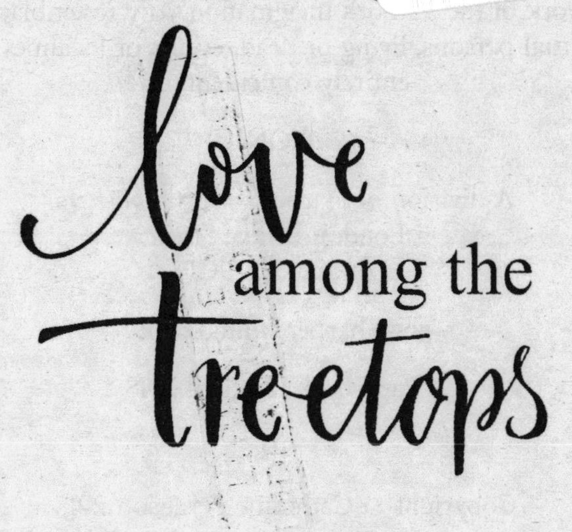

avon.
A division of HarperCollins*Publishers*
www.harpercollins.co.uk

This novel is entirely a work of fiction.
The names, characters and incidents portrayed in it are the work of the author's imagination. Any resemblance to actual persons, living or dead, events or localities is entirely coincidental.

AVON

A division of HarperCollins*Publishers*
1 London Bridge Street,
London SE1 9GF

www.harpercollins.co.uk

A Paperback Original 2018

1

Catherine Ferguson asserts the moral right to be identified as the author of this work

A catalogue record for this book is available from the British Library

ISBN-13: 978-0-00-826208-2

Typeset in Birka by Palimpsest Book Production Ltd, Falkirk, Stirlingshire

Printed and bound by CPI Group (UK) Ltd, Croydon, CR0 4YY

Prologue

They're catching up with me.

I'm trying to run faster but my heart is banging so hard it hurts, and I can't get my breath. And now Lucy's shouting at me to stop or else. She always makes her voice go deeper when she wants to really scare me.

Got to run faster!

The back of my leg stings where one of Lucy's stones just hit me. I can hear her laughing with her big friend, Sophie, that she's going to trip me up and send me flying, then they're going to pull my hair and pinch my arms until I beg them to stop.

Joanna should have been at the school gates. She's my cousin and she's twelve and goes to big school, and sometimes Mum asks her to bring me home. But I waited and Joanna didn't come so I started walking home myself. Mum will be cross if I tell her Joanna wasn't there, so I'm not going to tell her. I don't want Joanna to get into trouble.

Nearly home now!

If Mum's at the kitchen window, peeling the potatoes for dinner or doing the dishes, Lucy and Sophie will slow down and act like they haven't even noticed me. I'll tell Mum that Joanna left me at the end of our street because she's going to her friend Amy's house for tea. Then Mum won't be cross with her.

But Mum's not at the window today and I feel sick. What if she's got the hoover on and doesn't hear me ringing the doorbell?

If I dodge round the corner and take the short cut to the back of my house, I might get there before they catch me. They'd never dare come after me into the garden. I'll be safe there. I can see my treehouse now, sitting high above the fence. A few more steps and I'll be through the garden gate and safe.

But the back gate always sticks. *Please* let it open for me today.

I close my eyes and push myself against it.

Yes!

I run in and slam the gate shut behind me.

Made it!

The ladder up to my treehouse is a little bit wobbly and scary sometimes but Dad says it's perfectly safe. He knows because he made the treehouse for me himself and he's really clever at stuff like that. He does woodwork when he has time off from selling things to farm people in our shop at the bottom of the garden.

I'm so hot. As I climb up into the sky, the whole treehouse seems to sway, the bright green summer leaves sort of shivering as I move.

I'm crouched down on the wooden floorboards now, hidden among the branches, breathing in the lovely cool leafy smells coming in through the slightly open window. I can tell it's been raining because the woody scent seems much sharper and tickles my nose. Dad built the treehouse for me when I was just six. That's a whole year ago now. I'll stay here for a bit so my face isn't red and sweaty when Mum sees me – otherwise she might guess that something bad has happened.

Slowly, I stand up and peep through the big square window, getting ready to duck down if Lucy and Sophie are there. But they're not.

They must have gone!

My eyes are suddenly wet with tears. Lucy Slater is in my class at school and she hates me. She told everyone I smelled like a dustbin and all her friends laughed, so now they call me Stinker Wilson instead of Twilight Wilson, which is my real name.

I feel better now, although my heart is still beating fast and my legs feel funny, like they probably won't work properly if I try to climb back down the ladder. I'll just stay here a bit longer to make sure they've really gone. I could put the kettle on and have a pretend tea party for my dolls. Mum always says a cuppa makes things better.

If Lucy Slater knew I had my dolls up here, she'd think it was really funny and she'd tell everyone in my class. Like the time she told one of her fibs and said I'd had a wee in my pants in the middle of the shopping centre. It wasn't true, but it made my face really hot when everyone pointed at me and laughed.

I know I'm too old, really, to play with dolls. But I like them. They make me remember the time when I didn't have to go to school and see Lucy Slater. I could just play in my treehouse instead. I don't know why Lucy hates me. I gave her sweets once, but she just made a face and said they looked horrible. Then she threw them over the school wall and ran off with Sophie.

I love my dolls because they never laugh at me or say they're going to get me on the way home from school. We just sit here quietly and I pour tea into their cups (it's just water, really) and I tell them what I've been doing at school that day. I don't tell them about the nasty things because that would make them very sad.

Today, I tell them Mum wants me to make the cake for Dad's birthday on Sunday. She's going to let me mix the icing and decorate it and everything!

I'm so lucky to have my treehouse. I think maybe the reason Lucy Slater is angry with me is because her dad didn't make her a treehouse like mine ...

Chapter 1

I'm about to spread snowy white icing onto the perfect fairy cake, before adorning it with a sugary, melt-in-the-mouth pink rose, when a rail official walks into the carriage.

'All tickets, please.'

Pulled from my daydream, I sit up and start scrabbling through my belongings, panicking that I might have lost my ticket. If only I could be more practical and less prone to disappearing into my imagination.

As an only child, I tended to escape into a comforting fantasy world in times of stress, and now – at thirty-two – I'm still a bit of a dreamer, although the days of being bullied at school are thankfully long behind me.

Something tells me I'll have to start being super-practical if I'm going to run a successful café ...

I boarded a train four hours ago in Manchester, where I've been studying at catering college for the past year, then I switched to this local line that will take me to the village of Hart's End in Sussex, where I lived all my childhood. I've spent the time scribbling away in a notebook, composing a list of cakes, scones and tray bakes that will look good on a café menu. There's a price beside each one, although I'm finding it hard to work out what customers would be prepared to pay. That's why the page is full of scorings out and question marks.

Keeping busy like this also means I'm not worrying about Dad all the time.

We're less than an hour away from Hart's End now and my stomach churns constantly as I think about the life-changing steps I'm about to take.

I really need this café to be a success.

Honey Cottage, our family home, will have to be sold if I can't step in and start paying the mortgage on it. With Dad in hospital, undergoing the cancer treatment that Mum and I desperately hope will save his life, the last thing my parents need is to be worrying that they're going to lose their house. So that's where I come in.

Twilight Wilson to the rescue!

My insides shift uneasily. I've always loved baking, but it's a massive leap from turning out my favourite cakes in the warmth of my own kitchen to becoming a successful café owner ...

Finally, I locate my ticket.

The only other passenger in the carriage – a woman who looks about my age, sitting further along, across the aisle – is having to buy her fare, and the rail official is gently reminding her that she really should have bought her ticket on the platform. He shrugs in a friendly way as he says it, and she pats her glamorous blonde up-do and gives him the benefit of a winsomely apologetic smile.

The instant he's gone, the smile vanishes, like a light bulb being switched off. She raises her eyes to the ceiling with a look of contempt and gets back to her sporty-looking magazine.

The train slows down, entering a tunnel, and my reflection appears in the window, staring back at me from the darkness beyond. Fine, strawberry-blonde hair brushing my shoulders, wide-set blue eyes and too-plump lips that I've hated all my life. The rest of me is probably a little on the plump side, too, mainly because I love baking and you can't be a baker and not sample the end results, can you? I'm also fairly short, so every calorie-laden mouthful tends to reveal itself elsewhere.

As a kid, I loved making cakes: experimenting with different flavours and textures. After a bad day at school, I could forget Lucy Slater and lose myself in the supremely soothing world of buttery cake mix, glorious home-baking smells and endless icing possibilities.

Baking is still my passion. It never fails to give me that comforting feeling of old. And I've been taking refuge in it even more lately, with Dad so very ill in hospital.

I hand over my ticket to be stamped. Then I sit back and close my eyes for a moment, allowing myself to be lulled by the gentle rocking movement of the train.

Minutes later, we pull into a station and people flood onto the train.

'Is this seat free?' says a deep voice.

I glance up. A tall man with dark hair and round, Harry Potter glasses is looking down at me quizzically, and I return his smile. 'No, feel free.'

'Thanks.'

He pushes the glasses further up his nose then hefts his sports bag onto the overhead rack. After zipping open the side pocket, he starts feeling around inside it. His pale blue T-shirt hitches up, revealing a glimpse of washboard stomach above long, muscular jean-clad legs. Quickly, I look away, out of the window.

But when he draws out a book and drops it on the table, the temptation to be nosy and read the title upside down is too great.

My brow knots in confusion.

Adventures with Crotches?

Crikey. That's the sort of book to read on a Kindle so no one can actually see the title! He flings himself into the seat opposite me and I'm enveloped in the scent of *eau de sporty man*. It's clear he's been doing an activity of some kind, what with the sports bag and the dark hair that's still damp from activity and curling on his neck.

The frosty blonde, I notice, is casting interested looks over in our direction – well, specifically *his* direction. He is quite attractive, I suppose, apart from the geeky glasses. Not that I'm at all interested. At the ripe old age of thirty-two, I've grown quite cynical about love. Don't get me wrong. I'm sure there are probably lots of men my age who are basically decent, caring human beings. It's just I've never actually met one that I was attracted to. The sad fact is, the guys I've been out with invariably end up being more of a disappointment than anything. And it's not because I'm too picky, either. I suppose I've just been unlucky.

I think of Jason, the love of my life. The man who *first* disappointed me by breaking up with me in order to take up with Lucy (Lucifer) Slater, the horrible bully who tormented me throughout my schooldays. We were just eighteen when we split up, but I truly loved Jason Findlay and I was completely and utterly devastated when it ended. He was the first boy I ever properly kissed. That momentous event happened when I was fifteen, round the back of Hart's End Youth Club, and after that kiss, we were inseparable for a long time. Until I decided to go away to university and Lucy Slater got her claws into him ...

The man opposite shifts in his seat – possibly getting a little over-engrossed in crotches ('gross' being the operative word) – and our legs accidentally collide.

'Sorry,' he says with a lopsided grin. 'I'm having trouble getting my muscles to relax.'

I shake my head. 'Sounds nasty.'

'It is. I've just run a marathon and they ache like crazy.' He shifts them around.

'Ah!'

'I guess I should have started my training earlier.' He grins and goes back to his book which, looking at the cover the right way up, I suddenly realise isn't about crotches at all. My upside-down reading clearly needs some work. The book he's so enthralled by is actually called *Adventures with Crochet*. (Which, to be fair, sets my mind boggling all over again.) There's a colourful crocheted doll on the cover and a jolly border made from one long line of crochet, like I used to make when I was a little girl and Gran taught me.

I observe him curiously beneath my eyelashes. He certainly doesn't *look* like a crochet enthusiast, with his rugby player's body and big hands that would surely be way too clumsy to wield a crochet hook. But appearances can be deceptive. For all I know, he might also be a whiz at macramé and enjoy whipping up the odd summer fruit soufflé in his spare time. It was probably very politically incorrect of me to picture a crochet enthusiast as an elderly lady with a cat curled at her feet. Yes, in fact, good for him!

His brow is tense as if he's concentrating hard. He's obviously a 'metrosexual'. The sort of man who'd feel perfectly at home exhibiting his macaroons in a Women's Institute tent. Although why I should be so curious about someone I don't even–

'Excuse me,' says a slightly breathy voice.

I glance up and so does Mr Needlepoint. The voice belongs to the blonde I spotted earlier.

'Sorry to interrupt, but did I hear you say you'd just run a marathon?' She bats her extensive eyelashes at him.

'Twenty-six miles of hell,' he says cheerfully. 'Usually I enjoy them but today's was tough going for some reason.'

'So you've run marathons before?'

He nods. 'Dozens.'

Her hazel eyes open wide in admiration, and I find myself fascinated by her make-up. Her eyelids are like two perfectly matching mini canvases, artfully brushed with shades of gold, pink and purple, fringed with dark, curled lashes. Mr Needlepoint seems quite taken with them, too.

'Sorry, I should explain.' She sits down next to me in a cloud of flowery perfume, while continuing to completely ignore me. 'I'm Olivia.'

'Theo Steel.' They shake hands and as an afterthought, she turns to me.

'Twilight.' I wait for the reaction. Most people smile in surprise at the unusual name, which is exactly what Olivia does. Her hand feels thin and icy cold. She turns back to Theo.

'So I have a friend who's spearheading a "Get Hart's End Fit!" campaign. I assume you live around here?' She includes me in this query.

I nod. 'My parents live in Hart's End.'

'Lake Heath,' says Theo, naming a neighbouring village a few miles from Hart's End, further along the track.

'Well, my friend wants as many people as possible to take part in a 10k run she's organising for charity.' She gives Theo a coy look. 'And you're obviously *very* fit.'

'Well ... I don't know about that.'

'Oh, but you must be. Running all those marathons.'

'I suppose ...'

'And those lovely, hard muscles must be the result of an awful lot of weight training,' she says, gazing admiringly at his arms.

I want to snicker, she says it so flirtatiously. But Mr Needlepoint seems to be lapping it up.

'So will you do it?' she asks.

He smiles. 'Sure. When is it?'

She gets up. 'I've got some leaflets in my bag.' Returning, she hands him one, then looks doubtfully at me. 'Would *you* be interested?' Her icy gaze slides over me then lingers on my arms and their distinct lack, in my short-sleeved top, of any obvious muscle definition.

I almost laugh out loud. 'Er, I don't think so.' I mean, I'm all for charity fund-raising, but *running when you don't have to*? Isn't that a bit perverse? No, the only exercise I get these days is transporting tins of cake mix from the bench to the oven, and that's quite enough for me, thank you very much!

Her eyes are full of disapproval so I lean closer and murmur in a confidential manner: 'Mind you, I did get on the exercise bike the other day. For a whole forty-five minutes!' I smile modestly. 'Next time, though, I'm going to try making the pedals go round.'

There's an awkward silence as Olivia stares at me in a

bemused fashion, not getting the joke at all, and I feel an embarrassed heat washing up my neck. Thankfully Mr Needlepoint lets out a burst of laughter. At which point Olivia, presumably taking her cue from him, makes her mouth smile as if she's terribly amused, too. Which she quite clearly isn't.

'But listen, Dawn, exercise is *extremely important* to overall fitness,' she says, eyeballing me urgently, as if I'm in danger of keeling over from ill health at any second.

'It's Twilight. And I *have* got stamina,' I tell her confidently.

'Oh?' She frowns, clearly thrown by this unexpected nugget.

'Yes, tons of it.' I once heard my dad telling a neighbour that while my running technique might not be the best, I did at least have great stamina. Admittedly, I was only seven at the time and the race in question was a modest egg and spoon. But for some reason, this idea stuck and has since become part of family folklore. (I imagine my descendants, years from now, being impressed to learn of their great-great-grandmother's quite astonishing reserves of stamina.)

'Right. Good.' Olivia moves swiftly on. 'And obviously clean eating is also absolutely vital to good health. Do you eat clean food?'

I'm a bit taken aback. What on earth is she suggesting? 'Well, I always wash my strawberries.'

Theo laughs, obviously thinking I'm cracking another joke.

Olivia shakes her head. 'No, no, no. I'm talking about a *clean diet*. No processed junk. Just fresh food and preferably raw, whenever possible. Actually, it's not a diet, it's a *lifestyle*. I never touch sugar these days. Or gluten. Or dairy. Ugh!' She gives a little shiver of disgust. 'Clean eating is absolutely the way forward for a healthy mind, body and soul. Wouldn't you agree?' She addresses Mr Needlepoint. Obviously. Because why would a chunky, doughnut-scoffing no-hoper like me have anything interesting to say on the matter?

Theo clears his throat. 'Well, I'm not convinced cutting out whole food groups is necessarily a good idea, but you can't go wrong with plenty of exercise and your five-a-day.' He glances at me for confirmation.

Obligingly, I nod and say the first thing that comes into my head. 'Five-a-day. Absolutely. Wouldn't touch cake with a bargepole.'

There's a flicker of approval in Olivia's eyes – then she lights on my open notebook. 'What's this?' Picking it up, she reads aloud from my list. 'Sultana scones with raspberry jam and whipped cream (extra thick).' She gazes at me in mild alarm then goes back to the list, reading each item in a tone of increasing disbelief. 'Traditional butter cake, layered with white icing and sprinkled with hundreds and thousands. Buttery cherry and coconut cake. Gooey double chocolate fudge cake with a topping of milk chocolate ganache, decorated with chocolate buttons.' She looks as if she's about to faint.

Theo is trying not to grin but failing miserably. I wish this Olivia person would just bugger off. I'm feeling about three inches tall and very guilty, which is ridiculous. It's a café *menu*, for goodness' sake. Not what I'm planning to have for my dinner later.

'Right, well, each to his own, I suppose.' She drops the notebook as if it's contaminated and stands up, brushing imaginary fluff from her impossibly neat rear end. 'Personally, I always carry an emergency salad,' she confides, reaching into her handbag with a satisfied smile. She draws out a small Tupperware box and snaps it open. 'Celery anyone?'

It seems only polite to take some. 'Nice.' I nod, crunching

my bite-sized stick. Actually, I'm not joking. It tastes deliciously fresh.

'Organic,' she says, offering the box to Theo, who declines with a polite smile.

As she leaves, she glances over her shoulder (obviously not at me) and purrs, 'Do phone if you've any questions about the 10k. My number's on the back of the leaflet.'

Theo assures her he certainly will and even gives her a cheerful little wink. I conclude he probably fancies her. And let's face it, it would be a bit rude not to. Olivia is blonde, willowy slim and very pretty. She could be a model.

I bet Theo gets in touch with Olivia, 10k or not. I stare out of the window, wondering why I feel deflated.

The fields and houses rattle past and I think about Mum and Dad in London, facing the biggest hurdle of their lives.

'The trouble with celery,' murmurs Theo suddenly, 'is that it's ninety-five per cent water and one hundred per cent *not pizza*.' I look over and he bestows a wink on me, too, which cheers me up no end.

He gets back to his adventures with crochet and I apply myself with renewed enthusiasm to expanding the list of mouth-watering carbs in my notebook.

But the gentle rocking of the train is dangerously soporific. The words in blue Biro keep blurring into one – 'chocolate honeycomb slice' merging with 'buttery cherry and coconut cake'.

I haven't slept properly for weeks. I've been waking monotonously regularly at some ghastly pre-dawn hour, my brain leaping instantly into worry mode. If I were to close my eyes now, I'd probably end up in Lake Heath, which is the end of the line. I need to stay awake.

In less than half an hour, I'll be alighting at Hart's End Station and walking back into the old family home, with all its familiar nooks and crannies and memories. But with one big difference.

There'll be no Mum to fuss over me and put the kettle on. And no Dad to greet me with one of his big, comforting bear hugs.

A pang of grief hits me.

I wanted to be with them at my aunt's house in London. That's where they're staying while Dad has the pioneering medical treatment that we desperately hope will improve his quality of life. (I try not to dwell on the very best scenario – that the treatment could actually halt the cancer in its tracks and send Dad into remission. I tell myself it would be enough just to have him back to his old, energetic self, able to go fishing and do his wood carving in the man-cave.)

My plan to open a café in Dad's old shop premises means I can't join them in London. Instead, I'm coming home to Hart's End to put my last year in Manchester – training as a pastry chef – to good use.

The advantage of using Dad's empty shop is that it already has planning permission for a café – so that's the plan! Hopefully, if it goes well (and to be honest, that's an 'if' the size of a small continent), I might be able to earn enough money to save my parents having to put Honey Cottage up for sale. It all sounds fairly logical in my calmer moments. But waking in the middle of the night, frantic over my family's uncertain future, the idea just seems pie-in-the-sky ridiculous.

Do people *really* open cafés and make a living from them? I mean, clearly, they do. There are café owners all over the UK who can attest to it – but my worry is this: Am I deluding myself, imagining I can be one of them?

Honestly, I haven't a clue.

But since I can't think of a better idea, then I'm just going to have to go with it. Because Mum and Dad have got quite enough to worry about – in just a few days, Dad starts his treatment – without thinking they're going to lose their lovely home as well. They've lived at Honey Cottage all their married lives and it would break their hearts to leave. Plus, it's always been a secret dream of mine to open a café and spend my days up to my elbows in flour.

It was my love of baking that led to me giving up my public relations job in London a year ago – at the age of thirty-one – and enrolling at catering college in Manchester, with the intention of becoming a pastry chef. And it's also why I've now decided to change direction again and put those baking skills to practical use.

We will not lose the family home!

I lean back my head, my shoulders slumping, finally giving in to exhaustion. I'll close my eyes for just five minutes ...

*****

I'm woken by a giant pig snorting into a microphone.

What the ... ?

My startled gaze falls on Theo. He's still concentrating on his book but there's a suspicious tension about his mouth. He's trying not to smile.

Oh God, the great snuffling pig must have been me. How bloody mortifying.

Theo removes his glasses and rubs his eyes. Then he glances

over and I notice they're an incredible deep blue colour. Quite mesmerising. 'I was just about to wake you up. We're here.' He nods outside as the train glides into Hart's End and comes to a stop by the big, ornate station clock.

Eek!

I grab my notebook and pen, and stuff them into my handbag, along with all my other bits and pieces. To my surprise, Theo appears to be getting off at this stop, too. I follow him along the carriage, noticing Olivia also getting up to leave the train. Theo courteously ushers her out into the aisle in front of him and she says something I can't quite catch and they exchange a smile. I feel like a peeping Tom, intruding on a private moment between them, and a feeling of irritation rises up from nowhere. I wish I was off this damned train and walking up the path to Honey Cottage!

I try to peer round Theo to catch sight of my backpack in the luggage rack at the end of the carriage, but he towers above me, his broad shoulders blocking the view, so I give up.

When I get to the rack, panic sets in because I can't see my backpack at all. Then I realise that someone has dumped their enormous black suitcase on top of my modest-sized bag, squashing it underneath. So then, of course, I have to try and heave the massive monster off, which – ten sweaty seconds later – I'm realising just isn't going to happen. It's stuck. There's probably a dead body in this bloody suitcase, it's so immovable!

The train is going to leave any second!

I need my backpack!

Suddenly, two strong arms are moving me gently but firmly

aside. Dazed, I watch as they proceed to haul the evil black suitcase off the top of the pile. Quickly, I grab my backpack and turn to find Theo sliding the case back onto the rack. Then he guides me firmly towards the doors, leaps down onto the platform, then half-pulls, half-carries me off the train in the nick of time, just as the electronic whistle announces the doors are closing.

As the train moves slowly off, I find myself staring up into Theo Steel's deep blue eyes, still clasped to his powerful chest and trying – with limited success – to get my breathing under control.

'Thank you,' I gasp, and he lets go of me.

'No problem.' He smiles lazily. 'Didn't want you ending up in Lake Heath. It's a long walk back.'

'True.' I turn to hoist the backpack onto my shoulders, which conveniently hides my blushes. 'But didn't you say you live in Lake Heath? Why get off the train one stop early?'

Backpack secured, we start walking towards the station exit. Olivia and her irritatingly pert bottom are sashaying along just a few yards ahead of us and I'm quite certain Theo Steel is taking full advantage of the view. This makes me feel unaccountably cross. Probably because I'm shattered after the long journey.

'I live in Lake Heath but I work in Hart's End,' says Theo. 'I'm a personal trainer at the sports centre there.'

'Oh, right. *Olivia* will be impressed.'

He laughs. 'But you're not.'

'Well, I wouldn't say that. Anyone who can run a marathon then go straight in to work afterwards deserves a medal in my book.'

He shrugs his big shoulders. 'I've just got one client then

I'm off home for a soak.' He grins. 'Five hours in a hot bath should see to the aching muscles.'

'True.' I do a little mini jog to keep up with his long stride, doing my very best *not* to think about Theo Steel stretched out in the bath. *What's wrong with me? I definitely need a lie-down!* 'Epsom salts are good in the bath. Or so I've heard, never having run a marathon.'

'You should come along to the gym. I could put you through your paces.'

'Er ... ooh, I don't think so. Me in a gym would be like a giraffe in Sainsbury's. Just not normal.'

'No?'

'No. It's all those mirrors. Ugh! I mean, I *know* what I look like. I don't need my nose rubbed in it.' I'm wittering on, but I can't seem to help it.

'You look all right to me.'

I glance up and Theo Steel is assessing me with an approving look on his face. I blush as red as a letterbox and can't think of a thing to say. He's just being kind, obviously. We walk along in silence for a moment.

The fact is, I *have* been in a gym. Hasn't everyone? I joined one January along with about twenty-five thousand others determined to make this their year to adopt a healthier lifestyle. I went three times then gave up, mainly because it was winter and far too cold to venture outdoors after work. Which is a pretty pathetic reason, I know.

I give Theo a sneaky sidelong glance. I can't imagine *him* letting the temperature put him off working out.

Finally, we catch up with Olivia, despite my very best efforts not to. (I've already stopped to rummage around for my ticket – which I knew was safely in my jeans pocket –

then wasted more time checking that my backpack was zipped up properly.)

She dazzles Theo with a smile. 'Don't forget the 10k.'

He smiles back. 'I won't.'

She turns to me. 'I could email you the clean diet sheet if you like? And send you some muscle-toning exercises.'

'Er, no, you're all right, thanks,' I say perfectly calmly, while inside I'm literally growling.

Theo is walking along as if he hasn't heard a thing.

'Always remember,' says Olivia, as if she's addressing a classroom of five-year-olds, 'that what you eat in private, you wear in public.' She grips my upper arm and squeezes hard enough to make me yelp. Then she leans closer and says in a loud stage whisper, 'Banish those bingo wings before they really take a hold, Dawn.'

'Twilight,' murmurs Theo and I swing round in surprise and gratitude.

'Right, I'm off to do some courgette shopping,' says Olivia. 'I've just bought this incredibly clever machine that turns them into courgetti!' She gives a mad laugh that would put Mary from *Coronation Street* in the shade. 'Just like spaghetti but none of the *horrible gluten*. And it's so tasty, you'd hardly know!'

She gives a cheery wave and disappears into the supermarket.

'*I'd* know,' I mutter darkly, and Theo Steel grins.

Chapter 2

Walking along the road from the station to Honey Cottage, after saying goodbye to Theo Steel, I'm feeling a confusion of mixed emotions.

On the one hand, this picturesque little village is the place I associate with all the love, happiness and support of growing up with two wonderful parents. I'm an only child and Mum had three miscarriages before she had me, so it was probably inevitable we'd be a really close-knit family unit.

But passing the schools and the shops, jarring memories from schooldays keep punching their way into my head, making me feel queasy.

Like the time Lucy Slater dragged me into the school toilets one break time, with two of her mates, and told me they thought my hairstyle was weird so they were going to flush my head down the loo. I must have been about eight. They did it silently, I suppose thinking they might get caught if they made a noise. I can still recall Lucy's hand forcing me down and the dirty water rushing up my nose and stinging my eyes. And the blind panic I felt, thinking I was going to be drowned. I threw up afterwards, over my shoes, and they all thought this was hilarious.

Usually, the marks didn't show but this time, with my

streaming hair and eyes, it must have been clear to the teachers that something punishable had gone on. But I knew that if I snitched on Lucy, the misery she inflicted would only get far, far worse, so I pretended I'd ducked under the tap for a bet.

The head was obviously concerned enough to phone my parents, though, because I remember when I got home, Mum wanted to know exactly what had happened. I managed to convince her and Dad it was all just a joke. I dreaded them finding out what was going on and marching down to the school, mistakenly thinking they were making life better for me, demanding the bullies be punished.

I thought going to the high school might change things – that Lucy Slater would find other people to pick on. But the sly digs and nasty remarks continued unabated, for a while at least.

And then a boy called Jason Findlay finally turned things around for me.

Jason was a boy in my year, who I'd worshipped from afar for a while, and I finally got talking to him in the library one day. We found we were both huge fans of *The X-Files* and when he told me he thought I looked like Gillian Anderson's Scully, I was floating on air for days afterwards.

He found out about the bullying and he basically told Lucy and her mates to stop tormenting me. And, unbelievably, they did. I couldn't understand it at the time. It seemed amazing that they'd bullied me for so long and then one stern word from Jason and their active dislike turned instantly to indifference.

It was only later that I realised Lucy had a crush on Jason herself and would have done anything he asked her to do.

Anyway, overnight, my life changed. I was dizzily, ecstatically in love for the first time and Jason felt the same way. At fifteen, I was happy and confident at school for the very first time and my grades improved in leaps and bounds – enough to make university a possibility.

I thought Jason and I would be together forever ...

I've tried hard over the years to play down the bullying and put the taunts and the painful attacks behind me. But coming back to Hart's End always makes the dark days of my past loom a hundred times more vividly.

Sometimes I wonder if that will ever really change.

*****

The house feels shivery and bleak without Mum and Dad, so I go around turning on table lamps and radiators to make it cosy – even though it's the middle of May and it won't be dark for a few hours yet.

Then I make a cup of tea and sit in Dad's old armchair, smoothing the arm and trying to look on the bright side. It's going to be fine. The café will be a success and I'll be able to pay off the mortgage arrears so we won't have to sell the house. They don't have a big mortgage, but the illness forced Dad to stop working and close down the business. They lived off savings for a while but for the past few months, they've been sliding slowly into debt.

The treatment he's about to undergo sounds horribly invasive but my dad has always been strong – in body and in spirit. He'll take the discomfort in his stride – I know he will. I try to ignore the nagging little whisper in my head that says, *What if the treatment doesn't work?*

We have to be positive. The doctors wouldn't have recommended Dad for the trial if they didn't think he stood a big chance of benefiting from it, would they?

The bond I have with my dad is special.

When I was little, he'd take me fly fishing, usually right after tea, and we'd sit there, side by side, watching the surface of the river for any slight movement, Dad making me laugh with his daft jokes. (He didn't seem to mind that my giggles probably scared the fish away.)

Fishing as it grew dark was the way to go, Dad said, because fish loved evenings, especially after a hot summer's day spent lazing around. As a child, I loved this image of lazy fish getting their groove on as dusk fell. And of course, whatever we caught, we always returned to the water to swim another day.

Mum used to go fishing with Dad when they first met. I tend to picture it as quite romantic, the two of them sitting together on the river bank, talking about their lives and waiting for a bite – but Mum always laughs and says she was only there for Dad and that, actually, she hated the cold and the wet and all the fishy smells! (Prawns make the best ever bait, according to Dad.) I think Mum was quite glad when he started taking me fishing instead.

When they were thinking of a name for me, Mum joked they should call me Dusk or Twilight because that was the time of day they did a lot of their courting, right there by the river. Even before I arrived in the world, they were apparently patting her swelling tummy and talking to 'Baby Twilight', and the name just stuck.

They're well matched as a couple. Mum is the practical one, while Dad has a more reflective, dreamy nature, like me. I love that he believes in following your dreams, whatever the cost. When I was little and we sat on that riverbank, he'd tell me that life was precious and should be lived to the full. He'd encourage me to smell the rain and feel the wind, and throw my dreams into space to see what came back to me.

It was Dad who first gave me the idea about switching careers and studying to become a pastry chef. When he said it, I laughed, wondering why I hadn't thought of it first. I sometimes think Dad knows me better than I know myself.

He'd always been in great health. Never went to the doctor. His other hobby, apart from the fishing and wood carving, was walking. He and Mum both loved the holidays they spent in the Lake District, getting hot and breathless scaling the peaks and enjoying the panoramic views from the top. At home, when he wasn't busy with the shop, he'd often walk for miles in the country lanes around the village. He was a fit man. Everyone said that. So I didn't have to worry about him.

Then, a month after I started at catering college, Mum phoned to say she'd have to cancel our forthcoming weekend in Amsterdam because Dad was feeling a bit under the weather. I remember thinking it must be a *really* bad dose of cold or flu to make Dad give up a trip to one of his favourite cities. We'd been looking forward to it, all three of us, for ages.

Then came the news that Dad had diabetes.

I was quite shocked because Dad lived such a healthy life. Okay, he usually had the sticky toffee pudding when he and Mum went out for dinner about once a month, but that was hardly sugar overload.

But after the initial bombshell, I got used to the idea. Dad had diabetes, which wasn't good. But it wasn't the end of the world, either.

Then Mum phoned and mentioned he was going into

hospital for more tests, and that was when I started to really worry. If diabetes had been diagnosed, why the need for further tests?

It turned out the diabetes was an underlying symptom of something much more serious.

Mum very rarely cried. But that night, when I took the train back to Sussex and Dad was in bed, too exhausted from the effects of the cancer to even stay up to greet me, we clung to each other and she sobbed her heart out.

Now, the only thing keeping us all going is the thought that this revolutionary new treatment will somehow make a difference. His age – fifty-nine – meant it was touch and go whether he would even be accepted on the trial, but their lovely GP was adamant he was a good candidate for the treatment. The day we heard it was full steam ahead – two months ago, in March – we cracked open a bottle of champagne Mum had been saving for their anniversary, and even Dad managed a glass.

Dad's sister, my Auntie June, lives in North London, so hers was the obvious place for them to stay while Dad underwent his three months of treatment.

But their financial situation was becoming more urgent by the day. Dad had closed the business three months earlier, finally accepting he wasn't well enough to continue working. It broke my heart when he had to sell off his stock just to continue paying the mortgage.

And now it's up to me to save Honey Cottage.

The pressure makes me feel as if I'm carrying a boulder on my shoulders. I know Dad feels utterly useless, not being able to work and provide for them, and that can't be good for his health.

So it's up to me to take the load off his shoulders.

Whatever happens, I can't let my lovely dad down ...

The phone rings and it's Mum. 'We're just back from our appointment with the consultant,' she says, 'so I thought I'd ring. Make sure you'd settled in.'

'I'm fine, Mum. What about you? Both of you?'

'Us? Oh, yes, we're okay, Twilly love. And listen, your dad thinks what you're doing is *wonderful*. Coming back home to open a café.' She lowers her voice. I assume Dad must be somewhere in earshot. 'He hates the thought of that shop unit of his lying empty. It makes him feel completely useless, bless him. So when I told him the news that you wanted to do something with the space, it brought the biggest smile I've seen on his face in weeks. He's so proud of you, love.'

A lump rises in my throat, making it painful to swallow. 'I'm really glad, Mum. Tell him I'm going to do my best to make it work.'

'Yes, but are you sure that's what you really want to do? You were halfway through your pastry course and you seemed to be loving it.'

'I was. And I'll finish the course some time in the future.'

'Have you talked to your tutors? Have they said you can do that?'

'Yes, Mum. Honestly. It's fine.'

'Well, just as long as you're *sure*.'

I smile. Mum's the worrier: the sensible one. She always has been. Dad is the adventurer: the risk-taker. Mum manages for the most part to keep his feet on the ground. They complement each other perfectly. I've always regarded their relationship as something to aspire to, although so far, I've failed spectacularly in my quest to find a member of the opposite sex to share that same magical togetherness with. Perhaps I'll just get a rabbit instead.

'Betty and Doreen will definitely be regular customers at your café,' Mum's saying, referring to her two best friends in the village. 'You know how they love their cream teas. And I'll get the Women's Institute on side as well.'

'Great! Thanks, Mum.'

She sighs. 'Well, we're all in this together, aren't we, love?'

'Yes, we are.' My heart feels heavy. I appreciate Mum's support but it's going to take a lot more than Mum's best friends, and Winnie and Rose from the WI to make this venture a success! I'll need to get word out to all of Hart's End and the surrounding villages, too. And I'll have to attract the passing tourist trade – but how do I do that? I'll need some signage, directing potential customers from the main through-road into our quiet cul-de-sac. Fortunately, it's the beginning of May so the holiday season is only just starting ...

Oh God, am I completely deluding myself, thinking I can actually pull this off?

'Are you still there, love?'

'Yes. Sorry. I was just – thinking. About the café.'

'Ah, yes. We've been trying to come up with a good name for it. I was thinking, "The Twilight Café".'

'Mum, that's perfect!'

'Do you think so? Oh, it's such a tonic, talking to you, love.'

'You, too.' I pause. 'How's Dad feeling?' There's always an element of fear in the question these days.

'Your dad? Oh, yes. According to him, he'll be back in his garden by the autumn. He's got great plans to pull out the hedge and build a rockery with a pond and a waterfall, no less!'

'That's great, Mum.' I'm gripping my phone really tightly. 'Honestly, if anyone can get through these next few months, it's Dad with his positive attitude. 'Everything's going to be fine, I'm sure of it.'

There's a tiny pause and my heart lurches into my throat.

'Of course it is, love.' Mum's forced cheeriness is like a stab in the heart. 'We'll be home and fighting fit by Christmas. You can count on it!'

Chapter 3

At eleven, I switch off the TV and head upstairs to my old room with the single bed and the complete works of J. K. Rowling dominating the bookshelves.

The house phone rings by the bed and I dive on it, knowing who it will be. No one else would call so late and expect me to answer.

It's my old school friend, Paloma, who's been in a state of high excitement ever since I phoned to tell her I was coming back to live in Hart's End. Paloma always cheers me up, and we've been the best of friends ever since the day I discovered she was using the same trick as me to get out of PE at school – faking a twisted ankle. We both got away with it and spent the rest of the day trying to outdo each other on the hobbling front and escaping to the loos to squeal with laughter.

'You've arrived!' she cheers. 'When can I come round?'

I laugh. 'Not now. And not because I don't want to see you, but because I'm planning on being fast asleep in about – ooh – three minutes.'

Paloma is very much a night owl, still full of life in the late evening when most people are drifting off in front of the TV. (Mornings, she resembles a creature from the deep. Silent but scary.)

'I didn't mean *tonight*. You must be absolutely shattered. How was your journey? Boring, I imagine.'

A memory flashes into my head. Theo making his comment about celery being one hundred per cent *not* pizza and winking at me.

'Actually, no, it was okay,' I muse. 'There was this bloke called Theo who helped me off with my case. Otherwise I'd have missed the stop.'

'Theo, eh? Tell me more.'

Her tone is loaded with innuendo and heat floods into my cheeks. 'Nothing to tell. He's just ... um ... nice.'

'Nice? Is that all?'

'And quirky. He was reading a book about crochet.'

She laughs. 'He sounds fascinating. And how's your dad?'

'Oh, you know. Putting on a brave face, I think. They both are,' I say, relieved she's dropped the subject of Theo.

'Your dad is just the best. Remember he used to cut sticks of rhubarb from the garden and give us a little bag of sugar each to dip it in? We must have been about ten.' She sighs. 'Those were the days.'

I laugh. 'Yeah, and when you crunched it, you felt like you were stripping the enamel off your teeth. And if you ate too much you were awake all night with a sore stomach. Those "good old days" had a lot to answer for!'

Paloma gets quite sentimental over her childhood, but as my own memories tend to feature a lot of Lucy Slater in a starring role, I much prefer to look to the future.

We decide to meet for brunch at eleven, and I switch off the light, feeling so much better for having spoken to her. Coming back to Hart's End alone, without Paloma in my corner, would have been a whole lot more difficult ...

Paloma was there for me through my darkest days at school. She made me laugh through my tears and even squared up to Lucy sometimes on my behalf, although I knew she hated fighting – was against it on principle. She's much more resilient than me. Refuses to let anything get her down. And it's not as if her own childhood was exactly a walk in the park, either.

Born in Hart's End, she was given away at birth and moved soon after, with her new family, to Scotland. But her adoptive dad, Bill, died when Paloma was only six, and her heartbroken mum, Linda, decided to move them both back to the familiar surroundings of Hart's End. Then, last year, Linda – who Paloma adored – died after a short battle with breast cancer.

I came back to Hart's End for the funeral, then offered to stay on a few days to help Paloma clear out her mum's house because I knew she had no relatives to rely on. But she wanted to do it herself. It would help her draw one phase of her life to a close, ready to start the next, she explained. There was something about the calm, logical way she said it that made me uneasy, but I told myself people coped with bereavement in all sorts of different ways.

Then something happened that made me realise Paloma was far from okay.

Six months after Linda's death, she had what I later realised was a sort of breakdown.

I was at her flat one morning when the doorbell rang, and listening from the living room, I gathered it was one of her female clients. After a minute, Paloma's voice started to rise and to my alarm, I heard her shout, 'And *never* come to my home with your *stupid questions*!' before slamming the door.

I rushed to the window. The poor, bemused woman was hurrying away as if a psychopath was after her.

When I questioned Paloma, she insisted she was in the right. The woman shouldn't have come to her flat, no matter how urgent the matter was and however many emails were bouncing right back to her. I asked her if she'd managed to get a new broadband provider (she'd thrown the router at the wall in a fit of annoyance over a weak signal a few days before). She hadn't.

Retreating to the kitchen, I put the kettle on and stood there worrying about how to help my best friend. With no email contact, it was no wonder the poor client felt she had no option but to pay Paloma a visit in person to discuss her account. But Paloma wasn't thinking clearly. She was missing Linda so much but refusing to give in to the feeling and actually grieve for her mum.

The next day – a warm and sunny Saturday in early August – I told Paloma we were going on a mystery tour, down to the south coast, and I took her to Bournemouth, where she'd spent many happy holidays with Linda in a little B&B there called The Bay View Guest House. I was nervous about how she'd react. But when she realised where we were heading, she fell silent, staring out at scenery that must have been heart-breakingly familiar.

We sat on the sand and shared the picnic I'd brought, and I could tell she was growing emotional because she kept losing track of the conversation and staring out to sea, a wistful look on her face. The memories, I could tell, were flooding back.

In the end, her shoulders started to shake, and she dropped her head on her knees and wept for the mother she'd lost. We sat there for a long time, my own throat hurting in empathy with her sobs, as I rubbed her back gently from time to time.

At last, she stopped crying and looked up at me with red, swollen eyes and asked if I had a hanky.

'No, but you can use my sleeve if you like,' I joked, and was rewarded with a watery smile.

She gave a giant sniff and lifted her T-shirt to dab her eyes. 'I need something to drink.'

I dug in the bag for the flask of coffee and started unscrewing the lid.

She shook her head. 'I want to get plastered.'

So we gathered our things and went to the nearest pub as the light was fading and drank far too much for our own good. Then we walked back to the beach, arm in arm (mainly because we'd have fallen down otherwise), kicked off our shoes and went for a paddle in the sea, which we both found hysterically funny.

Next day, over breakfast at The Bay View Guest House, Paloma was subdued. But she talked a bit about Linda and the fun times they'd had in Bournemouth. And when we were leaving, before she got into the car, she stared out across the blue sea that glittered with diamonds in the sunshine, and said softly, 'I miss you so much, Mum.'

On the journey home, she said the first thing she was going to do when she got back was telephone her client and apologise for her outburst.

That's when I knew Paloma was going to be all right ...

Chapter 4

'Use the pulley! Go on, *please*. For old times' sake.'

It's the following day – a sunny morning in early May – and we're in the garden of Honey Cottage, Paloma beaming down at me from the open window of the treehouse.

She lowers the basket on a string, a remnant from when we were kids, and I plonk the box of freshly baked cookies inside, along with the two portable coffees I've made. Then I stand back, arms folded, grinning as she makes a big ceremony of hauling up the goodies.

'Double chocolate chip?' she calls, rescuing the coffees then pulling off the cookie box lid. 'Gorgeous. You can charge a fortune for these in your café.' She waves one around and starts munching.

'I'll be charging what they're worth, no more,' I call back, climbing Dad's home-made ladder. 'Otherwise the customers won't return. If they come at all.'

'If you build it, they will come,' she quotes from the movie *Field of Dreams*.

'I don't have to build it. It's already there,' I call up to her. 'And I'm not sure my café will be in the same league as a magic baseball stadium and a delicious Kevin Costner in his much younger days.'

She laughs. 'Well, maybe. But I bet he didn't sell the best strawberry and dark chocolate shortcake this side of the English Channel. Which yours will be, of course.'

Smiling, I clamber up onto the treehouse platform. Paloma has always been the biggest fan of my baking, ever since we were kids and I discovered how to make tray bakes based on melted Mars Bars. She and Dad are both convinced this café venture of mine can't fail.

I walk round to the door on the other side of the platform, feeling the usual heady rush of being high off the ground, among the rustling treetops.

Dad built the structure out of green oak because it rarely rots and the timbers it produces are really strong. The result is that it's weathered the storms perfectly, the exposed wood on the outside turning a lovely silvery grey over the years, which only adds to its charms. The wooden ladder was made to look rustic but actually it's incredibly solid, leading up to the broad platform, which appears to be magically suspended among the trees. If you look closer, you can see that the structure of the house is held firmly in place by three solid oak trees, one of them rising right up through the centre of the space.

You enter the house by a small but perfectly formed door, with three carved hearts fixed to the front. Dad used cherry wood for these. The door, which has a cute, fairy-tale quality about it, was the perfect height for a ten-year-old, but now, as adults, we have to duck a little to get in.

Paloma comes out and joins me on the wooden verandah and we lean on the sturdy rail and look down towards Dad's old country store, visible over the fence at the bottom of the garden. It's the building I'm crossing my fingers will soon house a busy and successful café.

Dad built his business premises on a plot of land adjacent to ours and people came from miles around to buy their farm supplies, pet paraphernalia and waxed jackets. On dry days, he'd have all sorts of interesting objects for sale, laid out on benches and racks outside the store like a colourful market, enticing people to come and browse.

The building lies stark and empty now.

Every time I catch sight of it – just a characterless box, the front doors bolted and padlocked – my heart twists. It's a constant reminder that Dad's no longer there, whistling cheerfully as he unpacks deliveries, arranging the displays and going out to greet customers, most of whom he'd known for years.

'I don't know,' I murmur, full of doubt. 'Do you really think I can turn that uninspiring building into a thriving coffee stop for locals and tourists?'

'Yes, of course you can. With my creative help, of course.'

I turn and smile at her. 'I'm counting on it.'

Paloma is a graphic designer. She's self-employed and works from her home in a block of modern flats on the edge of the village. The fact that she can work hours to suit herself is a big plus, and she will often still be up at three in the morning, finishing a project. I don't think Paloma would last a month if she had to be at an office every weekday for nine a.m. sharp.

'We can source tables, chairs and lovely old china from car boot sales and charity shops,' she's saying. 'And lots of rugs and wall hangings to make it look cheerful and cosy. It's a perfect size – not too cavernous, but still big enough for about fifteen tables. It's going to look great by the time we've finished!'

'I hope so.'

'We could get *Theo* to crochet some placemats,' she adds, giving me an arch look.

'Oh, ha ha!' I blush stupidly once again. Why on earth did I even *mention* the guy?

We bring out some big patchwork cushions and sit on the verandah with our coffee and cookies, the sun filtering through the canopy of leaves around us, dappling our faces.

'I've missed this.' I set down my cup and stretch luxuriously. 'Gossiping with my best mate in the treehouse. I think we solved all our teenage problems up here.'

She laughs. 'And plotted revenge on a certain Lucy Slater that we never, ever carried out. We were wimps in those days.'

My insides shift uneasily. *Lucy Slater*. It's strange how just the mention of those times is enough to cast a shadow over the day.

Paloma sees my face. 'Hey, you're not worrying about *her*, are you? She's just someone from the past who can have no effect whatsoever on you in the here and now.'

I shrug it off. 'I know.'

'And anyway, she's changed. When I bumped into her a couple of months ago, she actually asked after you.'

'*Really*?'

Paloma nods. 'And when I told her you were coming back to turn your dad's shop into a café, she couldn't have been more pleased for you.'

I stare at her in horror. 'You told Lucy Slater my plans?'

Paloma looks crestfallen. 'Oh, God, sorry, me and my big mouth. I should have kept it to myself, shouldn't I? It's just I thought it was common knowledge, what with your mum talking about it in the village and at the WI ...'

'No, it's fine, honestly,' I rush to reassure her. 'It's my

problem, not yours. I shouldn't be so touchy about Lucy.'

'Well, I still shouldn't have told her. But she has changed quite a lot. Actually, she's become quite the pillar of society.'

'Yeah, right.' I can't keep the scorn from my voice.

Paloma grins. 'Well, okay, I probably wouldn't go that far. But at least she's a bitch with a heart now.'

I swallow. 'What about her and Jason?'

'They seem ... okay.' She frowns and I can tell she's choosing her words carefully, not wanting to upset me. Not that I would be. Jason and I are history.

I grin. 'Are they still the Posh and Becks of Hart's End, then?'

'Oh, yes. They live in a huge house by the river now.' Her mouth quirks humorously. 'Thanks to rich Daddy's desire to spoil his darling daughter. And they both drive top-of-the-range Jaguars.'

'Courtesy of Lucy's dad again, no doubt.'

'Yeah, Jason certainly fell on his feet joining the Slater dynasty. He's director of IT now, apparently. A real rising star in Lucy's dad's business.'

'I don't suppose Lucy has to work, then.'

Paloma shakes her head. 'She did try to set up an on-line fashion retail business, but it didn't take off.' She grins. 'Her designs were ridiculous. Far too whacky for us common folk to wear.'

'And she's a pillar of society?' I can't help a slight sneer.

Paloma grins. 'Sort of. She's started raising money through charity events for this poor little kid who needs to go to America for life-saving treatment.'

I almost laugh, it seems so unlikely.

School bully Lucy Slater? Doing something good for others?

It flashes through my head that maybe she's doing it to atone for all her past actions.

I wasn't Lucy's only victim. There was a girl in the year below me whose parents removed her from the school because she was so unhappy. Everyone knew it was because Lucy Slater had taken a dislike to her and made her life hell.

'I know. Amazing, isn't it?' Paloma shakes her head as if she can't believe it either. 'Anyway, as part of her fund-raising effort, she's organised a little class reunion in the back room of The Three Blackbirds, with a buffet and a fashion show.'

My stomach turns over. I don't like the sound of this at all. Surely Paloma's not expecting *me* to— ?

'Everyone's been asking if you'll be there.'

'And what have you told them?'

She looks sheepish. 'I said you would be. Sorry.'

'So when is it?' A feeling of dread is already building at the thought of seeing Lucy again.

Paloma grimaces. 'Tomorrow night?'

'You're *joking*!' Hot tears prick my eyes and Paloma's guilty look switches to alarm. 'So I haven't even got any time to prepare for it?'

'Hey, it's okay.' She links an arm through mine and squeezes. 'It'll be fine. I'll be right beside you and if Lucifer bloody Slater puts one dainty size four out of line, she'll have *me* to answer to. I promise. I can't even rule out a good old-fashioned, pierced-ear-ripping scrap.'

She nudges me, and I smile through my tears, feeling a bit stupid now. I'm not seven any more. Of *course* I don't need Paloma's protection!

'Did you say a fashion show?' I frown.

'Yeah, I think Lucy still fancies herself as a bit of a Vivienne

Westwood.' Paloma grins. 'I don't think she ever forgave you for winning that school competition to design a ball gown for Princess Diana.'

'Oh, yes. That was in first school.' A memory flashes into my head. I was so pleased when the teacher announced to the class that I'd won, but then Lucy – who was runner-up – followed me home with her mates, jeering and laughing at me, making damned certain I paid the price for winning.

'Your ball gown entry was really dreamy,' says Paloma. 'A pink fairy-tale dress with a crystal-studded bodice.'

'Gosh, I'd forgotten about that. My memory isn't as good as yours.' *Except for recalling the bullying. It's funny how I can remember every single detail of that.*

A little later, when Paloma is leaving to get back to work, she gives me a stern look. 'See you tomorrow night?'

I swallow. 'Do I have to?'

'Yes. You do. You'll see lots of people you actually like, who've been asking after you and are looking forward to seeing you. You'll enjoy it. You'll see Zoe and Diana.'

'I suppose.' Zoe and Diana were my other good friends at school. It will be great to catch up with them.

'And anyway, I'm not going without you. Toodle-oo.'

I wave her off, close the front door, then lean back against it, suddenly exhausted. I can't believe that all these years later, I still get a sick feeling in the pit of my stomach at the mention of Lucy Slater. But perhaps if I make myself go along tomorrow night, I'll be able to lay the ghost to rest.

Paloma's right. People change. Of *course* Lucy won't be the same nasty bully of old.

Growing up was hard for everyone, slaves as we were to our unpredictable hormones. We were all trying to work out who we were and, naturally, that resulted in certain kids lording it over the rest of us.

But school bullies don't stay bullies forever. They grow up. Get older and wiser and regret their teenage behaviour.

Don't they?

Chapter 5

'I'll go in the pub on *one condition*.' I glare at Paloma, as if it's entirely her fault that I have to psych myself up to brave the class reunion.

We're perched on the car park wall round the back of The Three Blackbirds. Inside the pub, Lucy's charity event is presumably already under way.

'And the condition is?' Paloma folds her arms and eyeballs me kindly. She's being incredibly patient, considering we've been lurking here for the past ten minutes while I decide if I want to go in or not.

I hate myself for being such a cowardy custard, but I can't seem to help it.

I narrow my eyes and mutter, 'If skanky Lucy Slater looks at me in any way weirdly, I'm out of there immediately, no questions asked. Okay?'

Paloma nods. 'Okay. And I'll be right behind you. I promise.'

Attempting a smile, I jump down from the wall and brush imaginary leaf mould off my black trousers, impatience with myself resulting in me slapping my bum much harder than strictly necessary. I'm aware I must seem ridiculously neurotic, but I guess that's the effect ten years of dodging a nasty bully like her will have on a person.

'All set?' asks Paloma. 'Look, we don't need to stay long.'

I brush off her concern. 'It's fine. Come on. Let's go in.'

We walk through the bar to the function room at the back. And – oh joy of joys! – Lucy Slater herself is waiting in the doorway to greet us, along with another girl who I vaguely recognise.

'Hello! How lovely to see you both,' cries my archenemy, and it all floods back to me how Lucy's voice used to grate on me, with its slightly high-pitched, whiny tone. I take in the slinky black dress, ripples of raven hair and gash of red lipstick, before she envelops me in a brief but enthusiastic hug. She smells, appropriately enough, of Poison.

As I'm crushed against her, I make eye contact with the other girl and my heart sinks. It's that Olivia person from the train. The one who's obsessed with 'clean food' and fancies the arse off Theo Steel. We acknowledge each other with a half-nod and a raise of eyebrows.

Lucy sets me aside so she can give the same treatment to Paloma. Then she beams at us in turn. 'So ... almost everyone is here. Such a *fabuloso* turnout! And this is Olivia, my right-hand woman, so to speak. She's been totally invaluable with regards to raising local awareness of our charity 10k. Olivia, you've met Paloma, I think. But not Twilight?'

'Oh, but I have. We're almost old friends!' cries Olivia, linking my arm. 'We had quite a chat the other day on the train, didn't we? How's Theo?' She beams at me expectantly.

The question throws me completely. Why would she think *I* would know how Theo is?

'Er, I've no idea.'

'No? Oh well. Never mind.' She pats my arm, as if I need consoling.

'Right, help yourself to drinks and the buffet, ladies,' trills Lucy, holding the door wide for us. 'The fashion show will begin at eight prompt. And we'll be drawing the charity raffle straight afterwards.'

I follow Paloma into the function room, my head in a bemused whirl. Is that really Lucy? With the posh voice and saintly ways? And the invitation to go right ahead and eat her food? It's all very puzzling. In the old days, she'd probably have dragged me behind the door (by the hair), told me not to even *look* at the cold salmon if I wanted to walk home unaided, then given me a swift kick in the shins to emphasise her point.

'Oh, Twilight?'

I spin round to find Lucy's heavily kohl-rimmed eyes boring into me, and I freeze. I'm back to schooldays, every muscle in my body rigid because I've no idea what nasty surprises she has up her sleeve for me.

She walks over with that air of superiority, and I have a sudden urge to slip my bare arms behind my back so she can't give me one of her expert Chinese burns. She used to grab me, her dark eyes narrowed and mean, twisting the flesh hard until I squealed ...

'Let's have a proper catch-up later,' she murmurs, patting my arm gently and giving me a smile. Then she glides off, leaving me staring after her. I may have imagined it, but there might have been a hint of warmth in her tone.

I glance at my arm, feeling silly for over-reacting. It's probably at least twenty years since Lucy delivered one of her famous Chinese burns. My instinctive reaction shows just how deeply embedded childhood traumas can be.

But I'm sure Paloma's right and Lucy is different now ...

I feel myself relax after that.

It's lovely to see my other friends again and we're so busy catching up, I'm not even aware that Paloma has disappeared. Then I suddenly notice her in deep discussion with Lucy by the cold salmon and cucumber dip. A moment later, she comes over.

'Lucy wants us to take part in the fashion show.'

'Who?'

'You and me.'

I'm instantly suspicious. 'But why? It's such ridiculously short notice.'

'Two of the girls haven't shown up. So she wants us to fill in.'

I laugh. 'No way.'

'Why not? It'll be fun.'

'*Will* it?'

Paloma grins. 'If her designs are awful, it'll be a scream. And I have very high hopes that they might be.'

'No. No way on this earth.' I shake my head firmly. Lucy has to be joking if she thinks I'm going to do that. Really, wild horses couldn't drag me onto—'

Someone puts their arm round me and squeezes hard.

Lucy.

'Twilight! Thank you *so much* for agreeing to rescue me and my little show!'

I turn and Lucy's face is right there, looming large, a little scary in its proximity. But at least her hand is clamped around my shoulder on this occasion, not my neck.

So I gnash my teeth and endure it.

'You can't *imagine* how grateful I am,' she says as I practically gag on her perfume with all its horrible associations.

Paloma, in the background, is mouthing, 'Do it! Just do it!' with a big grin on her face. So I find myself relenting.

'Fabulous! Oh, you'll be brilliant. Trust me.' She hurries over to Olivia, doing a thumbs-up, and the tension in my body subsides.

Paloma comes over. 'It'll be a hoot. Honestly. The collection's called "Space Exploration Goes to the Movies".'

'What does that even *mean*?' I whisper.

Paloma grimaces. 'Beats me. Just a load of pretentious bollocks, I imagine.'

'Okay, ladies.' Lucy is back and my teeth clamp together again. 'Twilight, you're on last as it happens. I always like to end on a witty note. And guess what? You're it!' She rubs her hands together gleefully.

I force a smile and follow Paloma and Lucy into the little kitchen area off the main room that seems to be serving as a dressing room.

Paloma, who has an amazing figure, looks quite magnificent in her outfit. It's the sexiest take on a Princess Leia dress I've ever seen, all skin-tight silvery Lycra with slits to the thigh and white platform boots.

She does a twirl.

'Lovely.' I nod approvingly. 'Maybe I'll be Darth Vader.' Something black and voluminous would be just fine for covering up all the squidgy bits that haven't seen the light of day for years, and which I'd rather remained a mystery ...

'And here we are!' announces Lucy, producing my outfit with a theatrical flourish. 'I call it "Big Breakfast at Tiffany's". What do you think?'

I stare dumbfounded at the contents of the hanger.

And carry on staring ...

My face must seriously look like it belongs to Elastigirl; it's pulling in so many different directions at once as I try to work out what's actually going on there.

She has to be joking.

It's a 'big breakfast', all right, although the only nod to Audrey Hepburn's elegant attire in the movie is a black T-shirt dress that looks at least three sizes too small for me. Surely she doesn't expect me to—

'Oh, don't worry,' says Lucy, clocking my doubtful expression. 'There's such an enormous amount of "give" in this fabric. Look. It's quite extraordinary.' She stretches the garment out to really ludicrous proportions, so that even a portly walrus could be shoehorned into it at a pinch.

I shoot her a suspicious glance.

But she just smiles and murmurs, 'D'you know, Twilight, I think it's going to look *fabulous* on you.'

That's when she turns it around and I realise I was looking at the back view. The front is something else altogether ... and are they my *shoes*?

'Come on, off with the clothes!' Lucy urges me, with a glance at her watch. 'Don't be shy, we're all girls together here.'

There appears to be a lull in conversation. And when I look up, everyone – without exception – is turned towards me, watching, as if I'm the hired stripper for the evening or something. There's nothing else for it. Breathing in for all I'm worth, I start undressing. The zip sticks on my trousers and as I'm frantically trying to make it go down without breaking it, I can sense Lucy giving my figure the once-over.

'Mm, the trousers are a little – um – *snug*,' she comments, far too loudly. 'I can let them out for you, if you like. I'm a whiz with a needle and thread.'

I smile at her through gritted teeth. 'It's all right, thanks.'

She frowns at my bottom but thank heavens, at that moment the zip unfurls and I'm free.

Finally, after lots of wriggling and twisting and panting and straightening of fabric, I'm standing there, catwalk-ready, staring at myself in the full-length mirror.

This is Lucy's version of 'fabulous'?

The dress might have looked okay with some armour-plated underwear and a pair of skyscraper heels. But with my legs in yolk-yellow tights disappearing into over-sized tomato-red trainers, and three fabric bacon rashers appliquéd onto the front of the dress, along with two enormous, strategically placed fried eggs, I'm clearly the comic turn of the evening.

Paloma takes one look and guffaws so loudly, I worry for her vocal cords.

No one could blame her. I look like a mobile hangover cure.

I nod urgently at the kitchen door, through which Lucy just vanished, looking for Olivia. 'She designed this specially for me,' I hiss. 'I know she did.'

Paloma grins, shaking her head. 'You're just being paranoid.'

'I am *not*! She wants to make me a laughing stock.'

'Honestly, you're imagining it.'

'Oh, so you really think it's a coincidence that *you* get the gorgeous diva outfit and *I* get the *greasy fry-up*?'

Paloma snorts with laughter, tears in her eyes. But she nods. 'I do. You were the last to be kitted out, so you got the 'witty' costume. It was just bad luck, that's all. Nothing personal.'

'Hm.' I actually feel quite shaky and, to my horror, on the verge of tears.

'It's true. Honestly,' insists Paloma gently, seeing my face. 'If

I'd been last, *I'd* have been lumbered with the "transport caff extravaganza". Honestly, I wouldn't worry. You can really camp it up on the catwalk in a get-up like that!'

I attempt a smile. She's right. Of course, she's right. It's all just a bit of fun. I'm daft for taking it so personally.

Lucy bursts back into the room. 'Don't forget the hat!' she calls gaily.

And marching over, she slaps a giant baguette on my head.

*****

'It was really nice of Lucy to let you borrow those recipes of her grandma's.'

'Hm?' I murmur distractedly. We're walking back from the pub and I'm only vaguely aware Paloma just said something.

'What are you doing, Twi?'

I glance up sheepishly from Lucy's grandma's recipe book. 'I'm – er – examining the ingredients for anything suspicious.'

Paloma grins. 'What, like: *Victoria sponge cake. Butter, sugar, eggs, large pinch of arsenic (optional)*?'

'You never know with Lucy,' I mutter darkly. But I put the little notebook away, in my bag.

I didn't know what to think when Lucy produced it earlier in the evening, saying she thought my café idea was fabulous and that she'd be so thrilled if her lovely late grandma's recipe book could help inspire me to even greater things.

'Gosh, well, thanks!' I said, taking the small blue notebook and leafing respectfully through the pages of spidery writing. The gesture had taken me completely unawares and I wasn't sure what to say. Now, I was starting to wonder if trusting me with her grandma's book of recipes was Lucy's way of saying sorry for all the horrible things she'd done to me in the past.

Her fashion show certainly rounded off the evening in style. A very peculiar sort of style, admittedly, but at least it got everyone nice and relaxed and chatting away as if we only left school the week before.

I did what Paloma said and camped it up in the Big Breakfast outfit and everyone roared with laughter, which made me feel tons better. I almost felt I'd got one over on Lucy in deciding to just go with it and not show I was embarrassed or uncomfortable wearing something so preposterous. When everyone was laughing and applauding me, my eye landed on Lucy at one point, and she was standing there, straight-faced, arms folded, just staring at me, a cold, intense look on her face. A bit like creepy Mrs Danvers in *Rebecca*. It freaked me out for a second, but then I remembered what Paloma said about being paranoid and I told myself not to be so silly.

It was Lucy's show. She was frowning because she wanted it to be a success. Of *course* she wouldn't be able to kick back and have fun like everyone else.

'I might try this clean eating plan of Olivia's,' says Paloma, snapping me back to the present. 'If I'm going to be training for a 10k, I might as well go the whole hog and start eating healthily as well.'

'Really? But you won't be able to eat carbs.'

'Won't I?'

'No. That's the point of it. Nothing processed. No gluten. No sugar. No dairy. And the thing is, I really need your input this weekend, testing all the cakes and tray bakes I'm thinking of putting on the café menu.'

Paloma's face lights up at the thought. 'Yeah? Oh well, bugger clean eating.'

'So you're seriously going to train for this 10k?'

She shrugs. 'Why not? It's all in a good cause. Sending little Harry to America. And I sort of feel if Lucy and Olivia are spurring on the whole village to get involved and get fit in the process, I'd quite like to be part of it?'

She has a point. It's just the last time I took any serious exercise, I was running around a tea room garden in Devon, on holiday with Mum and Dad, trying to escape from a wasp that had taken a fancy to my strawberry jam scone with lashings of clotted cream.

Mind you, I *have* got stamina.

'We all agreed we'd sign up,' Paloma reminds me, nodding back at the pub. 'And to be honest, I'm quite looking forward to Lucy's boot camp training sessions.'

'You are?' I stare at her, aghast. I can't think of anything worse than Sergeant Major Lucy Slater breathing down my neck, yelling threats and making me run faster. (Actually, that just about sums up my schooldays in a nutshell.)

'Yeah, I thought I might go dressed as a chipolata,' says Paloma, straight-faced. 'You know, continue the Big Breakfast motif. With perhaps a side order of fried onions on my head?'

We look at each other and snort with laughter.

A car draws up alongside us just as I'm doing an impression of Lucy introducing one of her fashion designs. 'Ladies, this is my take on practical footwear with a twist. Mops for the feet! Get the housework done in no time and look super-uber-stylish while you do it. Note the *fabulous grey fringing*—'

I frown at Paloma, who's stopped laughing and is now digging me urgently in the ribs. 'What?'

I turn towards the car and my heart nearly gallops out of my chest when I see who it is.

My 'childhood sweetheart' as Mum quaintly describes him.

The only man I've ever really loved ...

Chapter 6

Jason Findlay is smiling up at me through the open car window with that thoroughly kissable mouth and those lovely, warm brown eyes. Eyes that used to gaze at me so lovingly from behind his glasses, my heart would turn somersaults of joy.

He must wear contact lenses these days ...

And then my face turns into a scorching radiator on max when I realise he's just witnessed me making a total arse of myself, *ridiculing his girlfriend, Lucy*.

Not that he looks anything but delighted to see me.

'Well, hello,' he says. 'If it isn't Scully herself.'

A stupid smile spreads across my face at the mention of our heroes back in the day, Mulder and Scully from *The X-Files*.

'Mulder.' I swallow hard. 'How are you?'

'I'm good, thanks. All the better for seeing you. I hear you gave up a high-flying PR career to make pastries. Brave move.' His eyes twinkle.

I laugh. 'Yeah, some might say stupid. But hey, you've got to follow your dreams.'

'And you always were a bit of a dreamer.'

We lock eyes and a wealth of memories shimmers in the space between us.

Me at fifteen, on the miraculous day Jason approached me shyly after school and asked if I wanted to go to the cinema with him. I'd liked him for ages but never thought I stood a chance. After saying yes, I walked on air all the way home and squealed into my pillow when I got to my room. The movie was *Harry Potter and the Philosopher's Stone*, but I don't think I heard a word of it – I was so delirious with happiness just to be with Jason.

Then at sixteen, listening to music with Jason in my bedroom after school, laughing, kissing and lounging together on the white fluffy bedspread, eating Screwball ice creams with bubble gum at the bottom.

And at seventeen, losing my virginity in the back of Jason's Ford Escort. People said the first time was always a disappointment, but it wasn't like that for us. I was madly in love and thought it would last forever.

At eighteen, I went off to university in Manchester, assuming we'd be true to each other in spite of the two hundred miles separating us. Then the horrible phone call from Paloma, six months into my course, telling me Jason had been seen out with Lucy. She'd agonised about whether or not to tell me, but I told her she'd done the right thing, letting me know.

I phoned Jason and challenged him, and he admitted they'd gone out just as friends and that was all it would ever be as far as he was concerned. But the thing was, I knew how mad Lucy was about Jason and I just knew, deep down, that with me at a distance, she would use every trick in her power to steal him from me ...

To be fair on Jason, he ended our relationship before anything happened with Lucy, although it came as a horrible shock to me.

I'd taken the train home for a weekend in the middle of the summer term, a few weeks after Paloma's revelation. I'd assumed that after my stressful phone call with Jason about Lucy, things were okay between us again. More than okay. Jason and I were meant to be together; I couldn't imagine us ever splitting up.

We'd gone for a long walk in the lanes around the village, ending up in our special place – a secluded spot in a pretty little wood by a stream, just beyond the village boundary.

We'd sat down and I'd leaned against him in the dappled sunlight beneath the trees, listening to the lazy gurgle of the water sliding over the stones, and Jason took my hand and told me he was finding our long-distance relationship much harder than he thought it would be.

While I was in Manchester, he said, Lucy was still there, in Hart's End. They'd been friends first, before he started to develop feelings for her, and he swore nothing physical had happened with Lucy. I believed him because Jason always told the truth. That was one of the things I loved about him – his total honesty and inability to tell a lie.

Now, he looks up at me with a wistful smile. 'You're looking great, Twi. We should get together for a drink. For old times' sake.'

'You think?' My tone is laden with cynicism because I really can't see Lucy allowing that. Paloma reckons Jason is completely under her thumb and I can well believe it. Jason is sunny natured, the eternal optimist and, if he has a fault, it's that he can sometimes be way too easy-going and forgiving for his own good. I can imagine Lucy taking full advantage of this.

'With Lucy as well,' Jason adds swiftly.

I nod. 'Of course.'

We smile at each other, acknowledging that nothing to do with exes is ever that simple.

'Oh, there you are!' a bossy voice screeches. 'We thought you were never coming, so we decided to walk.'

I swing round. Lucy is tapping daintily along the pavement towards us, with Olivia in tow. (I'm guessing she'd gallop in her eagerness to stop Jason and I talking, if it weren't for the skyscraper heels she's wearing.)

'Hi, love.' Jason's smile is a little sheepish. 'I spotted Twilight and I couldn't resist pulling up for a quick chat.'

Lucy's eyes sweep over me, like a cold front blowing in from a northerly direction. She leans down to speak to Jason. 'Olivia's coming back for a drink. To talk about the 10k. She'll probably stay over.' She opens the back door for Olivia to get in.

Jason looks surprised. This is obviously the first he's heard about it. But he says, 'Yeah, fine. I've got an early start in the morning anyway, so I'll leave you girls to it and grab an early night.'

'The bin needs putting out,' she snaps. 'Please don't forget to do it like you did last week.'

He grins. 'I won't.'

Hurrying round to the passenger side, she flicks her eyes over me. 'If you want those trouser seams taking out, Twilight, give me a call and I'll come round and collect them.' I notice she doesn't suggest I drop them off because, presumably, there would be a chance I'd bump into Jason again.

'Oh, right, thanks.' I have absolutely no intention of calling her for this or any other reason.

'I think your trousers look perfectly fine as they are,' says

Jason, grinning at me, and I wonder if this is his small revenge for Lucy's snippy comments about the bin.

'There'll be no nooky for *him* tonight,' mutters Paloma as we watch them drive off, Lucy with a face like thunder.

Chapter 7

It's three days since Lucy's fashion show and all the buzz around the 10k charity run has had an effect on me. I have decided – albeit reluctantly – to get fit for the first time in my life.

But I'm not as fearless as Paloma.

She's started running every evening, through the village and out along country lanes, but I'm not terribly keen on putting my wobbly bits on public show like that. So, I've decided to join the gym instead. I figure if I go prompt at seven in the morning, when it opens, there'll be fewer people to observe me tackling the treadmill. (I'm thinking particularly of Theo Steel. I really do *not* want to bump into him in my baggy T-shirt and tracksuit bottoms.)

Leaving the house, I give the milkman a cheery wave and head for the sports centre. Avoiding the main gate and taking a short cut through the bushes into the sports centre car park, I do a quick scan of the few cars parked there at this evil early hour. A pink Porsche, a clapped-out old Fiesta that looks as if it's been abandoned and an ugly, shiny people carrier. In other words, none that screams 'Theo Steel'.

Phew!

I whip off the dark glasses, which are probably a *little* over the top at seven in the morning, with the sun just a cheery promise lurking on the horizon. Then I change my mind and put them back on. At least they mask the puffiness from a very late night spent perfecting my scone selection.

By the time I crashed out around three, I had five different varieties cooling on wire trays. The date scones are my personal favourite, although I know Paloma prefers the cherry and coconut. Throw in a savoury flavour – cheddar, parmesan and cracked black pepper – plus blueberry lemon cream, and classic sultana, and hopefully, there will be a scone to suit every customer's taste.

What prompted this morning's early rise was Paloma knocking on my door last night, just before six. She was hoping to persuade me to join her on a jog around the village, but I despatched her speedily on her way, joking that I had far more enjoyable things to do with my time, such as cleaning the hard-to-reach bits behind the radiators and watching paint dry.

But after she'd gone, I decided that if I was to take part in Lucy's 10k with everyone else and not totally show myself up, I needed to do something about my lack of fitness because I suspected you needed a bit more than natural stamina to run all that way.

Walking into the sports centre, I find reception deserted, except for a model-like girl leaning on the other side of the desk painting her nails. Dressed in a skimpy bright pink leotard, she's wearing massive rollers that look more suited to flattening road surfaces than styling hair.

'Hi, you're an early bird.' She beams at me. 'I'm Lorena. I suppose you're wanting to bag the anti-gravity treadmill before anyone else!'

I give a nervous laugh. 'Sounds like an instrument of torture if ever there was one.'

'Have you tried it? No? Oh, it's amazing. You can beat world records on it.'

'Really?'

She nods. 'You run at eighty per cent of your body weight, so you're much lighter and therefore you can run faster.'

'Right. But isn't that cheating?'

Lorena bursts into peals of laughter at my witty jest (I actually wasn't joking) and waves her hands in the air to dry her nails.

I clear my throat. 'I just want to join the gym and use an – er – *ordinary* treadmill if possible. Do you have ordinary treadmills here?'

Another peal of laughter. 'About a hundred and twenty.' She looks at me kindly, as if I'm several dumb-bells short of a complete workout.

'Oh. Great.' I put my thumb up awkwardly. 'Well, I just need the one.' Honestly, I am *so* out of my depth here. I feel like this girl's grandma even though we're probably about the same age.

I must get myself some new workout gear. My outfit today is circa turn of the century, from the one and only other time I joined a gym (although I wisely left the matching sweatband at home in the bag). I'm going to stand out like the complete novice that I am.

I'm also terrified Theo Steel is going to walk in at any moment and think I'm stalking him ...

'I'll book you in for a seduction,' Lorena says.

Confused, I whip round to the door. *Is Theo here?*

Lorena runs a perfect nail down a column and looks up. 'Induction at ten-fifteen with Gerry?'

Ah! I breathe more easily. An *induction*.

I actually just want to go home and forget this whole idea. But Lorena is already writing my name in the diary and handing me a membership form.

I go home and fill the time until ten-fifteen making a Bakewell tart cake, which smells heavenly baking in the oven. Not having had time for breakfast earlier, I end up 'testing' two large slices of the jammy, almond-cake lusciousness and deciding it should definitely feature on the café menu. I make a note to bake two more for the 'tasting party' I'm planning.

Just before my appointment with 'Gerry' at ten-fifteen, I brave the gym again, register at the desk with a girl called Charlene, and scuttle through to get changed into my sad gym gear.

Gerry turns out to be a guy of about twenty with a broad Yorkshire accent and a lovely self-deprecating sense of humour, which puts me immediately at my ease. He takes me on a tour of the machines and how they work, and I spend my time nodding and looking knowledgeable, pretending I've memorised his instructions perfectly. There's not a sign of Theo Steel and I start to relax a bit and feel less awkward. Maybe it's his day off.

Gerry starts me off on a treadmill, very slowly at first then increasing the speed, and actually, I'm doing fine. I was worried I'd collapse, breathless, after ten seconds, but my legendary stamina appears to be serving me well. Gerry leaves me on my own to attend to another novice and that's when I get a bit too confident, pumping up the speed and almost falling off the back of the machine because my legs can't go fast enough.

Feeling silly but relieved to still be in one piece, I glance around nervously. I've got a muscle-bound Trojan pounding a machine on each side of me, sweat raining down like two mini cloud-bursts, but they're both so doggedly focused on getting in their mileage, they haven't even registered my mishap.

I climb back on and do another mile, then decide that's probably enough for my first day. Feeling rather proud of myself, I grab my towel to wipe my brow and exchange a smile with another novice. I'm not the only new girl – and soon, if I stick with it, I won't actually *be* the new girl at all. I'll show Lucy Slater that I'm more than capable of running for ten kilometres without stopping!

Feeling much better, I loop the towel round my neck, the way I've seen other people do, and swig down a cup of water at the drinks machine.

What on earth was I worried about? This is a breeze.

And Theo Steel was nowhere in sight!

Entering the changing room, all I'm thinking about is trying out one of those lovely power showers I spotted earlier, then going home to start painting the café walls with the pretty pale lilac paint I've chosen.

As I push confidently through the door, I'm rooting around in my bag for the locker key. So I've walked a fair way into the room before I finally look up and notice all is not as it should be.

Realisation engulfs me slowly, like treacle poured onto me from a height.

This – is – not – the – ladies' – changing – room.

All the men turn in my direction, innocently displaying their nakedness.

I gulp. *Suffering bed snakes!*

I'm staring at them and they're staring right back, frozen

in time. We're like some weird tableau in an edgy, fringe theatre production. One man has the presence of mind to whip a bag of crisps in front of his privates. (Sadly for him, his packet of Wotsits does a pretty good job of concealment.) At least three of the men are completely stark bollock naked.

But it's the one with his foot up on the bench, pausing in the act of drying his thigh with one of the gym's white towels, who turns my face the deepest shade of crimson.

Theo Steel.

Chapter 8

Plastering on a smile, I raise my hand in a general greeting. 'Hi. Sorry. Got the wrong door. Sorry.'

They all just stare at me. Except Theo Steel, who's grinning down at the floor.

I start backing apologetically out of the door, like I'm exiting a room with the Queen in it. 'Nice to see you. Enjoy your day.'

Fleeing into the corridor, I blunder in completely the wrong direction, then have to double back to find the women's changing-room door. Just as I'm charging past the scene of my nightmare, Theo emerges with a towel round his waist.

'Whoa! Steady on.' He grasps my arms as we collide and it flashes across my mind that if his towel should slip, my humiliation would be complete. 'Do you know where you're going now?'

I nod, pointing mutely along the corridor, my power of speech compromised by the experience of glimpsing more naked men in the last thirty seconds than I've seen in my entire life.

'I've just finished with a client,' he says. 'Do you fancy meeting in five for a drink in the bar?'

I smile regretfully. 'Bit too early for me.'

'I meant a soft drink.'

'Oh. Yes, of course.'

'They do fresh juices. Very healthy.'

I swallow hard. With my hair plastered to my forehead and my décolletage an attractive shade of blotchy red, due to my recent exertions on the treadmill, I don't think I've ever felt less like being sociable.

'I'm sure they'd make you a juice with celery if you asked nicely.' There's a glint in Theo's eye and I can't help smiling back at his reference to Olivia and her little Tupperware box of celery sticks on the train.

I nod. 'Okay.'

We part and I dash off, wondering if five minutes is enough time to shower, wash my hair and dry it, and reapply my make-up.

When I walk into the bar seventeen minutes later (a personal record), my hair is swishing softly round my shoulders, smelling all herby from the shampoo in the shower cubicle. The blotches on my chest have gone, and I'm glowing with a lovely sense of achievement at having run a couple of miles this morning.

Theo is sitting at a corner table, reading a newspaper, dressed in jeans and a pale green T-shirt. He throws the newspaper onto the table when he spots me. 'I assume you'd rather skip the celery juice?' He smiles, his deep blue eyes raking over me, making me glad I washed my hair.

I swallow. 'You assumed right. Actually, fresh orange would be nice.' I glance at the selection of fruit piled up on the bar near the industrial-sized juicing machine.

He nods. 'Back in a sec.'

My eyes follow him to the bar, although when he turns to

point out the table to the bar person, I swiftly avert my gaze and snatch up a menu.

Once we're settled, me with my deliciously cold orange juice and Theo with watermelon, I feel I have to apologise again for barging into the men's changing room.

'I wouldn't worry,' he assures me smoothly. 'It happens all the time.'

'Really?'

His blue eyes sparkle mischievously. 'Actually, it never happens. I was just trying to make you feel better.'

I grin sheepishly. 'Gee, thanks.'

He takes a long swallow of juice and sets down his glass. 'So how are the plans for the café coming along? Am I invited to the opening ceremony?'

'I'd like to open in June, as near to the start of the tourist season as possible. But I hadn't thought about a special opening ceremony. That's an excellent idea.'

He gives a modest nod. 'I'll send you my bill.'

'Why didn't *I* think of it, though? I could invite the village to a ribbon-cutting ceremony with a free glass of Prosecco for everyone and a competition to win a prize.'

'What's the prize?'

I frown, thinking. 'How about a complimentary slice of cake every week for a year?'

He nods. 'I'd enter. I assume you're a good baker.'

'My friends say I am.'

'Sounds like I might become a regular at your café, then. What's it called?'

'The Twilight Café.'

He nods approvingly. 'Perfect.'

I flush with pleasure at the compliment.

'You're based in that shop that used to sell all sorts of country goods, aren't you?'

I smile, surprised. 'You've been doing your homework. Yes, it used to be my dad's shop.'

'Has he retired, then?'

I shake my head. 'He's not been well.' I'm about to leave it at that, but something about Theo Steel's sympathetic expression makes me continue, and soon, I'm telling him the whole story about Dad's cancer and how this experimental trial might be his only chance of survival.

'That's really tough.' He shakes his head sadly when I've finished. 'And I suppose the pressure to succeed with the café is so much greater when you're doing it for the people you love.'

I nod. 'Got it in one.' My throat aches with emotion but I swallow hard and cast around for something upbeat to talk about. The last thing I want to do is to break down in front of Theo when I hardly know the man. 'So, have you always been really creative?' I ask, remembering him on the train, studying the book on crochet so intently. 'I could probably knit a scarf but that's about it by way of making things. Apart from baking, of course.'

He's looking at me oddly, clearly not having a clue what I'm talking about.

'The crocheting? I was saying to my friend, Paloma, how unusual I thought it was for a man to be so – er – creative, and she suggested you might make some placemats for the café.' When he still looks nonplussed, I shrug and smile. 'She was joking.'

'Oh, the book?' Light dawns.

'Yes. *Adventures with Crochet*.'

He grins. 'I don't crochet. At least, I probably could now, but it wouldn't be my – um – pastime of choice, shall we say?'

'So why read it?'

'I translated it. From Spanish into English. It was my first job as a freelance translator and I'd just had some copies delivered that day, fresh from the printers.'

'Oh, wow. How exciting.'

He laughs. 'Actually, the subject matter was dull as ditch-water. But the publisher seemed pleased with my work. And beggars can't be choosers. If I want to make a real go of a career as a translator, I need to start somewhere.'

'Do you know lots of languages, then?'

'I studied Spanish, French and Italian at university with the idea of doing something with languages. But I trained in fitness in order to pay my way through university, and I ended up falling back on that when my plans didn't pan out the way I hoped. And I'm still a personal trainer to this day. I like it, though. It suits me. It's good being my own boss.'

'Having your own business can be scary, though. You've got to be successful otherwise you don't get paid.'

'I don't mind the pressure. Or putting in the hours. In fact, I thrive on it.'

'Paying your own way through university is such an achievement.' I raise my glass to him. 'Most people rely on their family to fund them.'

A shadow passes over his face. 'I don't have family,' he says, matter-of-factly, and my heart pings with shock at the words.

'Oh. I'm sorry.' *Does he mean he's estranged from his family? I hope so because the alternative is awful ...*

He's frowning down at his hands. Then someone laughs loudly at the bar and he looks up. 'It's fine. Not having anyone else to please can be a real advantage. And I work better alone, in all areas of life. If you cock up, the only person you've let down is yourself.' There's a slight bitterness in his tone and when he smiles, it doesn't quite reach his eyes.

'Right.' I study him thoughtfully as he swallows down the rest of his watermelon juice.

'So, has this sudden desire to get fitter anything to do with the 10k Olivia's hell-bent on me doing?' he asks, setting his glass down.

I grimace. 'It has, actually. I went to a pretty horrendous class reunion the other night and found myself agreeing to take part.'

'So are you doing the boot camp training a week on Sunday?'

I groan. 'Can't think of anything worse, to be honest. But maybe I will. I quite enjoyed my run on the treadmill today.'

'Olivia says she's persuaded about fifty people to come along to her friend's training session.'

So he's been in touch with Olivia, then. Either she must have tracked him down at the gym or he phoned her on the number she gave him on the back of the leaflet that time.

I nod. 'Olivia's best friends with the organiser.' I look down and study my nails. 'Lucy Slater.'

'You're not keen on this Lucy Slater?'

I look up at him, surprised he could tell that from my face. 'No. I mean, well, she's—' I glance down at my hands again. 'She bullied me at school, that's all.'

'Then I'm not surprised you don't like her,' he says. 'Life can be pretty bleak anyway, without people like that making it worse.' The edge to his tone is back.

I nod, not knowing what else to say.

'Anyway, can I tempt you to another?' He points at my empty glass. 'Celery juice with extra celery on the side?' The shadow has lifted from his face. He smiles at me, eyes crinkling attractively at the corners.

But I can't help wondering what private torment Theo Steel is concealing from the world ...

Chapter 9

'You know, what you really need is a USP,' murmurs Paloma thoughtfully. She stops painting and leans back on the ladder to admire her handiwork. 'Lovely colour, this Hillside Heather.'

'USP?' I glance up from where I'm painstakingly sanding down an ancient brown table in Dad's old shop. 'Is that some kind of new-fangled coffee machine? Because I can't afford that!'

Paloma knows I'm joking and normally, she'd laugh. But she carries on painting as if she hasn't even heard what I said.

I glance at her, puzzled. Perhaps she's thinking of her latest graphic design project.

It's over a week since my unexpected encounter with a naked-but-for-a-towel Theo Steel, and although I've pounded the treadmill at the gym a few times since then, our paths haven't crossed again. Not that I've been looking out for him. I've had other far more important things on my mind – namely making list upon list and carrying out the thousand and one tasks that are apparently necessary to get a café up and running.

After much deliberation, and getting the opinion of practically everyone I've met – from our regular postman to the woman I sat next to on the bus home from a shopping trip to Chichester – I've chosen 1st June as the café's grand opening day.

I've already spent a worrying amount of my savings on paint, cutlery and gorgeous flowery china cups, saucers and plates, transforming Dad's premises into The Twilight Café.

'A Unique Selling Point,' I murmur. 'Something that makes my business different from the rest. I know! It's the only place you can buy coffee in the village, now that the ice-cream parlour has closed down!'

Paloma turns with a vague, slightly puzzled look.

I frown. 'Are you all right? You seem ... distracted.'

'Do I?' She looks surprised. 'No, I'm fine,' she says and turns back to her painting.

Distracted or not, I'm so grateful for Paloma's help with the café.

She's full of great ideas and common sense, and because she tends to do her graphic design work in the late afternoons and well into the night, she's got into the habit of coming over to Honey Cottage at around noon most days. As a result, my plans for the café – less than two weeks after arriving in Hart's End – are starting to take shape. Which is just as well, since I'm planning to open in ten days' time!

We spent a hilarious afternoon trawling round what felt like all the second-hand shops in Sussex with Paloma driving the big old estate car she inherited from her mum, Linda. We returned with some old tables and chairs, and boxes of crockery, including lots of lovely old-fashioned china teacups and saucers: mostly mismatching, of course, but I'm hoping that will add to the charm of the place.

The furniture was all in a pretty bad state, but Paloma

assured me we could work wonders turning it into 'shabby chic' designer pieces. I laughed and said there was surely a limit to what you could do with a pot of paint and a bit of sandpaper, but she only smiled smugly and murmured, 'Oh, ye of little faith.'

Sadly, despite our best efforts, the three small tables and six rickety chairs still look as if they were bought in a junk shop. Even Paloma was forced to admit that – especially after she sat down too enthusiastically on a chair and one of the legs fell off. I'm trying to stay calm at the thought that in just over a week, I'll be selling cappuccinos and lattes from our splendid but scary-looking industrial-sized coffee machine (bought second-hand on-line from a former café owner in Brighton), while my customers will have nowhere to sit.

But the décor is coming along nicely. It's going to be fresh and summery and inviting. The sort of place where friends will meet to chat over coffee or fruit teas. Where shoppers will drop in to take the weight off their feet and enjoy a slice of cake while browsing through our selection of magazines. Where frazzled mums will take a breather, watching their toddlers play happily in our mini soft play area. I'm also hoping to tap into the summer tourist trade with an eye-catching sign on the main road through the village, spotlighting our little cul-de sac café. It's being taken care of by the local print firm and I'm really excited to see it.

A car draws up outside and seconds later, the door bursts open and in strides a familiar figure. My stomach shifts queasily.

Lucy Slater has always enjoyed making an entrance, and her dramatic appearance normally ensures she gets the attention she craves. She's not conventionally pretty. Her long dark hair is certainly striking but its thick, coarse texture meant it looked bushy and wild when she was a kid. She must spend a fortune taming it these days.

She wears a lot of long, expensive layers in black, oatmeal and white that accentuate her tall, slim figure. Today's outfit is a loose black trouser suit, the jacket open to reveal a white silk blouse and a dramatic blood-red crucifix necklace swinging as she walks.

But it's her eyes that draw the most attention. They're green with flecks of silver, and their tone changes like the sea, depending on her mood. A dark circle around the colour of the pupil gives her an eerie, other-world look, and she accentuates them with so much thick black eyeliner and mascara, I swear she must have shares in the make-up company.

They might be Lucy's best feature, but those eyes gave me nightmares when I was a kid.

She ignores me and walks over to Paloma. 'Nice colour,' she says, standing on tiptoe to examine the paint tin perched on top of the stepladders.

'Hillside Heather,' says Paloma obligingly. Then she looks back at me and we shrug as if to say neither of us has a clue why Lucy is here.

She starts chattering on about the merits of plain white versus colour on a shop wall and Paloma says she thinks a little colour gives a room warmth and makes it seem cosier, which is exactly what I want for my café. Not that it's any of Lucy Slater's business.

A second later, Jason walks in, swinging his car keys. He smiles warmly at me and, seeing Lucy bending Paloma's ear, wanders over to see what I'm doing.

'It's a bit rickety.' I feel I have to apologise for the state of the chair. 'But we're hoping that with a makeover ...' I shrug.

He considers the chair on its spindly legs from all angles. Then he grins. 'Do you think it would take my weight?'

I groan. 'Oh, don't!'

'Rowena's got a load of furniture and crockery to sell, you know,' he says.

'Oh, I hadn't thought of that.' Rowena, a lovely woman in her fifties, ran the busy ice-cream parlour on Hart's End High Street for the past three years, but recently decided it was time she retired. The shop has been vacant for a couple of months now and every time I walk past its blank façade, I feel sad. 'That's a great idea. Thanks, Jason. I'll phone her and find out what she's done with it.'

'You should. I spoke to her the other day and she was thinking of putting it all for sale on-line, but if you get in quick, you might find some stuff you can use at a bargain price.'

I smile and offer him a mint, which he takes. They happen to be his favourite brand, and we exchange a look, acknowledging this. Even after all this time, there are so many little things I remember from our time together. I can't help but wonder if Jason feels this, too.

Out of the corner of my eye, I spot Lucy giving us shifty looks, so I turn away from Jason and get back to my sanding. I don't want to get him into trouble. She's probably desperate to know what we're talking about.

'So, I brought some curtain material for you to look at,' says Lucy, finally announcing the reason for her impromptu visit. She comes over with a plastic bag from a high-end fabric shop and shows me the material inside. It's a vertical stripe pattern in pretty pastel shades of lilac, pink and blue. 'Paloma mentioned you were needing curtains and I remembered we had this curtain material that we never used. You can have it if you like it. I could measure up and make the curtains for you.' She glances around at the room's four large windows, two ranged either side on opposite walls. 'Consider it an opening gift.'

I'm confused. Why is Lucy being nice to me?

I shake my head. 'I couldn't possibly – unless you let me pay you.'

'I said you can have it,' she says, snippily, looking anywhere but at me. And it suddenly occurs to me that maybe she finally feels guilty for making my life a misery at school. 'I bought it to deck out our summer house, but I went off it, so it's going spare.' At last, she meets my eye. 'Do you like it?'

Feeling pushed into a corner, I nod. 'It would tone in with the colour on the walls perfectly.'

'Right, well, have it. As I said, I can run up some curtains and bring them back in good time for your opening day.'

'Well, I will *definitely* pay you to do that,' I tell her firmly.

'Okay. Fine. I'll stick the money in the charity fund. You open on 1st June, don't you?'

'Yes.' I paste on a smile. 'Gosh, news travels fast. I've only just decided the opening day myself. However did you find out?' I swivel my eyes at Paloma, but she shrugs, disclaiming all responsibility.

'Oh, it's all round the village.' Lucy waves her hand impatiently. 'You can't expect to keep anything quiet for long round here.'

'Right, well, thank you.' It costs me to say it. I hate being beholden to bloody Lucy Slater. Whatever Paloma might say about me being paranoid, I still can't help being suspicious of her motives in suddenly being nice. But I suppose people do change sometimes ...

'It's fine.' Lucy waves her hand dismissively 'We're going to be moving soon, to a much larger property in Lake Heath. Five bedrooms. Triple garage. So we're hardly likely to need that.' She looks down her nose at the stripy fabric, which – frankly – is a godsend to me. Then she links arms with her man, gazing up at him adoringly. 'We can't wait to move, can we, Jason?'

Jason pats her hand and smiles. 'Whatever you say, darling. You're in charge of the purse strings.' He grimaces jokingly at Paloma and me.

Lucy's message to me is very clear: She has her man and they're doing brilliantly well in life. I catch Paloma's eye and she does a funny finger-down-the-throat mime from her perch on the stepladders, which makes me feel slightly better.

'Help me measure up and then we'll be off,' Lucy orders, and Jason dutifully toes the line.

I watch as he humours her. He's so patient and doesn't seem at all put out by her domineering manner. Perhaps he's so used to it by now, he's able to let it wash over him.

'Right, come on, the Jag awaits!' Lucy gives a little screechy laugh. 'I'm terrible, I know, but I never get tired of saying that. Do you have a car at the moment, Twilight?'

'Yes, she does,' jumps in Paloma, before I can open my mouth. 'It's a Lamborghini but she doesn't drive it much because she doesn't like to show off.' She smiles radiantly at a bemused Lucy, and I clamp my lips together to stop myself smiling.

Jason shakes his head at Paloma, clearly amused.

'So where is it?' Lucy wants to know. 'Is it in the garage?'

'Let's go.' Jason grins at me and starts steering Lucy towards the door.

As they walk out to the Jag, Lucy's voice drifts back: 'Oh, I see. She was making a joke. Well, it wasn't very funny.'

Paloma makes a comical face at me. 'Lucy never could understand irony.'

I shake my head. 'I just wish you wouldn't talk to her about my business, that's all.'

'But I don't.' Paloma sounds indignant. 'I just happened to bump into her on the high street the other day and it's kind of of hard not to answer questions when someone is grilling you.'

'Lucy was *grilling* you?'

'No.' Paloma holds her head in frustration and pretends to scream. 'I meant she was asking about you and the café. She's *interested*, Twi. Just like everyone else in the village.'

'You obviously didn't see the look she gave me when they left,' I mutter darkly.

'But she brought you material. And she's going to make curtains for you. Give her a break, for God's sake.'

She sees my face and instantly looks contrite. 'Look, I know she treated you horribly at school and I can never, ever forgive her for that. But things have changed. We're not school kids any more. I still can't stand the woman, but she's not that vicious kid any more.'

'Yes, but the look she gave me would have turned the milk sour,' I mutter.

'Oh, well, if a dirty look is all you have to worry about, you should think yourself lucky!' retorts Paloma.

'*What?*' I can't believe she'd say something so insensitive.

'Oh God, sorry, Twi. Forget I said that. My head's all over

the place today. Of course I know you're going through hell right now. How *is* your dad? Have you heard anything today?'

I swallow hard. Mum phoned last night in a panic, worrying about him, and it was all I could do not to leap on the first train to London to be with them.

'Is he okay?'

I wobble my hand to indicate so-so. 'It's all a big stress on his already weakened system. Mum's going through hell, wishing she could have the treatment instead of him. I wish I could be there.' I feel hot and anxious suddenly. 'I shouldn't be here, painting this stupid chair! I should be with them at the hospital, holding Mum's hand and being there for Dad. What if it's all too much for him and something terrible happens and I never see him again?'

A tear brims over and slides down my face as I stare in anguish at my best friend.

Paloma comes over and gently removes the sandpaper from my hand, then leads me over to a chair we haven't started on yet. Crouching down beside me, she puts her arms around me and lets me sob into her shoulder until her shirt is wet through.

*****

Next afternoon, as we put the finishing touches to the tables and chairs, we're both still a bit subdued.

There's something troubling Paloma, I can tell, but there's no point trying to force it out of her. She can be quite stubborn and she'd only clam up. I know she'll tell me when she's ready.

As for myself, I just can't stop thinking about Dad, hoping and praying the treatment will make a difference. Even just a small difference. Just so I can see a spark of life behind his eyes and have my vibrant, energetic dad back again, telling his awful jokes and whistling tunelessly around the place. It's funny the things you miss when someone isn't around ...

Later, we retreat to the treehouse where I've left cookies and an ice-cold thermos flask of home-made lemonade for our break. We sip the lemonade high up on the verandah overlooking the back garden that's beginning to give a hint of the riot of summer colour to come.

'Cookie?' I hold the box out to Paloma. 'They're raspberry and white chocolate. Your favourite.'

No reply. She's staring out, past Dad's old country store, at the clear blue sky beyond, a deep furrow between her brows.

'What is it?' I ask gently.

'I don't know.' To my dismay, her eyes fill with tears. 'I just feel ... weird.'

I grasp her hand, wanting to help. Paloma hardly ever cries. I never even saw her break down when Linda finally succumbed to the cancer last year. She didn't let out the tears until long afterwards.

'Tell me.'

She shrugs. 'All this stuff you're going through with your dad. Since you've been back, it's been playing on my mind and I really feel for you because it's so horrible watching someone you love going through hell. And I suppose Mum dying last year made me realise how important it is to have family.'

She draws a deep breath and lets the air out slowly, still staring into the distance.

Then she turns, an urgent look in her eyes. 'I want to find her, Twi.'

My heart lurches. 'Who?'

'My birth mum.'

Chapter 10

'Wow.' My mouth opens in total surprise. I never thought I'd see this day.

As long as I've known her, Paloma has always been absolutely adamant she already *had* a wonderful mum and wasn't at all curious about the woman who gave her up at two weeks old. It was just biology, she insisted, not the loving and nurturing of a true parent.

I take her hand and squeeze it gently, realising now that she probably only said those things because she didn't want to hurt Linda.

But now that Linda is gone ...

She grins at me. 'I know. Bit of a bombshell, eh?'

'It certainly is. But if you're serious, I'll help you any way I can.'

She leans sideways and nudges my shoulder. 'Thanks. I could do with my bestie's support in this. Because I'm scared. And when I say scared, I mean *terrified*!'

'Yeah?'

She nods and I can see genuine fear in her eyes.

'You've got nothing to lose, though,' I tell her gently.

'But I have! Don't you see?' She looks up at the sky in despair. 'Even though I've never looked for the woman who gave birth to me, I've *imagined* what she'd be like. What if I find her and she's nothing like my image of her?' She grabs my hand. 'Oh, Twi, what if I never find her? Or what if I do find her but she doesn't want to know me? At least if I don't look for her, I can cling on to the fantasy ...' She shrugs hopelessly and collapses back against the wall of the treehouse, staring up at the sky.

There's a long silence.

Then I say carefully, 'The thing is, a fantasy mother isn't much use. You need a *real* one.'

She says nothing but her mouth twists in acknowledgement.

'So if she's out there, I really think you have to try and find her.'

*****

The next day is Saturday, the day of my cake-tasting party. I'm awake early to bake scones and ice the cakes I baked yesterday.

As I work away, I'm feeling a mixture of nervousness and excitement because the café is now no longer just a whacky concept in my head. After all our hard work over the past few weeks – mine and Paloma's – my plan is slowly taking shape and becoming a reality.

If the people today give my cakes the thumbs-up, I'll be a step nearer the big opening day, a week tomorrow!

I've issued a casual invitation to around twenty people to drop in some time today, any time after two o'clock, to sample my cakes and, for fun, to score each bake a mark out of ten. Along with my old school friends, I've invited some of Mum's friends from the village. The plan is to find out people's preferences while at the same time, throwing a spotlight on the opening of the café the following week. A gorgeous poster, full of cupcake lusciousness and designed by Paloma, went up yesterday in various locations around Hart's End.

Mum phones at lunchtime, just as I'm cutting the tray bakes and slicing the cakes, ready to display on the gorgeous vintage rose-sprigged cake stands I picked up at a car boot sale. 'Your dad was back to charming the nurses this morning, poor things,' she jokes.

My heart lifts. 'That's great, Mum.'

'He's having a little nap right now, so I thought I'd phone and see how you were getting on, love.'

'I'm almost ready for the pretend customers. I just hope the cakes go down well.'

'You don't want them going down. You want them to *rise*.'

'Oh, funny.'

'Twilly, they're going to absolutely *love* them. You're a fabulous baker. Your dad says he can see this café of yours getting awards and everything!'

'Aw, bless him.' My throat feels suddenly constricted. If my café's success depended solely on the love and support of Mum and Dad, it would indeed be an award-winner!

'I just wish I could be there to help you today,' Mum says.

'To snaffle the chocolate cakes, you mean?'

She laughs. 'You know me too well. Are they filled with chocolate ganache?'

'But of course.'

When I hang up, a feeling of uncertainty pulses through me. It's great that they believe in me, but I just wish I could be sure it was justified. Because right now, the fate of Honey

Cottage rests solely in my hands, and that's quite a terrifying thought. What happens if the café fails to take off? What will we do then?

Paloma comes over just before two o'clock, and soon after that, two of Mum's friends arrive, both very excited about being cake judges. I pour them a glass of Prosecco each and after they've hugged me and asked about Mum and Dad and remarked on how strange it feels to be in their house without them there, we get down to the serious business of sampling the cakes and marking them out of ten.

'It's high time the village had a proper café,' says Betty, picking up a bite-sized square of lemon drizzle cake and popping it into her mouth with a swoony expression. 'Oh, that's utter heaven, Twilight, my love. What do you think, Doreen?'

'Marvellous. My favourite is the coffee and walnut. But I do love that gingerbread.'

Mentally, I thank Lucy. The traditional gingerbread recipe came from her granny's little notebook. Perhaps I've misjudged her. Maybe she has changed, as Paloma keeps assuring me.

I'm busy making tea for everyone when Betty follows me into the kitchen.

'It's such a lovely thing you're doing, setting up this café for your dad. And I *love* the name. The Twilight Café.' She wanders over to the window and peers out. 'That's a big garden,' she murmurs. 'Just as well you've still got that man – Terry, is it? – coming in to keep it tidy.'

I nod. 'He's great. But I'm not sure how long I'll be able to afford him.'

'Once the summer is over, of course, you won't need him for a while.'

'True.' I stare at my reflection in the shiny aluminium kettle. Paying Terry is the least of my worries. The mortgage arrears are piling up – and there's another payment due next week. I've set aside a small budget to pay for things like the café signs, the curtains Lucy's making for me, and the huge list of ingredients I'll need, to bake for opening day. I've calculated that after that, I've got just enough money left in my savings account to pay the mortgage arrears, which I will do this week. But unless the café turns in a decent profit in week one, I'll be unable to meet the regular monthly payment.

'Isn't that treehouse wonderful?' sighs Betty. 'Your dad is such a clever man.' She turns, a gleam in her eye. 'Why don't we take our tea up there?'

'Into the treehouse? The last time I had a tea party up there, the conversation wasn't exactly stimulating.'

Betty raises a querying eyebrow and I laugh. 'I was about eight and the guests were all dolls.'

'Ah!' She nods.

'But you're right, Betty. It's much too lovely a day to stay inside. If you're game, so am I! Do you think Doreen will be up for it, though?'

'There's only one way to find out.' Betty winks, then nips off into the living room, and the upshot is Paloma and I steadying the ladder while two ladies of a certain age tackle the ascent to the treehouse platform, giggling and in generally high spirits thanks to the Prosecco. Betty manages it without too much difficulty. But Doreen has to be steadied from behind on her way up by Paloma and me. Luckily, she's wearing trousers.

Once we're all safely up there, the treehouse works its magic, making everyone smile and relax. Betty and Doreen sit on the window seat inside, on the soft tartan cushions, and lean out of the window, enjoying the breeze rustling the leaves and drinking their tea from floral-patterned cups. Paloma and I sit on fold-out chairs on the deck beyond the window and we all chat about how sad it is that the ice-cream parlour has closed, but how fortuitous it is that I'm going to be filling the gap. Betty and Doreen seem really excited that they'll have somewhere new to meet for coffee, and their enthusiasm fills me with confidence that maybe – just maybe – things will turn out all right.

'It's so lovely and peaceful up here,' sighs Doreen.

Betty nods. 'It's perfect. All you can hear is the rustle of the leaves and the birds chirruping so close by. There's something really soothing about sitting in the treetops. Things really do look different from up here. In more ways than one.'

'Ooh, get you!' Doreen laughs. 'A regular little philosopher, you are.'

We all laugh. But I, for one, think Betty is right. Taking my worries to the treehouse always seems to help ...

*****

My mind flashes way back in time, to the eve of the school leavers' ball. Being in the treehouse with Paloma, terrified that Jason was about to break up with me.

We were eighteen and we'd been together for three years by then. The ball marked the end of school and the beginning of a whole new life for both of us, but I'd never had any doubts that whatever Jason and I did, we would do it together.

But the week before the ball, he seemed odd. Distracted. I kept asking him if he'd sorted out his suit for the night, but he just kept saying there was plenty of time to think about that, which there quite obviously wasn't. I asked him if things were okay between us and he said of course they were. He thought he had a cold coming on and was feeling a bit low, that was all.

But I remember feeling so uneasy, I confided in Paloma.

We were up in my bedroom and she'd brought over the dress Linda had bought her for the ball – a long, silky creation in deep pink that contrasted wonderfully with her dark hair.

'What's wrong?' she asked, sensing I wasn't myself.

And then it all came out, in between sobs. How Jason had been so distant lately and I was terrified he was going to end our relationship. Mum knocked on the door and asked if I was all right.

'Just a bit of boy trouble,' sang out Paloma.

Then she whispered, 'Come on. Let's go out to the treehouse.'

So, we escaped to my little world among the branches and as my best friend gave me a pep talk, I stared out over the garden, hoping Paloma was right and that my worries about Jason would turn out to be nothing at all.

Up in the treehouse, breathing in the scented air that rustled through the leaves, I always felt calmer and more able to think straight. I decided that if we made it to the school leavers' ball, things would be okay. If not – well, I didn't want to think about what would happen then. Jason was my first love and I could never in a million years have imagined being in this position, worrying that he might be going off me.

But if it happened, I'd cope ...

As it turned out, I *had* built a crisis out of nothing. I phoned

Jason and asked him if he really wanted to go to the ball with me, and he said of course he did and what a strange thing to ask.

He sounded quite cross with me for doubting him, and I remember the relief flooding through me. Things were okay between us after all.

I said he'd been distant with me and he explained that he'd been worried about what would happen to us, now we were leaving school and everything in our lives was about to change. I knew he hated the idea of me going off to university. But that night, at the ball, I did everything I could to reassure Jason that even though our relationship would be long-distance for a few years, the way I felt about him would never change. We'd survive the separation because we were so strong together.

He still seemed a little quiet. But then the next day, he came down with a horrible dose of flu and I told myself that must have been the problem all along ...

*****

When Betty and Doreen leave, Paloma and I tidy up and wash the glasses while we wait for more people to turn up.

Paloma seems distracted now that the visitors have gone, and she washes the same glass for ages while I wait with the tea towel. At last, she turns and hands me the glass. 'I went to Old Mill Road yesterday.' Her eyes sparkle with excitement. 'I think I know which house Mum lived in. My *birth* mum, I mean.'

'Really? Oh my God.' I grasp her arm and throw down the tea towel. I've got butterflies and it's not even my mum! 'How did you know which house it was?'

Paloma abandons the washing-up. 'The only thing Mum remembered from the time she adopted me was seeing a blurry photo of me in my birth mum's arms in front of a red door with an old-fashioned bell-pull in Old Mill Road. When I got there, there were no red doors in the street, so it's obviously been changed – *but* ... there was only one house I could see that had—'

'An old-fashioned bell-pull!' My eyes widen. 'Bloody hell! So did you knock on the door?'

She shakes her head. 'I felt so sick with nerves and excitement to think I might be standing right outside the house where my birth mum grew up, I just couldn't do it. I couldn't bring myself to walk up the path.' She closes her eyes and swallows hard, remembering. 'But I will. I definitely will.'

I nod. 'I'll come with you, if you want me to. Or would you rather go alone?'

'No! Maybe. Oh, I don't know, Twi. It's all so weird. Can I let you know?'

'Of course!' I touch her arm. 'You do realise she probably won't live there any more?'

Paloma nods. 'I know. She was only sixteen in that photograph. She could be anywhere by now. But I'm hoping the people who live there will be able to tell me where the family went. And if they don't know, I'll knock on some neighbours' doors and—'

The doorbell rings. I give Paloma a tight hug. 'This is all *so* exciting. I'm sure you'll find her. We'll talk about it some more later, okay?' Then I hurry through to answer the door.

Becky, one of my best friends from schooldays, is beaming on the doorstep, with a gaggle of 'the girls' behind her. She hugs me and says, 'We all skipped lunch so we'd be able to do a good tasting job for you!'

It's all really relaxed, with everyone sitting round the big oak table in the kitchen or standing chatting, sipping tea or Prosecco, and stopping occasionally to scribble on their score card.

Everyone seems genuinely delighted I'm opening a café in the village.

'It's obvious you're filling a big gap in the market,' murmurs Paloma as we stand together, refilling the cake stands. 'And from the reaction to your cakes, it looks like you might be run off your feet when you open.'

'God, I hope so.'

My phone rings and I go to answer it, thinking it's probably someone apologising for being late. I don't know the number that flashes up.

'Hi, Twilight?'

'Yes.' My heart sinks. It's Lucy.

'A little bird told me you're having a cake-tasting party. Can anyone come?'

'Well, it's not really a party. Just a few people ...' I trail off awkwardly, wondering how on earth she got wind of it. You can't keep anything quiet in a village as small as Hart's End.

'I'm following a "clean diet" these days, but I'm sure I could step off the wagon for the afternoon, if it's in aid of helping a friend,' she says, and my eyebrows shoot up.

A *friend*? She has to be joking. Has she conveniently forgotten how she terrorised me for years? The only reason she's phoning is because she can't bear being left out.

'Well, I don't know ...' I hate myself for dithering. Why can't I just tell her straight that she's not invited? It's not as if I owe her anything, for goodness' sake!

Paloma is frowning at me. She's probably guessed who it is. No one else but Lucy would make me so ridiculously awkward.

'It would just be me and Jason. And Olivia,' Lucy says, sounding affronted that I'm not immediately welcoming her with open arms.

'Fine. Come round.' I hang up, hating myself for giving in so easily.

'What's wrong?' asks Paloma, seeing my glum expression. 'Was that Lucy?'

I nod. 'She heard I was having a party. She's coming over with Jason and Olivia.'

Paloma looks annoyed. 'What a cheek, phoning up to demand an invitation! I'd have told her where to go, although maybe not in so many words.' She shakes her head. 'Honestly, she hates to think she's not right at the hub of things. The queen of our little community!'

I respond with a weary frown.

'You'd already decided there was no way you wanted her here,' says Paloma. 'You should have just told her straight, Twi, that you wanted to keep the party small, so you'd only invited a certain number.'

With a sigh, I point out that Lucy did let me borrow her granny's recipe book and that she was also providing curtain material, which made it hard to say no to her.

But I feel weak, like I'm making excuses for giving in to her.

A feeling of despair settles over me.

Will things ever change?

Chapter 11

The afternoon, which was going so well, is spoiled now because I'm permanently on edge, waiting for the doorbell to ring.

What's Lucy's motive for coming here with Jason and Olivia? Because I'm damned sure it's not to tell me which of my cakes she prefers! Perhaps it's to lord it over me with her darling Jason dancing attendance on her. She didn't mention bringing the curtains over, even though she assured me I would have them in plenty of time.

A thought occurs.

What if the only reason Lucy offered to dress my café windows was so that she could leave me high and dry on launch day?

Paloma would say I'm being paranoid again. But what's that well-known saying? *Just because I'm paranoid doesn't mean someone isn't out to get me!*

The doorbell rings and I go to answer it, feeling heavy with dread.

The threesome on the doorstep are all linking arms, a beaming Lucy in the middle. They look as if they're about to perform a celebratory can-can in honour of my cake-tasting session.

Lucy sniffs the air appreciatively. 'Everything certainly smells good. But I guess the proof is in the eating.' She lets go of the other two and marches forward when I usher them in.

'Just go on through,' I say sarcastically to her back as she disappears into the kitchen, gravitating towards the group of chattering women. Olivia pinches my upper arm as she walks past and gives me a knowing look. 'Just checking those bingo wings.'

Jason hangs back and we exchange an amused look.

'It's like going out with twins,' he murmurs. 'They're never apart these days and they're always whispering, although they stop immediately when I walk into the room. Olivia sees far more of Lucy than I do. Especially now they've embarked on this mission to get the whole of Hart's End fighting fit.'

'Oh, poor you.'

He grins. 'Not really. I quite like it, actually. With Lucy engaged elsewhere, it means I can get out with the lads more often.'

I smile at him. He's the same Jason I remember of old. Laid-back and happy to go with the flow. It would take someone with a personality like his to put up with a demanding type like Lucy Slater.

'You're looking good,' he says, sweeping his eyes over me. 'Being an entrepreneur suits you.'

'Thanks. But I'm not *officially* an entrepreneur until next week when we open.'

He concedes this with a smile. 'I suppose not. June 1st, isn't it?'

'That's right.' I feel flattered he's made a point of finding out.

'I'll be there. And I'm hoping for double chocolate cookies.' His eyes twinkle at me. 'You see, I haven't forgotten.'

I laugh. 'Wow. I didn't realise my baking was *that* memorable!'

'The cookies were. You used to bake them every Saturday especially for me.'

We smile at each other. And just for a moment, looking into those lovely, kind eyes the colour of melting chocolate, it's as if the intervening fourteen years never happened and we're right back to the days of Jason and me. Wrapped up in each other. Inhabiting our own private little bubble of happiness.

The eye contact lasts a second longer than it should.

Jason coughs and looks down at his feet, and I launch into my party piece: 'So if you could taste everything in sight and give each cake a mark out of ten, that would be fab. Just a bit of fun, really.'

He grins and heads for the kitchen. 'My idea of heaven. And not a "clean diet" sheet in sight.'

With a heavy heart, I join them in the kitchen.

Lucy already has Jason welded to her side and is holding forth on the subject of her 'boot camp' training session the following day. She'll have to do without me, I'm afraid. I've got far too much to do to get the café up and running.

'I'm sure I can count on you all to attend my boot camp,' Lucy is saying. 'The 10k is in such a good cause and we have to set an example to the rest of the village. Get as many people joining in as possible.'

I happen to catch Jason's eye when she mentions boot camp, and he grimaces ever so slightly at the thought. I suppress a smile and look down at my feet.

'Wouldn't you agree, Twilight?' barks Lucy, and I glance up to find everyone looking at me. Why is she putting *me* on the spot? Or is that a stupid question?

I glance at Paloma but she's just grinning away at the thought of me being forced to do some exercise.

'Er, yes. Absolutely,' I bluster. 'It's a great cause. Children's charities.'

Lucy nods approvingly. 'So I can definitely count on you to be there tomorrow, then?'

Everyone is looking expectantly at me. So I nod. 'Yes, I'll be there.'

Lucy's small smile sends a shiver through me. Oh, God. What's she got planned? If it's as horrendous as the 'Big Breakfast at Tiffany's' nonsense, I'll be going straight home.

Soon after this, everyone starts making a move to leave, and I can't help wondering if it's 'the Lucy effect'. She always seems to hijack conversations, bringing all the attention back to herself. I don't know how Jason stands it. I glance over at him, just as he tenderly tucks a lock of Lucy's hair behind her ear. Lucy flaps at his hand in irritation and he just grins.

As it turns out, Lucy and Olivia decide they'd like to see the treehouse, so after waving the rest of the girls off, I'm obliged to take them up there, which actually really grates on me. It was my own private little hideaway for so long. It still is, if I'm being honest. I don't want Lucy Slater polluting it!

Paloma, bless her, tries to dissuade them, saying, 'The ladder sways a bit. So I'd hang on quite tightly if I were you, unless you want to come a cropper.'

Lucy hesitates, her foot on the bottom rung, but Jason, behind her, grabs her bottom and pushes her up. She squeals and pretends to be cross, but you can tell she quite likes it, and she makes it to the top no trouble at all.

'Oh, I never tried the lemon drizzle cake,' calls Olivia through the treehouse window, just as I'm about to follow them up.

'I'll get fresh supplies!' I say, heading back into the house.

I grab a plastic box and start filling it with an assortment of little cake squares, glancing out of the window towards the treehouse, wondering what they're talking about.

'So, a café owner, eh?'

I spin round. Lucy is standing right behind me, which is a bit spooky because I never heard her come in. She must have followed me down the ladder.

'Yes.' I force a laugh. 'Who'd have believed it.'

'Setting up a business isn't easy. You're very brave to do it.'

'Very brave or very stupid.'

She shrugs. 'You have to take a risk. I took a risk with my on-line clothing business and luckily, it's working out.'

I nod. 'Good for you.' I'd heard on the grapevine that in five years of business, Lucy has sold three tunic tops made out of black PVC and one skirt held together with giant safety pins. But at least she's doing what she loves. And it's not as if she and Jason need the money, by all accounts.

I busy myself cutting up a Madeira cake into squares. 'If your heart is in it, you should just go for it.'

'And is your heart in selling coffee and cakes?'

'Yes. It is, actually.' I glance over my shoulder at her. Is she belittling my ambition? Or just being curious? 'It's a bit of a dream come true, to be honest. And it's important to Dad. He's over the moon I'm making use of his shop.'

She nods thoughtfully then sits down on a stool and just watches me. Her silence makes me clumsy and the cake slice slips out of my hand.

As I dive down to rescue it, Lucy says, 'I do *hope* your café is a success.'

My eyes dart up to her face. It's a simple enough statement. But something in her tone makes me hear warning bells – like years ago, at first school, when she'd taunt me, saying softly, 'You *like* that pencil case, don't you?' then next day it would be found ripped and lying in a pool of mud.

I'm crouched on the floor and Lucy's staring down at me from her perch on the stool, an intense expression in those ethereal-looking, black-rimmed eyes. A feeling of nausea hits from nowhere. Grabbing the cake slice, I scramble to my feet and move away from her, over to the window.

'Gosh, it's hot in here.' I fumble with the catch and finally get the window open. I stand there, staring out, gulping in air. 'It must be because the oven's been on.' I glance back, forcing a smile. 'I suppose a day of seventy-degree heat isn't the best time to be baking for England!'

Her continuing silence is more menacing than any insults she could hurl at me.

With hands that tremble slightly, I snap the lid on the box and head for the door. How can it be that after all this time, whenever Lucy is in the same room, my heart is always in my mouth, just waiting for her to pounce?

As I pass, she grabs my arm, just above the wrist, and I stop in my tracks and turn to face her.

She smiles and hops off the stool. 'I'm sure it *will* be a success. Your café, I mean. Now, let's get back in there, otherwise there's a danger we might miss out on some juicy gossip.'

She links my arm and squeezes it lightly and we walk out to the treehouse.

Paloma, leaning on the windowsill, smiles at us from on high.

We must look, for all the world, like old friends happily catching up on the years in between ...

Chapter 12

When I wake up, I realise it's Sunday and I give a thankful yawn and stretch. Even with a café opening frighteningly imminent, and dozens of jobs still to tackle before then, surely a small lie-in on a Sunday is allowed?

Then two things occur simultaneously to flatten my prospects of a well-earned snooze.

Someone bangs on the front door.

And I remember it's Lucy's boot camp day.

Groaning, I pull the duvet over my head, hoping Paloma will take the hint and jog off to the assembly point on the village green without me. But no such luck. After a blissful few seconds of silence, my phone starts to ring.

Ten minutes later, we set off on the short walk to the village green.

A rumbling noise in the distance makes me grip Paloma's arm. 'Thunder.'

'Really?' Paloma shakes her head and gazes up at the sky. There are still patches of blue in between the grey clouds. 'I don't think so.' She grins. 'Is this an excuse to get out of training?'

I shake my head, my eyes trained on the suspiciously murky horizon. 'It was definitely thunder. And no, it's not an excuse.'

It's been hot and humid for days now and on the news last night, they were predicting a storm. That's another reason – actually the *main* reason – I wanted to just hibernate indoors today.

Storms really freak me out.

'If there *is* a storm brewing, it looks pretty far away to me,' says Paloma, and I feel my shoulders relax. She's right. It looks miles away. I need to forget about it and concentrate on the more immediate crisis – surviving Lucy's boot camp.

'The exercise will be good for you,' my dear friend adds, far too cheerfully for my liking.

She looks as fresh as the proverbial daisy in her dark blue and cute pink top baring her very flat midriff, whereas 'bedraggled dandelion' feels like a more apt description for me – not great when I'm having to psych myself up to face the Vile Twins, Lucy and Olivia, and no doubt have my upper arms 'jiggle tested' at random.

I haven't had time to iron my shorts and T-shirt – or my face, for that matter. There's a big red crease down my left cheek where I must have been lying on my arm. A bit of make-up would have worked wonders, but Paloma wouldn't let me. We didn't have time, apparently. We needed to join the keep-fitters. Get into the community spirit. Show that Lucy Slater what we were made of.

My answer to that was a rebellious grunt.

When we arrive, the first person I see is Theo Steel, looking Olympics-ready in proper running gear. My heart lurches when I see who he's talking to: Olivia. She's looking up at him with a little coquettish smile, twirling a lock of blonde hair as he regales her with some story, using his big hands expressively. My teeth gnash together. Olivia couldn't look more perfect in a skimpy jade green top and little black Lycra shorts that show off her tiny peachy bum. As I watch surreptitiously, Theo Steel leans closer to her with one of his big, sexy smiles, and drapes his arm casually around her shoulders ...

'What's wrong?' asks Paloma. 'Have you spotted Lucy? You look like an alpha male tiger who's just set eyes on an arch rival.'

I clear my throat awkwardly. 'No, it's – um – Olivia. I'm worried she'll come over and start telling me off for not having lost a stone since she last saw me.' I bend down to retie my shoelaces and hide the weird flush that's crept into my cheeks.

If Theo Steel wants to mess around with Olivia, that's entirely up to him. It's absolutely none of my business. I won't even look at them. They are of no interest to me whatsoever ...

Paloma laughs. 'Stop glaring at her. You really don't like her, do you?'

I feign nonchalance. 'Who? Olivia? Never really thought about it to be honest.'

A surprising number of people are already assembled on the green – probably around fifty or sixty of them – and from what I can make out, they seem to fall into one of two categories. There are the ones standing round in little groups, looking stiff and awkward, probably because the last time they went out so skimpily dressed was on the beach in Magaluf. And then there are the ones who are limbering up, proving they can touch their toes with ease and generally showing off.

I look around for Jason, but he doesn't seem to be here. Wise man. He must have come up with a solid excuse because I can't imagine Lucy letting him off lightly.

Paloma does a supple jog on the spot.

'Don't.' I glare at her. 'Just *don't*.'

She grins. 'Okay. Keep your hair on. Christ, I wonder what torture Lucy has in store for us.'

We soon find out. After a group session of stretches, led by Olivia, Lucy announces that we're going to attempt a five-mile run through the lanes around Hart's End.

'The route is clearly marked. Just look for the yellow stickers on fences and tree trunks.' Lucy raises her slightly screechy voice to be heard at the back and I want to put my fingers in my ears. 'Although if you follow the person in front, you're not likely to get lost. And it goes without saying, you should all run at your own pace. If you've been sticking to our suggested training schedule for the past few weeks, you should be getting into fairly good shape by now.' She glances at Olivia. 'We've seen a lot of you out running through the village in the evenings and at weekends, so well done! Although I have heard through the grapevine that some of you seem determined to remain couch potatoes.'

A titter goes round the assembled group and there are a few guilty smiles.

'I've heard a few interesting excuses why people haven't got time to exercise. But being forced to bake cakes all day, every day, is probably the best one.'

Lucy looks 'jokingly' in my direction as she says this, and more people laugh. A few who know about me setting up the café turn to grin at me, and my face flushes the colour of pickled beetroot.

Then I catch a familiar eye and wish the ground could swallow me and my blushes right up. Theo Steel is grinning over at me, having clearly got the joke.

'You know who I'm talking about – *Twilight*!' calls Lucy as I grit my teeth. More laughter. 'But hey, listen, don't worry about it. Just take it slowly. Even if you have to *walk all the way*, that's absolutely fine.' She's talking directly to me now, which is so bloody mortifying. 'Remember, finishing the course is the important thing. All right?' She cocks her head to the side and smiles at me as if I'm five years old.

'Fine,' I mumble.

'Great!' She rubs her hands together, murmurs something to Olivia, then announces, 'Okay, let's get going. Remember it's not a race. This way, people!'

'God, she's loving this.' Paloma grins as we set off. 'Being in charge.'

I curl my lip moodily in the direction of Lucy's slender form as she runs effortlessly towards the group of trees at the edge of the village green, pursued by her eager band of followers, including Theo Steel near the head of the pack. 'Why am I doing this?'

'You'll be fine. Exercise is a fantastic stress reliever,' says Paloma. 'It'll give you a lift. Help you meet the challenge of your café opening next week head-on.'

'Hm.'

'Are you all right?' she asks a minute later, looking genuinely concerned, and I nod. I'd like to expand on this, but I've run about fifty paces and already breathing has become a scarily strenuous effort.

'Listen, I might ... walk a bit,' I gasp. 'You ... just run on ahead. I don't ... want to hold you up.'

'Are you sure?'

'Yes.' I attempt a grin, although it takes up *far* too much energy. 'Go on ... bugger off ... you're showing me up.'

She laughs and accelerates off. 'See you at the finish line,' she calls, turning to smile then sprinting for the trees.

I want to shout, *Yes. A week next Tuesday!* But I fear the effort would finish me off. Panting along resignedly, I stare after Paloma.

Lucy, Olivia and Theo have disappeared into the trees, but my heart is going to literally explode out of my chest if I don't slow down a bit. I keep up the pretence of jogging normally until everyone else has overtaken me – even old Stan, who has dodgy joints and celebrated his ninetieth birthday last week. He gives me a cheery wave as he power walks past.

I come to an abrupt halt then start walking very slowly to get my breath back. It's my own fault. I should have kept training like Paloma, who's probably halfway round the course by now. It's just every time I think of the gym, I remember the look on Theo Steel's face when I barged into the changing room and I cringe with embarrassment all over again. One thing's for sure: I definitely *haven't* got stamina! I can no longer rely on that stupid myth to get me through. I need to actually get out there and *move* to get myself fit, and I will. I definitely will. I'm not having bloody Lucy Slater making a show of me again.

For now, though, my aim is to get round this 5k course without expiring in the process.

The route is nicely scenic, winding in and out of the trees by the village green then along country lanes in the direction of Lake Heath. I walk at a brisk pace, keeping my eye on Stan up ahead. He keeps disappearing round a bend and at those moments I start to feel uneasy, wondering if I'll be doomed to pound the lanes around Hart's End forever, totally lost, like the conclusion to some weird horror film. Then Stan pops up again in the distance and my panic subsides.

At one point, the route takes us up quite a steep incline, which slows me down a bit. I'm sweaty and out of breath when I get to the top, but it's worth it for the lovely view over Lake Heath. I'm getting the hang of spotting Lucy's markers now, on trees and churchyard walls, and a few of the runners who started off enthusiastically have slowed right down. I can see them up ahead, although it's still going to take me a while to catch them up.

After we've passed through Lake Heath, the route doubles back towards Hart's End, crossing several fields. I nearly get lost at that point because the track is practically non-existent. Then I spot Stan's white peaky cap up ahead by a gap in a hedge and breathe a sigh of relief.

The main road into Hart's End is on the other side of the hedge and I spot a signpost that says the village is one-and-a-half miles away. My heart sinks. I'm not sure I've got another hundred yards in my tank, never mind over a mile! My legs feel like jelly.

A squeaky noise makes me turn. A woman on a bike is pedalling very slowly up the slight incline. She's red in the face and sweating with the effort, and I feel an instant solidarity. As she passes, we exchange a knowing smile.

'Hellish this, isn't it?' she shouts cheerfully.

'Bloody awful. Especially when you haven't done any training.'

She slows to a stop and gets off the bike. 'I'm meeting my friend for lunch.' She nods at a country pub in the distance. 'Wish to God I'd brought the car instead.'

'Know what you mean.'

'Where are you going?'

'Hart's End. The other runners are probably back there by now.'

She makes a sympathetic face. 'I'm Sue, by the way.'

'Twilight.'

Her eyes open in surprise. 'Lovely name.'

'Thanks.'

'You can borrow my bike if you like.'

'What? Really?'

She shrugs. 'You'd get back a bit faster, wouldn't you?'

'Well, yes, I suppose so.' It's extremely tempting. But I can't. *Can I?* 'But what about you?'

'Oh, I'm getting a lift back with my friend. I'm not getting back on *this* bloody thing. I'll give you my address and you can drop the bike back any time.'

I smile. 'It's a lovely offer. Thank you so much. But I can't. I'd feel terrible cheating like that.'

'Sure?'

'Sure. But thanks!'

'Okay.' She clambers back on the bike and pushes off, calling back cheerfully, 'Have a good one!'

'You, too. Enjoy your lunch!'

She waves energetically and gets a bit of a wobble on before managing to straighten up.

Mournfully, I plod on as my new friend disappears from view, round a bend in the lane. Why didn't I say yes to the bike? I'm on my own again now. Even Stan's cap is nowhere to be seen. Will everyone be waiting for me when I get back to the village green? Oh God, yes, they will. Lucy will make sure they are. I'll no doubt get a welcome committee and a round of hilarious applause for coming in last. Theo Steel will be there, grinning away and clapping and thinking I'm a total plonker.

A mechanical noise behind me distracts me from this nightmare vision.

I turn and spy the number forty-five bus to Hart's End rumbling slowly up the incline, and my heart leaps in my chest. It's like when the cavalry turns up in those cowboy and Indian movies my granddad used to love.

My tired brain is suddenly razor sharp. There's a bus stop a few yards ahead and if I hurry, I'll just make it. It would be rude not to! Fumbling in my shorts pocket, my hand closes on the pound coin I use to work my locker at the gym. Yes! I start to run, frantically sticking my hand out to stop the bus.

It grinds to a halt, the doors open and I clamber on.

'One-fifty,' says the driver, unsmilingly.

My heart sinks. 'But it's only a mile to Hart's End.'

'It's still one-fifty.'

I clutch my stomach. 'I think I'm going to be sick,' I tell him truthfully. 'But if I could just sit down, I might be okay.'

For one terrible moment, as he glares at me under his mono-brow, I think he's actually going to get up and manhandle me off the bus.

Then he jerks his thumb backwards with a disgusted look, waving me on.

'Really?' I'm so grateful I want to kiss him.

I fall into the nearest seat, ignoring my gawping fellow passengers, and stare out of the window as my heart rate slows and the nausea subsides. My ankle is throbbing gently.

As we approach Hart's End, I catch sight of several groups of runners jogging wearily to the green and I quickly slide down in my seat to avoid being seen. I'm planning to get off at the high street stop, then jog the rest of the way, mingling with the other runners so Lucy won't be able to single me out.

Approaching the stop, I glance this way and that along the high street. The coast is clear. No one will ever know I cheated a little bit! Feeling pleased with myself, I step off the bus – and the first person I spot, coming out of the newsagent's with a paper under his arm, is Theo Steel.

I dive behind the bus shelter and hide until he's safely on his way, then I start jogging after him, smiling at my lucky escape. Thank goodness he didn't see me!

Finally arriving at the green, I join Paloma who's flopped out on her back on the grass. She sits up, shading her eyes against the sun. Luckily, the threatened storm has passed. 'Hey, well done. You did it. Not bad for someone who never exercises.'

'Aw shucks,' I say, feigning modesty. 'It wasn't too hard at all, really.'

'Glad to hear it,' says a voice at my shoulder, and I spin round to see Theo Steel standing there.

'Oh, hi. Yes, I finished just behind you, I think.' I laugh nervously. 'What took you so long?'

He grins. 'I did the course twice.'

'Ah! Right. Of course.' I swing round to Paloma. 'You two haven't met, have you? Paloma, this is Theo.'

Paloma gets to her feet and they shake hands. 'The man who reads books about crochet,' she says, smiling up at him.

'He was translating it,' I explain hurriedly. 'He's a book translator.'

'Really? How fascinating.'

'Is it?' He laughs. 'Well, thank you. I don't think I've ever been described as fascinating before.'

I feel a stab of irritation. Paloma's staring up at Theo Steel as if he's the eighth wonder of the world. 'Right, well, I'm off home. I need to put some frozen peas on my ankle.' I smile at them and start heading off across the green.

'Wait up!' Paloma runs after me. 'Have you hurt yourself? Let me see.'

'Congratulations on your time, Twilight,' calls Theo, and we both turn.

He's standing with his hands on his hips, grinning over. 'Very impressive. If I didn't know better, I'd think you must have come by bus.'

Chapter 13

When I get into Paloma's car next morning, I heave a sigh of relief and slump back in the seat. 'I can't believe I'll finally have proper furniture for the café.'

We're on our way to Lake Heath to collect it from Rowena.

'And it's not too shabby, either!' Paloma grins. 'Except that it is.'

'Yeah, shabby chic. Just the effect I wanted – and I won't have to do a thing to it because it's already in such great condition.'

'Just as well since it's only two days until the grand opening!'

It's been a real roller coaster of a week on all fronts.

Mum was worrying me. She kept saying everything was fine when we spoke on the phone, but for some reason I started to suspect she was protesting too much – and eventually, after a bit of delicate probing, it emerged that Dad isn't responding to the treatment the way the consultant had hoped he would, and Mum has been trying to protect me from this news. We were both in tears on the phone and I made Mum promise never to keep the truth from me again.

Things on the café front weren't going swimmingly, either. The big 'Twilight Café this way' sign that Paloma created is a real triumph, but it kept on falling down from the fence where we were trying to moor it. So in the end, I gave in and hired a local hoardings company to fix it in place. It's all money, though, and the cash is slipping through my fingers at an alarming rate.

So when Rowena Swann said I was welcome to look at the furniture she'd had in her ice-cream parlour with a view to taking it off her hands, I practically cheered down the phone. Paloma and I went to see it and it was perfect. When I asked Rowena how much she wanted for it, she mentioned a cash sum that was so reasonable, I took her hand off there and then – although I insisted on throwing in a free cake and coffee every week for a month, which she seemed quite delighted about. I think she was just really pleased to get the furniture out of her garage.

And now, Paloma and I are off to collect it.

I'm expecting her to start the engine and drive off. But instead, she takes a deep breath and turns to me, her eyes sparkling.

'I did it!' She clutches my arm. 'I knocked on the door with the old-fashioned bell-pull.'

My eyes open wide with shock. 'Oh my God! What happened? Did you find out about your mum?'

Paloma shuffles in her seat so she's angled towards me. 'Well, a lovely woman called Sylvia answered the door and we had a long chat about my search. She said the people she bought the house from were called Banbury, but that obviously wasn't Mum's family because her name is Margaret Green. At least, it *was*. Obviously if she's married, her name will have changed.'

'So what's next?'

'The woman, Sylvia, is going to ask around her neighbours and see if anyone can shed any light on where the Green family went. I gave her my number to text me if she finds anything out.'

'Gosh. That's so great. I guess the more people who know you're searching for her, the better.'

Paloma gives an excited little nod.

I lean over and give her a quick hug. 'I'll keep my fingers crossed.'

'Come on, then. Let's get this furniture.'

When we arrive at Rowena Swann's modern semi-detached in Lake Heath, she already has the garage door open ready for us. She greets us with a big smile and a thumbs-up and helps us load the furniture into the back of Paloma's estate car. It's like a giant puzzle, trying to fit as many chairs in as possible at weird angles and it's fairly clear it's going to take several trips to collect the whole lot.

When we're loaded up, we stand chatting in the driveway.

'So are you putting your feet up now you've retired?' asks Paloma.

Rowena laughs. 'I hate that word "retirement". It makes me feel as if I'm a poor old horse being put out to grass. No, there'll be no lazing around. I plan to stay very active and take up loads of hobbies I've never had time for.'

I smile. 'That's what my Auntie June was planning – until she stepped into the role of chief babysitter for her grand-daughter. Not that she minds, of course.'

'Of course not.' A shadow passes across Rowena's face. 'I don't have any family, so I guess my time is my own.'

There's a brief silence. Then Paloma says, 'I'm not even sure I want kids, but I suppose I've got a while to decide.'

Rowena nods, a pensive look in her eyes. 'Children are such a blessing,' she murmurs. 'I never realised that until …' She breaks off and smiles. 'Anyway, hope this furniture is okay for you!'

'I hope you'll be there on opening day,' I say as we get back in the car. 'Remember your free coffee and cake.'

'I'll be there, Twilight!' She waves gaily. 'Along with hundreds of others, dying to sample your coffee and your baking!'

'Hundreds?' I turn to Paloma as she motors carefully down the driveway, mindful of the shifting load in the back. 'I wish.'

'Hey, you never know.' She grins and turns slowly out onto the road. 'We've put up all those posters in prominent places. It wouldn't surprise me if you had a queue out the door on Saturday.'

I'm thinking about Rowena. I glance behind and she's still standing there, staring after us. I wave but she mustn't be able to see me because she doesn't respond.

'Rowena seemed sad when we talked about family,' I murmur.

'Yes, I think she lived in Brighton until she moved here to take over the ice-cream parlour a few years ago. Perhaps her family is back in Brighton.'

I frown. 'But I'm sure she said she didn't *have* any family, full stop. Which is sad.'

Paloma nods. 'Family is certainly an emotional topic. Speaking of which, have you heard from your parents lately?'

'Just last night, actually. Dad's got a surprise for me, apparently. Mum said she's sent it in the post.'

'Aw, bless him. He's so lovely, your dad. He really doesn't deserve …' She trails off.

A lump fills my throat. '*You* don't deserve the hand fate

dealt you, either. You must miss Linda so much.' Her adoptive mum was such a lovely, kind-hearted woman and so full of fun. I can't imagine the chasm she must have left in Paloma's life. 'I so hope you find your birth mum.'

Paloma pastes on a smile. 'Well, if I do, she couldn't possibly be as lovely as Mum. Linda, I mean.'

I nod sadly. 'You're probably right.'

*****

We've just finished unloading the third and final batch of furniture when a familiar car drives up and parks on the forecourt.

'Oh, great,' I murmur, agitation rising up inside me. 'My all-time favourite person.'

I only hope Lucy has come to bring me the curtains. The café is going to look pretty bare without some form of window dressing. Although I'm still not sure I trust her, despite her kind offer to donate the curtain material free of charge.

She emerges with a bag and I can see she has the curtains inside.

'I just need to check the length against the windows,' she says, brushing straight past me and making for the café entrance, her high heels tapping on the concrete. She's wearing a couture trouser suit in navy with cream braiding.

'Feel free.' I roll my eyes and we follow her inside. Paloma shakes her head in amused disbelief at Lucy's rudeness.

'She's a little charmer all right,' I mutter, and Lucy swings round suspiciously.

'With ears the size of dinner plates, apparently,' murmurs Paloma, without moving her lips.

'Who's a little charmer?' Lucy demands.

Paloma shakes her head and says, with a charming smile, 'No, no, Twi was just saying she's feeling *a little calmer* now you've brought along those gorgeous curtains. She's been so stressed out about the café opening. Haven't you, Twi?'

I nod solemnly. 'Very stressed. So thank you, Lucy, for lightening my load.'

'It's no problem,' she says, narrowing her eyes at us in suspicion 'Come here and hold this end, would you?'

We do as we're told, and I wonder for the millionth time how Jason can go to bed with someone so glacial every night.

I suppose she isn't cold with him, though.

Immediately, I brush the thought away.

I really don't want to think about that ...

Once Lucy has established the length is correct, she bundles the curtains back in the bag and clack-clacks her way over to the door, clearly not intending to give me any idea of when they will be back and in position.

'Erm, when will you be bringing them back?' I ask nervously, not wanting to rock the boat. I'm hoping she'll say tomorrow morning, then we can get them up in good time. I'm still half-expecting her to snatch the curtains out of the bag and drop them in a muddy puddle out of spite.

She doesn't even bother to reply until she's back in the car. Rolling the window down, she shoots me a frosty look. 'I'll put them up for you tomorrow night.'

'But we open the following morning,' I say, dismayed, thinking of all the other things to be done the next day.

'Yes, I know that.' She sounds impatient.

'Well, it's just that we're cutting it a little fine, that's all. And I'll be so busy.'

'I don't need you there,' she snaps. 'I can do it myself.'

I nod, still not sure. But she's doing me a big favour, so I can hardly say it's not convenient for me.

'I hope you're not suggesting I'll muck it up,' she says, frowning.

'No, of course I'm not.'

'You're just nervous about Saturday, aren't you, Twi?' puts in Paloma, and I nod gratefully.

Lucy gives me another look that would instantly freeze the water in a hot tub, and drives off furiously, scattering gravel everywhere.

'Bloody hell,' breathes Paloma. '*She's* a bit stressed. Perhaps life chez Lucy-and-Jason isn't the bed of roses she'd like us to think it is.'

'Maybe.' I turn away to start setting up the tables and chairs. The state of Jason's relationship with Lucy is not a road I want to venture down ...

Chapter 14

Friday rolls around – the morning before Saturday's big café opening – and I bound out of bed. Standing in the shower, I tick jobs off on a mental list.

The cakes and scones need to be perfectly fresh, so I'll be baking and icing all the cakes today, then getting up very early tomorrow morning to bake the three different flavours of scone.

Adrenalin is already pouring through my system, making me feel nervous, excited, apprehensive and ecstatic all at the same time. I can't believe my dream of owning my own café is finally coming true! I suppose I always thought of it as just a lovely fantasy, but now circumstances have conspired to turn that dream into a reality.

I think of my parents and the excitement subsides. If only those circumstances didn't involve my lovely dad's fight for survival. A lump fills my throat. I need to phone Mum when I've got a minute, so they can feel involved in tomorrow's big opening. I know Mum really wishes they could be here, but it just wouldn't be wise for Dad to make the tiring and uncomfortable journey to Hart's End. In any case, I don't think the hospital would allow it.

Paloma comes over soon after eleven. When I open the

door, she walks in sniffing the air appreciatively. 'I could smell the aroma of baking frenzy just walking up the garden path.'

We go straight into the kitchen, where my two Cherry Bakewells in the big, shiny new flan cases I bought are almost ready. I peer into the oven. They're beautifully golden on top and I reckon they're done, so I grab the pink gingham oven gloves Paloma presented me with yesterday and take them out. My brand-new mesh trays are lined up on the bench, ready to be laden with cooling bakes. I go to my list and tick off 'Cherry Bakewells'. So far, so good. I need to work steadily and methodically today and keep a cool head. Then, hopefully, I'll be all prepared for tomorrow at ten a.m.

Tomorrow at ten a.m.! It seems a long way off. I might actually expire with excitement before then!

Before I start on the next bake, I grab the keys and we head over to the café to admire the work we did the previous afternoon.

Rowena's tables and chairs seem as if they were bought specially to fit the space, they look so perfect. And there's a single purple freesia in a little vase on every table, along with a simple white menu with navy type, designed by Paloma. I pick one of them up and try to imagine I'm a customer, looking at the menu for the first time. Would I be impressed?

'Oh God, you haven't found a spelling mistake, have you?' asks Paloma anxiously.

I smile and shake my head. 'No. It's just perfect.'

I glance around at the lovely polished wood counter with the pretty cake stands on top and the second-hand till that scrubbed up really well. The shiny knives and teaspoons standing to attention in their stainless-steel containers alongside the white dish full of tiny paper tubes of sugar. The large pastel pictures of single flowers on the walls and the pretty pale wood flooring. The only thing needed now is the curtains to make the place perfect. And Lucy has said she'll be here at seven this evening to hang them herself.

A strange feeling trickles through me. A sort of foreboding that takes me by surprise and makes me shiver. It's all *too* perfect. What if something goes wrong? What if I've forgotten something vital? What if I've spent all my savings on a café that turns out to be a failure?

Next moment, Paloma shouts, 'Is there any of that lilac paint left? I've missed a spot over here.'

'Jeez, you just can't get good staff these days,' I joke, heading into the back room to look for the paint can. The uneasy feeling has passed. I'm just super nervous about tomorrow, that's all ...

Paloma gets to work touching up a dodgy area near the skirting board while I make yet another of my lists. I need to go to the bank later so I have plenty of change for the till. Phone Mum. Check the big sign on the main road is still in place ...

'By the way, I bought this,' says Paloma, pressing the top on the paint tin, then pulling what looks like a rolled-up poster out of her bag. 'I couldn't resist.'

She grins at me. There's a smudge of lilac paint on her cheekbone, which – weirdly – tones in with her eye-shadow. She opens out the poster to show me. It's a picture of a giant cupcake with pink frosting, and the words: The More You Weigh, The Harder You Are To Kidnap. Stay Safe. Eat Cake.

I giggle. 'That's brilliant.'

'I saw it and thought it would be perfect for the café.'

I pause, thinking. 'It would be far more perfect in my kitchen.'

'Not in here?' Paloma frowns.

I sigh, not wanting to rain on her parade. 'It's just I'm not sure that's the message I want to put across, is it? Come here and eat cake and put on weight?'

She laughs. 'You sound like Olivia.'

'I know. Weight is such a tricky subject, though, isn't it? It's hard to know what you can and can't say without offending.'

'You've got a point,' she says cheerfully, rolling up the poster. 'Best just keep the message simple: Cake is brilliant!'

I nod. 'A little of what you fancy does you good?'

'Everything in moderation.' She hands me the poster. 'For your kitchen wall. Consider it a launch gift.'

'Thank you.' I smile, taking the gift. 'I'll treasure it. By the way, you've got paint on your face.'

Back at the house, I get on with the mix for my chocolate fudge cakes, which came out on top on cake-tasting day. Paloma lingers over a coffee, checking her phone for messages. I know she's hoping to hear from the bell-pull lady, Sylvia, with news of where her birth mum moved to. She puts down her phone looking dispirited, so there's obviously no news. To cheer her up, I kid her that the only reason she's still here is because she's waiting for the chocolate cake bowl to lick. She firmly denies it but when I go to put the empty bowl in the sink, she shouts, 'Oh no you don't!' then grabs it out of my hand and gets to work with the wooden spoon, scraping it out.

I can't help laughing. Paloma is like a big kid sometimes.

I just wish she could meet a nice guy to appreciate her

amazing qualities, but every time I bring up the subject, she says she's far too busy with work to even *think* about romance.

I blame Rufus Black, the egotistical artist she went out with several years ago.

She was in awe of his talent and he swept her off her feet with his charm and his intensity. Paloma is quite a practical – some would even say cynical – sort of person. Definitely not a romantic like me. But she fell heavily for Rufus and I'd never seen her so deliriously happy. Their relationship lasted a year, during which they even talked about moving in together ... until Paloma discovered that on the nights he told her he was 'working', he was actually paying sneaky visits to his ex-wife for bondage sessions.

Rufus was arrogantly unapologetic. He seemed to think Paloma should *understand*. She had, after all, laughed at the pink wireless vibrating nipple clamps he gave her for her birthday, telling him she'd sooner wear them as earrings if it was all the same to him. Surely Paloma didn't expect a man like him – a true *artist* – to suppress his natural creativity so brutally? His self-expression absolutely *had* to be given free rein, otherwise his art would suffer and his devoted fans would pay the price. Surely Paloma didn't want that?

Paloma held out the nipple clamps and told him to shove them where the sun never shone.

'Actually, don't,' she amended furiously, snatching them back. 'Because you'd probably enjoy it *way* too much. I'll take them to remind me of the twelve months I wasted, going out with the most self-centred, arrogant, deluded man on the planet.'

And with that, she swept out ...

I'd like to have been a fly on the wall for that. I never warmed to Rufus Black.

Paloma turns to me now and beams. The paint on her cheek has been joined by a splodge of chocolate cake mix by the side of her mouth. I indicate its presence by pointing at my own mouth and she flicks out her tongue. 'Right, must dash or I'll miss my deadline and lose a client.' She hops off the stool and disappears, calling, 'See you later!'

When the doorbell rings a few minutes later, I assume Paloma must have forgotten something. So you could knock me down with a feather when I open the door to find someone else standing on the doorstep.

Jason.

Chapter 15

'Hi! What are you doing here?' I feel unaccountably nervous.

'Just came to wish you luck for tomorrow.' He gives a sheepish smile. 'I know I could do that tomorrow, but everyone else will be there and you'll be busy.' He shrugs. 'We haven't really had a chance to chat, just the two of us, since you've been back.'

I nod. It's funny but I'd been feeling exactly the same. 'Come in. I'll put the kettle on.'

When we broke up all those years ago, I was absolutely distraught but deep inside, I remember thinking it was probably for the best in the long run. In our last year together, the passion had waned and we'd become principally great friends rather than romantic lovers. I bore Jason no ill will for ending our relationship – despite the fact it was to start seeing Lucy, my archenemy. It was just one of those things. Our relationship had faltered under the strain of being long-distance, with me away at uni. And I grudgingly acknowledge that the fact he and Lucy are still together after all this time probably means he made the right decision.

But it still feels like there's unfinished business between us. Nothing major, but it would be nice to really talk. I loved

Jason for a long time, and if I'm being honest with myself, I think I still do on some level ...

'Sit down.' I pull a chair out from the kitchen table and Jason flops into it, and I'm aware of his gaze following me as I fill the kettle and gather cups and coffee and teaspoons.

'I never thought you'd come back to Hart's End. Not properly, like this,' he says. 'I knew how much you hated what Lucy did to you as a kid. I suppose I assumed that as long as she was living here, you never would.'

I turn, fixing on a smile, bringing the coffee over. 'Well, it just shows you should never assume things. And anyway, that's all in the past.' I wave my hand as if it's of no consequence to me that, already, we're talking about Lucy.

'Well, I'm glad you're here,' Jason says with a shy smile, stirring his coffee. 'How does it feel to be back in the village after life in the big city?'

I laugh then glance at the ceiling, considering. 'It feels ... okay, actually. I mean, I was nervous about coming back but people have been really welcoming on the whole, so ... yes, it's fine.'

'On the whole?'

I feel my face flush. The only person who's made me uneasy since I've been back is Lucy, but I don't want to talk about her to Jason, so I say, 'No, *everyone* has been nice about my return. Sometimes, it feels as if I've never been away.'

He looks at me without speaking for a moment, his brown eyes sad. Then he shuffles in his chair and says, 'I never wanted to hurt you, Twilight. I loved you so much, but ...' He shakes his head, almost angrily.

I swallow hard on the sudden constriction in my throat. Then I force myself to say brightly, 'I know, but long-distance relationships are a killer. It would never have worked. It's probably just as well you started to have feelings for Lucy.'

He glances down. 'But that's the thing, Twi. I didn't. Not really. At least, not at the start.'

I stare at him in surprise. 'What do you mean?'

He takes a deep breath and blows it out slowly. Then he looks at me and says, 'I didn't cope well with you leaving for university. I ran up debts, drowning my sorrows in drink and buying expensive toys to dull the pain of not having you there all the time. It was a bad time. And I wasn't earning much as an apprentice in the IT company.'

'I never knew,' I say, dismayed. 'You always sounded so cheerful on the phone.'

He laughs bitterly. 'Of course I did. It was an act. The last thing I wanted was to make you feel guilty about following your dreams.'

'So what happened? You got out of debt, didn't you?'

He nods. 'Yes, with Lucy's help.'

This is all news to me.

'She'd liked me for a long time.' He purses his lips. 'Well, you knew that ...'

I nod, not liking the direction this is going in.

'So she got her dad to give me a job at his petrochemicals plant. He didn't really want to. I don't think he trusted me, to be honest, and who could blame him? But she kept going on at him to give me a chance and finally, he relented.' He sighs. 'It was a big increase in responsibility and salary, and I grabbed the opportunity with both hands and managed to get back on track financially.' He glances at me sheepishly. 'I owed it all to Lucy, didn't I?'

I can't quite believe what I'm hearing. 'So you ended our

relationship to be with Lucy because she got you out of *debt*?' I ask, horrified.

He grimaces. 'It sounds terrible when you say it like that. But I guess that was part of it.'

There's a long silence as I absorb all of this.

'But do you love her?' I ask at last.

He nods. 'Yes, I do. Not like I loved you. I'll never love anyone like that.' We lock eyes and my stomach lurches.

Jason sighs and looks away. 'I know Lucy's a pain in the arse at times but she's really sweet with me. Well, not always, obviously. She has her moments.' His mouth twists. 'But it's because she has so many hang-ups about not being good enough. She hates herself most of the time. She used to be so jealous of you.'

Laughter bursts from me. 'Jealous? Of me? You've got to be joking.'

He shakes his head. 'I'm not. Her parents were great at buying her things, but they never had much time for her. They were far too wrapped up in each other. It's sad, really. You were such a contrast, with your close family unit.'

'Hang on, so I'm supposed to feel *sorry* for Lucy? Well, forgive me if I pass on that one. It wasn't *her* whose childhood was ruined by the relentless bloody bullying.' I shake my head incredulously, my throat tightening.

Jason is staring down at the floor, a strange look on his face. 'Don't be too hard on Lucy. There are other things. Things you don't know ...' He trails off and looks up.

'What things?'

He looks confused for a second. Then he seems to realise he's said too much because he pastes on a smile. 'Nothing. At least, nothing for you to worry about.'

He leans over and grasps my hand. The warmth of his fingers curled around mine makes my insides jolt with longing and a single tear leaks down my face. Gently, he strokes a lock of hair behind my ear and my whole body quivers, feelings of long ago rushing right back at his touch. *Lying entwined on my bed, listening to music, talking about anything and everything, and those endless, languorous kisses* ... 'Can I smell burning?' Jason breaks into my memories.

'What?' I stare, bemused, deep into those brown eyes I could never quite forget.

'The cakes?'

'Oh.' Snapped right back to the present, I scrape back my chair and dash to the oven. Both cakes are charred on top, beyond rescuing. I pull one out in a panic then reach for the other but manage to catch the top of my thumb on the shelf above. Yelping, I drop the second spoiled chocolate fudge cake in its tin on the hob and cross to the sink where I stick my thumb under cold running water.

Jason is there in a heartbeat, asking if I'm okay. I nod and try to smile, hoping he thinks the reason there are tears in my eyes now is because of the burn on my thumb – and not because of what he's just admitted to me. That part of the reason our relationship ended was because of stupid money!

He says he'd better leave me to sort out the cakes, and we part with a wistful smile.

My head is still reeling from what he told me. We could have sorted out his problems between us. If he'd told me how much he missed me, I might even have switched to a uni or college nearer so we could have seen each other more often. But he hadn't given me that chance because he hadn't told me. Instead, he'd allowed bloody Lucy Slater to insinuate her way into his life and save him, effectively tying him to her side by luring him into the family firm. That's what it sounded like to me, anyway.

What a horrible mess.

And now I've burned my chocolate fudge cakes.

I force myself to concentrate on the baking ... to think about measurements of butter and sugar rather than how things could have turned out so differently for Jason and me. It's hard, though.

Then, just as I'm checking on my Victoria sandwich cakes in the oven, Paloma pops her head round the back door and calls through. 'Lucy's just arrived with the curtains. She wants the keys to the café.'

I'm thrown into an instant panic. 'But she's early. She said seven and it's only four, and I can't leave because I've got cakes in the oven!'

'She doesn't need you there, Twi. She can put the curtains up herself. She just needs the keys.'

I stand there, dithering. I don't want to give Lucy Slater the keys to my café. It's probably completely irrational, I know, but that's how it is. On the other hand, can I risk leaving the kitchen while I've got things in the oven, even for ten minutes? There's nothing worse than a dry, over-baked cake.

Paloma is looking at me expectantly.

'Can you go over there and open up for her?' I ask at last.

She glances at her watch and frowns. 'I've got a deadline of half an hour ago for a really important client. But okay.' She holds out her hand. 'Keys?'

Sighing, I snatch them off the bench and hand them over.

Paloma smiles. 'It'll be fine. I doubt Lucy plans to trash the café while you're not there.'

Feeling silly, I nod and she dashes off.

I tell myself to relax. All will be fine. The café will have some lovely curtains to complete the look. But every now and then I feel compelled to run upstairs and peer out of my bedroom window to check if Lucy's car is still there.

After I've done this three times, I hear the letter slot rattle and something falls onto the mat. Going through to the hall, I see that she's pushed the café keys through the front door. Once all the cakes are out of the oven, I slip out the back door then through the garden gate and along to the café.

Holding my breath, I open up and walk in.

I'm not sure what I was expecting, but actually, Lucy has done a brilliant job. The curtains are really beautiful, long swathes of soft fabric billowing all the way down to the floor, in lovely pastel-coloured stripes. They're absolutely perfect.

I look around at my lovely café and my heart swells with happiness and pride. It's time to put the past well and truly behind me and concentrate on the future. Paloma is right. Lucy has changed. She didn't have to offer me the curtain material, but she did and it turned out perfectly.

A calm feeling settles over me.

It's high time I forgave Lucy ...

*****

Later, around eight, when all the baking is done for the day, I head out into the mild summer evening to make sure Paloma's café sign is still in place. I know it will be because I paid a local company to do the job. Secretly, I just want to stare at it again and marvel at what it represents. *My very own café*.

I'm standing there in front of it, shaking my head in wonder at the word 'Twilight' in such large letters, when a voice behind me says, 'The Twilight Café. What do you think? Will you be risking it?'

Turning, I find Theo Steel standing there, dressed in track-suit bottoms and T-shirt, a sports bag slung over his shoulder.

'Ooh, I'm not sure. The owner sounds a bit weird. But apparently she can bake good scones.'

He grins. 'Yeah, I heard that.'

'She's not great at 5k runs, though.'

He shrugs. 'It shows great ingenuity, though, hopping on a bus to save her injured ankle.'

'You think so?'

'I do.'

'I think she'd like to get fit, actually. At long last.'

'Really?' His brow knits. 'Why hasn't she wanted to before now?'

I frown and look away. 'The problem was,' I tell him a moment later, meeting his steady blue gaze, 'she spent so many years trying to escape from the clutches of a school bully, she went right off the whole idea of running.'

He looks at me thoughtfully. Then he nods. 'I can see how that might happen. What's changed her mind?'

'Oh ... she's fed up with letting the past get in the way of her future.'

'Very sensible. Do you think she might accept some free personal training sessions in exchange for regular supplies of cake?'

I make an awkward face. 'Seriously?'

He nods. 'It had better be good cake, though.'

'Oh, it will be.' I smile at him. 'Trust me.'

'Great. Well, wish her luck for tomorrow if you see her and tell her to save me a slice of cherry and coconut cake.'

I gaze at him. Cherry and coconut cake was on my list. The one Olivia read out with such disgust on the train that time. I can't believe he actually remembered that.

He grins, holds up a hand and strolls away, along the high street.

I stare after him for a moment, admiring his back view for a little longer than I probably should. Then I laugh out loud at the bizarre nature of our exchange. I think he just offered to be my personal trainer for free.

Thoughtfully, I pinch the flesh at the sides of my waist. I hate to admit it, but Olivia's right. I could afford to be leaner and an awful lot fitter.

But do I really want to be Theo Steel's charity case?

Chapter 16

The big day dawns.

I'm a bundle of nerves and excitement as I rise with the alarm at five to bake my three varieties of scone. I glance out of the bedroom window. It's going to be a beautiful day. You can just tell. The sky is clear, the crescent moon still faintly visible, and the sun, poised on the horizon, is a sphere of molten gold.

It's a good omen, I decide, as I pull on shorts and T-shirt and run downstairs to the kitchen. It's day one of a brand-new life for me. I've had a bit of a cold over the past few days but luckily it hasn't developed into anything bad. A blocked nose I can cope with!

The postman rings the bell just as I'm taking the last batch of cheddar, thyme and cracked black pepper scones from the oven. They look golden and inviting but I couldn't eat a thing, my stomach is in such turmoil. I transfer them to a rack, quickly because they're piping hot, then dash to the door. The postman hands over three cards in pastel envelopes and a parcel.

'Your birthday?' he asks.

I smile. 'No. My café opening.'

'That's today?'

'Yes. Haven't you seen the posters?'

He frowns. 'What posters? I saw the one you put up a few weeks ago in the post office but it's definitely not there any more. I thought you'd taken it down for some reason.'

'No way.' I stare at him in surprise. 'Who on earth would remove it?'

'Beats me.'

I wave him off and close the door, my mind working overtime. The fact that our postie wasn't aware of the date the café opens is quite worrying because he, of all people, should have noticed the posters Paloma put up around the village. If the one in the post office has gone, have the others survived?

There's only one way to find out.

Abandoning the letters and parcel, I grab my bag and head out along the high street to the village hall, where I know for certain Paloma placed a poster on the notice board. I pop my head into the entrance hall. No poster.

There's no one around to ask about it, so I head along to the newsagent's.

No poster there, either. And Val, the owner, is unable to tell me what happened to it.

'I know it was there last week,' she says, puzzled. 'Maybe my husband took it down, but I don't think so.'

I arrive back home feeling utterly despondent.

All the posters Paloma pinned up have been mysteriously removed and no one seems able to shed any light on the situation. It's extremely worrying. If no one knows about the café opening, except the people I've told in person, what sort of turnout can I expect?

Standing there in the hall, I make myself stop and draw in a long, steadying breath. Then I breathe out again, very slowly, trying desperately to calm the panic that's rising inside. I can't afford to fall apart at this late stage! There's still work to be done before I officially open those doors in just over an hour.

I open the parcel, which I know is a gift from Dad. Drawing out a simple wooden bowl with 'The Twilight Café' carved in tiny letters along the front, I gasp at its perfection. He said I needed something for tips and I laughed and said *I should be so lucky*. He must have created this specially, despite getting tired so easily these days, and it would have taken him ages to make it. A lump fills my throat. I'll phone him later to thank him.

There's a big good luck card from Mum and Dad and one from Paloma. The third is from Lucy and Jason. *Thinking of you and wishing you well for today*.

I stare at the message, hit by a pang of sorrow mixed with regret. I run my fingers over Jason's familiar handwriting. It would have been his idea to send me a card, of course. A warm feeling envelops me like a hug and tears prick my eyes, but I tell myself not to be so ridiculously sentimental. It's just nice to know he still thinks of me, that's all. We were always such good friends as well as lovers ...

I shake myself and head back into the kitchen to start packing the scones into boxes ready to transport. And by nine-forty-five, I'm standing behind the café counter in my new pale blue summer dress, patterned with white dragonflies, teamed with practical navy ballet pumps. My hair is twisted up, off my face, and at the last minute I cut my nails short and applied a coat of clear polish.

I've put a fresh hand towel and matching soap and hand cream by the mirror in the newly decorated 'rest room'. (Paloma painted the walls cream and I put up a pretty yellow, white and green daisy border.) There's cash in the till, the scones and iced cakes are all laid out under the pristine glass case along with several stainless-steel cake slices, and there's fresh milk in the dinky little jugs for customers to collect with their hot drinks. I've been practising with the coffee machine and can now deliver the perfect cappuccino with a cocoa sprinkle smiley face on top.

I'm all set for my first customer!

I potter around, straightening up the magazines on the side table and turning the cake forks so they all face upwards and look pleasingly uniform, and as ten o'clock approaches, the butterflies in my stomach go quite manic and start flapping about in there like nobody's business. I know that no one is likely to pitch up the instant I'm open. But after unlocking the door and turning the sign hanging there to 'open', I can't help peering along the road to see if I can see any cars or people on foot. Of course, there's no one. It's only two minutes past ten.

Shaking my head at my own daft impatience, I take my position behind the counter again, quickly checking my reflection in the shiny aluminium coffee maker, making sure my hair is still hygienically in place, with no wisps escaping. No, it's fine.

At ten-forty-five, I'm drumming my fingers on the counter in the rather eerie silence, when I suddenly remember Dad's old stereo system. Digging in my bag, I find the CD of popular jazz songs I'd thought would be a good choice of background music and I go through to the back and slide it into the player. It belts out of the speakers far too loudly, so I turn it down low until it's perfect, then I collect a magazine from the table and read it behind the till. I'll push it under the counter when a customer walks in.

And then, at last, I hear footsteps outside and the door opens.

I glance up, big smile at the ready, my heart racing.

It's Paloma.

'Looking good!' she says approvingly, glancing around. 'No customers yet?'

I shake my head, determined to remain upbeat. 'It's still early, though. Mum's friends said they'd pop in about eleven.'

'I guess I'm your first official customer, then.' She grins and sits down at a table near the counter. Then she sniffs. 'What's that smell?'

'Can't smell anything. My nose is still snuffly.' I frown at her. 'What is it?'

She sniffs again and shakes her head. 'Place has been empty for ages. It just needs to be lived in probably.' She sits up straight, hands folded in her lap, and studies the cakes under the glass. 'Right. The important stuff. Could I please have a latte and one slice of your finest double chocolate fudge cake?'

I laugh. 'Certainly, Madam. But chocolate cake so early in the day? Not that I'm complaining.'

Paloma sighs. 'I've been up most of the night working. Got just three hours' kip before I came over here. I'm absolutely starving!'

I'm just bringing over her latte when the door opens and in come Betty and Doreen, with Rowena Swann in tow.

'Oh my days!' sighs Betty, looking around her. 'How beautiful you've made it! Hasn't she, girls?'

'*Love* the curtains,' says Doreen, nodding. 'And your colour scheme. And the floral art on the walls.'

Rowena smiles. 'I recognise those tables and chairs. Don't they fit the space well?'

'They do indeed. Thanks so much, Rowena. And it's lovely to see you all, ladies.' I beam at them. Even though I know them, my heart is jumping around at the idea of serving my first 'proper' customers. 'Welcome to The Twilight Café! Have a seat. What can I get you?'

'Can I smell kippers? Are they on the breakfast menu?' asks Betty, her nose in the air.

'Er, no. I don't have a breakfast menu as such,' I say, surprised. 'Just cakes and scones.'

'Ah. Must be the savoury scones I can smell,' she says, pointing at the cheddar variety. 'Actually, I'd love one of those, please.'

They stay for almost an hour, chatting over cups of tea. Doreen and Rowena opt for toasted teacakes, then they all sample slices of my gingerbread, which was Doreen's favourite at my cake-tasting session. They all declare the complimentary shortbread to be the most buttery and melt-in-the-mouth they've ever tasted.

Paloma stands chatting to me at the counter for a while.

'Where are the customers?' I murmur.

She glances at her watch. 'It's not quite noon. I bet by one o'clock, you'll be rushed off your feet.'

I nod, although I'm not convinced. 'I wonder if the sign is still up.' I call over, 'Excuse me, ladies. On your way in, did you notice the big sign advertising the café on the high street?'

'Oh, we didn't drive that way, dear,' says Betty. 'I picked up Doreen and Rowena in Lake Heath and we came here by the back roads.'

Rowena goes off to use the loo, while Betty comes to the counter to settle up. It feels good putting money in the till. A few more payments like that one and I'll have broken even on the day!

'Lovely woman, Rowena,' says Betty. 'But I do worry about what she'll do now she's not got the ice-cream parlour to run any more.'

I nod. 'I know. It's not as if she has family to take up her time.'

'No.' Betty looks sad. 'She did, apparently. She had a daughter, but she doesn't see her any more. She doesn't speak about it so I never like to ask. Oh, here she comes—' She plasters on a smile and starts talking about the weather, wondering how long the sunny spell will last.

My mind is ticking over. Poor Rowena. I wonder what happened to separate her from her daughter? Did it happen recently, after a fallout? Or was it a long time ago?

But I haven't got time to ponder because at that moment, a car draws up and four people get out – all ladies from the WI. And then just as I'm tending to them, settling them at a table with fresh scones and butter and a big pot of tea, some old school friends drop in, all smiles and excited to sample what my new café has to offer. I saw them all at Lucy's charity fund-raiser – some of them also came to the cake tasting – and I'm so glad they made the effort to come on opening day.

After that, there's a steady stream of customers and I'm kept constantly busy until just after five, which is almost time to close up anyway.

After the last two customers have left, promising they'll be back the following week, I make myself a coffee and wander over to the door, opening it to let in a warm summer breeze. And after a few moments of reflection, the buzz of being busy dies down and what I'm left with is a sad feeling of anticlimax. Because it's gradually dawning on me that yes, I had a fair few customers through the door today – but not nearly as many as you would expect on opening day, and I guess that's partly down to the mysteriously vanished posters. If no one knew the café was opening, it's hardly surprising I wasn't overwhelmed with curious villagers. Also, every one of those people who turned up today was someone I knew, and they came because they promised me they would.

After all the stress and effort of the past few weeks, I'm shattered and a feeling of bitter disappointment descends. My eyes feel heavy with unshed tears, but I blink them away. It will be fine. Of course it will. It's only day one! I'll get more posters made, and this time I'll make sure they don't disappear.

I'm glad when Paloma arrives.

She walks in and immediately sniffs the air with disgust. 'Bloody hell, what *is* that smell?'

'My nose is blocked,' I wail. 'What does it smell like?'

She sniffs again. 'I don't know. It's a fishy smell. Are you sure there's nothing going off in the fridge?'

'Positive. I gave it a thorough clean the day before yesterday.'

'Maybe it's the drains. Perhaps you should call—'

My mobile starts ringing and I grab it, vainly hoping it might be someone wanting to know my opening times.

The voice sounds far away. But eventually I realise it's Jason.

'Hi, Jason. Thanks for the card.'

'No problem.'

I take a deep breath. 'If you're phoning to see how it's going so far, it's been not too bad.'

'Good. Because I was worried.'

'Worried?' I shrug at Paloma.

There's a silence and I think I must have lost him. 'Jason?'

Paloma is frowning at me, wondering what's going on.

'Look, I hate being the one to tell you this, Twi, but I'm afraid you've got competition.'

'Competition?' I stare in alarm at Paloma. 'But who? Where?'

'Just get along to the high street,' he says flatly. 'The old ice-cream parlour.' There's a pause and my brain whirrs into overdrive. 'Sorry, Twi. You're the last person in the world who deserves this.' And he rings off.

Swallowing down my panic, I tell Paloma what Jason has just told me.

'Come on,' she says, and I grab my bag and keys and follow her out of the door. My fingers fumble over the key in the lock, but at last, we're marching along the street in the direction of the high street.

My heart is banging against my ribs and I feel sick, wondering what I'm going to find. Neither of us says a word.

We emerge at the junction onto the high street and the first thing I notice, looking along the road, is a queue of people outside one of the shops. My heart drops like a stone.

'Bloody hell, Jason's right,' says Paloma. 'Something's happening at Rowena's old ice-cream parlour.' She looks both ways as if to cross the road, but I pull her back.

'Don't go over there. Not yet.'

'Okay.'

We draw level with the long queue of people waiting outside, chattering and laughing and reading the special offer in big bold letters splashed across the window: *Super-healthy dining, 50% off!*

And that's when I see the brand-new sign in quirky colourful text above the shop front.

Paloma and I gasp in horror at exactly the same time.

The old ice-cream parlour has indeed been let again. And the names above the window make my heart drop like a stone.

Lucy & Olivia's Clean Food Café.

Chapter 17

'Oh my God! She wouldn't,' breathes Paloma, while I just stare at the café front, my legs feeling like jelly, as the horrible truth slowly sinks in.

Lucy has set this café up deliberately to hamper my chances of success. What other explanation can there be?

'My God, she kept *that* under wraps, all right! What a cow!' explodes Paloma. 'Right, I'm going over there to tell her exactly what I think of her, the scheming, two-faced, pathetic little bitch!'

'No!' I grab her arm and she turns, stopped in her vengeful mission by the look of pure shock on my face. I'm struck temporarily dumb. I can't believe that even *Lucy* could stoop this low – could act with such breathtaking maliciousness.

But her name is right there, above the window alongside Olivia's, so incredibly, it must all be true. I shake my head slowly in disbelief. Maybe I'm in the middle of a nightmare and I'll wake up soon.

One thing's for sure, though – we definitely shouldn't be waltzing over there right now, kicking up a fuss.

Paloma takes a deep calming breath. 'You're right. We need to think about this logically, instead of diving straight in, on the attack, and making things worse.'

I swallow down a feeling of nausea. I can't think calmly. Not yet. Not while my head is still spinning with shock. How could Lucy be so cold-bloodedly devious, pretending to support me in my new endeavour while all the time plotting my downfall with Olivia behind my back? I've had my doubts, but I allowed Paloma to talk me into trusting Lucy.

More fool me!

I should have realised, better than anyone, the depths Lucy Slater is capable of sinking to.

I trail back along the high street with Paloma in silence.

'I can't believe she and Olivia kept their café plans a secret until today,' says Paloma when we arrive back at the café. 'I mean, I'm certain no one in the village knew what they were planning to do. News travels like wildfire here, but there wasn't a peep, was there?'

I shake my head, rattling the key in the lock in frustration as it sticks.

'Here, let me.' Gently, Paloma takes over and we step back over the threshold.

I glance around the empty café, trying to push down the wave of panic rising up inside me. *What if Lucy has ruined my plan to save Honey Cottage*?

Paloma heaves a sigh. 'I suppose it was all designed to have maximum negative impact on you,' she murmurs. 'What an evil bloody witch! There must be something we can do, though.' She flumps in a seat and stares into space.

'And what *is* that disgusting *smell*?' I shout, all my bottled-up anger at Lucy suddenly bursting out. 'Even *I* can smell it now!'

'Drains,' says Paloma absently.

I frown, shaking my head slowly. I'm certain it's not the drains, but what— ?

And then it comes to me in a flash.

The curtains!

Getting up, I push back my chair so abruptly, it topples over.

I go to the nearest window and grab a length of fabric, bringing it to my nose and sniffing hard. There's definitely an odour of rotting fish there, but maybe that's just because the whole place smells of it now.

Paloma joins me and bends to lift the curtain up from the bottom. Sniffing the hem, she makes a revolted face and passes it to me.

I breathe in the horrible stench and recoil. 'What the ... ?'

'Hang on, I've got nail scissors in my bag.' Quickly, Paloma starts snipping at the thread, releasing the hemmed fabric, and that's when Lucy's dastardly deed is revealed.

'Oh my God, it's *kippers*.' She pulls more of the stitching away and we stare at the disgusting slivers of slippery yellow flesh sticking to the fabric. 'I can't believe this.'

She must have painstakingly sewn the fish into the curtain hems!

I stare at Paloma. I want to laugh but it's just too horrible.

I picture Lucy slicing the fish and carefully stitching it into the hems, and the premeditated nature of it makes me feel sick to my stomach. Does she really hate me that much? I was starting to agree with Paloma that Lucy had changed towards me. But we were wrong. So very wrong ...

'Jeez,' breathes Paloma, her eyes glazed with disbelief. 'No wonder she wanted to put the curtains up herself at the very last minute. She must have planned for the stink to sabotage opening day and drive away any customers you might actually have.'

I try to swallow but my mouth is dry as dust. 'And you thought I was being paranoid,' I whisper.

Paloma shakes her head. 'It's incredible. I mean, what the hell does she hope to gain from opening a café the same day as you? I'd never have believed it before now, but ... she's done it all deliberately to hurt you, hasn't she?' She turns, her face aghast. 'What have you *ever* done to Lucy Slater to warrant this?'

'Nothing. Apart from loving Jason.'

'And Jason loving you,' murmurs Paloma. She shakes her head. 'I'm going to have it out with her. Ask her what the hell she's playing at.'

'What's the point?' I smile sadly. 'You know Lucy. She's a master at wriggling out of trouble. She'll only deny any wrongdoing.'

'Well, she'll be smiling on the other side of her face when everyone finds out she sewed fish into your curtain hems!' Paloma gives a frustrated sigh and we both stare into space for a long moment.

Then Paloma grabs the complimentary shortbread from a nearby saucer and starts munching furiously. 'The best way to get even,' she says at last, 'is to make damn sure your café is a massive success.'

I stare at her wordlessly. I know I should probably be fired up with determination to battle on in spite of everything, but right this minute, all I want to do is close up the café, go home, get into bed and blot out all the horror of it with sleep.

Then a little knot of fury begins to unfurl inside me. It might feel as if Lucy Slater has me in a stranglehold all over again. But this time, I'm not going to take it lying down.

'Help me get these – *things* – down!' I drag a chair over to the nearest window and start pulling the curtains off the hooks as fast as I can. They're heading for the bin.

I'm shaking but determined. You have to stand up to bullies.

And that's exactly what I intend to do ...

*****

Over the next few days, I do my best to carry on, providing a service for the customers who come along, but it's hard knowing I'm barely breaking even, never mind making some sort of profit to pay the mortgage.

The worst part is trying to keep the truth from Mum and Dad.

I phoned on opening day to thank Dad for the lovely tips bowl, and Mum answered, sounding anxious.

'I'm trying not to panic,' she confessed. 'And I probably shouldn't be worrying you, but your dad's still not responding to the treatment the way they'd like.'

I felt a horrible twinge of fear, and was only mildly cheered when she added, 'But they keep saying it's early days and we'll have a much better picture a few weeks from now.'

'Right, well, give him my love, as always, and tell him the bowl is fantastic.'

Mum laughed. 'Bless him, he spent weeks making that for you.'

'Well, it was worth the effort because it's gorgeous.' I swallowed hard on the lump in my throat. 'And tell him I'd quite like a box with compartments for knives, forks and spoons if he's got time in his busy schedule!'

'I'll tell him.' She sighed. 'I wish we could come and see you, love, but your dad's too weak at the mo to make the journey. And to be honest, I'm quite exhausted myself what with all the hospital to-ing and fro-ing. Still ...' She injected a note of brightness into her tone. 'We'll get there! Your dad's been as strong as an ox all his life – that's bound to stand him in good stead, don't you think?'

'I do, Mum. Nothing can keep that fella down for long. Not even bloody cancer! Sorry for swearing.'

'Oh, don't worry about that, love. I've said some pretty choice words myself over the past six months. I stood in the empty house and told the cancer to fuck off back where it came from the other day!'

'Mum!' I hooted with laughter, both shocked and amused. My mum is the type of person who says 'shoot' instead of 'shit'.

Then she said, 'Sorry, I haven't even asked how today is going. Spectacularly, I hope?'

'Oh, yes, yes. Fantastic.' I was glad she couldn't see the awkward heat creeping into my face. 'We'll have those mortgage payments in hand in no time!'

I made an excuse to get off the phone so I didn't have to tell her any more lies. The last thing I needed was for them to be worrying about money, on top of everything else ...

Chapter 18

It's Friday afternoon, nearly a week after my decidedly unremarkable opening day, and The Twilight Café is having another of its all too frequent lulls in business.

In other words, it's empty.

'This is just a blip in your new career,' says Paloma, with an airy wave of her hand. 'Just a tiny fly in the ointment.'

I grunt. 'A bloody great giant hornet, you mean.' I pass her a complimentary espresso.

'*So* defeatist. Do you think Alan Sugar gave up at the first hurdle? No. He dusted himself off and came back stronger than ever.'

'You just made that up.'

'Well, yes, but it's probably true.'

I scowl at her. 'It's a big fat cliché. That's what it is.'

She folds her arms and fixes me with a penetrating stare. 'So let me get this straight. You're actually going to just sit back and let Lucy Slater steal your thunder and your customers? Without at least putting up a teeny-weeny little fight?'

I gaze at her unhappily. 'But what can I do? It's obvious Lucy's tapped into a whole new niche in the market. Clean eating is the buzz word of the moment.'

'Well, technically, it's two words.'

'But you must admit, it was bloody clever of her to highlight the whole issue of fitness and staying healthy with this charity 10k run of hers, before magically springing a clean eating café on everyone.'

'Sneaky, if you ask me. Everyone thought she was so good, raising money for children's charities with the run, but all the time, it was just a ploy to brainwash people into thinking they need the sort of food she's serving in her stupid café in order to be healthy.'

'I wonder what the food's like,' I murmur gloomily.

'Bean sprouts and cabbage, no doubt, with a side order of unseasoned bulgur wheat and cardboard.' She makes a face. 'Yuk.'

I smile at my best friend, grateful for her support. But I know she's only saying these things to make me feel better. Lucy's not stupid. 'The food must be good,' I point out. 'They've been open a week and yesterday when I lurked behind the post box to observe, the queues were showing no sign of diminishing.'

'Only because they're still offering a *ridiculous* fifty per cent off people's first visit. How the hell can they hope to make a profit like that? No, mark my words, all the excitement will die down when people start having to pay full price for a bowl of lettuce and turnip soup.'

'I'm desperate to know what really *is* on their menu.' I give a loud groan of frustration and droop over the table, burying my face in the soft wool of my sleeves.

Paloma grins. 'Well, be desperate no longer. Because I have a plan ...'

*****

I can't believe we're doing this.

We're in Paloma's car, parked in a side street a few doors along from Lucy & Olivia's Clean Food Café, and I'm admiring my startling reflection in the sun visor mirror. Paloma, who's sporting a long red wig, sunglasses and an enormous straw sunhat that flops over her face, is doing the same on the driver's side.

'Not bad,' she murmurs, adjusting the brim of the hat, turning this way and that in the mirror, and pouting ridiculously. She looks across at me and snorts with laughter.

Having closed the café for an hour to go on this mission, I've wound a big, poppy-splashed scarf around my head and tied the ends together at the side in a big floppy bow. My sunglasses are huge, covering most of my face. If I walked into a café like this, even *I* wouldn't recognise me ...

'You look like a pirate,' says Paloma.

'No I don't. I look ... glamorous. Like one of those movie stars from the nineteen-fifties. *They* wore turbans.'

'Which movie stars?'

'Marlene Dietrich? She made them famous.'

'Who?' Paloma looks mystified.

'Audrey Hepburn!' I shout out. '*She* wore them.'

'Yes, but I'm sure the elegant Audrey never resembled Long John Silver in drag.'

'Rude!'

She grins. 'Arrrr! Land ho, me hearties! Shiver me timbers and rattle me cannonballs.'

I start to laugh, although it borders slightly on the hysterical. 'Come on, then. Let's do this.'

'Really?' Paloma looks unsure, which is not like her at all.

'Well, it *was* your idea,' I remind her. 'Going undercover to stake out the competition.'

'I know, but looking like this, we stand out like bird poop on a black welly. What's the betting Lucy will take one look and rumble us instantly?'

I shake my head firmly. 'We can carry it off. Come on.' I'm already opening the door, extreme curiosity – at seeing the inside of the Clean Food Café for myself – propelling me out of the car. Lucy and Olivia are obviously pulling in the crowds and I need to know what they're doing right. Because if I don't want to end up with a total turkey on my hands, I need to somehow start drawing in the customers myself.

'You know, what you said about having a USP was absolutely spot on,' I say thoughtfully, as we brave the high street in our disguises.

Paloma nods. 'Lucy's Unique Selling Point is the "clean eating" angle. I hate to admit it, but it does make her café stand out from the rest.'

I almost chicken out as we near the entrance, my heart is racing so fast, but Paloma pulls me inside, on the coat-tails of a couple just going in. I shuffle along behind the man, who's very tall, taking quick peeks over my sunglasses to locate Lucy and Olivia. I spot them, standing behind the counter.

Paloma pulls her hat brim down so far, she walks right into the antique umbrella stand. It rocks alarmingly and looks like it might go crashing to the floor, but she grabs it and steadies it in time.

Lucy's hawk-eyed gaze swings over in Paloma's direction and my heart plummets. But a customer distracts her. I watch – through the ghostly gloom of my gigantic shades – as Lucy points over to the cutlery, plastering on a fake smile, which vanishes the instant the woman leaves the counter.

'Careful,' I hiss, nudging Paloma.

The place is heaving, so we sit down on the only two seats remaining – a couple of high stools at a long shelf-like table in the window, facing out onto the high street.

'This is good,' Paloma mutters, wriggling on the stool to get comfortable. 'It means we've got our backs to Lucy and Olivia. Less chance of them spotting it's us.'

'But it also means I can't get a proper look at everything.' I peer round in what I hope is a discreet manner, noting the fresh, airy feel of the décor, the French café posters on the walls and the simple but stylish pale wood tables and chairs.

'What do you think?' Paloma is also giving the place a subtle once-over, shading her face with her hat brim.

'They've done a good job.' I stare at her gloomily. 'I hate to admit it, but I actually like it.'

Paloma nods reluctantly. Then she grins. 'Shame the patrons are utter cows, though.'

'The customers don't know that.'

'True. But they'll no doubt show their true colours eventually – especially Miss Lucifer Slater – and then where will their business be?'

We glance at each other, uninspired. We both know Paloma is just talking bollocks to try and cheer me up.

'I suppose the testing time for them will be when the period of special introductory offers is over.' I pick up the cute white ceramic salt shaker and turn it around ruminatively in my hands. 'Will the customers pay full price for ...' I swivel to look at the day's specials on the blackboard menu '... tofu burgers with roast Mediterranean vegetables or Grilled

Halloumi cheese with a herby omelette, sweet potato fries and salad garnish.'

'Actually, it sounds quite nice,' says Paloma. Then she grimaces. 'Sorry.'

'No, it does.' I shrug. 'I'm depressed as hell. There, I've admitted it.'

'And how are you two ladies today?' Olivia's school-ma'am voice at our shoulders makes me freeze with fright, and my heart rate zips into overdrive.

I can't speak. She'll recognise my voice. And the last thing I want is Lucy knowing we've gone to such great lengths to spy on them, because then she'll know she's won!

Paloma clears her throat. 'Eeh, we're fair t'middlin', thanks fer askin'.'

I swivel my eyes at her in astonishment. Her voice has gone deep, like a man's. A man from Yorkshire, weirdly.

'Mind, it's chuffin' roastin' out.' She wafts her hat brim vigorously. 'Eeh ba' gum, I'm absolutely sweatin'.'

'Good, good,' murmurs Olivia politely. 'And what can I get you both?'

I turn slightly so I can see her expression. She's staring down at Paloma as if she can't quite believe her eyes.

'Eeh, gi'us one o' them butties each and a mug o' tea and we'll be 'appy as pigs in muck!' Paloma points at the food on the next table and a bemused Olivia goes to write something down in her order book then stops.

'Erm, those sandwiches are made from rye bread?' she says hesitantly, pen poised in mid-air, as if no one with such a thick Yorkshire accent could possibly want anything other than the sort of stodgy white processed bread that sticks to your teeth.

Paloma nods approvingly. 'Aye, that's champion, flower.' When Olivia walks off, Paloma says, 'Eeh, she were nice, considering she's not from Yorkshire!'

I hold in my laughter until Olivia walks away. 'I can't believe you did that. That accent was a sort of a weird combo of Geordie and Yorkshire.'

She grins. 'Aye, it's reight grand oop north, apparently.' She glances behind her and her face falls. 'Oh, bugger, I think she might have clocked it was us.'

'Really?' I look over at the counter. Sure enough, Olivia and Lucy are in deep discussion and they're frowning in our direction.

Lucy starts walking over and I groan.

'I *knew* this was a bad idea!'

'No, you didn't, you were all for it,' reminds Paloma, trying not to smile.

I adjust my sunglasses and look round at Lucy, psyching myself up for her catty comments.

'Ladies, hello,' she says. 'Was it the salad on rye you wanted or the humus?'

There's a brief silence.

I'm so relieved Lucy appears not to have recognised us, my whole body relaxes. 'Salad please.'

Lucy nods and turns away. Then she stops.

I gaze at Paloma in a panic. *Why didn't I let my Geordie Yorkshire friend answer?*

Lucy carries on walking, picks up a newspaper from a display by the counter, and walks back to our table. She opens the newspaper to a certain page, folds it over and beams at me. 'Nice to see you, Twilight. Having a morning off? Shouldn't you be catering to your hordes of customers right now? But maybe The Twilight Café is so popular, you've had to hire extra staff already.'

She drops the newspaper onto the table in front of us. 'A little reading material for you. I'm sure you'll find it interesting. I presume you'd like to cancel the sandwich order?'

She tosses her head and walks off, leaving Paloma and I staring after her.

Chapter 19

I turn to the newspaper story, swivelling it slightly so Paloma can read it, too.

Sparkling Clean Café is a Hit in Hart's End!

The heading, in big bold type, makes something die inside me. But I read on with a sort of horrible fascination.

'Clean eating' is the buzz phrase of the moment in the health and fitness world and two enterprising young women have brought this trend to Hart's End – with great money-spinning success.

Lucy & Olivia's Clean Food Café, situated on the village high street, opened just a week ago, but already, the establishment is proving to be a runaway triumph.

Lucy Slater and Olivia Bright, both 32, share a firm belief that 'we are what we eat', and they're on a mission to prove to locals that they can improve their health and wellbeing immeasurably, just by making changes to their diet, eating the kind of vegan-based food the café provides.

Says Lucy, 'All our food is extremely wholesome, but please don't assume we frown upon goodies like cakes and biscuits. We have an absolutely delicious courgette cake on the menu, or why not try our heavenly pumpkin breakfast cookies?'

On the opposite page is a cut-out coupon that announces:

Eat at Lucy & Olivia's Clean Food Café and feel on top of the world! Plus, bring a friend and they can eat FREE!

I stare at the advert, a queasy feeling inside. All my determination of earlier has vanished completely. How can I hope to compete with an offer like that?

Paloma slides off her stool, snatching up the newspaper, and I follow her out of the café with a heavy heart. She shoves the paper into the mouth of a public waste bin that's right outside the café.

'No, I want to keep it,' I tell her, pulling it out again, and in doing so, something underneath catches my eye.

Staring into the bin, I can't believe what I'm seeing. It's one of my missing posters.

'Look at this,' I say to Paloma, pulling it out. 'Is it a coincidence that this should be found in the bin outside Lucy's café? I think not!'

Paloma looks amazed. 'The scheming little cow. So *she's* the one who made your posters "disappear". Might have bloody known.'

Now that I'm out of sight of the windows, I tug off the scarf part of my disguise. I never suspected Lucy of removing the posters because at that stage, there was no reason to. But now ... well, now it's fairly obvious it was her.

'I'd like to know how she managed to get that story in the paper,' grumbles Paloma. 'I mean, really it should be an advert, not bloody *news*!'

'I know exactly how she managed it.' Irritably, I smooth my hair down and pull off my sunglasses. 'Her dad's a businessman with fingers in so many pies, he should be running a bloody bakery! No doubt he's done a "favour" in the past for some head honcho on the paper and now it's *his* turn to get the preferential treatment.'

Paloma nods. 'Namely a glowing advert in the form of a "news story" for his darling daughter's brand-new enterprise. Ha! Nice publicity if you can get it.'

'Got time for a coffee?' I ask on the way back in the car.

She glances at her watch. 'Wish I did, but I've got this impatient client chomping at the bit for something to look at by the end of the week, so it'll be nose to the grindstone for the next few days.'

'Have you heard from that woman, Sylvia, with any news about your birth mum?'

Paloma's eyes light up. 'No, but I'm convinced I will. I can just feel it. My real mum's out there somewhere, Twi, and I'm going to find her!'

I smile at her, sensing a new energy about my best friend. She's never referred to her birth mum as her 'real mum' before. For some reason, I think of Rowena and her lost daughter ...

'Can you imagine?' she says. 'If I find Mum, I might even discover other relatives I never knew I had! Wouldn't that be amazing? We could have proper family Christmases together!'

My smile slips. I can't help worrying for Paloma. She's so enlivened by the prospect of finding a family, but what if the trail goes cold, right there on that woman's driveway? How devastated will she feel then?

Softly, I say, 'I know. It would be incredible. And in the meantime, you've got me and my family. We love you.'

She leans over to hug me, her eyes bright with tears. 'I know you do. Thank you.'

I wave her off and let myself into the café, keeping the 'closed' sign in place for a little while longer so I can drink a strong coffee and get rid of my disguise. It's not as if I'm in danger of losing customers by having closed up for an hour or so. I'd bet not a single person has been along during the time I've been away with Paloma, scouting out the competition. Except maybe Betty and Doreen, who call in most days for refreshments. I doubt they'd be surprised to find me closed, though. They fully understand that I'm just treading water here really, while Lucy and Olivia continue their crusade to take over the village with their café and their charity run.

Both Betty and Doreen are disgusted at what Lucy has done, deliberately sabotaging my efforts in such a two-faced, diabolical way, but I've made them promise not to mention any of it to Mum. They understand my motives because they're so protective of Mum and Dad themselves, especially recently, with what Dad has been going through.

Much later, at four-thirty, after another agonisingly slow afternoon, I'm just thinking of closing up and going home, when I hear a car draw up and park outside.

It's Jason.

I haven't seen him since the night before opening day, and I've sensed he's been avoiding me. I really don't think he can have known about Lucy and Olivia's plans to open their own café the same day as me. If he did, surely he wouldn't have come to the house the night before my opening to wish me well? He'd have given me an embarrassed wide berth.

I remember the night of Lucy's fashion show in the pub. When I was chatting to Jason through his car window, Lucy arrived and announced to him that Olivia would be staying the night. They were probably planning their café opening even then, and I had no idea.

'Hi, Twilight.' Jason's expression is hangdog and his eyes look puffy as if he hasn't slept. He might as well have 'guilty' stamped on his forehead.

'Hi, Jason.' I try to gauge his body language. Either he feels guilty because he knew all along about the Clean Food Café, but his conscience got the better of him at the last minute, leading to his phone call to enlighten me. Or he *didn't* know and he feels embarrassed about Lucy's shocking behaviour. I'm inclined to think it's the latter. I know Jason of old. He's not a schemer and he can't lie for toffee.

'Can I get you something, Jason? Coffee? Tea? I think I *might* be able to fit you in.' I smile ironically, throwing out my arm to indicate all the empty tables.

'A stiff drink would be preferable.' He falls into a seat and rubs his face wearily. Then he meets my eyes properly for the first time since he walked in. 'Twi, I'm so sorry. About Lucy. I'm stunned and ... well, horrified she could do this to you.' He laughs bitterly. 'I mean, I've always known she was a handful, but I never thought she could do something so calculated and hurtful. I know you two have never got on but *this* ...' He shakes his head.

'*Never got on*?' I jump instantly on the defensive. 'I should have thought you, more than anyone, would know it's nothing to do with Lucy and I not getting on, and *everything* to do with your girlfriend's totally illogical hatred towards me.'

He nods swiftly. 'I know, I know. That came out wrong.' He sighs. 'I suppose I just don't want to believe that it's all her because that means I'm living with a callous, scheming monster.'

He looks so defeated, my heart goes out to him. It's clear Lucy kept him completely in the dark about the café, presumably because she knew he would be against it and would probably warn me about it.

'Monster might be a *little* strong,' I say, hoping to make him smile.

'I don't know,' he murmurs. 'If it's any consolation, we had a huge row about it and Lucy's taken the hump and moved out, back to her parents.'

'Wow. Gosh, I'm sorry.'

He curls his lip. 'Don't be. I'm not. We're not exactly a match made in heaven, Lucy and I.'

He gazes up at me, a mournful look on his face, and I'd give anything to know what's going through his mind right this minute.

Does he think *we* were a match made in heaven?

Our eyes lock and my heart gives a funny little skip. Back in the day, we used to crave time alone together like this, away from family, teachers, school friends. We had our favourite places to meet. There was a secluded spot by the stream running through the woods in Lake Heath. It was our special place ...

'Penny for them?' I whisper.

He smiles sadly. 'We were good together, you and I. Weren't we?'

'We were,' I agree, giving him the reassurance he seems to need. I sit down next to him and we smile at each other. He reaches over and takes my hand, and my heart does another funny little flutter.

'I'm sorry about you and Lucy,' I say carefully. 'But maybe it's for the best? I always thought you were much too good for her.'

He squeezes my hand and shifts in his chair, never taking

his eyes off my face, and I wonder if he's going to kiss me. My heart starts to beat faster.

Then the door opens and in walk Doreen and Betty, exclaiming over how hot it is outside. Betty fans her face with her purse.

For a moment, I feel disorientated, still inhabiting the distant past, down by the stream with Jason. Then I remember where I am and rise swiftly to my feet, clicking smoothly into professional mode.

'Ladies! Great to see you. What can I get you today?'

*****

That night, I lie in a bath of scented bubbles, reflecting on the day.

My eyes feel heavy with tiredness.

It was a real body blow, seeing that article in the local paper about Lucy and Olivia, reporting how well the Clean Food Café was performing. That kind of publicity is like gold dust and will no doubt have even more intrigued customers beating a path to their door.

I hold up the soggy sponge and squeeze it slowly, watching the hot water cascade down my arm. There's no doubt about it. Lucy is winning the battle of the Hart's End cafés hands down, and I've no idea what to do to reverse the trend. Or even if it's possible. Maybe Lucy possesses an instinct for business that I just don't have.

I throw down the sponge, making a satisfying splash.

I will *not* be beaten by a horrible bully like Lucy Slater! Business acumen can be learned, can't it? Just like most skills. I'm certainly not giving up – not yet, anyway. I just have to find that Unique Selling Point that Paloma is always talking about.

Thinking of Paloma, I start wondering whether she's heard anything from Sylvia. Paloma's been so bloody brave, forging on with her career and life in general since Linda passed away. It would be so wonderful if she were to track her birth mother down. But what are the chances? For every ecstatic reunion, there's sure to be a not-so-happy ending also. That's just the way life is.

I lever myself out of the scented water and reach for a bath towel. Family is everything. I can't imagine what it's like to feel totally alone in the world. The thought of losing Dad makes my heart contract painfully.

Paloma is amazing. I don't think I'd be half as brave as her if the worst were to happen ...

Chapter 20

A week goes by and the buzz around Lucy & Olivia's Clean Food Café is showing no signs of dispersing.

In humiliating contrast, business is far from brisk at The Twilight Café. Starbucks, it's fair to say, can definitely rest easy.

I can actually count the number of regular customers on the fingers of two hands – possibly three, if you factor in our local postie, who often calls for a quick espresso after finishing his rounds. I feel silly now thinking of how excited I was before the café opened – what high hopes I had for its success.

On the plus side, after doing the accounts, I was able to report to Paloma that the café *almost* broke even last week.

That, of course, was down to the loyal patronage of friends like Betty and Doreen, who've been in for coffee and cake practically every day since I opened. The girls I was friendly with at school have also been great at showing their support. Some of them are mums now, and they've started meeting here several times a week. They bring their toddlers and babies to play in the pre-school activity area I've set up, while they drink strong coffee and chat gloomily about how lack of sleep can actually kill you.

Some of Mum's friends from the WI also come in from time to time. They think it's an absolute scandal how Lucy sabotaged my big opening day, and they're apparently spreading the word, hoping that people will start boycotting the Clean Food Café. (She's not just 'Lucy' to them any more, she's '*That Lucy Slater*'.)

I'm so thankful to the people who are supporting me. They keep me going through my most despairing times, such as the mornings when I don't have a single customer through the door.

Today, I've got the 'mums and babies' in, which I like. It's a stark contrast to the dead silence I've grown to dread. Betty is also here with her daughter, Jess, and sitting at another table are a couple I don't know at all, which is quite a novelty. I'm relatively run off my feet this afternoon!

I'm through the back, stacking cups and plates into the dishwasher when I hear the door open. Checking my reflection in the little mirror by the fridge, I try out a welcoming smile and then hurry through to greet the arrivals.

One customer. My heart skips nervously.

Theo Steel.

He's dressed in worn jeans and a white polo shirt, the usual sports bag hitched high over his shoulder. He glances around him then spots me behind the counter and strolls over, fixing me with one of his lazy smiles. Several of the mums lose track of their conversation, I notice, preferring to study Theo's progress instead.

'Twilight. Hello. You're busy.' He glances round approvingly.

'This is unusual,' I confess. 'But it makes a nice change. What can I get you?'

'Something to sort out an afternoon energy dip,' he says, surveying the cakes under the glass. His eyes light up. 'Cherry and coconut. My favourite. Bit of luck it's on the menu today!'

Warmth creeps into my cheeks. 'Yes, how about that? It's your lucky day!' No need to mention that cherry and coconut cake has been available every single day – ever since that time he told me to keep him a slice of it!

'And a large cappuccino, please.'

I cut him a generous piece that has four glacé cherries on top instead of the normal three. Unfortunately, my hand wobbles as I pick it up, which means it slides off the cake slice far too quickly and lands upside down on the plate.

Aaargh! Bloody typical!

Flustered, I abandon the disaster and reach for another plate. But before I can even pick up the cake slice, Theo gives a throaty chuckle and says, 'Er, I'd like that one, please.'

'No, I'll get you another one.'

'That one has four cherries on top,' he says solemnly, pointing at the upside-down mess. 'You're not going to deny me, are you?'

I hesitate, smiling awkwardly.

'I could complain to the manager. Oh, hang on, you *are* the manager.' He grins and points to the splodge. 'Just hand it over.'

With a shrug, I do what he says and watch in amusement as he casually picks up the cake and turns it the right way up. 'There you go. No harm done.'

As I'm making his cappuccino, he says, 'So when are you coming for this free training session?'

'I don't like gyms.'

He grins. 'Or changing rooms?'

I gulp as a memory of my most embarrassing moment ever zips into my head. Theo, naked apart from a towel that only just covered his modesty. I turn to grimace at him and the froth-maker dips too low, making a horribly loud sucking sound that echoes around the café. 'Better concentrate,' I mumble, blushing to the roots of my hair.

'Great, thanks,' he says when I finally deliver a coffee I'm quite proud of. 'Listen, you don't have to work out in the gym. How about some stretches then a jog on the village green?'

'Okay.' This sounds slightly better. At least there'll be no one there to watch me sweat my arse off. Apart from Theo, of course, which is bad enough. But as I've already decided I'd like to be fitter, I'd be a fool to pass up the chance of a free session, wouldn't I?

'I'm free tonight, actually. About seven?'

I glance outside. 'It looks like it might rain later.' I've been keeping a nervous eye on the sky all day. Over the past hour, it's been growing oppressively darker in the distance over Lake Heath.

He shrugs. 'A bit of rain won't matter, will it?'

I swallow. 'Er, no, I suppose not. As long as it's only rain. I – um – I'm not a fan of thunder and lightning.'

He nods. 'I promise we'll retreat indoors the instant it starts to look threatening.'

'Okay.' I force a smile, trying to shrug it off.

It's high time I got over my childhood phobia of thunderstorms. I'm told they're really nothing to be afraid of, unless you happen to be hugging a tree or raising your metal club on a golf course! I just wish I could believe it.

'Great. Seven it is.' Theo digs his wallet from his pocket. 'How much do I owe you?'

'What? No, it's free. In exchange for the training session,' I remind him.

'You sure?'

'Absolutely.'

'Well, thanks.' He smiles at me, deep blue eyes crinkling at the corners as he transports his cake and coffee off to a nearby table.

One of the mums, my old school friend Diana, winks at me and glances knowingly over at Theo, and I shake my head at her, blushing a deep shade of scarlet. She's got the wrong idea altogether. Theo is just being nice and taking pity on me, that's all. He's probably never had such a challenge on his hands in his entire career as a personal trainer.

His slice of cherry and coconut cake disappears in a flash, I'm pleased to note, and so does the coffee. Not that I'm watching his every move. (Mind you, I wouldn't be the only woman in here doing so, if I was.)

I do like to check how well my baking is being received ...

I'm delivering a second round of coffees to the mums' table when Theo gets up to leave.

'Village green. Seven o'clock?' he murmurs, as he passes me, and I nod, trying to look enthusiastic. What on earth have I let myself in for? I want to get fit, but do I really need a big, sporty, hard-muscled personal trainer like Theo Steel witnessing my shameful lack of fitness and flabby bits? I close my eyes, feeling quite sick at the thought.

'He doesn't go in for relationships, apparently,' says one of the women.

Her neighbour sighs. 'What a waste.'

'Bit of a lone wolf. Gorgeous, though,' says Diana. 'Thanks, Twilight. You didn't have to bring the coffees over.'

'Hey, it's no problem.' I start placing the cups on the table, one by one, as it dawns on me they're discussing Theo.

'He was married, though, wasn't he?' says the first woman, just as I'm putting down the final cup. It rattles in its saucer and slops hot coffee onto my hand and onto the table.

'Oh, I'm so sorry.' Flustered, I mop my hand with a napkin from my tray, then attack the spillage with a few more. 'I'll get you another coffee.'

'No, honestly, Twi, it's fine,' says Diana, then she turns to her friend. 'No, they were engaged, I think, and madly in love, but it all ended tragically.'

'Really? How?'

I linger by the table, going over the spillage again and again, just to hear the reply.

'I can't actually remember. It was a good few years ago now. But the woman's no longer on the scene and I know it didn't end well.' They exchange a frown. 'I think that's why he keeps himself to himself.'

My head is reeling.

Theo was going to get married?

I don't know why I feel so shocked.

I suppose I had an impression of him as a fairly easy-going, laid-back sort of guy, happily living the single life. But his apparently tragic past would indicate otherwise.

'Twi? Are you all right?' Diana frowns up at me. 'Don't worry about the spill.'

Her words filter slowly through to my brain, as if she's talking under water. I remember where I am and paste on a smile. 'I'll get you another cappuccino. Honestly, it's no trouble at all.'

I retreat behind the counter and start making the coffee. My hand stings a little where the hot liquid landed on it, but I'm too preoccupied with the heartbreaking image of Theo as a 'lone wolf' – because of losing his fiancée – to do anything about it.

When the drink is ready, I realise I forgot to put in fresh coffee grounds so I have to pour it away and start all over again ...

Chapter 21

The training session isn't as bad as I imagined it would be.

It's a whole lot worse.

I turn up at the green in shorts and T-shirt, expecting to spend a leisurely ten minutes chatting about the great weather we've been having and possibly watching Theo flex his muscles, demonstrating the exercises he wants me to perform. (I'm quite looking forward to that bit. From an educational viewpoint, of course.) But within sixty seconds of establishing that I haven't done any formal exercise for years, I'm thrown straight into stretching out muscles I never knew I had.

As I feel the burn in my hamstrings, pivot round at the waist and do 'lunges' that push my thigh muscles to the limit, Theo keeps up a reassuring commentary, giving me tips on technique and making encouraging noises, like he's impressed with my efforts. This, of course, makes me want to perform even better, which is a very cunning move on his part. I'll be aching all over tomorrow, that's for sure, but that's fine because it's all in a good cause.

Clearly, my technique leaves a lot to be desired, but as I huff and puff and gasp, I'm finding there's one part of exercising that I'm *really* good at.

The sweating bit.

All great athletes sweat like mad. And I'm brilliant at it!

Honestly, my body is so efficient at cooling me down, you just wouldn't believe it. Of course, it is the middle of June and fairly humid, which probably accounts in part for the moisture that's making my T-shirt cling. And there's also the fact that Theo Steel is undoubtedly 'hot' in a very different way to me. (Those subtly defined biceps and long, muscular legs are enough to make any woman 'come over all unnecessary', as my granny used to say.)

Not that Theo Steel's muscles have anything to do with the soaring temperature inside my T-shirt. No way. I'm not like those mums in the café with their tongues practically hanging out as the 'gorgeous lone wolf' passes close by.

'Great,' says the man himself, nodding approvingly. 'With an enthusiastic attitude like yours, Twilight, we'll get you fit in no time.'

I give him a modest smile and keep my arms clamped to my sides. Big wet patches under the arms are *not* a good look. Neither is hair plastered to a glowing forehead. On the other hand, they do show how hard I've been working. Maybe I should be *proud* of my wet patches.

'Next time, make sure you bring a bottle of water and sip it throughout your workout,' says Theo. 'Never wait until you're thirsty because that's a sign you're already depriving your body of the fluid it needs.' He's quite stern when he's in professional mode. I bet his female clients find it disturbingly sexy. It's lucky I'm completely immune to his charms ...

The mention of water makes me realise how thirsty I am. As soon as I get back, I'll have a long, cool drink. As I glance in the direction of Honey Cottage, I'm already anticipating quenching my thirst and having a lovely shower ...

'Okay, let's do some warm-ups before we run,' Theo says, and I do a double take as he starts jogging on the spot.

I thought we were finished, but apparently we haven't even started yet.

It turns out star jumps and something called 'burpees' are what's next. The star jumps I can handle but these bloody burpees are torture, especially the bit at the end where you have to leap in the air. And he's ordered me to do *ten*!

I'm beginning to think I've ended up with the raw end of the deal. Theo gets all the cake he can eat and I get ... pure knackered.

*****

An hour later, we're sitting on the deck of the treehouse, our backs to the wall, legs stretched out, quenching our thirst with glasses of home-made lemonade over ice. The first few sips that trickle down my parched throat, while the ice cubes clink in the glass, are as deliciously welcome as rain after a drought.

'You did well.' He grins across at me. 'Considering you've never exercised.'

I smile modestly. 'Thank you.'

There's a brief silence then he says, 'You know, it might sound obvious but eating well and exercising are great ways to keep stress at bay. I think you should continue with the running.'

I nod. 'And stop eating so much cake and eat carrots instead.'

He smiles ruefully. 'I'd never advocate that. You wouldn't

be able to stick to it. But the occasional carrot would work wonders.'

I sigh. 'I know. You're right. Perhaps I'll give it a go.' I close my eyes and turn my face up to the sun. Vitamin D from sunlight is another way to boost your health. And with all the stress in my life right now, I need all the help I can get.

'This is a great place,' murmurs Theo.

I open my eyes and glance at him as he gazes out over our garden and the café to the fields beyond.

'I know. I used to look out when I was a kid and think I could see the entire world from here. It was only later I realised it wasn't Australia in the distance. It was Lake Heath.'

He looks across at me and grins. 'You're funny. Attractive *and* funny is a wicked combo. Did you really think it was Australia?'

I nod, covering my blushes and sudden confusion by sticking my nose in my empty glass. *Attractive and funny?*

'Easy mistake to make when you're a kid, I suppose. Is there any more lemonade in that flask?'

I shake it, unscrew the lid and pour the remainder into his glass.

'You should have saved some for yourself.' He turns slightly, offering to tip some into my glass and his thigh brushes mine.

An odd little shiver runs through me. 'Sorry? No, no, it's fine.' *Theo thinks I'm attractive and funny.*

'You look a bit dazed. Have I worn you out with the run?' He smiles apologetically.

'Well, yes, *obviously*,' I joke. 'But it's fine. It's high time I did something about my fitness.'

Does he really mean it? Or was he just being kind? Trying to boost my confidence in myself, the way a good personal trainer should?

He takes a long drink of the lemonade and my eyes are drawn to his strong, tanned throat, the leap of his Adam's apple as he swallows. His dark hair is raked back, slick with perspiration after our session. The strong chin and jaw line hint at determination but there's something attractively vulnerable about his blue eyes that I hadn't noticed before, possibly because he's not wearing his glasses today. (He told me he wears contact lenses to work out.)

Of course, now that he's said I'm funny, I'm racking my brains to think of something hilarious to say, but my mind is a complete and utter blank.

'So, it's a shame more people don't know about The Twilight Café,' he says, putting his glass down on the deck. 'I can't imagine Olivia is your favourite person right now, after the trick her friend Lucy Slater pulled. If it's any consolation, she feels really bad about it.'

'She told you that?' I shoot him a glance, feeling my stomach plummet. Theo and Olivia seem very friendly. Does he know how catty she can be? But perhaps it's not strictly her personality that's the draw ...

The thought makes me feel ridiculously cross.

I might have known Theo would be a typical man and succumb to Olivia's obvious attractions!

He nods. 'I kept bumping into her on the high street and at the gym. We laughed at the coincidence. Then the last time, she was feeling a bit faint, so I drove her home and she made me lunch.'

Coincidence indeed! She's probably been stalking him!

'I asked her what they were playing at, launching the Clean Food Café that Saturday, but she swears she didn't even know yours was opening on the same day.'

I almost laugh out loud. Of *course* she knew! 'So she got over her fainting spell fairly speedily, then? Enough to cook you lunch?' As soon as it's out, I could kick myself for sounding so waspish. 'What did she make you?'

'Tofu pancakes.'

'Ooh, how ... *healthy*!'

He's silent for a moment, observing me with a little smile, while I cringe inwardly and concentrate hard on spooning a lemon pip from the jug.

At last he murmurs, 'I much prefer your cherry and coconut cake.'

My heart does an odd little leap. 'Only because it doesn't contain celery.'

He laughs softly. 'Well, there is that.'

I'm partly mollified, although I can't believe Theo would fall for Olivia's lies. But it's good that he's seen Lucy's foul play in action and is fighting my corner. I wish more people would see her for what she is.

'The tide will turn,' says Theo.

'Wish I shared your confidence. I really need the café to do well.'

'For your dad?'

I nod, feeling my throat thicken with emotion. I'm hovering on the brink of tears just at the mention of him. I twist my mouth into a bitter smile. 'We're hoping for a miracle.'

He looks genuinely sorry. 'I hope things work out.'

'Don't be nice to me or I might cry.'

'I don't mind if you do. I've got a choice of two fairly broad shoulders here if you need them.'

He regards me solemnly, and I stare up into the depths of his blue eyes and my head spins. For a second, I can't even remember what we were talking about. *Dad. That's right.* I can't seem to drag my eyes away from Theo's – and neither, it seems, can he. My heart is suddenly beating so incredibly fast ...

Then a crow caws loudly from a nearby tree and Theo's eyes flicker. He clears his throat and leans back against the treehouse, staring out over the garden.

In the silence, my heart slows its beat, finally steadying to its normal rate. *What's wrong with me? I can't be attracted to Theo Steel! It's obvious he fancies Olivia, however disparaging he might be about her food preferences!*

'You need an angle,' says Theo after a while.

'An angle?' I look at him, confused.

'Yes. Something different that sets you apart.'

I realise he's been thinking about The Twilight Café.

'A USP, you mean?' It rolls airily off my tongue.

He grins at me. 'Exactly.'

'Yes, but what?' I shrug. 'What could my angle be?'

He leans his head back, thinking. 'Something that would get you in the Guinness Book of World Records,' he says at last. 'What about the smallest café in the world? Just the one table.'

I laugh. 'Doubt if I'd make a great living.'

'True.'

'Or a café where the staff are all movie star lookalikes?' I suggest. 'That would be different. I could have Melissa McCarthy waiting on tables and Tom Hiddleston showing people where the toilets are.'

'Wages bill might be a bit steep.'

We exchange a warm smile and my insides respond by turning a pleasurable little somersault.

'Of course ... there *is* an answer that's staring you in the face.' He frowns.

'Go on.'

'To be accurate, it's not staring us in the face. We're actually leaning against it.'

Automatically, I glance behind me.

'The treehouse. Have your café in the treehouse.'

I stare at him. 'Are you mad?'

'No.' He laughs. 'I'm actually being serious. Think about it. A treehouse café. You can't get more unique than that.'

My mind is still rejecting the idea as ludicrously outlandish. But when I begin to imagine what he's suggesting, I find my heart swelling with excitement. Could it be possible?

'But how would it work?' I ask with a doubtful laugh.

My brain is coming up with all sorts of reasons why it absolutely couldn't. It's a lovely, romantic idea, but completely nuts.

'I'd have to have a system of pulleys to bring up the coffees and the cakes. Or one of those dumbwaiter lift-type things. Except it would be cunningly disguised as a tree.' I nod, grinning up at Theo. 'Yes, I can definitely see that working.'

He shrugs, conceding it's a bit far-fetched. 'I'm not sure the elderly population would spring up the treehouse ladder with the greatest of ease.'

'Oh, I don't know. My mum's friends, Betty and Doreen, managed it the other week. They just needed a very small shove from behind.'

'You could have a Tom Hiddleston lookalike on double duties at the bottom of the ladder.'

'Yes! He could be Chief Shover-Upper!'

'Sounds painful.'

We catch each other's eye and laugh.

After a while, Theo says, 'I've got a good mate who's a carpenter. I reckon he could extend this treehouse into an amazing café with a proper walkway and everything.'

'Walkway?'

'You know, like one of those swing bridges, where you hold on to the rope at either side.'

I stare at him. He can't be serious. But there are two deep grooves between his eyebrows as if he's actually pondering the idea, ridiculous at it sounds to me.

I grin. 'With a swing bridge entrance, the liability insurance would be through the roof.'

He shrugs. 'Jake's clever. He could make it secure enough to pass any health and safety inspection.'

'Jake?'

'My carpenter mate. He lives on the south coast.'

I smile. 'And you're living in cloud cuckoo land if you think I really could have a café in a treehouse!'

He leans sideways and lazily bumps my shoulder with his. 'You, Twilight Wilson, clearly have no imagination whatsoever.'

My skin, where he makes lingering contact, fizzes and burns, and I have to stop myself from leaping away in shock.

'That's ... that's very unfair,' I protest stiffly, choking out the words, my throat suddenly as dry as the desert. 'I have a fantastic imagination.'

Theo moves away slightly and I breathe more easily. 'But – I also have a foot planted firmly in reality and something tells me a treehouse like that would cost an absolute fortune to build.'

He frowns. 'Not necessarily. You've got the basics here already.'

'Yes, but it would cost thousands, not hundreds. And I don't have that kind of money.'

I can't even pay off the mortgage arrears, never mind fund the sort of project Theo is talking about. Sadly. Because the more I think about it, the more amazing it seems.

Theo is still close enough for our arms to be touching, and I'm breathing in his lovely masculine scent and something lemony that must be his body spray. A surge of desire springs from deep within and spreads like wild fire through my entire body. Stunned, I glance up at him and at the very same moment, he turns his head a fraction to look at me. My heart gives a giant leap at the intensity burning in his eyes.

We stare at each other for a long moment, our eyes locked. My head is swimming and my whole body is pulsing wildly with a desire I haven't felt in forever.

He moves towards me, his mouth only inches from mine, and when I arch my neck in response, he slips a hand around my waist. A second later, I feel his strong arms pulling me towards him ...

I'm slowly melting with desire, past the point of return, aware of Theo's powerful body pressing into me. His breathing is ragged and suddenly his mouth comes down hard on mine and I feel myself transported on a tide of desire too powerful to resist.

I cling to him, kissing him back as my head spins off into space.

Then abruptly, he pulls away.

Bewildered, I stare up at him, gasping for breath. Despite the warmth of the balmy evening, I feel the chill of the sudden separation keenly.

Theo makes a rasping sound in his throat and springs to

his feet, avoiding my eye. I'm at a loss to know what I did wrong. Because it must have been something I did, to make him pull away so abruptly ...

'I'd better be going,' he says matter-of-factly, looking at his feet, the wooden railing, the garden. Anywhere but at me.

'Right,' I mutter at my hands. 'Yes, of course.'

He stares down at me for a moment, a peculiarly intense expression in his blue eyes, and I wish I were a mind-reader because I'm floundering here, wondering what just happened between us. Then he holds out his hand and after a second, I reach up and he pulls me to my feet. Nervous, I wobble slightly and fall against him, and he steadies me, holding both my arms. But then very deliberately, he steps away from me.

'Don't bother coming down,' he says, heading for the ladder. 'I can see myself out.' At the bottom, he walks round so he can see me.

'See ya!' He holds up his hand, his usual relaxed smile back in place now there's a safe distance between us. 'And think about The Treehouse Café! It could work.'

When he's gone, I sit there for ages, staring out over the garden, my head a whirl of confusing images and emotions.

He couldn't wait to get away from me.

What the hell just happened there?

Chapter 22

It's only when there's a rumble of thunder, and my heart nearly jumps out of my chest at the sound, that I realise rain has been falling while I've been sitting here in a trance.

I'm not sure how long it's been pattering against the leaves, but it must be a while by the look of the dripping garden. It wasn't raining when Theo left. I must have been sitting here for a lot longer than I thought.

My chest flutters with panic. I look up at the sky – and at that moment, a fork of lightning splits the heavens directly overhead, lighting the sky like a scene from a horror movie. I freeze, closing my eyes tightly and counting the seconds, which – Dad told me when I was little – is the way to work out the rough proximity of the storm. I barely get to 'one' when a long rumble of thunder seems to vibrate through every bone in my body.

The storm is right overhead.

Standing up slowly, my knees are trembling so much, I know there's no way I'll be able to get down the ladder and into the house before the next bolt of lightning strikes, so instead, I push open the entrance to the treehouse, stumble over the threshold and slam the door behind me, leaning back against it with relief. I feel frightened and sick, but at least I'm inside now and relatively safe.

The rain is battering on the treehouse roof. The noise is quite incredible. I slide to the floor and sit cross-legged in the middle of the space, with my head buried in my hands.

I can't believe it.

All the time Theo and I were talking, the thunderous clouds must have been gathering on the horizon and moving stealthily overhead until the sky was turbulent and black, yet I hadn't even noticed. It had started to rain and I still hadn't realised. I was so deep in thought about the hasty way Theo left.

And now I'm trapped alone in the treehouse with no safe bed in which to take cover.

That's what I do usually. I pull the duvet right over my head and lie there, my heart beating frantically, hugging myself tighter when the thunder crashes overhead. Until the storm passes and it's safe to come out. I feel so ashamed of myself at those times. I know it's such a ridiculously childish fear to have, but I can't help it ...

*****

The night it happened, I was about ten and I'd been invited to a party.

I remember being excited because Mum had bought me a brand-new red velvet dress and I couldn't wait to wear it. (Even now, just the feel of velvet makes me shudder.)

It was my friend Diane's party. She'd turned nine that day and about ten of us were invited to her house for a birthday tea and old-fashioned games like pass-the-parcel and musical chairs. Lucy was invited with her friend, Sophie, but Mum said not to worry. They wouldn't be able to get at me at someone else's house. I'd be perfectly fine. I think she secretly didn't want me to go because she knew what a bully Lucy could be. But she could tell I really wanted to go to the party, so she agreed and tried to reassure us both.

I should have known Lucy wouldn't waste an opportunity to scare the life out of me.

There was a storm brewing that November afternoon and by the time Mum and Dad dropped me off at Diane's house around four, the trees were waving their branches angrily and freezing rain was bouncing off the pavements. It was pitch-dark and we had to run to get inside before we got soaked. Mum sheltered under the porch to chat to Diane's mum, with her coat collar pulled right up, while I said goodbye and ran inside to the cosy room with the Christmas tree, where everyone was gathering.

At first it was lovely. We played games and Diane opened all her presents. Then her mum and auntie went to get the sausage rolls and bowls of crisps and jelly and ice cream ready in the next room.

That was when Lucy came over and whispered in my ear that she had a special surprise for Diane and she wanted me to help her fetch it, without the grown-ups or any of the other girls finding out we were gone. I remember feeling proud that Lucy had chosen to share her secret with me and not the other girls, and I followed her out into the cold hallway, while everyone else was playing a noisy game of blind man's buff in the cosy living room.

Lucy put her finger to her lips and guided me along the corridor towards the back door. 'The surprise is in the greenhouse,' she whispered, struggling to turn the key quietly in the lock. She pulled the door open and we looked out. It was no longer lashing down with rain, but it was pitch-dark. The faint light shining through the curtains in the living room illuminated the garden path. The stones looked treacherous and slippery. The greenhouse itself was just a shadowy shape at the bottom of the garden.

Lucy told me there was a parcel in the greenhouse and I had to collect it.

I remember staring down the garden path, feeling sick, trying to pluck up the courage to go out into the darkness.

'Go on. Quickly.' Lucy was getting impatient. 'I'll wait here until you come back.'

So I did. I left the warmth of the house and started slip-sliding along the garden path towards the greenhouse. The bitter December wind tugged at my hair that Mum had curled specially for the party, and blew it wildly around my face. The walk seemed to take a long time and I screwed my eyes almost shut so I didn't have to see the ghostly shapes of the plants and trees on either side of me.

When I reached the greenhouse, I couldn't get the door open. I thought it must be locked. I remember pushing and pulling to no avail. I glanced nervously back up the path, knowing Lucy would be angry if I came back empty-handed. But she wasn't there, and my heart rose up into my throat. The oblong of light where she'd been standing was gone. She had shut the door and left me outside in the pitch-black.

I started to walk back up the path, my heart racing, and that's when the first drops of rain fell. Big, icy drops bouncing furiously off my head. The whole sky lit up as lightning forked overhead and then came the long crash and rumble of thunder.

I'd seen a story on the news about a man who'd been struck by lightning in his garden and he'd died right there. Panic choked my throat as the second bolt of lightning lit up the scary landscape around me. I tried to scream but I couldn't. Then my foot caught something and I tripped and fell hard onto my knees.

The thunder crashed overhead, louder this time. As I scrambled to my feet, my hands touched something slimy on the path and it moved. I screamed because I thought it must be a rat.

I was going to die.

No one knew I was out here in the thunderstorm and the darkness. Except Lucy, but she wouldn't care what happened to me.

I made it to the house, tears mingling with the icy rain on my face. I made my numb hands into fists and banged as hard as I could on the back door. The sound of 'Jingle Bells' was blaring out from inside, and another wave of panic seized me. I would be out here all night in the storm. No one would hear me because of the party music. I was going to die and Mum and Dad were going to be so sad ...

Looking back, I think Lucy must have deliberately turned the music right up so no one would hear me battering on the door.

It probably wasn't that long before I was missed, but for ten-year-old me, standing outside as the storm raged around me, it felt like hours. Finally, the door opened and there was Diane's mum, standing in a pool of light. She pulled me in and all the kids came into the hall and stared at me because I couldn't stop sobbing. Diane's mum led me into the kitchen and gently dried my face and my hair with a towel. She fetched some clothes of Diane's but I folded my arms and refused to take off my red velvet dress, even though it was all muddied down the front from when I fell.

Mum and Dad came to pick me up soon after that and took me home. For weeks, I was scared to go outside if it was raining. Even now, I get a slightly panicky, choked-throat feeling if I'm out and the sky looks threatening, especially if I'm a long way from home.

And I still can't handle thunderstorms ...

Chapter 23

As I curl myself into an even tighter ball, pulling my knees to my chest and burying my head there, I'm hoping and praying the storm will be over as swiftly as it arrived.

My neck and back ache where I'm stretching the muscles, bending over to protect my head with my arms. I've been on-line so many times, anxious to know how to survive a lightning strike, and most of the advice is the same: sit on the floor, then the lightning will probably rush up one leg and down the other, leaving your vital organs untouched. I'm not sure if that applies when you're twelve feet in the air, in a treehouse, though. Perhaps what I'm doing is the worst thing of all ...

Another huge lightning flash penetrates my screwed-up eyes and I tense my body even more, waiting for the long crashing noise that sounds like a monster hurling heavy furniture down the stairs. It's so frighteningly close. The storm must be directly overhead, and I'm in the trees, which must be the worst place to be. But I can't move from here. I just couldn't make my legs do what I want them to do.

I'm stuck here until it passes.

Fuck! I can't bear it!

The mantra! Say the mantra!

Slowly stirring the fruit and spices into my Christmas pudding. Smells so good!

A cold hand is gripping my insides, squeezing ever tighter. The panic is rising. Being alone in the storm is the very worst thing. When I was a child, Mum would come and sit on the bed and sort of hug me through the duvet. These days, I make sure I'm indoors with other people, preferably people who know about my phobia and will distract me and cluster round protectively and tell me I'm going to be fine.

I once read that if you're alone, it helps to think of a calming image, so I know it sounds daft, but I always think of Stir-Up Sunday, the day I make my Christmas pudding.

Slowly *stirring the fruit and spices into my Christmas pudding. Smells so good!*

It's not working.

I remember my phone in my pocket. I could call Paloma. She would come. Then my heart sinks. She's away tonight at some graphics event in London. Oh God, who else ... ?

I can't phone Betty or Doreen and ask them to brave the raging storm for me. They'd think I was mad. And anyway, they'd never be able to climb up here without some help.

A vision of Jason swims into my head, sitting in the café with me earlier. Feeling that strange sensation that the years had magically rolled away and we were strong as ever. Still together.

I pull out the phone and stare at it.

Lucy has moved out, so Jason will be alone in the house. He's a kind man. That's one of the things I loved most about him. His kindness and gentleness. He understands my fear and he wouldn't want me to be here, alone. I glance at the time. Just after ten. He'll definitely still be up. Jason is a bit of a news junkie, so if he's at home, he'll be watching TV right now.

I draw a deep breath and find his number. Lucy gave it to me when we were arranging for her to bring the curtains round. It's ringing ...

I press the phone tightly to my ear to block out the sound of the rain peppering the treehouse roof. Jason, when he answers, sounds distracted at first but as soon as I mention I can't move from the treehouse, he gets it instantly.

'Oh God, Twi. The thunderstorm. Poor you. Look, I'll be over in five minutes, okay?'

'Okay,' I repeat, not wanting to lose contact with him but knowing I have to. He ends the call. But he'll be here soon.

I listen to the storm rushing relentlessly through the trees. It almost seems to be calling my name, but I'm obviously imagining it, desperate for Jason to be here already.

I lift my head and really listen. Someone *is* calling my name.

I shout back, as loudly as I can, 'I'm up here!'

The wind carries my voice away, so I shout again. And again. I don't know how Jason got here so fast and I don't care. He's here and that's all that matters.

'I'm coming up,' he calls, and I hear him scaling the ladder fast, paying little heed to how slippery it must be in the rain. This surprises me. Jason is usually far more cautious than that. He must be just desperate to get to me! A lump fills my throat just thinking of this.

I turn my head with a rueful smile, feeling embarrassed he's had to come out in the storm, but knowing he understands me of old ...

'Twilight. Christ, are you okay?'

Theo Steel is standing in the doorway, staring down at me.

I gulp. 'Yes. No. What are you doing here?' I feel exposed. Vulnerable. And humiliated.

'Is it the thunderstorm?' He comes and crouches down beside me. 'I was halfway back home when I realised I still had your bag in my backpack, so I turned around. I saw the house was in darkness and I remembered you said you hated thunderstorms, so I came round the back and found the door was still open from earlier.' He lays his hand on my back. 'Come on. I'll help you get back to the house.'

I shake my head. 'I'll just stay here.'

He thinks for a second. Then he nods and sits down next to me, folding his long legs in the same way I have, arms casually round his knees, sitting close enough for our arms to be touching. It feels so blissfully good after being alone with my fear that my heart gives a little lurch of something approaching happiness, which feels unbelievable in itself.

Instinctively, I lean against him, taking comfort from the solid weight of him next to me. We stay like that for a while and gradually, a feeling of calm settles over me. I have the strangest feeling that as long as Theo Steel is by my side, nothing bad will happen.

When he finally murmurs, close to my ear, 'I make a mean hot chocolate. Just so you know,' I realise he's gently suggesting we make a move indoors, but I don't want to. I know I *could* get down the ladder and into the house with Theo's help, but I'd rather stay here, right where I am, leaning against him like this, feeling his solid, reassuring presence.

But I know it's silly. The storm has passed over and there's no longer any reason to stay here.

Getting up, my legs feel stiff from sitting in a cramped position for so long. Theo holds out a hand and pulls me the rest of the way, then guides me onto the deck, closing the treehouse door firmly behind us. Then he descends the ladder first, staying just below me as I climb gingerly down the slippery rungs. If I miss my footing in the dark, he will catch me.

As we go in through the back door, I hear a car draw up outside.

Jason!

I go straight out through the front door to meet him as he gets out of the car.

'God, sorry it took me so long,' he says, taking my arms, concern written all over his face. 'I couldn't find my bloody door keys and I couldn't leave the house unlocked.'

I smile. 'Of course you couldn't.' I'd have run out of the house and left the door on the latch and to hell with it. But everyone is different. I'm just touched he got here.

'Are you okay?' He starts leading me back to the house. 'I hated to think of you here alone, knowing how much you hate storms. But I'm here now. You're not on your own any more.' He looks over at the house and his expression changes. 'But I see you're not actually alone at all.'

When I glance over, I see Theo standing in the doorway, watching us.

I start talking, far too fast, feeling the need to explain to Jason. 'Oh, yes. Well, I *was* on my own. When I called you. But then Theo – Theo Steel, that's his name – well, he arrived and he sort of got me down from the treehouse.' I give a little nervous laugh. 'Thankfully. Otherwise I'd still be up there, a quivering wreck.'

'Who's Theo Steel?' asks Jason lightly.

'He's – erm – a personal trainer.' I laugh awkwardly. 'I know. Imagine. Me working out! So basically, Theo's getting me all hot and sweaty in return for as much cake as he can eat!' *Damn, that sounded terrible!*

'Right.' Jason smiles and takes a step back. 'Well, I can see you're all right, so I'll – um – leave you to it.'

'Come in for a drink!' I feel really bad now. Flustered at what Jason must think. 'Oh, you're driving. Well, a coffee, at least?'

Theo starts walking over. 'Hi, I'm Theo. I take it you came to the rescue as well?' He grins and the two shake hands rather stiffly.

'This is Jason,' I say quickly, and when Theo looks expectantly at me, I add, 'My childhood sweetheart, you might say!'

Jason laughs, a little too heartily. 'If you were acting in a movie from the last century!'

We all laugh then. It's all so hilarious. (Not.)

I can feel this weird tension in the air and I can't wait for them both to bugger off so I can be alone. As soon as I have this thought, I feel really guilty. Both of these men went out of their way to rescue me tonight!

What the hell is wrong with me?

'Right, well, nice to meet you, Theo,' says Jason. 'I'd better be off.'

I glance at him sharply. Was it my imagination or was there an edge to his tone?

'Yeah, me too,' says Theo. He nods and smiles but there's an odd tension to the set of his mouth and he continues to stand there beside me. We wave Jason off together, which feels weird, as if we're a couple.

'Hope I'm not encroaching on something,' he says, as Jason's car disappears.

'No, no, of course not. Jason's just – well, he's a friend now.'

An awkward flush stains my face. 'It's a shame, actually. He's had a row with his girlfriend and she's walked out so he probably feels a bit lonely. But he'll be fine. She wasn't good enough for him anyway.'

Theo gives me a piercing look with those deep blue eyes, and I can't fathom what he's thinking.

Then he says, 'Of course. His girlfriend is Lucy.'

'Yes. How did you know?'

We walk back to the house and he ushers me over the threshold first. 'You told me about a girl called Lucy who bullied you and stole your boyfriend, so I put two and two together.'

'Well, you're right. And Jason's far too good for her.'

Theo walks on ahead, over to the counter. 'Seems like you still really like him.'

'Yes. I do. But as a friend.' I'm not sure why I feel the need to add that last bit. Theo says nothing, just gets on with pouring out hot chocolate into two mugs he's found on the kitchen dresser. They're just there for display really so they'll be in need of a dust, but I'm not going to tell Theo that after he's been kind enough to make me a drink in the first place!

He brings the mugs and we go through to the living room, and I quickly draw the curtains to block out any evidence of storm still visible outside. I sink onto the sofa, and after a quick glance at the seating, Theo hands me my mug and sits down next to me, lounging into the corner so he's almost facing me, long legs spread out and almost touching mine.

'I used to have a weird fear of buttons when I was a kid,' he says. 'Grown out of it now, thankfully, otherwise I'd be spending my life in a onesie.'

I've just taken a sip of hot chocolate and almost choke

with amusement at the thought. 'I can see you as Superman. Or maybe Rudolph with the furry antlers on your hood.'

'Thanks.' He nods with fake modesty. 'Yes, I've always been quite stylish.'

'Buttons is a strange one, though.'

'It is. At least yours is slightly more common.' He raises his mug. 'Here's to weird phobias. So have you always been scared of thunderstorms?'

I don't really like talking about it, but I give him a brief description of being stranded in the garden in the middle of a humdinger of a storm, thanks to Lucy. I try to laugh it off, but I think he can see right through my bravado because he doesn't even smile.

'Kids can be so cruel,' he says, shifting his position and leaning over to place his empty mug on the coffee table. When he sits back, he's closer to me on the sofa, his thigh brushing mine, and suddenly, I'm acutely aware of his nearness. It's like a giant hoover has come down from the sky and sucked all other thoughts right out of my head.

Every time he shifts slightly, I get tantalising wafts of shower gel or body spray blended with his own scent, which I very much like. It's all in the nostrils for me, this attraction thing. And I think it's the same for most people, even though they might not even realise it. Nothing personal but some people just *stink*! (And yet to someone else, they might smell like a garden of roses.)

'Are you feeling better now?'

I'm so lost in the sensation of actually being attracted to a man after so long, it takes me a while to process the question.

'Much better.' I smile shyly, risking eye contact. 'Thank you for rescuing me. And for the hot chocolate. I feel fine now.' And it's true. I do.

'Good.' He's leaning sideways, his arm on the back of the sofa, looking at me with a strange intensity in those mesmerising blue eyes, and a powerful longing surges up and engulfs me. Suddenly I'm wondering what it would feel like to unbutton his shirt and run my hands over his broad bare chest and kiss the side of his neck right where his hair curls, soft and dark ...

The eye contact goes on and my skin is tingling with an overwhelming desire to be touched. When he reaches over and gently shifts a strand of hair out of my eyes, the feeling of his fingers lightly brushing my temple makes my whole body quiver. He runs his hand down my cheek, cupping it in his palm for a moment and instinctively, boldly, I turn my lips towards it.

'I need to be going,' he murmurs, and his words are confusing, disorientating to me. His body seems to be saying one thing and yet ...

Abruptly, he gets to his feet and clears his throat. 'You must be exhausted after tonight.'

I try to smile but a feeling of despair is creeping over me. I'm back to feeling cold and frighteningly alone, like I felt in the treehouse before he arrived.

'Right.' I stand up, too, but my legs are a little shaky and I stumble slightly. He catches me, his hands firm around my waist, and we laugh, and then our eyes meet and the laughter dies away. The space between us is bridged at long last as our mouths meet, hard and passionate, longing moulding our bodies ever closer.

Then suddenly, he breaks away and pulls me into an

embrace, so that my face is against his chest, his fingers in my hair. 'I can't,' he murmurs.

'Why not?' My plea is muffled by his jumper.

'It wouldn't be fair. On you.' He holds me for a moment and I can feel the strong, quick beating of his heart.

'I don't understand.'

He gives a deep sigh and I long to see his face, to try and understand him. But the way he's cradling my head so tenderly against his chest makes it impossible for me to even think about moving away.

'I'm bad news,' he says at last. 'Just being friends is better. For both our sakes.'

I look up at him and he bends and kisses me chastely on the forehead.

'Sure you'll be all right?' he asks.

I nod and follow him to the door.

'Think about the café in the treehouse,' he says again.

The storm has passed over. All that's left of it is a stiff breeze rustling the trees. Theo walks out into the scented, rain-soaked night, gets into his car and drives off at speed.

I retreat indoors, feeling oddly empty, as if my insides have been hollowed out. It's been an emotional night, what with Jason turning up and so clearly resenting Theo's presence.

And then Theo ...

Sighing, I switch off the lights and head upstairs to bed.

Theo might be thinking about a café in the treehouse. But to be honest, that's the very *last* thing on my mind ...

Chapter 24

When I finally fall asleep, after tossing and turning most of the night, I have a horrible dream that bailiffs are kicking the front door down and marching through the house, taking an inventory of everything.

I wake in a sweat with a raging headache, all the events of the day before tumbling chaotically around in my mind.

Theo coming into the café and offering me a training session. Diane and the other mums nudging each other and winking, saying what a waste that Theo was a 'lone wolf' due to his tragic past. Chatting to him about the café after the session, up in the treehouse, followed by his swift departure. And then being caught outdoors in the thunderstorm, Jason coming to my rescue and being so obviously disgruntled because Theo was already there.

And then the really embarrassing encounter on the sofa. Heat washes into my face just thinking of it.

Not that the kiss was embarrassing. If I'm honest with myself, I didn't want it to end. It was the way Theo deliberately extracted himself from my clutches. I don't think I'll ever be able to face him again.

I glance at the clock. It's already eight-thirty on a Monday morning, and in an hour or so, I should be heading over to the café to get ready to open up. But for the first time, I'm actually wondering if it's really worth it. At a guess, I'll have maybe a dozen customers through the door today. And that's if I'm lucky. I hate to think of Betty and Doreen feeling obliged to call in and order something most days, so they can help me shore up the business. That's not how it's supposed to be!

Trailing downstairs, I put the kettle on and fetch the post from the doormat in the hall. My heart stalls. There's one from Mum and Dad's building society. I stare at it, my mouth bone dry. I should open the letter, I know – Mum and Dad would want me to – but somehow I can't summon up the strength.

It's probably time to admit that I've failed in my bid to save Honey Cottage. I had such a marvellous vision of how it could be – a café serving wonderful cakes and the best coffee, a meeting place at the heart of a thriving community. What an idiot I was to think it could be so easy.

It might have worked – if Lucy hadn't gone out of her way to ruin everything as she always did. I can't believe I was starting to give her the benefit of the doubt ... thinking that Paloma was probably right and that Lucy was no longer the vindictive schoolgirl bully she once was; she was sure to have matured and left those days behind her. How wrong could we have been! And, of course, the people who will suffer because of her nastiness are Mum and Dad, who never did Lucy any harm in their lives! How am I going to break it to them that my café idea has failed? That they will lose Honey Cottage after all?

I go back into the kitchen and throw the letter from the bank onto the table. It slides along the surface and falls onto the floor, but I turn my back on it, resolutely making my tea.

But even before I start drinking it, good sense gets the better of me and I reach down and rip open the letter, reading the inevitably bad news with a sinking heart.

It is, as I knew it would be, a reminder that the mortgage arrears requested have not been paid. I have fourteen days to settle the account, otherwise 'further action' will be taken. Somehow seeing it written in black and white makes it suddenly very real.

Who was I kidding thinking I could succeed? Me, a successful café owner? What a joke!

I sink down at the table as the tears begin to slide down my face. My throat hurts, thinking of Mum and Dad so far away. It's probably just as well they're in London right now, so they can remain in ignorance (for a little while longer) of what's really going on here, with the cottage and the café. But all the same, I'd give anything to be able to see them. Dropping my head on my arms, I finally give in to my grief, sobbing loudly in the stillness of the house, letting out all the sadness and the frustrations of what has been the most challenging time of my life.

It's time I admitted it.

Once again, Lucy has won ...

I'm drying my face on kitchen towel later when the doorbell goes.

Instantly, I think it's Jason, come to quiz me about Theo. I'm not sure I'm up for that. Hopefully, it will be Paloma back from London, although I doubt it. She would have had to get a very early train, and Paloma is very definitely not a morning person ...

When I open the door, I truly can't believe my eyes.

'Oh my God, Mum!'

She's standing there on the doorstep with her small overnight bag, and my heart contracts because it's so good to see her and she's lost so much weight. She's wearing a navy sundress with a little turquoise cardigan and navy sling-backs, and her mid-brown hair has been given soft blonde highlights that really flatter her face shape. But however much of an effort she's made with her appearance, there's no disguising the prominent dark circles of worry about Dad around her pale blue eyes.

'Surprise!' She steps over the threshold, drops her bag and enfolds me in the biggest hug. I hug her back, clinging tightly, breathing in her achingly familiar, comforting scent, tears of relief at seeing her dripping down my cheeks. She's smaller than me by a couple of inches and having lost the weight, she feels angular and a little fragile.

'I can't believe you're here!' I stand back to look at her, and she keeps tight hold of my hands. 'I was only just wishing I could see you – and here you are!'

'Why were you wishing you could see me?' She looks worried. 'Has something happened?'

'No, no, of course not.' I brush away her concern. 'Things are hunky dory here. Come on, I'll put the kettle on.'

'Lovely! I left so early, I didn't have time for breakfast.'

'How's Dad?'

Her smile freezes. 'Well, you know, he's in fairly good spirits, considering.'

A cold hand grips my heart as we walk into the kitchen. 'Still no improvement, then?'

She gives her head a quick shake then says, 'But it's early days, love. He'll be fine, I'm certain of it.'

'He will.' *If we keep on believing it, maybe it will come true.*

She sits at the kitchen table and kicks off her shoes with

a sigh while I make the tea and keep up a constant stream of chat about Betty and Doreen – and what they've been getting up to in their retirement – to distract Mum from the subject of Dad. A break from all the stressful hospital visits will probably do her the world of good. It must be so hard keeping cheery and strong for Dad's sake.

'I get the feeling they're both at a bit of a loose end,' she says. 'Betty and boredom really don't go well together! I think she wishes she was still the terrifyingly efficient PA she used to be, except with plenty of days off to get up to all sorts of mischief with Doreen.'

I laugh. 'Yes, well, they're in the café pretty much every day, so I gathered they were probably short on excitement!'

Mum's eyes gleam. 'I decided to come early so I could help you open up.'

I stare at her blankly.

'The Twilight Café?' She laughs at my expression.

'Oh yes, of course.' I swallow and glance down at my hands.

'Is there something wrong, love?' She takes my hand and squeezes it and for a moment, the only sound is the ticking of the clock on the wall as I stare at my lap. It's no use. I'll have to tell her. She's about to see for herself how popular The Twilight Café *isn't*.

Finally, I look up and my expression must say it all.

'What?' she asks in alarm.

'It's ... the thing is, Mum, it's not going so well. Do you remember Lucy Slater?'

Her face turns instantly thunderous. 'I *do* remember that little witch. How could I ever forget her? She *terrorised* you throughout your schooldays.'

'Well, it wasn't that bad.'

'I think it was.' Her look is razor sharp. 'You just didn't tell us the extent of the bullying until after you left school. I've felt bad for years that I didn't realise at the time.'

'But how could you have known? I kept it from you because I didn't want you to worry.'

'Yes, but that's what mothers *do*; they worry about their kids. That's their *job*! So, come on, love, I need to know.'

With a sigh, I describe the damp squib that was launch day, and her face falls even further when I tell her about Lucy & Olivia's Clean Food Café.

'The place is packed every time I go past. I just can't compete.' I shrug hopelessly.

Mum frowns. 'Of course, Lucy's dad is a businessman with contacts all over the place. No doubt he'll be using his influence to make sure his darling daughter's café is a raging success.' She shakes her head. 'But it makes my blood boil that she opened the same day to sabotage your success!'

'I know. I've been planning all sorts of murderous revenge.' Grinning, I add, 'But I value my freedom, so it looks like she's got away with it.'

She reaches over and presses my hand. 'Honestly, love, I don't know how you can be so calm about it. If she did that to me, I'd be tearing my hair out.'

'Oh, I've done plenty of that, believe me. It's just I've got to the stage where I'm wondering if it's worth carrying on with the café. Perhaps it's time I accepted that it was a lovely idea but thanks to Lucy, it's not going to work.'

Mum studies me, thinking hard. 'There must be *something* you can do to draw people to The Twilight Café.'

'If there is, I can't think of it. And I've thought about practically nothing else for the past few weeks.'

She pats my hand. 'Well, don't lose hope. Not yet.'

'Actually, someone *did* suggest a solution.' I swallow hard. 'He said I should put the café in the treehouse instead.'

She frowns and looks at me for a minute. Then she gives a bark of surprised laughter. 'Well, it would certainly be unusual.'

I nod. 'I can see the headline now. Local girl turns childhood treehouse into a café.'

'Shame it's not big enough.'

'Oh, Theo has a friend who's a carpenter. He reckons his mate could extend the treehouse into a viable structure to house a café. All pie in the sky, of course, because it would probably cost an absolute fortune!'

She nods. 'Interesting. Who is this Theo, by the way? Someone nice?'

'Oh, not really.' I shrug awkwardly. 'I mean, yes, he is nice. He's a personal trainer and he gave me a free session, and we ended up having a drink in the treehouse, that's all.' I get up to make some tea and to conceal the annoying blushes that have just flooded my cheeks for no good reason.

'A free session? Hmm, very good.' I can tell by her tone she's dying to know more about mystery man Theo, but she's going to be disappointed! In any case, I barely know anything about him myself.

What I do know is that every time I think about him pulling away from me, I feel stupid and embarrassed all over again. And I can't stop wondering what he meant when he said he was 'bad news'. Did he mean he stays away from relationships because he's not the faithful type? But it was only a kiss. I wasn't proposing marriage or anything. It was a kiss that happened on the spur of the moment, probably

– from my side anyway – because of the build-up of emotion. I was so scared of the storm, I'd have clung to *anyone* who offered to prop me up and see me through the worst of it ...

I bring our tea and some gingerbread to the table, and Mum says, 'We'd better not be too long. When do you open up?'

I glance at my watch. 'Ten. In half an hour.'

'Right, well, you never know, there might be a queue a mile long when we get there!'

I smile at her determination to remain positive. She might feel differently after a day of kicking her heels behind the till of a deserted café, as tumbleweed rolls along the street outside. But whatever happens, I'm so very glad she's here with me.

'Mum?'

'Yes, love?'

'We don't need to mention to Dad that business isn't exactly booming, do we?'

She shakes her head firmly. 'Definitely not. It's our secret, for now.'

Chapter 25

After a day spent in the café, reading magazines and chatting in the long gaps between customers, Mum and I decide to cheer ourselves up with a couple of our favourite movies and a Chinese take-away. We get into our pyjamas and I open a bottle of wine and we have such a lovely, relaxed evening.

Halfway through *Sleepless in Seattle*, Mum falls asleep – curled into the corner of the sofa – and I watch her with an aching heart. She must be utterly exhausted, looking after Dad, but at least she's had a chance to escape the hospital routine for one night. We have my Auntie June to thank for that. She's looking after Dad while Mum's away.

Mum wakes up around ten, long enough to drink some tea before I shoo her off to bed with strict instructions to sleep for as long as she needs to, then have an easy day while I'm at the café. We'll have a meal together when I close up in the afternoon, then I'll walk her to the station around seven for her train back to London.

The following morning, Paloma comes over to the café around eleven and it's pretty clear she's not in a great mood. When I mention that Mum arrived unexpectedly and is staying for a while, her face lights up and she hugs me, saying what a lovely surprise.

But she continues hugging me long after she normally would, and that's when I realise, to my horror, that her shoulders are shaking.

'What's wrong?' I hold her arms and pull away from her vice-like grip so I can see her face. Sure enough, tears are leaking down her face, and I can't help feeling alarmed. Paloma very rarely cries. Apart from breaking down over losing Linda and before she told me about looking for her birth mum, I've only ever known her to cry once. That was when her ex, Rufus, revealed his prize knob-head status by expecting her to tolerate his kinky sex sessions with his ex-wife, which he insisted were a vital part of his ongoing psychotherapy treatment.

'Sorry.' She dashes the tears away and tries to smile. 'I'm so pleased for you that your mum is here, Twi. It's just I haven't heard a thing from Sylvia and I just keep wondering if I'm ever going to find my mum.'

'Oh God, poor you. And here's me going on about how great it is to have Mum here.'

Why didn't I think?

But Paloma shakes her head. 'Don't be silly. It's not your fault. I've just been feeling really despondent about the whole thing. I've started to think I should probably just forget about trying to find her if it's going to cause me so much grief.'

'No, don't give up. Not yet,' I urge her. 'Sylvia could unearth something at any time.'

Paloma attempts a smile, but it changes into a huge yawn and it turns out she's been working most of the night on a project. I pack her off home with a bag of freshly baked cheese and thyme scones and she promises to go to bed and get some sleep.

After she's gone, there's a bit of a lull and then Rowena Swann arrives. She orders three cappuccinos, explaining that Betty and Doreen are on their way and will be here any minute.

She walks around looking at the wall art while I set to, making the coffees.

'I'm so glad Jason pointed me in your direction for the furniture,' I call over, above the noise of the coffee machine. 'It fits in here perfectly, don't you think?'

She smiles. 'It does, doesn't it? I really love how pretty and cosy the place looks.' She lingers by the children's play area, stooping to pick up a picture book. Watching her leafing through it with a distant look on her face, I can't help myself. I have to ask.

'Did you say you had children, Rowena? I couldn't remember.' I busy myself wiping up coffee spillages, my heart beating fast.

She walks over to collect her coffee and for a moment I think she's not going to answer me. Then she stands by the counter, drawing her coffee towards her, and says, 'I had a daughter.' She picks up the spoon and starts carving through the froth, making patterns in it.

The silence in the café, now that the machine noises have stopped, is absolute.

'What ... happened to your daughter, Rowena?' I ask.

She looks up at me and says simply and matter-of-factly, 'I let her go.'

My heart lurches. I don't know what to say, so I just reach across and press her arm.

She gives a sad little smile. 'It was for the best. I can see that now, but it was so hard at the time.'

My heart is beating very fast. I look at her lowered head as she stirs the coffee. She has short dark hair, the same shade as Paloma's, although no doubt both women use colourants to enhance the shade. Paloma said her birth mother's name was Margaret, but perhaps Rowena changed her name or goes by her middle name.

'Do you ever wish you hadn't?' I ask softly. 'Let her go, I mean.'

Her eyes fill with tears and she laughs and grabs a paper napkin to dab them with. 'Every day, but that doesn't mean it wasn't the right thing to do.'

At that moment, the door opens and Betty and Doreen come in, which means I can't ask anything else.

The three friends greet each other and I stand there, thinking: *What if it really is her? What if Rowena Swann is Paloma's birth mum and neither of them even realises it?*

Should I mention my suspicions to Paloma? But immediately, I decide against that. The chances of it being true are slight, and the last thing I want is to build Paloma's hopes up only for them to be dashed. But it's so frustrating, not being able to ask outright if her baby was adopted and if so, when?

I'm so lost in thought, I don't even notice Rowena's purse on the counter until they've all gone.

After leaving her a message saying I've found it, I decide to close up for an hour so I can nip over and see how Mum's getting on. I'm expecting her to be in, perhaps lying on the sofa watching some daytime TV, but she's left a mysterious note on the kitchen table saying she's nipped out but will be back later.

I'm wiping the tables in the café just before five, ready to close up, when she walks in.

'Hi, Mum. Had a nice afternoon?'

There's an odd look on her face, an expression somewhere between nervous and excited.

'What is it?' I ask, pausing with the cloth in my hand.

She stands in the middle of the café and looks around her. 'This place is so absolutely wonderful. What an amazing job you've done, love, and the cakes are second to none.' She smiles at me, her eyes misting over. 'When you told me what you planned to do, I never imagined something like this. I'm so proud. You deserve to do really well.'

I'm almost tearful myself at her enthusiasm. But I shrug. 'I just don't think it was meant to be.'

'Well, I think you're wrong.' She flashes a mischievous smile, then says impulsively, 'Let's go up to the treehouse!'

'What, now?' I stare at her, puzzled. 'But I'm making a pasta carbonara for dinner—'

'Just humour me, love?'

'Okay.' Grinning, I drop the cloth on the table and collect my keys and bag. 'You haven't been up in the treehouse for ages.'

'The last time was when you came home for your birthday last year, and we had cake and champagne up there, remember?'

I nod wistfully. Dad seemed well then, the life and soul of the party, telling his bad jokes. None of us had any idea ...

I swallow hard as I lock up and we walk along the street and in through our back gate. Mum climbs up the treehouse ladder with ease, and soon we're standing on the deck in the late afternoon sunshine, looking out over Dad's leafy domain.

'I miss the garden,' she says wistfully. 'It's just as well your dad still has the gardener coming in every week, otherwise this view would be nothing but wilderness!'

'Where were you this afternoon?' I ask, leaning on the railing, curious to know what's going on in her head.

'Well, Betty and Doreen called in after they saw you at the café and took me out for lunch, and we had a lovely old catch-up. We were talking about The Twilight Café and I told them what your friend, Theo, said about putting the café in the treehouse instead and that he had a carpenter friend who could work on extending it and making the structure sound enough for purpose.'

'Right,' I say slowly, wondering where on earth all this is leading.

Mum turns to me and takes hold of my hands. 'Betty and Doreen want to invest in The Twilight Café. You can get Theo's friend to start work immediately. If that's what you'd like.'

I stare at her, trying to process what she's just told me.

Her eyes are shining with expectation, but all I can do is frown. 'What? Really? Did you *ask* them to invest?'

She shakes her head. 'No, of course not.' She smiles, remembering. 'I actually told them they were mad to even *think* of using their precious retirement funds to finance such a project. But they wouldn't listen. Betty said – and I quote – "What's the point of having money in the bank if you can't put it to good use? We've been looking around for the perfect investment opportunity – and I think we've just found it! Eh, Doreen?"'

I can't take it in. I'm still too dumbfounded to speak.

Mum rushes on, 'You'd still be running the place and making all the decisions, but Betty and Doreen would finance the initial stage and help you out in the café. You wouldn't mind that, would you?'

'No, of course not. But ...'

'But?'

'It's far too big a gamble, Mum. What if they invest their money, thinking it's all going to be fabulous, then it fails spectacularly. I'd feel absolutely terrible. And I wouldn't be able to pay them back. At least not straight away.'

She nods. 'I know. And of course nothing is guaranteed in business. But Betty and Doreen are both intelligent women. They know all about the risks in ventures like this, but they're both convinced that a treehouse café would be something really special and they want to be part of it.' She smiles. 'I think they're looking for a bit of excitement in their lives. You wouldn't deny them that, now, would you?'

'But how would I pay them back?'

Mum frowns. 'I'm not great with legal stuff but Betty seems to think there's a way for you to pay them back gradually, from the proceeds of the business.'

I shake my head slowly. 'But you're always so cautious, Mum. It's Dad who's the adventurous one. I can't believe you're so enthusiastic about this ... this wild idea!'

She smiles sadly. 'Listen, love, if I've learned anything from your dad being so ill, it's that you only have one life to live and it can be over in a flash. Just like that.' She snaps her fingers. 'So why not really live it while you can? Have an adventure. Take a risk.' She shrugs. 'As long as it's a *calculated* risk, of course.'

I take a deep breath and stare out over the garden to the fields beyond, and Lake Heath in the distance. Something stirs inside. A little leap of excitement at the thought of what a café in Dad's treehouse could be like.

'Well, what do you think?' asks Mum.

'I think ... ' Turning towards her, I can't believe what I'm about to say. I'm quivering inside with a strange sort of nervous exhilaration 'I think Betty and Doreen are right. People would be fascinated to come up here and drink their coffee among the treetops.'

I swallow hard.

'I think it might actually work, Mum.'

*****

Later, after I've waved Mum off on the London train, I walk home, deep in thought. Wandering out into the garden, I climb the ladder to the treehouse and sit on the window seat inside, staring out at Honey Cottage. A summer breeze drifts in through the open window and I try to imagine what it would be like to have enough room up here for tables and chairs, and a proper walkway entrance so everyone – young and old – was able to come inside.

Could it really work?

Before we parted, Mum said she was going to transfer a little money into my account so I could keep going financially while I decided what to do. I hated the thought of taking what little savings she had, but she was really insistent.

She took my hands and said, 'I believe in you, love. Your dad and I both do. You'll be a success, whatever you decide to do.'

I grimace, remembering her words. They both believe in me. *No pressure there, then!*

One of the things that makes me very wary is having to get Theo involved. I'd need his carpenter friend's contact details.

My heart sinks every time I imagine seeking him out at

the gym. I'm not at all sure I *want* to see Theo again after what happened the other night. It will just be so awkward. I'll have to make it very clear that all I need from him is his help with the treehouse café – namely, an introduction to his friend, Jake.

From now on, as far as my relationship with Theo Steel is concerned, it has to be strictly business ...

Chapter 26

It's a week later, and I'm sitting in the back seat of Theo Steel's car, trying to hear what he and Paloma are talking about in the front.

We began by trying to have a three-way conversation, but I was finding it too much of a strain having to lean forward all the time to hear, so eventually I sat back and took out my notebook and pen, pretending I needed to plan my baking for the following week. The week since Mum dropped the bombshell that Betty and Doreen wanted to invest in the café has taken its toll on me and I feel really tired. All I want to do is relax and watch the scenery go by. The trouble is, I also want to know what's being said in the front!

We're on our way to meet Theo's carpenter friend, Jake, who lives near Brighton and has a business creating bespoke playhouses. Apparently, Theo knows him from way back, when they went to school together in Lake Heath, and he's already spoken to him about the possibility of building a treehouse big enough to house a café.

I love the whole idea of extending Dad's lovely treehouse into a café and my heart beats a little faster every time I imagine what it would look like. But it still seems pretty unreal to me somehow. There are so many practical uncertainties to consider, and the financing of it is worrying me the most. I mean, a bespoke treehouse is not going to come cheap, and it's Betty and Doreen's money!

Feeling a bit left out, I lean forward slightly and manage to catch a snatch of their conversation.

'Oh God, what a poser!' Paloma turns to Theo's profile and laughs.

'I know. So this poor guy is lying trapped under a massive set of weights, while his mate ogles a girl on the treadmill.'

I stare glumly at the backs of their heads. They have the same dark, glossy hair and the same taste in jokes, apparently, if the merriment in the front of the car is anything to go by. *A match made in heaven!*

I check myself. What's wrong with me? I should be really grateful to both of them. Theo is doing me a big favour, giving up his afternoon off to take us to meet Jake, and Paloma is coming along to provide support and give me her opinion. The only reason she's sitting in the front seat is because Theo happened to pick her up first. Not that it makes any difference whatsoever!

I suppose I'm still confused about Theo's behaviour towards me. His passion tells me he's attracted to me, but then he says it's best 'for both our sakes' that we stay friends. This irritates me – and it's not because I'm interested in getting involved with Theo. Not at all. I'd just like to make my *own* mind up about what's best for me, thank you very much!

Mind you, would I actually *want* to be with someone who describes himself as 'bad news'?

I think of how he is with Olivia. Has he told *her* that he's 'bad news'? I get the feeling that even if he did, it wouldn't stop her flirting with him every chance she got. Would Theo repel her advances? I'd like to think so, because then I could stop thinking that the reason he backed off was because I'm not attractive enough ...

'Okay in the back there?' Theo asks, and I jump, thinking he must have been reading my mind. Or my expression, at least.

'Yes, I'm fine, thanks.' I paste on a smile to prove it. His deep blue eyes seem even more intense because I can only see the top half of his face. 'It's really nice of you to do this.'

He shrugs. 'It's a pleasure. I haven't seen my old mate, Jake, in years. It'll be good to catch up.'

We drive through a small village and then here we are, turning off the road at a sign saying, *Jake Fellows, Wood Creations*, bumping along a short track to our destination.

We head for a small visitors' car park at the side of what is clearly Jake's workshop, and as we're getting out, a man in a pair of khaki green overalls emerges from the cottage, which is just a hundred yards or so from the workshop. Theo walks over to greet him and they shake hands and pat each other's backs in that very male, slightly self-conscious way. They turn to Paloma and I, and Theo does the introductions.

Jake has green eyes, longish auburn hair and a rugged, square jaw that hasn't seen a razor in a few days. He doesn't look in the best of moods.

'I gather you're looking to build a treehouse café?' he says, turning his cool gaze on me.

When I smile and concur, he murmurs, 'Interesting concept,' and I can't tell whether he thinks it's a good or bad idea. 'I'll show you some of my work and you can see what you think.'

'Okay.' I nod cheerfully, and Jake indicates where we're going with his thumb before striding off, Theo alongside him.

Paloma calls after him, 'It would be a real first for the area, don't you think? A café in a treehouse. I don't know of anything similar, do you?'

'No, I don't,' says Jake without turning round. 'But maybe there's a reason no one's done it before.'

Paloma and I are hurrying to catch up.

'Perhaps they haven't thought of it?' she ventures.

He grunts. 'A treehouse is quirky by nature and "quirky" doesn't necessarily translate into the most practical of business premises.'

We're walking by the side of the house to a field at the back and, breaking into a little jog, Paloma finally manages to walk alongside our rather less than welcoming host. 'But surely,' she says, trying to make eye contact with him, 'if the concept is sound, you can find ways to work around any physical obstacle?'

I can tell she's needled by his brusqueness. I'm quite surprised myself. I would have thought the prospect of a big new commission would make him happy. But perhaps this *is* Jake happy!

'Only if the end result is worth the hard work,' he says.

'But how can you know that unless you've tried?' she persists, and I smile at her determination as I follow on a few steps behind.

'Experience,' he says flatly, before turning his back on her to open a gate into a display area.

I glance at Paloma, intending to grimace in amusement. But she's glaring at Jake's back. *If looks could kill ...*

The creations before us take my breath away and are a complete contrast to the surliness of their creator.

There's a cute log cabin with three rocking chairs on the

front porch and a sign carved over the door that says *The Three Bears Playhouse*. And next to it is an amazing structure, built entirely of wood, which makes you smile just to look at it. Everything about it is lopsided – from the shape of the windows and the door, to the higgledy-piggledy writing on the sign that says, *The Crooked Playhouse*.

'Oh, I love that. It's stunning,' I say. 'They all are.'

'Yeah, you've got some talent there, mate,' Theo says, laying his hand on Jake's shoulder and shaking his head in wonder at a house in the shape of a huge shoe with three rows of windows, and a slide emerging from the top level.

I nod in agreement. I'd have had huge fun as a kid, scrambling up the wooden stairs inside the shoe then sliding right down to the bottom. This man has some imagination! 'What do you think, Paloma?'

She gives a stiff little smile. 'They're great. Although they're not quite what you'd want for a café.'

'Well, obviously not,' says Jake, walking over to *The Three Bears Playhouse* and opening the door for us to see inside. 'This is just to show Twilight my range of techniques in wood.' He gives me a grudging smile. 'I envisage we'd have a chat about your vision for the café, then I'd draw up some plans for you to look at and we'd go from there.'

I nod happily, already carried away by the idea that Jake can clearly work wonders, and really wanting him to work his clever magic on The Treehouse Café!

Theo and Jake wander over towards the house, chatting and catching up on the years in between their last meeting, while Paloma and I wander in and out of the playhouse exhibits.

'Is it just me, or is that guy totally up his own arse?' says Paloma.

I laugh. 'Jake? He seems all right to me. A bit of a sense of humour bypass, maybe, but he's incredibly talented at what he does.'

She shrugs. 'Jake Fellows is the sort who always has to be right. You'll need to be careful he doesn't ride roughshod over your ideas for the café because, of course, *he's the artist*, don't you know!' Her sarcasm is accompanied by a sneer in his direction.

I grin at her. 'Aren't you jumping the gun a bit? I haven't even decided if the project is a goer yet.'

She twists her lips.

'Presumably Jake *wants* the commission? In which case he'd surely listen and be respectful of the client's ideas?'

She shrugs.

Jokingly, I say, 'Hey, artists are *allowed* to be grumpy and temperamental – didn't you know?'

She snorts. 'He's a *knob-head* artist. Just like Rufus Knob-Head Black,' she says, referring to her despicable former lover, who kept going back to his ex-wife for bondage sessions. 'And he's got nothing to be superior about. Have you seen his website? A five-year-old could have designed a better one.'

I laugh. 'Just because he's bad at computer stuff doesn't mean he's a bad person!'

We leave soon after, and Paloma ushers me into the front seat this time with a knowing smile. I throw a quick glance at Theo but he's starting the engine and waving at Jake. To be honest, I'd rather be in the back where I could spend the journey thinking about what we've just seen.

But front seat it is. And it gets even more awkward when Paloma realises she's left her phone in the giant shoe and hurries off to collect it.

Theo switches off the engine and in the silence that follows, we both stare ahead, Theo tapping the steering wheel.

At last, he clears his throat. 'Twilight, I want to apologise for leaving the way I did that night. The night of the thunderstorm. It's been on my mind ever since.'

I glance at him, cringing at the memory. 'It's no problem. Honestly.' I'd rather just forget it ever happened.

He heaves a sigh. 'Look, I have my reasons. And it's not you, I assure you. I meant it when I told you I'm bad news.'

There's another brief silence and I wait for him to elaborate. Why would he be 'bad news'? Maybe he's just come out of a relationship and doesn't want to get involved with anyone else so soon? Is it to do with him being a 'lone wolf', as the mums in the café described him?

We glance across at each other at the precise same moment.

He smiles sheepishly. 'It's definitely not you. You're gorgeous.'

A little jolt of shock runs through me. I wasn't expecting that. I wish I could read his mind. We lock eyes and his smile slowly vanishes, just like on the night of the thunderstorm when neither of us could break away.

But this time, he does.

'Friends?' he says, snapping me out of my reverie, and it's like he's thrown a bucket of cold water over me.

His smile seems strained.

'Friends,' I repeat.

Thankfully, Paloma comes back at that moment, which saves me from having to think of something else to say – and having to examine the awful hollow feeling inside ...

*****

The following morning, early, I receive a phone call from Jake asking if he can come round to look at the site for the tree-house café. We decide on six o'clock, after I've closed up for the day.

The meeting starts off well. He's really taken with the tree-house – how sturdy it still is after all these years and such a clever design. My eyes fill with tears several times when he refers to dad and how impressed he is at his handiwork.

'I'll make sure to keep the character of the original,' he says, which reassures me hugely. I'd had visions of him wanting to knock it down and start all over again from scratch, which I just couldn't bear. 'I'll incorporate it into my design.'

I nod happily and he shrugs. 'It makes sense. And the structure is so solid, it will make my work a lot easier.' He winks. 'Therefore cheaper.'

I laugh. 'Even better!'

He smiles. 'I'm going to enjoy this commission. *If* you give me the go-ahead. This café of yours could be absolutely stunning.'

It's the first time I've seen him smile and it transforms his whole face and demeanour. Maybe it's the passion for his craft that's shining through.

'Sorry I was a bit gruff the other day,' he says, as if he's just read my thoughts. 'I'd just finished a commission that took weeks, and right before you arrived, the client phoned to say she'd changed her mind and didn't want it after all.'

'Oh God, that's terrible. Will you lose money on it?'

He shrugs. 'She'd paid a hefty deposit, which she'll obviously lose, and I'll be able to sell the playhouse to someone else. But that's not the point. I made it to her specifications, so it just seems like a complete waste of my time and effort.'

I nod. 'I can see that. Well, rest assured if I give you the commission, I won't be backing out!'

'Good.' We exchange a smile.

'So how long do you think it would take you to complete the work here?'

He stares up at the sky, doing mental calculations. 'Two months. I've just started a job that will take me the best part of a month, then I could start on yours.'

I do a quick calculation in my head. That would mean the structure would be finished by September, but by the time we decked it out and got ready to open, we'd be into the autumn.

I stare at Jake in dismay. 'I was hoping we could open during the summer, to take advantage of the rest of the tourist season, but ...'

He frowns and shakes his head. 'Couldn't do it. If the job I'm on goes well, I might be able to shave a week off the times, but not much more, I'm afraid.'

After feeling so optimistic, my heart is suddenly heavy in my chest. 'So realistically, I'd be better opening in April, at the start of next year's tourist season.'

But the money from Mum will have run out long before then. And then there's the mortgage arrears to pay. It just can't be done ...

I keep up a happy front until Jake has gone.

Then I climb up into the treehouse and sit on the deck, staring out over the garden, wondering what on earth to do now.

I decide to go and grab some cake to cheer myself up, so I climb down and head along to the café, checking that I still have the keys in my pocket. As I arrive at the door, a car draws up and Rowena Swann gets out.

'I was in the village so I thought I'd pick up my purse, if that's okay?'

'Of course. Come in. I put it in a drawer in the kitchen for safe-keeping.'

Now's my chance. I need to find out once and for all ...

I collect the purse and Rowena looks so relieved to have it back.

'I don't know what happened.' She laughs. 'I think I got distracted, talking about Melanie.'

'Melanie?' *That must be her baby's name*.

She nods. 'My daughter.'

'Have you never thought about trying to get in touch with her?' I ask gently, and she shakes her head.

'She didn't want me to. You know what teenagers are like. I'd forbidden her to see this waster of a boy who she professed to be madly in love with, so that was it as far as she was concerned. She never wanted to see me again.'

For a second, I'm baffled.

What about the baby?

'Her dad and I divorced years earlier, and when Melanie and I had our bust-up, she decided she wanted to go and live with him in Scotland.'

The truth is gradually dawning on me.

There *is* no baby. No adoption. I'd just assumed there was. It was wishful thinking, of course – desperately wanting a happy ending for Paloma.

Talk about jumping to conclusions!

Rowena is explaining about Melanie. 'We'd had a massive row over this boy. I could tell he was just using her but being only sixteen, of course she couldn't see that. We fell out big time and she declared she never wanted to see me again.'

'That's awful. How long ago did she leave?'

'Three years,' she says. 'When she'd gone, I knew I had to have a change of scene, so I came here and took over the lease on the ice-cream parlour.'

I stare at her sadly. 'And you haven't see her in all that time?'

Rowena shakes her head, looking as if she's about to break down in tears. 'She made me promise not to contact her.'

'But she was angry with you then. Things will have changed,' I murmur. 'She probably misses you like mad. Can't you just try phoning her?'

Rowena shakes her head. 'I'm scared she'll just put the phone down on me, the way she used to in the weeks after she left, and I couldn't bear that.' She gives a long, shaky sigh. 'I just keep praying that one day, Melanie will turn up on the doorstep and things will get back to normal. And if that happens, I swear I'll never criticise her boyfriends ever again ...'

She attempts a smile but her face crumples and a tear rolls down her cheek.

I rush to hand her a paper hanky. 'You should phone her.'

'I can't,' she whispers. 'I'm not brave enough.'

Chapter 27

'Turn on your TV!' shrieks Paloma down the phone line.

'What? Sorry?' It's seven-forty-five in the morning and I'm eating breakfast in the kitchen, not even fully awake.

Obeying her command, I hurry through to the living room, toast in hand.

'Is it on?' she demands.

'No, I can't find the remote!'

'Look down the side of the seat where you were sitting last night!'

'Okay, okay! Keep calm! Who's on anyway?'

'Lucy bloody Slater, that's who. With that "Z" list local "celebrity" who slimmed down to a size zero using a clean food diet! Have you got it yet?'

My fingers close on the remote down the side of the seat. After fumbling slightly, eventually I manage to turn it on.

Lucy Slater looms at me in enormous, full-colour close-up, just like she does in my worst nightmares. Instinctively, I back away from the TV. Clutching my stomach, I abandon my toast and stare at the screen in horrified fascination.

The interviewer on this local morning news programme is talking about someone who's donating money to help send a little boy to America for life-saving medical treatment. He's called Harry and he's seven, and he's sitting there on the sofa with his mum, looking cute as a button. His poor mum is clutching him tight and is clearly so grateful for the help, she looks as if she's having a hard job holding back the tears. I feel quite emotional for her.

'What's Lucy got to do with this?' I ask Paloma, though the story does seem familiar. I remember something about a boy needing medical treatment in connection with the 10k run.

'She's donating a percentage of her café funds. Quite the little saint on the sly, isn't she?'

Flashing onto the screen is the sign above the café doorway: Lucy & Olivia's Clean Food Café. And then Lucy and Olivia are there, standing behind the counter with someone I recognise but can't quite place. The interviewer is talking about what a popular trend clean eating has become and how Lucy and Olivia's café is filling a big gap in the market. And how determined they are to put some of the profits towards helping others. Hence the trip to America for Harry and his mum.

I frown at the screen. 'Who's that woman with them?'

'Don't you recognise her? It's "B" list celebrity Meghan Sparkle. She lives in London, but she grew up in Lake Heath, apparently.'

'What does this Meghan Sparkle *do*?'

'Nothing, as far as I can make out. Except lose tons of weight.'

'So how is she famous?'

'Because she was on a certain reality TV programme a few months ago where you spill your guts in the name of entertaining people? Don't you remember her?'

'I didn't watch it. I've been too busy baking.'

'Well, apparently she's a "firm friend" of Lucy's and will be "working" at the café over the next few weeks to attract more customers, so Lucy can donate even more money for Harry's cause.'

'A firm friend of Lucy's?' I burst out. 'What a load of old bollocks! You mean Lucy's got in touch with her, and they've cooked this stunt up together in order to get their names in lights!'

'I imagine that's pretty much the size of it,' says Paloma gloomily. 'Her ears look weird, don't you think?'

'What?'

'Meghan Sparkle. Now that she's slimmed down, her ears look like jug handles.'

'Er, never seen her before. But they do look on the large side.'

'She needs to grow her hair longer to cover them up.'

'Ssh! I'm trying to listen.'

'You can watch it on catch-up.'

'I want to watch it now.'

Lucy is speaking. She's putting on a really false posh accent and I'd laugh if I didn't find the whole thing so annoying. 'So anyway,' she's saying, 'Meghan and I want everyone in the local area to join us in our "Turn On to Sparkle-ing Health" campaign. She gives a little wink to camera at the 'Sparkle' witticism. 'All to raise money for little Harry here.' She smiles sadly at Harry and his mum and, right on cue, a single tear rolls down her perfectly made-up face.

'Oh, for God's sake!' explodes Paloma.

I'm too stunned to speak.

Is Lucy seeking all this publicity just so she can continue reigning supreme in the Hart's End café wars? Because there's no doubt the addition of Meghan Sparkle to the staff is a bit of a triumph. Having followed her warts-and-all conversations on that reality show, people will be eager to see her in the flesh. Especially if they can lose weight like Meghan did by eating at the 'clean food' café.

The queues at Lucy and Olivia's are unlikely to die down any time soon. In fact, I wouldn't be surprised to hear that Lucy's next move is to plan a whole *chain* of clean food cafés! Not that it matters much to me any more, since – thanks to Jake's busy schedule – The Treehouse Café is unlikely to happen now.

'There's one small consolation,' says Paloma with a sigh.

A chink of hope pierces my gloom. 'What's that?'

'Lucy obviously has no idea that the letters of her shiny new campaign spell out TOSH.' She gives an amused snort, but I'm too downhearted to even dredge up a smile ...

I draw a deep breath. 'By the way, it's going to be autumn before the treehouse café is ready. *If* I go ahead with it.'

There's a second's silence, then she explodes in my ear. '*Autumn!* But it's only the end of June! Does he work at a *snail's pace*? That's ridiculous! Sack him instantly.'

'I haven't even hired Jake yet,' I remind her.

'Well, good. Because you need to catch the tail end of the summer tourist trade if you want to stand any chance of getting up and running straight away.'

'My thoughts exactly. Which is why I think I might have to shelve the whole idea.'

'But why? Surely Jake isn't the only treehouse builder in the country!'

'He's the only one I know about. All suggestions gratefully received.'

Paloma has a call waiting so she rings off, while I continue to sit there, listening to Lucy talking in her gratingly posh voice about the 10k charity run.

'We've got a *fantastic* group of people, some of whom had never run before but who are now fighting fit, thanks to my training sessions on the village green and the wonderful green juice we serve at' – she pauses and smiles directly into the camera –'Lucy & Olivia's Clean Food Café.'

I want to reach into the TV and wring her stupid alabaster neck, which is obviously so flawless because of the thick layer of professional make-up she's wearing. Not that I'm at all bitter (or possibly even the tiniest bit twisted) about this whole damn scenario.

'And of course,' she purrs, 'it goes without saying that the sponsorship money raised by these lovely, dedicated people will also be used to get one very special little boy all the way to America.' (Cue another meltingly sentimental gaze over at Harry and his mum.)

Honestly, I'd be sick if I could actually scrape together the energy ...

*****

I'm still sitting there, stunned and staring at the TV, when the doorbell goes.

Realising they've moved on to a news bulletin, I flick it off on the remote and go to the door. It's Paloma, looking flushed and wide-eyed with excitement.

'What?'

'I heard from Sylvia. She's got some news about my birth mum.'

'Oh my God.' I reach for her hand and squeeze it tightly.

'She wants me to go over and see her.'

'Couldn't she tell you the news on the phone?'

'She says she doesn't hear so well, so she dislikes the telephone and would rather talk to me face to face.' She swallows hard. 'Will you come with me?'

'Yes, of course I will. Right now?'

Paloma nods. 'You could just sit in the car while I go in? Is that okay?'

I laugh. 'Of course it's okay. I'll just get my bag and keys.'

We're silent on the drive over to Sylvia's, each of us absorbed in our own thoughts. The tension in the car is like an elastic band, stretched to the max. Paloma has coped so well with the death of her adoptive parents. She so deserves to find her birth mum. I send up a silent prayer that this story has a happy ending. What if her birth mum doesn't want to be found?

I sneak a glance at Paloma. Her hands grip the steering wheel and there are spots of bright colour in her cheeks. If I'm thinking these thoughts, I can't imagine what's going round in *her* head right now.

She parks outside Sylvia's house, switches off the engine and takes a deep breath in then releases the air very slowly. Turning to me, she says, 'I'll be back soon.'

I hold up two sets of crossed fingers. 'Good luck!'

She nods and disappears. I watch her walk up Sylvia's garden path, my heart beating fast, hoping ...

I must have been sitting there about five minutes when someone taps gently on the window. Turning, I see Jason bending to look in at me. Grinning, he makes a winding-down-the-window gesture.

'Hi,' he says. 'What are you doing here?'

'Oh, just waiting for Paloma. She's – er – in there at her friend's.' I point at the house.

He nods and looks about to say something then stops.

'Thanks for coming when I phoned the other night,' I say. 'I didn't realise Theo was going to arrive, otherwise I wouldn't ...'

'Hey, you can call me any time. You know that, don't you?'

His eyes burn into mine and I nod, knowing he means it.

He sighs. 'Look, if there's something going on between you and Theo Steel, I'll just walk away and be happy for you.' He grimaces. 'I'll try, anyway. But if you're free and you'd like to have dinner with me ... ?' He shrugs, looking so vulnerable and nervous, my heart contracts.

Dinner with Jason?

'Just for old time's sake?' he says, seeing my hesitation. 'Or are you and Theo ... ?'

I shake my head firmly. 'There's nothing whatsoever going on between me and Theo. But what about Lucy? I don't think *she'd* like it if we dined out together.'

He shrugs. 'It doesn't matter what Lucy thinks any more. We're over. For good.'

'Really?' I stare at him, shocked. I'd thought they were just having a break from each other ...

He nods. 'I should have broken it off a long time ago. We were never really right for each other.' He smiles sadly. 'If I'm honest, it was a bit of a rebound thing after you left for uni.'

'Well, it's certainly lasted a long time. There must have been something there.'

Reluctantly, he nods. 'I suppose. She can be a horror, I know, but she was always good to me.'

'Except when she was bossing you around?'

He looks sheepish. 'I got used to that. Water off a duck's back.'

'You're too easy-going for your own good sometimes,' I tell him with an affectionate smile.

'So is that a yes to dinner?'

I look up into his hopeful brown eyes and a warm feeling spreads through me. 'Okay. Let's do it. For old time's sake.'

He nods, looking pleased. 'I'm away on business next week, but as soon as I get back, I'll phone you.' He straightens up and raises his hand, and as I watch him walk away, a torrent of emotion rushes through me. Jason was my first real love. Actually, my *only* real love. But it was all so long ago.

Is it ever wise to turn back the clock?

What would love be like for us the second time around?

I watch Jason until he disappears, leaning back in my seat, trying to make sense of my feelings.

A movement to my left catches my attention. Paloma is walking quickly along the garden path towards me. She's looking down so I can't see her expression.

Please let it be good news ...

I turn in my seat as she gets in. But one look at her tear-stained face tells me it's not the news she was hoping for. Without even looking at me, she starts the engine and we move off.

'What happened, love?' I ask gently, wishing she'd stop the car and tell me. But she doesn't reply; she just carries on driving, an awful dead look in her eyes, dashing away the tears as they roll down her face.

We draw up outside Honey Cottage and she turns to me at last, her face white as a ghost's. 'Mum died.' She shrugs helplessly, staring at me as if there might be something I can say to prove her wrong.

'Oh, Paloma. Really? Oh, God, I'm so sorry.' I reach over and try to hug her, but her body is rigid. She must be in shock. 'Look, come in and we can talk about it. I'll make some tea. Or something stronger? A brandy? I think Mum's got some in the cabinet.'

I'm talking too much, not really knowing what to say, and Paloma is just sitting there, bolt upright, her head in another space altogether.

She turns as if she's just realised I'm there. 'I'm all right. I'll just go home if it's okay with you.'

'Of *course* it's okay.' I press her hand. It feels icy cold. 'But are you sure you want to be alone?'

She nods, attempting a smile. 'I'll be fine.'

There are so many questions I want to ask her, but I can't. Not until she's ready to talk about it.

After I get out, I lean back in. 'Look, if you need *anything*, you just pick up the phone and I'll be right over, okay?'

She nods, her hands on the steering wheel, holding it together. 'Thank you, Twi. I'll phone you.'

Watching her drive off, I feel helpless and absolutely gutted for her. I have an awful feeling she'll break down completely the instant she's alone.

Chapter 28

I drag through the next few days, crushed that the treehouse café is now unlikely to become a reality, and increasingly worried about Paloma.

I resist the impulse to go and knock on her door to make sure she's all right. She made it clear she would phone me when she was ready, so I need to respect that. I can't help feeling she'd be better actually *talking* about her birth mum, though, and getting it all off her chest.

It doesn't help my low mood that three days after Jake's visit, he emails me some rough plans for the treehouse café. I stare at them for a long time, thinking that he must be a mind-reader; the artist's impression looks so beautiful, I really wouldn't change a thing about it. Then I get a lump in my throat when I realise how I'm going to have to disappoint Mum. And Betty and Doreen. I'd need to launch the café in high summer to give the project the best possible chance of success, and clearly, that's not going to happen. So there's no point in dreaming ...

On Wednesday afternoon, the café is so dead that in despair, I get on my laptop and write an email to my old catering college, saying I'm considering returning in the autumn to complete my studies and would this be possible?

I desperately don't want to have to give up my dreams and go back to Manchester, but I must face facts. The café is barely breaking even. I'm nowhere near bringing in the sort of cash I'd hoped would mean we could put an end to thoughts of selling Honey Cottage.

I send off the email and snap the laptop shut, feeling slightly sick.

Then I turn the sign on the door over to 'closed' and go home early, spending the rest of the afternoon on the phone to some of my old friends from college, which lifts my mood a little.

On Thursday morning, I decide to clean out the fridge for the second time that week, just for something to do. It's nearly eleven, and my only customer is a dark-haired pleasant-faced woman in a smart business suit, sitting at a table by the counter reading a newspaper she pulled out of her briefcase and drinking a cappuccino. She's been in a few times before and it raises my spirits to see her back again. I must be doing something right!

While I'm busy out the back, I keep popping my head round to make sure she's okay, and on one occasion, she looks up and smiles. 'Could I have the same again, please, and a slice of that gorgeously sinful-looking chocolate cake?'

'Of course you can.' Smiling, I set to at the coffee machine then cut her a big slice of cake.

'Delicious,' she says, taking a bite. 'This is the best coffee stop I've discovered in a long time, and I travel all over the country with my job.' She glances around her admiringly. 'Lovely décor, so relaxing and the best cake for miles around. I don't know why you're not busier.'

'Gosh, thanks.' I feel quite flustered at such high praise. 'I'm so glad you like it.'

'Oh, I do. I tried that café on the high street once. The one that sells only "clean food", whatever that is.' She grimaces. 'Wouldn't go back. No atmosphere and the customer service isn't great.'

'Really?' *Ooh, tell me more!*

She shakes her head. 'You feel as if you're on a conveyor belt. In and out, so someone else can have your table, and you feel slightly guilty if you linger over a second coffee.' She shrugs. 'Their dishes are full of very noble ingredients, but for me, a courgette really has no place at all in a Victoria sandwich cake.'

I smile a little awkwardly. I'm longing to say, 'Yes, I think it's pretty shit as well.' But obviously that wouldn't be very professional.

'Oh, sorry, is the owner a friend of yours?' She frowns. 'I never thought. A small village like this. Everyone knows each other.'

I laugh, rather too loudly – bordering on the hysterical, actually – and she looks a bit surprised.

I shake my head. 'No, no, Lucy and I definitely aren't friends.'

'Ah! A bit of café rivalry going on?'

'Something like that.'

'Well, you definitely have *my* vote. Your café is the clear winner by a country mile.' She smiles. 'Right, I'd better be off.' She slides her paper into her briefcase and pays the bill, popping a very generous sum into Dad's tip jar. 'I'm Carole, by the way.'

'Twilight.'

We shake hands and her eyes widen. 'Lovely name!'

I beam at her. 'Thank you so much.' *For everything!*

'See you again very soon,' she says, leaving with a cheery little wave.

After she's gone, I go over to clear her table, but instead of stacking plates and cups, I slip into her chair and sit there, resting my chin on my hand, thinking. Carole has given me a totally different perspective on my situation here. She actually prefers The Twilight Café to Lucy's place – *by a country mile!* And she definitely seems like a woman of taste. It's interesting that she doesn't think much of Lucy's customer service, either, although obviously, I'll do my very best not to rejoice at that.

Woo-hoo!

If only I had more time, I'm sure I could build up a loyal clientele – not based on special offers galore and 'celebrity' gloss, but through good old-fashioned care for the customer, a relaxing atmosphere and great food.

But unfortunately, time costs money. And money is something I don't have.

Later, after closing up, I walk into the village to pick up a few groceries, and coming out of the supermarket, I bump into a friend of Mum's called Marilyn, who lives in Hart's End.

'Twilight, love, so good to see you!' After we hug, she frowns and digs in her shopping bag. 'Look at this. I was reading it while I was in the hairdresser's.' She opens the magazine out at a full-colour spread and we look at it together. The heading in bold red type shouts, 'No more cake for us (unless it's a delicious parsnip sponge)' There's a big photo of a beaming Meghan Sparkle in the café with her hands on Lucy and Olivia's shoulders, and the article is all about the café's rise to fame, thanks to bride-to-be Meghan's regular visits.

Marilyn reads a bit out loud in a fake posh voice. '"I'm determined to slim right down for my wedding day," says lovely reality star Meghan, "and Lucy and Olivia's Clean Food Café is the perfect place for guilt-free eating!" *Guilt-free eating, for goodness' sake!* What's so great about that, I ask you!'

I laugh. 'I've seen Meghan Sparkle on YouTube and you sounded just like her there!'

'Well, it makes me mad what that Lucy Slater did to you on opening day, making sure everyone went to her café and not yours. I've been in Spain for the past few weeks, but Betty told me all about it. And *this*—' She flicks the magazine article distastefully. 'Well, it's nothing but a big, tacky publicity stunt, Lucy being friendly all of a sudden with a so-called "celebrity". It's so obvious Lucy's just out to make money and get famous and that's not what you want in a village café, is it? I've started telling everyone to boycott that place and go to yours instead, although of course, people do love a bargain. But mark my words, once there aren't any more "introductory two-eat-for-one offers", the tide will turn.' She pops the magazine in her bag and pats my hand. 'It will, you know.'

I smile gratefully, glad of Marilyn's staunch support, and wave her on her way. That's exactly what Theo said. *The tide will turn ...*

Thinking of Theo makes my insides churn like a washing machine.

I'd love to believe he and Marilyn are right. But a few minutes later, when I walk past Lucy's place, I can see that, as usual, most of the tables are occupied. They seem to be doing a roaring trade and I can't help a little twinge of envy.

Not that it really matters any more, because by October I'll probably be back at catering college and Honey Cottage will be up for sale.

A lump fills my throat and I have to put my head down and hurry back before the tears start. Safely home, I curl up in a ball on the sofa and sob as I haven't done for a very long time – not since we first got Dad's diagnosis a year ago. My bare arms are wet with tears and they just won't stop. All the kind comments in the world won't change things if I can't get customers through the door ...

The only bright spot on the horizon is my dinner with Jason, once he returns from his latest business trip.

At last, I get up and walk slowly to the bathroom, intending to wash the mascara streaks off my face. On the way through the hall, I notice the post on the mat. One of the letters is addressed to me. As soon as I pick it up, I know what it is.

Feeling sick, I yank it open. It's from the building society, threatening action if no settlement of arrears is received within a fortnight. Even though I was expecting something like that, it's still a shock to read the cold, hard words on the page.

Next moment, when my mobile phone rings, I actually laugh out loud. No doubt this will be Jason, calling to say he's had second thoughts about dinner!

I'm tempted to ignore it, but something makes me pick up. If it's more bad news, I may as well face it sooner than later ...

It's not Jason.

It's Jake.

And what he tells me makes my head whirl madly like one of those old-fashioned spinning tops cranked up to high speed. I hang up and immediately start calculating timescales in my head.

Jake has managed to rejig his schedule. If I still need him, he can start work immediately. This is such amazing news, I feel like crying.

I pick up the phone to call my parents, picturing the delight on Dad's face.

The Treehouse Café will open for business in August!

Chapter 29

After a sleepless night, during which I build The Treehouse Café in my imagination and design an entire fairy-tale interior (if money was no object), I phone Mum then Betty to break the good news.

Betty, especially, is really excited and I know the instant I hang up, she'll be on the phone to Doreen to chat about it. Sure enough, ten minutes later she phones to tell me how delighted they both are that it's all finally happening, and that she'd like to make a suggestion.

'Of course. What is it?' I smile, expecting Betty to say something like she wants to make the curtains herself so there'd be no raw fish in the hems this time.

'Well, Doreen and I think you could do with a little break, what with all the stress you've been under. So we wondered if we could take over at the café for a couple of days.'

'Take over?'

'Yes. If we're going to be helping out in The Treehouse Café when it's finished, it would do us good to learn the ropes beforehand? So for those few days, we'd run the café and we could even do the baking if you like.'

'Oh. Wow. That's so kind of you. But are you sure you don't mind?'

Betty chuckles. '*Mind?* We can't wait!'

'Well, in that case – yes, please!' It's only now that it's being handed to me on a plate that I realise exactly how much I could do with a few days off from my usual routine.

They come round to the café later and during a quiet spell, I show them how everything works, and Doreen offers to bake the daily batch of scones, while Betty will make her favourite party piece, a black forest gateau.

I smile. 'Very retro. I like it.'

'You do?' Betty peers at me anxiously. 'We don't want to be pushy. It's your café.'

I laugh. 'Listen, girls, it will be your café, too, soon, when the new place is ready, and I'm really going to need your help. You can't expect me to cope with the hordes of hungry customers all by myself! I don't know about you, but I have a feeling we're going to make a brilliant team.'

*****

It feels odd having two days off and not having to think about the café – but in a good way.

My immediate thought is to go and see Mum and Dad. But Mum assures me she's fine, that Dad isn't really up to long chats, and that it would probably be best for me to just chill out at home for a while.

So instead, I take up Jake's offer to show me the plans for The Treehouse Café in detail by going back down to visit his workshop again. He's much more relaxed this time and I thoroughly enjoy my afternoon. He treats me to a ploughman's lunch in the garden of the local pub and we spend a couple of happy hours chatting about the work he's going to do, and poring over his sketches and detailed plans.

It's been another really sticky day with soaring temperatures and I catch the train back to Hart's End, arriving in the early evening. I like Jake, I've decided. I know Paloma decided he was a bit of an arrogant arse, but I think that's unfair. Anyway, it doesn't really matter what she thinks of him, as long as he builds me a beautiful treehouse extension!

Exhausted but happy, I crash into bed at ten and fall asleep instantly, despite the fact it's barely any cooler than it was during the day.

Next morning, the doorbell wakes me and, struggling up, I peer at the time on my mobile. Nine-thirty. I've slept round the clock! Diving into my dressing gown, I rush to the door, thinking it's probably Betty or Doreen with a query about the café.

It's Betty and she looks worried.

'So sorry to disturb you, love, but we're having trouble locating the cake.'

Puzzled, I laugh. 'It hasn't run off again, has it?'

She sighs. 'Doreen excelled herself, baking that black forest gateau yesterday. Beautiful it is. But it's gone missing. She put it in a box and asked her nephew to deliver it to the café on his way to work. He's got a refrigerated van for his catering company and I think she was worried about the cream melting in this terrible heat. But it hasn't turned up. She told him to leave it round the back of the café but when we got here, it wasn't there, even though Tom swears he delivered it.'

'Don't worry, I've got fruitcake left and some of those lovely double chocolate chip cookies that seem to survive the heat pretty well. Come in and I'll get them for you.'

Betty goes off with her Tupperware box, still apologising and saying she'll phone Tom again.

Twenty minutes later, she phones back, mystery solved.

'I can't believe it!' she wails. 'He delivered the cake to the wrong café!'

My insides shift uneasily. 'You mean Lucy and Olivia's?'

'Yes. What a bloody cock-up. Do you want me to drive round there and get it back.'

'No, don't worry. You just concentrate on opening up. I'll see to it.'

I hang up, feeling slightly sick at the thought of having to walk round there and demand my cake back. What if Lucy refuses to give it to me out of spite? But I can't just leave poor Doreen's lovely creation there – not after she's gone to so much trouble baking it.

Sighing, I get ready to go round there.

I'm just leaving the house when the phone rings again. It's Paloma this time, sounding much more like her old self. Tentatively, I ask her if she's okay. There's a slight pause then she says she'll tell me all about it, but not over the phone. We both know she's talking about her birth mum.

'I totally understand.'

'Are you still doing Lucy's 10k run on Sunday?' she asks.

'I wasn't going to. But if you are, I suppose I could.'

'Can you manage 10k?' She sounds doubtful.

'Er, I'll have you know I've been going out for a little run most mornings before opening up the café! I'm fitter than I've ever been.'

'Wow, that's great. Let's do it, then. So what else has been happening?'

I tell her that The Treehouse Café is going to become a reality and she's over the moon for me. She doesn't even slag off Jake. Then I tell her about the cake emergency, wanting to make her laugh.

'Christ, it's not a great start for poor Doreen, is it? Cake goes walkabout!'

'I know. Bless her. She's in a bit of a stew about it.'

'Why don't I drive you round there? I'll even go in and collect the cake if you don't want to face Lucy yourself.'

'You will?' Relief spreads through me. I've been dreading the thought of having to talk to Lucy. I hate myself for not being braver. It's just I never know what horrors she's going to spring on me next. Her illogical hatred of me seems to know no bounds, which is quite a scary thought when you really think about it.

'Of course I will,' says Paloma. 'Pick you up in five?'

We get there just before ten o'clock and the café isn't open yet. No one comes when Paloma knocks on the door, and in the end, I get out of the car, deciding I have to be brave. It's my café and my cake. I can't leave it up to Paloma.

'Let's go round the back.' I glance at my watch. 'Doreen said Tom left the box at the back door, so it might still be there.'

We walk down a side street and find the back of the building. Both of their cars are parked there and there's a light on in the window. There's no sign of the cake box and my heart sinks. We'll have to see Lucy after all ...

Suddenly, I realise Paloma is trying to get my attention, waving madly and putting her finger to her lips. She's crouched down, peering through the window, which I can see is open a crack. Curious, I sidle along next to her and look in, feeling like a regular peeping Tom.

The sight that greets me makes my eyes open wide in stunned amazement.

Lucy and Olivia are sitting at a table right next to the open window with their backs to us. Dressed in their smart black trousers, white shirts and long cream-coloured café aprons, they're in the process of devouring Doreen's black forest gateau as if it might be snatched away from them at any moment.

'Oh my God, bloody heaven,' drools Lucy, digging a huge serving spoon into the creamy cake and trying to cram it all into her mouth at once.

Olivia makes a grab for the spoon, but Lucy snatches it away, out of reach, and yells, 'Oi! Get your own spoon.'

'Fuck that,' says Olivia, plunging her hand straight into the cake. She grabs a creamy wedge and starts guzzling it down, throwing back her head and making noises that frankly wouldn't be out of place in a soft porn movie.

Eyes out on stalks, Paloma and I exchange a look. She mimes a belly laugh while I clap my hand over my mouth. It's pretty revolting but hilarious at the same time.

Paloma reaches into her pocket and pulls out her mobile phone. Then she grins wickedly.

'What are you doing?' I mouth.

'Ssh! Wait and see.'

Slowly, she reaches in, lifts the catch and pushes the window further open. It gives a tiny squeak.

'What was that?' mumbles Olivia through a mouthful of cake, and we freeze, holding our breath.

'Oh God, stop me. I think I'm going to be sick,' groans Lucy.

'Me, too, but I don't fucking care,' mutters Olivia, diving in for more, sending a splodge of black cherries and purple-tinged cream down her pristine apron.

Paloma positions the camera and calls out cheerily, 'Good morning, ladies!'

They both turn at exactly the same time, each with a mess of cake in their hand. And the horror on their guilty, chocolate-smeared faces is a sight to warm the cockles of my heart.

'Click' goes Paloma's camera.

She holds up her thumb. 'Great shot, girls. Enjoy your breakfast!'

And we both scuttle back to the car, almost peeing ourselves laughing.

'So much for clean eating!' snorts Paloma, starting the engine.

In between breathless guffaws, I do an imitation of Lucy's slightly grating, high-pitched voice. 'Oh, I *never* eat cake unless it's made from parsnips!'

*****

After driving to a nearby supermarket to top up on cake supplies, we're heading back to the café to break the news that Doreen's black forest gateau has sadly been demolished, when I see them.

Theo and Olivia.

They're walking along the high street, laughing about something, and my stomach lurches. Theo nudges her and squealing, she stumbles away then punches him playfully in retaliation. He pretends to be hurt, rubbing his upper arm and scowling at her.

There's an ease and an intimacy between them that's impossible to ignore.

I feel sick.

So it's true. Olivia has won him over. They're a couple.

'Is that Theo with Olivia?' Paloma is peering over. 'I would have thought he'd have much better taste.'

'Where? Oh, yes.' I swallow hard and make a show of finding my keys.

Just as we turn down into my cul-de-sac, I take a quick glance back. Just in time to see Olivia stretch up on tiptoes and kiss Theo on the lips ...

Chapter 30

The day of Lucy's charity 10k run dawns clear but with a cool breeze. It's a relief, quite frankly, after all the hot, sultry weather we've been having.

Not that the weather is uppermost in my mind.

If I had my way, I'd rather stick pins in my eyes than have to face Theo and Olivia after that display of affection I witnessed the day before on the high street. I know they'll both be doing the run.

But I owe it to Harry and his mum to do my bit for the fund-raising appeal.

'*You* look smart,' I tell Paloma when she arrives to collect me.

She does a quick pose in her new turquoise and black Lycra running gear. 'Thank you.' She grins. 'You don't.'

'Hey, thanks.' I grimace down at my running gear. The only runner's top I could find seems to have shrunk in the wash, which means I'm having to hoist it up at the front every five minutes so I won't be done for indecent exposure.

'When have *I* had the time and money lately to go shopping for new clothes? And new haircuts.' I glance pointedly at Paloma's chic new shoulder-length style.

She gives her head a little shake. 'Needed a fresh start.'

I nod approvingly. 'Well, it really suits you.' I'm so glad she seems to be moving on from the crushing news about her birth mum.

Walking along to the village green, where the run is starting, Paloma suddenly remembers she promised Olivia she'd collect in the remaining sponsorship forms. 'I'd better do it before the run starts or she'll tell tales to Lucy,' she grins, breaking into a jog. 'See you along there?'

There's quite a crowd assembled on the green when I arrive, even though it's still half an hour until the run kicks off at 11.30. The first person I recognise is Theo. He's so tall, his dark head is easy to spot in a crowd. He's standing chatting to Olivia, who's looking sleek and slender in little black Lycra shorts and a purple top that shows off her tanned midriff. I lurk on the perimeter, feeling like the ugly stepsister by comparison, preferring to remain anonymous in my grunge gear.

As I watch them furtively, Paloma goes up to Theo and is obviously asking him for his sponsorship form. Olivia smiles and leans towards him, then slides her hand into the small, zipped pocket of his running shorts and draws out what must be the folded-up form, holding it out to Paloma. It's such an intimate gesture, I feel my stomach lurch uncomfortably.

They're all laughing now, Theo more than anyone.

Olivia obviously meant it as a joke. I wish I could see the funny side ...

'Hey, you.'

Someone taps me on the shoulder and I turn to find Jason standing there.

'Changed days,' he says. 'You're the girl who used to say the trouble with jogging is that by the time you realise you're not in shape for it ...'

'... it's too far to walk back.' I laugh. 'Yeah, yeah. I know. But what about you? You weren't at Lucy's boot camp training session, so I just assumed you'd probably give today a body swerve as well.'

He shrugs. 'I started training on my own. It's a good thing that she's doing, helping send that little boy to America. I want to take part. I'm not a natural runner, though. As you know.'

'Me, neither. But I've actually started to enjoy it. I feel better when I'm exercising.'

He feels my forehead, jokingly.

'I know. Bit of a shocker, right? I hope you haven't forgotten we're going out for dinner,' I add, smiling to hide my slight awkwardness.

He looks at me with an expression I can't quite decipher.

'I need to tell you something,' he says, taking my hand and drawing me away from the crowd. Bemused, I go where he leads me, beneath the branches of a big oak tree nearby. And before I know what's happening, I'm in his arms and he's kissing me.

Taken by surprise, my brain instantly starts popping with questions. (Mainly, how can he possibly find me attractive wearing *this* lot?)

But very quickly, the lovely familiarity of kissing Jason takes over and after a moment, I start kissing him back. All the memories of when we were together start rushing back. Theo and Olivia are quite forgotten. Kissing Jason seems like the most natural thing in the world ...

'The run is beginning shortly.' A sharp voice at my back calls an abrupt halt to our amorous interlude. 'If you can bear to come up for air, of course.'

I break away and turn to find Lucy standing there, eyes

flashing with fury. Shock paralyses me, and for a horrible moment, I'm back at school in the toilets where Lucy has just dragged me – to warn me that if I dare go out with Jason, she will make sure I regret it.

I shake the memory, reminding myself we're all grown up now. It's a free country. I can kiss whomever I like and Lucy can't hurt me any more.

Calmly, I return her look. I'm expecting Jason to react by letting go of me, but to my surprise, his grip on my waist only tightens.

Lucy stalks off and Jason blows out a long breath. 'Good riddance.'

He pulls me against him again, murmuring urgently, 'Oh God, Twi, you do realise I'm falling for you all over again? I keep thinking how great it was between us. Do you remember? You must.'

I nod. 'I do. But—'

'It can be like that again. It can, Twi. I know it can.' He smiles and cradles my face. And I look into his kind brown eyes that are so lovely and familiar to me, and I can't help wondering ... It would be so easy to fall back into Jason's arms. Ours was such an easy relationship, full of warmth and fun. We were so close, we used to finish each other's sentences all the time.

Maybe we're right for each other, after all.

Perhaps we've wasted too much time already ...

A memory of my hot encounter with Theo in the treehouse flashes into my mind – the way his body and lips felt pressed against mine – but I force it away, leaning forward and kissing Jason firmly on the lips. 'Let's have dinner,' I murmur, 'and then we'll see.'

'There's Theo,' Jason says stiffly, looking over my shoulder.

I shoot Jason a sharp glance. 'There's nothing going on between me and Theo, you know. And there never will be.' I say it determinedly, to crush the pang of sadness.

'Really?'

'Really.' I turn slightly so I can see where he's looking. Paloma has joined Theo and Olivia in conversation. Theo is talking and the two girls are looking up at him, listening intently with serious expressions. Then, as I watch, I see Paloma's expression change to one of pure horror. At least, that's what it looks like to me, although obviously I have no idea what they're talking about.

She looks away after a moment, as if she's thinking about something, while Theo and Olivia continue to chat in their flirty way. I can't see Theo's face because he's facing away from me.

Next moment, Paloma looks around and spots me. She says something to the other two, then walks over and I smile expectantly, thinking she might tell me what's on her mind.

But all she says is, 'Theo's lovely, isn't he?' She says it in a weird, distracted sort of way, almost as if she's talking to herself.

I shrug. 'He's okay. A bit of a lone wolf, apparently. No point trying to get close to people like him.'

She gives me a slightly bemused look, and I feel my face redden. I don't know why on earth I said that. I suppose it still needles that while on his own admission, he considers me 'gorgeous', he has no intention of touching me with a bargepole!

Paloma glances from me to Jason and her expression changes. 'Oh, sorry. Was I interrupting something?'

'No, of course not.' I laugh a little too heartily. 'Jason and I were just talking about – er, old times. Weren't we?' I swing round and beam at Jason.

He smiles, his eyes fixed on me. 'Old times. And new.'

'Are we running together?' asks Paloma.

I nod. 'Feel free to speed off at your own pace if I hold you up, though. Coming, Jason?'

'No, I'm going to linger at the back.' He grins. 'Then if I decide to stop off at the pub, no one will notice.'

Paloma and I set off, running with the pack, Lucy and Olivia right up at the front, leading the way. Theo isn't far behind them. I spot someone else I recognise running just behind him, but I can't put a name to the face.

'I'm sure I've seen that woman before.' I point her out to Paloma. 'But I can't for the life of me think where, can you?'

'Sorry?' Paloma seems miles away.

'That woman. Do you know her?'

She frowns and looks where I'm pointing. 'It's little Harry's mum. The one we saw on TV, who we're all raising money for today.'

'Of course. How much do they need to get to America? Do you know?'

When she doesn't reply, I glance at her worriedly. 'Are you okay? Has something happened?'

She looks at me vacantly. Then she shakes her head. 'No, everything's fine.'

'You sure?'

'Yes. Absolutely. So I hear Jason and Lucy have broken up for good?' She grins. 'I couldn't help noticing the two of you getting very close back there. Something *I* should know about?'

'Maybe.' I give a mischievous smile. 'Rest assured, you'll be the first to know if there's anything to report. We're going out for dinner, though.'

'Nice.' She nods vaguely, back in her own little world.

After a while, I slow right down. 'Look, if you don't mind, I'm going to pace myself. Don't want to run out of steam and not be able to finish the course!' She slows down with me, but I shoo her on. 'I don't want to hold you up.'

'Okay. See you at the finishing line.'

I set off behind, watching her speed away.

There's something she's not telling me, but what? An image of her brand-new gear and chic hairstyle flashes into my mind. Her more upbeat manner. Is it all in an effort to move on after discovering the horrible truth about her birth mother? Or is it something more than that? She's been so secretive about this 'important client' of hers ...

I'm so deep in thought, I almost don't notice the figure leaning against a tree up ahead. But as I approach, the person – a woman – slides to the ground and buries her face in her arms. It's the woman from the TV. Harry's mum.

She glances up, startled, as I jog by – almost as if she's forgotten she's taking part in the run – and I see that she's dabbing at her eyes. Maybe she's not feeling well?

'Are you all right?' I ask, stopping. 'Do you need anything?'

She sniffs and gives me a sad little smile. 'Three thousand pounds should do it.'

'Sorry?'

She shakes her head. 'No, *I'm* sorry. I shouldn't have said that. Just ignore me; I'm having one of those days.' She gets to her feet. 'Actually, I'm not feeling so great. I think I'll just head back. I've lost my enthusiasm for the run all of a sudden.'

I stare at her, puzzled. This run is all for her and little Harry's benefit. What's happened that would make her feel like this on such an important day?

'Is it to do with Lucy?' I ask. 'Has she upset you?'

She nods, her smile freezing. A single tear slides down her face and drips off her chin onto the grass.

'I'm Twilight, by the way.'

Her eyes widen. 'Twilight? Lovely name. I'm Jane.'

'So what happened, Jane?'

Her face falls. 'Lucy's changed her mind about helping us financially. I sold our house to pay for the treatment, and friends and family managed to raise the money for the flights to America. But we're going to be living there for six months while Harry undergoes his treatment, so we need living expenses. Lucy said ...' She trails off, her voice choking with misery.

I nod. 'I saw you on TV. Lucy was going to donate the proceeds of this run and a percentage of her takings from the café. So what happened? Why has she gone back on her word?'

Jane shrugs helplessly. 'I asked her when the money would be in my account because I need it to pay a deposit on the little flat we were going to be staying in over there. But she just said sorry, things had changed and she couldn't do it any more, and ran on.'

'No explanation?'

She shakes her head.

'But millions of people heard her make her promise on national TV! She can't just cash in on the publicity then decide she's not going to give you the money after all. That's not the way it works.'

Poor Jane is white-faced, leaning against the tree as if she could barely remain standing otherwise. It's clear the shock has knocked her sideways, and thinking of how desperate she must be to get her son this vital treatment, I feel a surge of hot rage at Lucy's careless, selfish attitude.

How dare she dash this woman's hopes and dreams without even explaining why! What if it was Dad going over there for life-saving treatment and then he couldn't go in the end because someone reneged on their promise to help? I'd be absolutely devastated.

'Look, don't worry. You'll have those funds, even if I have to organise a sponsored run myself! Will you be all right to walk back, or shall I come with you?' I pass Jane a clean paper hanky and she takes it gratefully, giving her nose a noisy blow.

'No, I'll be fine, really. It was a shock, that's all. But thank you so much.'

'It's fine. Honestly. How long since Lucy left?'

'Oh, only about five minutes.'

I glance at the route ahead. 'Right. I'm going to get to the bottom of this. I'll see you later, Jane.'

She waves me off, a surprised look on her face, then I quickly double back and she fishes around to find a pen and paper to give me her mobile number.

'Great. I'll phone you and let you know what happens,' I call back, waving the piece of paper and pounding off after Lucy, suddenly very glad of all the training I've been doing lately.

My blood feels like it's boiling in my veins. How could she do this to Jane and Harry? Does she *never* think of the far-reaching and devastating consequences her nasty, selfish actions have on innocent people's lives?

Well, she'd better have a good explanation for this ...

Chapter 31

I pound along the path through the woods, catching up with a group of girls jogging along fairly slowly, laughing and chatting as they go. They all fall silent as I run past them, thundering along at top speed as if I've got a serial killer hot on my tail.

I'm determined to catch up with Lucy and demand to know what she thinks she's doing to poor Jane and Harry. She can't be allowed to play around with people's lives like this, and after years of being a victim of her spite, it's suddenly desperately important to me that *I'm* the one to make her see this.

My rage at the sense of deep injustice seems to be giving me wings, but after ten minutes of hard running, I begin to flag.

At last, just when I think I can't possibly keep up this speed for a minute longer, I catch sight of Lucy's red T-shirt disappearing round a bend in the path up ahead. Puffing like a vintage steam train, I put my head down and – my legs feeling as heavy as lead by now – I tank along even faster, overtaking several small packs of runners, amazed that I'm still going. Perhaps I do actually have stamina now!

Lucy is running alone, which I'm pleased about. It would be harder to tackle her if Olivia was there, supporting her.

When I'm finally in shouting distance, I call out her name.

At first, she doesn't hear me, so I keep on shouting until she finally turns her head. The instant she sees it's me, her face turns thunderous.

'What do *you* want?' she barks, showing her total disdain by running on and refusing to stop.

'There's a hole in your shorts at the back.'

'*What? Where?*' She halts and twists round to examine her own butt. She glares at me. 'There's no hole. What do you want?'

'I want to ask you a question, Lucy.' My heart is hammering so loudly, she can probably hear it. Even if she can't, she'll be able to tell from my face that I'm angry and upset in fairly equal measure.

'Oh, yes? And what question is that?' She smirks, hands on hips. 'Oh, I know. *How come you're always so much more successful than me, Lucy? Especially when it comes to setting up cafés*. Was that the question, *Twilight*?'

She spits out my name, contempt for me oozing out of every pore, and for the thousandth time, I wonder what I ever did to be the object of such never-ending hatred. My whole body is trembling and I worry my emotion will show in my voice. The last thing I want is Lucy thinking that after all these years, I'm still afraid of her.

I take a deep breath to calm my ragged nerves.

'Come on, spit it out,' she sneers. 'Or are you too scared?' She puts on a fake look of sympathy. 'Aw, poor little Twilight. Going to run home and complain about me to your mummy?'

I clench my fists at my sides. 'Lucy, for God's sake, we're not ten any more.'

'Sorry? What was that?' Lucy holds her hand exaggeratedly

to her ear. 'Did the timid little mouse speak there?' She shakes her head at me in disgust.

I swallow hard, remembering something Paloma is always saying. When faced with something or someone intimidating, imagine that person with no clothes on or dressed up as Mickey Mouse with a funny squeaky voice.

Actually, the squeaky voice thing is easy with Lucy because she often sounds like a recording that's been speeded up. I turn her into a pesky five-year-old and give her goofy teeth, and I actually find my shoulders relaxing.

'Well? Cat got your tongue?'

'Lucy, for fuck's sake, we're not in the school playground, so why not grow up, wipe that stupid smirk off your face, and listen to me? You never know, you might just hear something useful.'

A look of uncertainty flashes across her face for a brief moment. She wasn't expecting me to challenge her. But then next second, she's laughing in my face. 'Ooh, playing the tough guy now, are we? Do I look scared? I think not. Now, if you don't mind, I've got a run to finish.'

She turns, about to go, but I dash forward and grab a handful of her T-shirt at the back, stopping her dead in her tracks. She turns and for a brief instant, we lock eyes and I see her look of shocked disbelief. Then she starts shrieking with indignation, trying to wrench herself away from my clutches, but grimly, I hang on to the fabric.

I eyeball her as steadily as I can, feeling like I'm trying to tame a rebellious child. 'You're not going anywhere, Lucy Slater, until you've answered my question, which is this: Why have you gone back on your promise to help Jane and Harry?'

Her eyes slide away from mine, guilt written all over her

face. 'Get your hands off me, you pathetic excuse for a person.' Incensed, she slaps at my hands to make me let go but I hang on tenaciously, determined to get an answer.

'Tell me why you've left them in the lurch like this and I'll let go.'

She glares at me mutely but stops struggling so hard.

'Come on. I want to know, Lucy. Why would you do that to such lovely people? I want to hear your reasons.'

'I don't need a reason, except that I've changed my mind,' she snaps, turning the full force of her blazing white-hot fury on me, eyes flashing angrily. Shocked, I almost let go of her. But something deep within is giving me the strength to persist. It's as if all the heartache of those years of being tormented by her has been building up inside me, and it's finally risen to the 'full' level and has nowhere else to go. Except out of my mouth!

I'm not giving up. I want an answer. 'I should have thought you'd be making tons of money from the café, Lucy. It's been a runaway success, hasn't it? Not like your fashion design business.'

She narrows her eyes and stops struggling altogether, and I know I've hit her where it hurts with that last remark. She'd have given anything to be the next Alexander McQueen, but even Daddy couldn't fix that for her.

'The money must be rolling in, and then there's the funds you'll collect from this charity run, so donating a few thousand to a good cause like Harry's won't be much of a hardship, will it?'

'It's not rolling in!' she snaps. 'And anyway, it's absolutely none of your business what I do with my own money.'

'Possibly not. All I'm saying is you promised Jane and

Harry, and I don't know how you'll be able to sleep at night knowing you've let them down. I certainly couldn't.'

She laughs. 'Well, no, of course you couldn't. Because you're a saint and everyone adores you. You couldn't do anything wrong if you tried, little Miss Perfect. Perfect family. Adored by everyone. With Jason twisted around your little finger. God, you make me sick.'

I stare at her, taken aback by her fury.

'Oh, don't give me that innocent look. You always get what you want, regardless of how much your selfishness might be hurting other people.'

'*What*?' I stare at her, mystified. 'Lucy, what the hell are you talking about?'

She gives me a filthy look. 'You know exactly what I mean.'

I rack my brains but come up with zero. 'I actually don't.'

'You mean Jason didn't tell you? I thought he told you everything.' She practically spits out the words.

I laugh. 'Jason told me nothing. But I'd like to know what I'm supposed to have done, so why don't *you* tell me?'

I let go of her T-shirt and she makes a thing of furiously straightening it up. There's a wasp flying around and she swipes at it.

'Well?' I demand.

But she seems to have transferred her rage to the wasp instead and is flapping her arms around wildly.

'So you're not going to help Jane and Harry? Is it because the café isn't doing so well?' I ask, remembering her comment that the money wasn't rolling in.

'What makes you say that? We're doing brilliantly.' She shrieks as the wasp keeps buzzing around her head and she runs away to escape. Climbing on a nearby fence, she unscrews her water bottle and takes a long drink. 'We're packing them in every day, haven't you noticed?' She smiles smugly and turns her face up to the sun. 'Oh no, of course you won't have noticed because you can never leave that crappy building you call a café, just in case your once-in-a-blue-moon customer arrives.'

Grinning, she leans a little further back on the fence, and I glare at her, thinking how easy it would be to give her a little prod. There's a trough filled with something slimy and green just behind her in the field beyond the fence ...

She sits up straight, looks me straight in the eye and says, 'I bet your mum and dad are *so* proud of you for making such a success of it.' She says it slowly, with a triumphant smile, relishing every single word.

The blood rushes in my veins. If I take a deep breath, maybe I won't have to kill her.

I walk towards her and a look of astonishment crosses her face.

I don't know what she thinks I'm going to do, but she jerks fractionally backwards then seems to lose her balance, gripping on to the fence to try and stay upright.

But gravity wins. And with an anguished glance behind her, she sort of slides slowly off her perch, legs at a funny angle, and lands with an ominous gloopy splatter in the trough.

The indignant shrieks and threats that ensue turn the air blue. Struggling to get out of the trough, legs and arms flailing about, she's getting more steeped in green slimy gunk by the second and calling me all the names under the sun.

'Are you just going to stand there, you halfwit blockhead?' she splutters at last.

I walk slowly across and lean over the fence, offering my

hand to pull her out. But she ignores me and stubbornly manages to heave herself out.

Then without warning, she opens her mouth and lets out a deafening noise somewhere between a howl and a scream.

I stare at her in alarm. 'Keep the noise down. People will think you're being murdered.'

'I've been stung by that wasp, you freak!' she yells. 'Fuck's sake, it's bloody painful.' She's twisting round, lifting her T-shirt at the back to find the sting, and moaning that she's going to die.

I step forward. 'Are you allergic to wasp stings?' Frowning, I feel in my pocket and bring out my mobile phone, ready to dial for an ambulance.

'No, of course I'm not allergic, you stupid moron!' she yells in my face. 'It just bloody hurts.'

'Right.' Calmly, I slip the phone back in my pocket. 'Well, you're not going to die then, are you! Better get on. Got a run to finish.'

With a cheery wave, I jog off, leaving her standing there, wearing the contents of the trough, her mouth opening and shutting like a giant angry cod's ...

Chapter 32

I force myself to run normally until I'm out of sight of Lucy. Then I collapse weakly against the trunk of a horse chestnut tree, my heart banging against my ribcage.

My legs are trembling so much at the confrontation, I'm not sure I can go on yet. A couple of people are jogging towards me – and Lucy will be along soon, if she's not heading back – so I slip round the other side of the trunk and sink down gratefully onto a patch of green moss under the tree's sheltering branches.

I feel slightly sick. But the fearful look on Lucy's face when I started walking towards her was a revelation. You always hear that bullies are essentially cowards, but I never really believed that before now. It puts a whole new complexion on my attitude towards Lucy.

I might even feel a bit sorry for her.

Actually no, that's rubbish. I'd still like to punch her lights out ...

'Is this a private party or can anyone join?'

I look up and Theo is standing there, strong tanned arms folded, looking down at me. His face is dappled by the sun shining through the leaves and I have to shade my eyes to see his face and his lovely lazy smile. My heart lurches. He's wearing dark running shorts and a white vest top that show off his lean, muscular body to perfection. His blue eyes seem slightly lighter today. They're the same shade as the summer sky overhead.

'I'm just taking a break,' I mutter. 'Where's Olivia?'

He looks puzzled. 'Somewhere up ahead, I think.' He points at the mossy cushion I'm sitting on. 'Looks comfy. Do you mind ... ?'

I shake my head, not about to forgive him for having such bad taste as to take up with Olivia.

He sits down beside me, long muscular legs splayed out, almost touching me, then he stretches his arms upwards, turns his face to the sky and gives a great yawn. It sounds like a long, satisfied growl and it reverberates deep inside me.

'On the beer last night. Not entirely awake yet.' He grins. Then he studies my face. 'Are you okay? You look a bit flushed.'

I purse my lips ruefully. 'Had a run-in with Lucy. She fell into a trough of green slime.'

He laughs. 'Really? Hey, high five!' He holds up his hand and I oblige. When our palms collide, I feel his long fingers curl briefly around mine and the contact sends a little pang of longing through me.

'Nothing to do with me,' I tell him. 'She just fell.'

He chuckles. 'That's what they all say.'

'It's true!'

'She had it coming to her, from what I hear.'

'From what you hear?' I glance at him questioningly.

He nods. 'Pretty much everyone I speak to is coming over to your side. They think Lucy has behaved abominably, deliberately sabotaging your business.' He grins. 'It was the fish in the curtain hems that seemed to sway opinion in the end.'

‘Oh my God, everyone knows about that?’

‘I think so. A tale as juicy as that will spread round a village as fast as a salmon wriggling upstream.’

‘It wasn’t salmon. It was kippers.’ I correct him with a grin, feeling amazed that popular opinion seems to be on my side. ‘But why is Lucy’s place so full if she’s got a bad name?’

He shrugs. ‘People love a bargain, and Lucy seems to have a special offer on every day of the week.’

I recall her saying the money wasn’t rolling in, and an awful thought strikes me. If Jane and Harry aren’t getting the proceeds from this run, where is the sponsorship money going? Surely not directly into Lucy’s pocket?

‘I’m scared The Treehouse Café might flop as well,’ I admit, staring at him sadly.

‘It won’t.’ He studies my face, an expression in his eyes that makes the breath catch in my throat. ‘You’re lovely. You care about your customers and you make a mean cherry and coconut cake. It’s going to be a brilliant success.’

My eyes fill with tears at his obvious sincerity, and I laugh and brush them away. ‘I hope you’re right. We can’t lose Honey Cottage.’

‘Hey, you won’t.’ Gently, he cups the side of my face so there’s nowhere else for me to look but into the mesmerising depths of his blue eyes. I catch a flicker of torment in them, before his intense gaze drops to my mouth. My heart starts beating so fast I can barely breathe. The space between Theo’s strong lips and mine is so small and we’re moving towards each other, his hand tangled in my hair. For a brief second, I feel him stiffen and pull back, his eyes full of a savage emotion that makes my heart lurch.

Then his mouth comes down on mine and the passion

that flares between us makes my head spin off into another realm.

Then, just as quickly, he pulls away from me. His breath is rasping and jerky, like mine, and he's shaking his head, his hands gripping my arms so tightly, I yelp.

'Sorry.' He lets go. 'Look, I can't ...' I look up at him, desperate to know why, and my heart twists at the tortured expression in his eyes. He's in deep pain and I have no idea why. But I want to help ...

'What's wrong?' I whisper.

'I can't do this to you.'

'What? You can't do what? Kiss me?'

He shakes his head. 'You don't understand. I'm jinxed.' He laughs bitterly. 'I've tried to think of it differently but there's no other way to look at it.'

'Jinxed? But how? I don't know what you mean.'

He stares off into the trees, his face bleak, lost in some private torment.

At last he turns and shrugs. 'It's just that everyone I love ends up ... *suffering* ... and there's nothing I can do about it.'

I stare up at him. 'Not everyone, surely?'

He gives a bitter smile. 'Everyone I really love.' He adjusts his position so there's a distinct distance between us, then he runs his hands over his face and through his hair. 'I know people call me the Lone Wolf, but it's not through choice, believe me.'

I swallow. 'I heard that you were engaged ...'

The silence, as I wait for his response, is electric.

He closes his eyes, and immediately I wish I could take back what I just said. It's obvious he's still grieving – I just really want to understand.

'Her name was Rachel,' he says at last, opening his eyes and staring out at nothing.

'How did you lose her?' I whisper.

'She died.' He glances across at me. 'Sorry, I try not to dwell on the past. You've caught me on a bad day.'

I shake my head. 'There's nothing to apologise for. You've obviously been to hell and back and I'm so sorry for that. But I think ...' I hesitate, not wanting to give an opinion where it's not wanted. 'I think you shouldn't just rule out being in a happy relationship again. You shouldn't give up on love.'

My words sound horribly clichéd, I know. But maybe it's what he needs to hear.

He smiles wistfully. 'You know, sometimes I think I'd like to be able to give my love to one woman for life, instead of trying to convince myself that casual relationships are better.'

I nod and his eyes burn into mine, as if he's desperate to make me understand.

'So why can't you?' There's a note of desperation in my tone. 'Love one woman, I mean.'

He shrugs. 'Can't take the risk. Not just for me, but for ...' He swallows and looks away. 'For *that person*. I feel like I'm jinxed. And maybe I'm opting out of life, but I can't face another devastating loss, so it's easier to keep my love life simple.'

My head swims as I absorb his words. Finally, I croak a reply.

'But I really think you're wrong.'

'I'm not.' His tone is weary, but also resolute. This is a man who has made up his mind and will not be influenced by anyone ...

'Still, there's nothing wrong with casual relationships, is there?' he says, with a smile that doesn't quite reach his eyes.

‘I suppose not.’ I swallow, not much liking the waters we’re sailing into. ‘Speaking of casual relationships, are you and Olivia ... ?’

He shakes his head.

‘God, sorry, I shouldn’t have asked.’ *I don’t know why I did. It just came out!*

‘No, it’s fine. I’m not saying I’m not tempted.’ He smiles.

I try to smile back, to show I’m okay with the idea of him fancying Olivia. I wish I’d never started this conversation.

‘Olivia’s beautiful, yes, but she’s far too earnest about the wrong things,’ he says. ‘I like a woman with a sense of fun, who doesn’t take herself too seriously.’

A feeling of relief floods through me at his reply. I’d felt sure there must be something going on between them. Of course, it doesn’t mean he won’t give in to Olivia’s flirting at some point in the future. She doesn’t seem the type to give up on a man at the first hurdle. *But I’d really rather not think about that ...*

I want to ask him why he keeps on holding *me* at arm’s length. *I’m* not earnest about the wrong things, am I? And he does laugh at my jokes. So what is it that’s putting him off me? If all he wants is a casual fling, then I think I’d be all right with that ...

I try again. ‘You’ve been unlucky so far in life but that doesn’t mean you’re an unlucky person. Perhaps your fortunes are about to change.’ My words sound desperate even to me, but something makes me plough on. ‘I think ... I really think you should consider taking another chance on love. You owe it to yourself to be happy.’

I stare down at my hands, my heart beating uncomfortably fast.

After a taut silence, I look up at him. He's just staring into space.

Then he turns. 'I'm not unhappy. I've got a good life. But after what I've been through, it's just not worth the risk. The utter devastation you feel when what you loved slips away from you. All over again.'

He brushes a gentle finger over my cheek. 'And nothing you can say – lovely, funny, gorgeous Twilight – will ever change my mind.'

*****

I sit there by the tree for a while after Theo has left, thinking about the love he lost, and finally facing up to the terrible truth.

I've fallen hard for Theo Steel.

And in light of what he's just told me – that he's made up his mind to live a single life – it's the worst thing that could have happened. It's meant to be beautiful when you fall in love, but this ... this is just devastating.

My limbs feel like lead and my head is all over the place.

I'm trying to summon the energy to get up and run on, when my mobile rings.

As I fumble in my pocket, it flashes through my mind that it might be Theo, phoning to say he's changed his mind about being a lone wolf ...

But of course it isn't Theo.

It's Mum and when I say hello, she immediately launches into a panicky speech that at first I can't quite make sense of. Except that it's about Dad and I know it's not good.

'Mum, slow down. What's happened?' My heart is in my mouth.

Just don't let him be—

'Oh, love.' Mum's voice sounds high-pitched and far away.

A cold hand grips my insides and squeezes.

'Yes?' I stop breathing.

'He's gone down with pneumonia. The doctor's worried he might not even survive the night. Can you come straight away?'

Chapter 33

Somehow I make it to the hospital. And when I walk into Dad's room, he's just lying there with tubes coming out of him and so much machinery keeping him alive, it's completely overwhelming.

Mum gets up from his bedside, looking grey and worn out, and we fall into each other's arms, sobbing. I glance anxiously at Dad, suddenly wondering if he can hear us.

'Any change?' I ask.

Mum shakes her head. 'Apparently the next twenty-four hours are critical. If he survives, the prognosis is good, but ...'

I swallow hard and we leave the 'but' hanging in the air.

'So ...' She attempts a bright smile. 'How was your journey, love?'

'Oh, fine. Well, horrible, but ...' I shrug. No need to tell her I sobbed the whole way, my face turned to the window, curled in a seat at the back of the compartment.

'Have you eaten?'

I shake my head. 'I couldn't. However tempting rail food might be.'

This raises a small smile, although I've never seen Mum look so old. I can't imagine what it's been like for her this past year, looking after Dad and worrying constantly, and having no one to look after *her* ... and now this.

'Why don't you go back to the house, now that I'm here?' I suggest. 'Get a few hours' sleep?'

Even as I'm saying it, I know it's a stupid thing to say. Of *course* she wants to stay, however exhausted she is. The next twenty-four hours are critical for Dad ...

I take a seat in the green plastic chair Mum has pulled over to Dad's bedside for me, next to hers. She takes my hand and squeezes it. And we look at Dad's expressionless face, at the closed, lined eyelids that don't look like his at all.

'Don't worry.' I nudge Mum. 'He'll be awake soon enough and making one of his terrible jokes.'

I look at Dad, hoping for a response. A small miracle. But there's nothing.

Panic flutters in my chest. What if he never regains consciousness? What if we never even have a chance to say goodbye?

Beside me, Mum sighs. 'You know, I'd moan about him telling the same funny stories to everyone who came to the house. What I'd give to hear one of his shaggy dog tales now ...'

We make it through the night, taking it in turns to doze in the more comfortable, padded chair, and drinking scorching coffee in thin plastic cups in the bleak, unearthly hours before dawn when it seems as if we're the only people in the world awake.

At around six, I fall into an uneasy sleep, slouched in the chair. And I'm woken by Mum's voice calling, 'Nurse! Nurse!' followed by a sudden burst of activity around me. I sit up, startled, and see that Dad's eyes are open. My heart lurches as I watch the nurse checking his vital signs, and I pray she'll give us good news. Mum is gripping my hand tightly and watching with the same intensity.

The nurse turns and smiles at us, and a wave of relief floods through me.

He's survived the worst. It was touch and go but it seems that for now, at least, we've been given a reprieve, the three of us.

My little family.

Still together ...

*****

I stay in London for a week, taking the strain off Mum and Auntie June by sitting with Dad for hours at a time.

We talk about anything and everything, and once he's sitting up in bed and more like his normal chirpy self, I break the news about Lucy and her rival café. He listens in silence as I describe the disaster of opening day at The Twilight Café, Lucy springing such a devastating surprise on me, and how Lucy & Olivia's Clean Food Café has been in the local newspaper and on national TV, and how it's been choc-full of customers practically every day since it opened.

He knows a bit about the retail trade, my dad, having run his country goods store for more than twenty years. When I finish my emotional tale, he takes my hand and says, 'Those cut-price offers of hers will be squeezing her margins to practically zero. No business can survive long like that. She'll go bust within six months. Unless she keeps on throwing Daddy's money down the black hole.'

It sounds brutal the way he said it, but I know he's just

being really protective of me. And deep down, I hope he's right.

The trouble is, Dad doesn't know Lucy like I do. I got the upper hand when she plummeted into the trough at the charity run. Lots of runners must have spotted her up to her eyes in smelly green slime. I made her a laughing stock and knowing Lucy, I have an uneasy feeling there will only be one thing on her mind now.

Revenge.

Chapter 34

Sitting on the train as it speeds back to Hart's End, I've got a bad case of butterflies in my stomach.

I'm both excited and nervous about seeing how Jake's work is progressing on The Treehouse Café. Also, having left halfway through the charity run after receiving Mum's desperate phone call about Dad, there are certain things I'm going back to that were left up in the air.

My dramatic confrontation with Lucy.

And the realisation that I've fallen for Theo Steel.

I feel bad for Jason. He seemed so certain we had a future together when he spoke to me so urgently at the start of the 10k. But although it felt lovely and familiar kissing my first love, it was nothing compared to the way I felt just being close to Theo – every nerve ending tingling, feeling fully, ecstatically alive ...

When Theo sat beside me under the tree after my clash with Lucy, I knew without doubt that I was in love with him, but it was so bittersweet. I felt heady with the thrill of being near him but devastated at the same time, knowing there was no hope for us.

I've tried so hard over the past week to push him from my mind because there's really no point. Theo seems to have this unshakeable belief that he's cursed when it comes to people he loves, and I can't imagine where I would even *start* trying to convince him he's wrong. I've felt the sting of rejection by him several times already. I'm not sure I could bear it if it happened again ...

It was hard saying goodbye to Mum and Dad, and getting on the train, because I wanted to stay and be there for them.

But just before I left, I went in to see Dad, who was sitting in his favourite armchair, watching an old episode of *Inspector Morse*. When I sat on the arm to lean over and hug him, he held me really tightly and said, 'You know, love, the best thing you can do for your mum and me is to go back to Hart's End, get The Treehouse Café up and running, and show that Lucy Slater how it's done. Okay?'

I smiled at him. 'Okay, Dad.'

'And make sure Betty and Doreen are on standby because when I get home, I'm spending a whole day fishing on that riverbank. With you.'

I smile and nod, my throat closing up.

'It's been keeping me going ever since I've been down here,' he says. 'I've got the clearest picture in my head. It's going to be dry and sunny with not a breath of wind to ruffle the surface of the water, and we'll toast each other with hot coffee from my old flask and slabs of your home-made lemon drizzle cake.'

I laugh. 'Okay, Dad, I'm on it. Shall I dig out the hip flask as well?'

He grins and squeezes my hand. 'You're getting the idea. Now, get back to Hart's End and that treehouse. I can't wait to see it.'

*****

The train glides into the station and I alight, smiling wistfully as I recall Theo practically lifting me off onto the platform the last time. My foolish heart is beating faster, just knowing he's nearby and I could bump into him around the next corner.

Walking along the high street, I'm so deep in thought – wondering how long it takes to get over someone you've never even been out with in the first place – I almost don't notice the two people emerging from The Three Blackbirds pub. Then with a shock, I hear a laugh I recognise.

Theo.

He's lingering at the entrance, chatting with the woman, who has bright blonde hair and a very slim figure in jeans and a white T-shirt. Casually, he drapes his arm around her shoulders and she leans into his side, turning slightly so finally, I can see who it is.

My heart sinks like a lift plummeting all the way to the basement.

Olivia.

I nip into a shop doorway and watch as they walk together along the high street. They're on the other side of the road, walking away from me, so there's no chance I'll be spotted.

They look very at ease in each other's company, and a pang of pure, green-eyed jealousy punches me in the stomach. I didn't think it would be long before Olivia won Theo over ... and seeing them looking so cosy together, I was right.

I set off, following them, walking at a distance but keeping them in my sights all the time. I feel sick. I know I shouldn't be trailing them – I'm really not some sort of mad stalker – but my legs seem to have a will of their own. I need to know where they're going. If it's back to her place, I don't know what I'll do ...

They turn off the high street and head up a little alley, so I quickly cross the road and follow them. Apart from a church, there's little else along there except green fields.

As I round the corner, I'm just in time to see Olivia stretch up on tiptoe and kiss Theo on the mouth. He grabs her and kisses her back, and my heart turns over. Olivia does a cute, flirty wave and heads back up the alley, so I quickly nip back into another shop doorway until she's walked off along the high street.

Cautiously I peer round the corner, just in time to see Theo walking into the churchyard, through the little lych gate. My heart swoops in sympathy. Oh God, perhaps he's visiting Rachel's grave. Watching from a discreet distance, sure enough I see him standing, solemn and still, by a grave just inside the churchyard entrance.

My throat feels thick with emotion. How often does he visit Rachel's grave like this? I long to be there for him, to help him get over his grief.

But he doesn't want me ...

At last, he starts walking slowly back in the direction of the high street, and I go into the nearby newsagent's and buy a newspaper. When I come out, he's nowhere to be seen. I linger for a while. Then I start walking round the corner to the church. I don't know why, but I have to see for myself.

Slipping through the gate, I find the grave and when I read the words there, my heart starts beating uncomfortably fast.

Margaret and John Steel, loving parents of Theobald. Missed every day but you will live in my heart forever.

A lump fills my throat. It's not his fiancée, Rachel, as I'd assumed.

Poor Theo, losing both his parents ...

Then I read the dates, and two things strike me.

Margaret and John Steel died on the very same day.

And they were only in their forties.

I stand there, just as Theo did ten minutes earlier, staring at the gravestone, feeling utterly shell-shocked. His parents must have perished in some kind of accident. And saddest of all, if my calculations are correct, when the tragedy happened, Theo was little more than a boy.

After such a devastating blow so early in life, then losing his fiancée as well, I'm starting to see why Theo would feel so terrified to love someone ...

*****

I head back to Honey Cottage and start unpacking, my head full of Theo's sad past.

It's nearly five o'clock by the time I'm finished. Betty and Doreen will be preparing to close up the café. I decide to call in and see them.

They greet me like their favourite niece, fussing over me. Betty takes my backpack and Doreen starts brewing my favourite coffee, and after asking about Dad and anxiously enquiring after Mum, they chatter away about how much they're looking forward to working in the treehouse.

'Jake's been in here every day this week,' says Betty. 'Nice big strapping lad. Isn't he, Doreen?'

'Oh, yes. He's very partial to my cherry macaroons. And the treehouse is coming on in leaps and bounds. Have you seen it?'

'No, not yet. But I can't wait.'

A car draws up outside and Betty pops her head round the door. 'Another customer before we close up?'

To my surprise, in walks Jane. I haven't seen her since the day of the run when she told me about Lucy changing her mind and refusing the funds she promised for Harry.

'Hi. Betty said you'd be back this afternoon. How's your dad doing?'

'Better, thanks.' I grin. 'He's at home now, ordering everyone about from his favourite armchair.'

She nods. 'Good. I know how horrible it is, knowing there's nothing you can do but wait by the bedside. You feel so utterly helpless.'

'Will you still manage to get to America?'

She smiles grimly. 'Oh, yes. Even if I have to rob a bank. Look, I just wanted to thank you for being so kind to me on the day of the run. I was at my very worst ebb. I'm sorry I blubbed all over you.' She laughs. 'I don't normally do that to strangers.'

'Hey, don't apologise.' My heart goes out to her. I can't imagine how tough it must be for her, a single mum having to look after a child with a life-threatening illness all on her own. 'I'd like to help if I can,' I tell her on impulse. 'How about I do the same as Lucy was going to do? Five per cent of my share of the takings from The Treehouse Café, once it opens?'

She looks horrified at the suggestion. 'No, you don't have to do that. I hope you don't think I only came round here so that you'd ...' She shrugs helplessly and I rush to reassure her.

'Of course I don't. I just want to help, that's all. I'm not sure it will be much but at least it would be a start to your living expenses fund.'

'Count us in, too,' calls Betty.

We both turn, and Doreen says, 'Make it five per cent of *all* the takings, not just yours, Twilight.'

'Oh God, are you sure?' Jane is practically on the verge of tears.

'Definitely,' smiles Betty. 'I can't think of a better cause. We'll get that little lad to America yet!'

*****

On the way back, I nip in through the garden gate to see the work that's been done.

Jake has fixed up a big screen around the treehouse, presumably to keep people from staring over the fence and having a good old nosy. I like the air of mystery it creates, not knowing what's going on beneath the flapping covers.

His van's not there, so he must have gone home for the day. I pick my way through the garden and venture behind the screen, staring skywards at the magical scene before me.

'Oh my God,' I breathe, barely able to believe the transformation Jake has achieved in a little over a week.

Dad's original structure had a fairy-tale feel to it and I was worried that in catering to the practical elements necessary to house a café, Jake might obliterate this quality. But he hasn't at all.

The treehouse might now be ten times the size and have an impressive walkway entrance, a bit like a swing bridge, made from all natural materials, but it's clear that the magical essence of the treehouse has not been lost at all.

It's simply fairyland on a much bigger scale!

There's still work to be done on it, but already I can see what a gloriously romantic setting it will be for our new café. It will be so light and airy in the summer for the customers, drinking their coffee high up in the treetops with glorious views over Lake Heath. In the winter, I'll string fairy lights all along the walkway, and put candles under glass in the windows so that when it gets dark mid-afternoon, it will look so pretty and welcoming.

A little surge of happiness rushes through me. If I love it, other people will love it too, won't they? It's such an original idea, having a café in a treehouse. It will work, I'm sure of it.

It *has* to work ...

Of course, I have Theo to thank for this glorious plan. It was all his idea. A cloud moves across the sun and I shiver. Part of me desperately wishes Theo could be here right now to see all this. But what would be the point? I can't be with him the way I want to be. He's made that very clear ...

I'm aware of the doorbell ringing, and when I walk round the front of the house, there's Paloma.

'Hi, you're back!' she squeals, brandishing a copy of the local newspaper. 'I'm so glad your dad's recovered. I couldn't wait to show you this.'

I unlock the front door to let us in and take the newspaper, which is folded open at a particular page. In the living room, I dump my backpack and slump down on the sofa, and Paloma sits beside me to enjoy my reaction to the photo.

'It's that picture you took of Lucy and Olivia!'

Paloma nods gleefully. 'Stuffing their faces with cake.'

I peer closer at the photo and burst out laughing. 'Their *expressions*! Caught red-handed. Oh my God, that really cracks me up.'

I read the headline aloud. *Health Food Café Not Quite So Squeaky Clean!*

I gape at Paloma. 'So you gave the photo to the newspaper?'

She nods. 'And a reporter phoned me up for the story. Read

it!' She taps the text. 'I managed to get in a mention of The Treehouse Café. Look!'

I read it and sure enough, there's a paragraph about the treehouse café being built and mentioning that it's scheduled to open in mid-August.

'Did you tell them mid-August, then?'

She shrugs. 'I made it up, but I thought it would probably be around then. It will be, won't it?'

I nod, grinning at the sheer nerve of my best friend. 'I was thinking Sunday August 13th, if all goes according to plan.'

'And Lucy doesn't manage to sabotage it again,' says Paloma, looking suddenly serious. 'We're going to have to watch her like a hawk. You do realise that? The cow will stop at nothing to bring you down.'

I sigh wearily. 'I have thought about that, yes. I'm not going to let Lucy get within a hundred yards of the treehouse because I really can't trust her.'

'Are you worried about how she reacted to your shoving her in the trough?'

'I didn't *shove* her. She lost her balance.'

Paloma grins. 'Yeah, yeah, I believe you.'

'But it's *true*!' My face falls. 'Oh God, are people saying that I deliberately pushed her off the fence?' I groan. 'Lucy's going to *hate* that everyone's laughing and thinking I got one over on her.'

Paloma shrugs. 'I wouldn't worry. She deserves everything she gets.'

We grin at each other and fall silent, staring at the picture of Lucy and Olivia in the newspaper.

'You should issue invitations to the grand opening of The Treehouse Café,' says Paloma.

I nod. 'And I'm going to get people to RSVP so I can be fairly sure how many will be there on opening night.'

'You're having it in the evening?'

'Yes, early evening. I thought that would make it a bit more special. Summer berry Pavlova and a glass of fizz at six, then we can cut the ribbon and have a proper ceremony. I might even make a speech.'

'Invite the local press. I'm sure they'll be interested in taking photographs.'

I nod, excitement making my heart beat faster. 'I can't believe this is happening. Do you want to see the work Jake's done already on the treehouse?'

She grimaces. 'I've – er – already seen it. I hope you don't mind. I sneaked into the garden and took a look last night.'

'No, of course I don't mind,' I say, laughing at her awkward blushes.

'It's going to be incredible.'

'Praise indeed when you don't even like Jake.' I grin.

She frowns. 'He's an arrogant arse. But he can build a solid structure. I'll give him that.'

We look at each other and burst out laughing.

Chapter 35

Over the following two weeks, the treehouse slowly takes shape. Every day, there seems to be something else to admire and I grow more and more confident that we've done the right thing – Betty, Doreen and I.

I go out running every morning in the lanes around the village, and every time, I'm half-expecting to see Theo out running, too. But I never do, and eventually, I come to the conclusion he's avoiding me.

At least I have the new café to keep me occupied. I have a feeling that without all the buzz and frantic activity, I might just fall into a big black hole of despondency over Theo and never emerge again.

Paloma designs a beautiful invitation, which we send out to around fifty people – personal friends and family, business contacts, the local press and anyone who's been involved in The Treehouse Café project.

Betty and Doreen turn out to be full of fabulous ideas for the interior design of the café. We eventually go for a minimalist feel, with beautifully simple tables and chairs of solid oak, designed and made by a local craftsman Doreen knows. The eight tables will be ranged around a central serving area, dominated by our brand-new coffee machine that Betty tracked down for a bargain price on-line and a beautiful polished oak counter, on which will sit the cake display glass domes and all the other café paraphernalia. I've decided on a pretty posy of silk flowers in a simple glass vase on each table.

It's going to look gorgeous. I can't wait for people to see it ...

*****

I'm coming out of the village post office, a while before the grand opening, when the inevitable happens and I spot Lucy walking towards me. I immediately change my route and dive into a side street so I don't have to talk to her, but to my dismay, she comes running after me, calling out my name. So then I have no option but to speak to her.

'Twilight, I want to say sorry. For everything,' she says, panting slightly after her exertion.

I stare at her in disbelief. Then I laugh in her face. '*Everything*?'

'Yes. I should never have opened my café the same day as yours without telling you. I can see now that that was very sneaky.'

'*No*! Really, Lucy? You do surprise me.'

She hesitates, frowning. 'Well, I don't know why you're surprised. It must have been quite obvious I did it deliberately.'

'I was being sarcastic, Lucy. But then, you never did have much of a sense of humour.'

She drops the sorry act and glares at me. 'Well, there's no need to take that attitude when I'm being good enough to apologise.'

I laugh. Is this girl for *real*? 'Right, well, very nice of you to say sorry, Lucy, even though the apology is roughly twenty-four years too late.' I smile cheerily. 'Got to be going. Goodbye!' And I walk off, leaving her staring after me.

And I have to admit, refusing to take her crap, after all those years of feeling intimidated by her, feels good. Very good indeed.

On my way home, a journalist from the local paper calls, wanting to run a story about The Treehouse Café in this week's edition.

'Will you be in around four o'clock?' she asks. 'I'm going to try and bring a photographer along. Take some photos of the work in progress? Would that be all right? If I can organise it?'

Would that be all right?

'That would be absolutely perfect.'

'We might not manage it this afternoon, but we'll try. Because then we'd be able to get you in tomorrow's edition of the paper.'

'Fabulous!'

'I'll let you know if we're not coming. Then we can schedule it for next week instead.'

I feel like dancing the rest of the way home. It's really happening! People are becoming curious and every time I'm out, I have people asking me about the building work that's going on behind the tarpaulin in my garden, because they've heard it's going to be an amazing new café in the treetops! And now, with a story in the local paper, *everyone* will know about it!

I phone Betty's number and she squeals with delight when I tell her the news and she promises to get straight on the phone to Doreen. Then I phone Paloma.

'We might be in the paper tomorrow!'

'Sorry?'

'The Treehouse Café. I might have a reporter and a photographer coming round later.'

'Oh. Good.'

I frown. 'Did you hear what I just said?'

There's a silence on the other end, then a rustling noise as if she's shuffling through some papers.

'Paloma? Are you all right?'

'What? Oh, yes. Sorry, I was just – erm – looking out for the postman.'

'Oh. Right. Are you expecting an important letter, then?'

'A parcel, actually. Look, I've got to go. Talk to you later.' And she rings off.

When the phone rings again a few seconds later, I pick up expecting it to be Paloma with some explanation for her vagueness. But it isn't her. It's Rose, one of Mum's friends from the Women's Institute.

'Oh, Twilight, so glad I've caught you. I know you're busy these days, what with the new café and everything. Very exciting! Everyone's talking about it. We can't wait for you to open. I got your invitation, by the way. Thank you ever so much.'

'Oh, good, I hope you can come.'

'I'll be there!' she says cheerily. 'But, Twilight, I was hoping you could do me a huge favour?'

'Of course. If I can.'

'Well. We've got our craft fair today on the village green, as you probably know. We're raising funds for the village hall and we had Lucy Slater coming along to do the judging in the baking tent. The thing is, she's cancelled on us at the last minute and, well, we were hoping that we might be able to persuade you to step in. I know it's terribly short notice ...'

'Oh. Right. So Lucy just cancelled? Did she give you a reason?'

'None at all.'

Bloody typical!

I glance at my watch. It's just after three now. 'Well, I'm sure I could help. What time would you need me?'

'The prizes are being awarded at four-thirty, so if you could come along now that would be fabulous.'

'Oh. The thing is, I've sort of got a loose arrangement with a reporter. She might be coming round at about four.'

'Oh, right.' There's a pause and I can almost hear her brain ticking over, anxiously scrabbling for a solution. 'Well, don't worry. We'll try and find someone else.'

'Would it take long? The judging?'

'Oh, no, not really. There are five categories and you'd be tasting cakes from each. Half an hour, maybe?'

I hesitate. I like Rose and she sounds in a real predicament. It's typically selfish of Lucy to cancel at the last minute without a reason, especially when she seemed perfectly all right when I saw her in the street half an hour ago!

'Listen, I'll do it. I'll come along now.' *If I hurry, I can be back before four.*

'You will?' Rose sounds incredibly relieved. 'Oh, Twilight, that is *so* good of you! Thank you ever so much!'

It turns out to be good fun, sampling the cakes and scones and awarding them rosettes. Lots of people want to know about The Treehouse Café, which is very reassuring, so of course I stay to talk to them about it. By the time I finally leave the tent and head home, it's five to four.

When I get back, there's a note on the mat from the journalist.

They were here a little earlier than expected. Sorry to find I wasn't in but maybe they could come back next week sometime?

I could kick myself. Such a great opportunity gone to waste! I know it will probably still happen, but being in tomorrow's edition would have been amazing.

I shake my head in dismay. Even when Lucy Slater isn't even trying to, she still manages to muck things up for me!

*****

It's the following morning and I'm at Paloma's flat, helping her design a little flag with a floral border, on which I can write the name of each individual cake.

'Lucy apologised to me yesterday.'

Paloma is leaning forward concentrating on the screen. 'Hmm?'

'She apologised in the street.'

Paloma turns with a confused look. 'Sorry, I could have sworn you just said Lucy apologised.'

'I did.'

'*What?*'

'I know. Weird, huh? I mean, why now?'

Paloma sits back in the chair. 'What was she apologising for exactly?'

'God knows. Making my life a misery at school? Getting her claws into Jason? Sewing kippers into my curtains? Your guess is as good as mine.'

'Yeah, well, don't trust her.'

I laugh. 'Don't worry, I won't. She doesn't scare me any more. But that doesn't mean I won't be watching her like a hawk to make sure she doesn't come within a mile of The Treehouse Café!'

'Especially in the run-up to the opening ceremony.'

My heart beats faster at the thought of Sunday. 'Oh my God, it's really happening.' My insides shift uneasily. 'Mind you, I keep getting a worrying feeling of déjà vu. It's not the first café I've launched. And remember what happened last time.'

Paloma nods thoughtfully. 'The phrase "damp squib" comes to mind. But this time it's different.'

'How?'

She shrugs. 'There's a fantastic buzz about The Treehouse Café. Everyone's talking about it. You finally found your Unique Selling Point!'

'I hope so.' I swallow hard. 'I really do hope so.'

Paloma nips away to make coffee, leaving me to play about with the floral border. I notice that she's been looking at Jake's website, so I click on it, expecting to see something really basic. I seem to remember her saying it was rubbish and that a five-year-old could design a better one.

But to my surprise, it's really attractive, with photos of the treehouses beautifully laid out and headings in red, green, and blue, in a lovely, curly font reminiscent of a child's handwriting.

'I thought you said Jake's website was rubbish,' I say when she walks back in.

She colours slightly. 'It *was* rubbish. But I've revamped it.'

'Oh.' I'm taken aback. 'But I didn't think you liked him.'

She shrugs. 'Business is business.' Then she sighs. 'Actually, he didn't pay me for it.'

'What?'

She looks at me, quirking her lips at one side. 'I wasn't going to tell you.'

'What? You fancy Jake?'

'You're joking. Of course I don't. He's probably more of an arrogant arse than Rufus,' she says, scowling at the memory of her ex. 'No, when he told you he couldn't work on your treehouse for a while because he had another commission, I – um – phoned him up and offered to redesign his crap website if he managed to make you a priority client.'

I gape at her.

She shrugs, looking anywhere but at me. 'So he did. And that's why his shit website now looks half-decent.'

'Paloma! You didn't have to do that. But it's so lovely of you! I need to pay you for the work you did for Jake, though. Why didn't you tell me what you were doing?'

She grins. 'Because I knew you would react like this, and I don't want payment. What are friends for?'

I smile at her, feeling quite emotional.

'So ... you *don't* fancy Jake?' I ask a minute later, thinking of the surprise new hairdo and glancing at her brand-new top and dark red lipstick. Paloma *never* used to wear lipstick – just a slick of gloss when it was a *really* special occasion. But these days, she looks *groomed*.

She doesn't even deign to answer my question.

The disgusted look on her face says it all ...

Chapter 36

The day of the café launch arrives. And the heat is on. Quite literally, as it happens.

The newscasters are making a huge deal of the fact that it's set to be the hottest day of the year. This bodes well for entertaining the fifty guests due to arrive at six o'clock.

As The Treehouse Café seats a maximum of thirty-two people at eight tables, it's our plan to serve the refreshments in the garden, allowing people to mingle, then take small groups up to view the interior of the treehouse.

Summer heat waves always make me nervous because I associate them with thunderstorms, but thankfully, when I check the local forecast, there's no sign of a break in the perfect weather. So we should be fine for our al fresco celebrations later on.

Betty and Doreen arrive at mine at eight and we all set to, making the meringues for the summer berry Pavlovas we'll be serving at the opening ceremony later. I've never made a Pavlova before, but Doreen convinced Betty and me that it would be a real show-stopper, served with a glass of the Prosecco from the crates of bottles we carted back from the supermarket in Betty's car the other night.

By ten, the nest-like meringues are out of the oven and

cooled down, and we've filled them with a mouth-watering mix of strawberries, raspberries and whipped cream.

'They're going to wilt in this weather,' worries Betty.

I frown. Jake is organising last-minute snagging in the treehouse today, so the fridge there isn't in operation yet. 'Let's put them in the fridge over at the old café?' I suggest.

We cover them with cake domes and carry them carefully over there. Luckily, the fridge is just large enough to accommodate all eight. The old café is closed today while we prepare for tonight – and get ready for The Treehouse Café's first official day of business tomorrow!

Betty and Doreen go off to the hairdresser's for a spot of pampering, leaving me with my list of jobs still to do before tonight. I check the fridge to count the Pavlovas, hoping we've made enough. It's a relief to get the baking out of the way. I can check it off my list, along with the fizz that's now chilling in my own fridge back at the house. I've bought in a supply of pretty paper plates for tonight and hired glasses from the local off-licence ...

Then I remember something. *Cake forks!* We don't have enough.

Why didn't I think of it before? Damn, it means a trip into town to buy forks that match the ones we already have. My heart sinks. That's going to use up valuable time – especially since I don't have a car to get there myself. I'll have to wait till Betty comes back and see if she can whiz me into town ...

A car draws up outside and a door slams.

Instantly, my foolish heart is hoping it's Theo, come to wish me luck for tonight.

When Jason walks in, it's silly, I know, but I feel like crying with disappointment.

I paste on a smile. There's no chance for me with Theo. I know that. But it would really help if my mind could stop the eternal wishful thinking and get with the programme ...

Jason's smile seems a little strained. 'Just came to wish you well for tonight.'

'Aw, thank you. That's so lovely of you!'

'All organised?'

'Yes. Well, no, actually. I forgot to buy cake forks.' I laugh. 'You haven't got any, have you?'

He grins. 'Sorry, no.'

'Can I get you a coffee while you're here? A piece of fruitcake? The fridge is full of summer fruit Pavlovas but they're for tonight, I'm afraid. I'm just hoping they don't melt before then.' I'm aware I'm babbling, but it's been on my mind that I need to let Jason down gently, and I guess the time to do it has arrived. There's no point having dinner with him if I'm in love with Theo. The last thing I want to do is lead Jason on.

But he turns down the offer of coffee, saying he needs to get back.

'Off to work?' I ask.

He shakes his head slowly, looking at me with a strange expression on his face.

'Is something wrong?'

He gazes down at the floor, hands in his pockets, and when he eventually looks up, his eyes are suspiciously shiny.

'Jason?' I stare at him in alarm.

He sighs and takes a step towards me. 'I don't know how to say this, Twi. It's been so great having you back in Hart's End. I've missed you and I really meant what I said about us getting back together. But ...' He tails off miserably.

'But what?'

He shrugs. 'Lucy's moving back in.'

'Oh.' I stare at him, the wind taken right out of my sails. 'You're back together, then? Gosh, well, that's ... great!'

The expression on his face indicates he feels it's the opposite of great. 'She said she apologised to you. I told her she had to, otherwise there was no chance we could get back together.'

Ah, so that was the reason for the little performance of hers on the high street!

'What made you ... reconsider?' I ask carefully.

He sighs and flops into a nearby chair. 'Look, I know you probably think I'm mad, but – well, she came over to see me saying she's been missing me terribly. I decided I owed us both a second chance to make the relationship work.'

I nod slowly. 'So will you be moving into that big new house Lucy was talking about?'

He pauses. 'Actually, we're moving to Paris.'

My eyes are wide with astonishment. 'Paris? Really? But why?'

His gaze slips to the table top. He reaches for the salt shaker and starts turning it round and round in his hands. 'The thing is, her dad wants me to head up his new operation in Paris. It means more responsibility, a huge step up career-wise and more money, obviously.'

Ah, now we're getting to it!

He looks up at me and shrugs. 'I couldn't say no.'

'It certainly sounds like a great opportunity.'

'Yes.' His eyes slide away from mine.

'Jason, I hope you're not getting back with her just because of the job,' I say quietly, genuinely worried he's making the worst decision ever.

He shakes his head. 'I do love her, Twi. She's always there for me. You coming back stirred up lots of bad memories for her and – um – sent her off the rails a bit.'

'Bad memories?' A bitter laugh escapes. 'I think *I'm* the one with those. Not Lucy.'

He looks at me, a wealth of sadness in his eyes. 'She's not as terrible as you think, you know. If you need to blame someone for what happened with the café, blame me.' He shrugs helplessly.

'*You*? Why would I blame you for Lucy's actions?'

He sighs. 'Because I'm not the man you think I am. I'm weak and pathetic. And you, Twilight, deserve someone noble and strong.' His smile has a trace of bitterness. 'Some guy like Theo Steel.'

I swallow hard, pushing away the feeling of despair suddenly threatening to engulf me. 'Well, that's total rubbish,' I snap. 'You're a lovely man, Jason. And for your information, you deserve someone far nicer than Lucy.' I smile wistfully. 'It's just ... that someone isn't going to be me. I can see that now, however tempting it felt to fall back into our old relationship.'

'I know,' he agrees reluctantly. 'It would have been a mistake to go back.'

'But will you be happy? With Lucy?' I ask urgently, needing to know that he's going to be okay.

He smiles sadly. 'Look ... there are things you don't know about Lucy. Things that might make you understand a little about why she's so bitter. She's not the evil witch you might think she is. She's just ... desperately sad. Poisoned by the things that have happened to her. And I'm to blame, so I need to stick with her.' He shrugs. 'She needs me. And in a funny way, I need her, too.'

'What? Hold on. I don't understand.' My head is reeling. 'Why is Lucy so sad? What things have happened to her? And what have they to do with me?'

But he's already heading for the door.

He turns. 'I've said too much already. Look, Lucy and I will be off to Paris soon and I really think that's for the best.' His gaze as he looks at me is rock steady. 'For everyone.'

My eyes well up. 'Well, good luck with everything. I mean that.'

He looks at me for a long moment, his eyes full of sadness and affection.

Then he holds up his hand and walks out.

I take a huge breath and let it out slowly. Poor Jason doesn't look like a man in love, off for a new adventure. He looks sick of his life. Who knows what the mysterious dynamic is between him and Lucy?

He seems to have made up his mind, though, which to be honest, is quite a relief. I don't have to wonder how I'm going to let him down gently.

I go back in and start gathering up the cutlery, ready to take up to the new café, all the time thinking about Jason's news about Paris. And wondering about Lucy and what's happened to turn her so bitter and vindictive.

Jason has always tended to take the path of least resistance in life. He's easily swayed – the sort who'll just go along with the status quo, rather than take a risk that could improve his life. In some ways, he's a good match for Lucy. She likes being in charge and Jason's quite happy to be told what to do ...

Eventually, I manage to get hold of Betty in the hairdresser's. As she's already in town, it makes sense for her to pick up the cake forks we need. I'm just ringing off, when the door opens and someone breezes in.

Lucy?

'Cake forks,' she says brusquely, holding up a bag. 'Where do you want them?' Without waiting for a reply, she barges straight through to the kitchen.

I stare after her, stunned by her appearance, before realising that what I was determined would never happen is now taking place.

Lucy Slater is on my premises!

I hurry after her, in time to see her plonking the bag of forks on the counter beside the fridge.

She smiles serenely at me. 'Don't worry—'

'I'm not worried,' I snap, on the defensive.

She arches her eyebrows at me. 'If you'd let me finish? I was actually going to say, don't worry, we've got plenty of forks at the café. There's no rush getting them back to me.'

'Oh, right. Well, thanks.'

She heads back out into the café and I follow.

'By the way, there was a van parked in your driveway when I passed,' she calls back.

'Was there?' I rack my brains trying to think who that would be. Jake, perhaps? I watch Lucy until she's out of the door and walking back up the road. Even when she's apparently being helpful, she still freaks me out. (Although she couldn't possibly have sabotaged the cake forks, like she did with the curtains, so it should be all right to use them.)

I grab my bag and dash out to see who's at the front door.

When I get there, there's no sign of the van. So I have a quick peek behind the tarpaulin at the treehouse. It's hard to believe that in just eight hours, this garden will be milling with guests and I'll be able to unveil The Treehouse Café for all to see.

And with Lucy Slater well and truly banished from the premises, nothing will go wrong this time ...

*****

The afternoon whizzes by in a whirl of activity as Betty, Doreen and I rush around getting everything ready. In the humid heat, I feel constantly drenched, despite my sleeveless cotton T-shirt and loose, flowing skirt. But I'll be having a long, cool shower later, before the guests arrive ...

Jake does a brilliant job of finishing off and at just after four o'clock, when he drives off, the three of us climb up into the treehouse to admire our brand-new café.

The treehouse interior feels surprisingly cool and dim after the heat and glare of the afternoon sun. Wooden chairs and tables are ranged around the central serving island, formed from a smooth slab of polished oak, and four square windows, two on each side, allow a mellow, dappled sunlight to filter in. Now, a fresh scent of leaves and greenery wafts through the open windows on a warm summer breeze, mingling with the fragrance of dad's lilacs in the garden below.

It's so beautiful, all big expanses of burnished wood, the rich colour of chestnuts, and fairy lights twinkling wherever you look. It's like a scene from a whimsical fairy tale. Whenever I enter, I always think of a picture book from my childhood, that told the story of a little community of woodland creatures living happily inside the trunk of a giant tree.

'It was a stroke of genius studding the roof with those lights,' says Betty, and we all stare up at the ceiling.

Doreen sighs happily. 'They're just like tiny little stars.'

Glancing around, I suddenly remember something. 'What about the tips jar? The Treehouse Café isn't complete until my tips jar from Dad is in place!'

I run down the walkway and dash happily through the garden and out of the gate. When I reach the old premises, I suddenly realise I've forgotten the keys, but when I try the door, it's open anyway. Walking in, I pick up the little wooden tub and hold it to the light, admiring the sheen of the polished wood.

It seems very quiet in here. I glance around. It must be because I'm used to the music playing softly in the background.

Still puzzled at the stillness, I go through to the kitchen, and that's when I realise, with a jolt, what's different. The fridge isn't making its usual 'busy-doing-its-thing' noises.

I pull open the door and frown.

The light inside hasn't come on.

My heart lurches. The fridge must be broken.

I stare in horror at the Pavlovas. Without the chill temperatures, the stiffly whipped cream has wilted. The fruit, too, has lost its lustre.

Hot tears of panic prick my eyes.

Even if we take the Pavlovas over to my fridge at home, by the time they're in there, they'll already be a great deal less than perfect.

We can't possibly serve sub-standard food at a café launch. What the hell are we going to do?

Chapter 37

Betty and Doreen are horrified when I tell them what's happened.

'We'll have no food to serve to the guests!' wails Betty. Then she gets a determined light in her eye. 'I'm going to have a look at them. You never know, we might be able to salvage them.'

We all go over there and peer into the dead fridge.

'There's nothing we can do about those,' Doreen says, shaking her head sadly. 'All that effort wasted.'

'Hang on.' Betty frowns. 'What's going on here?'

I turn and she snaps on a switch at the wall. Instantly, the fridge hums into life.

'It was switched off at the wall!' I gasp. 'But how can that have happened? It was definitely on when we put them in, so how ... ?'

'Oh my God.' Doreen claps a hand over her mouth.

'What?' demands Betty.

'I can't believe I did that,' says Doreen slowly. 'I must be going senile.'

'What? What did you do?' I ask.

She looks agonised. 'I brought the food mixer up to the treehouse this morning. I unplugged it from this same socket, so I must have accidentally flicked off both the switches at the same time.'

We're all silent, staring at the socket, absorbing the explanation. My mind is already leaping ahead to tonight, wondering if there's time to bake something special.

Doreen grabs both our arms. 'I'm *so* sorry.'

'These things happen!' murmurs Betty, patting Doreen's shoulder and looking worriedly at me.

'Not to me, they don't!' wails poor Doreen. 'I've never done anything like that in my life. What on earth was I thinking?'

'Hey, don't worry. It was an accident.' I give her a hug, trying to make light of it, while inside, I feel like running away in a panic.

'Yes, cheer up, Doreen,' says Betty. 'We're resourceful women, aren't we? We'll just have to get our thinking caps on, smartish!'

We take the Pavlovas back to the house and I make room for them in the fridge there. But it seems a pretty pointless exercise. They'll taste good, but there's no way we can use them, looking as they do.

After a brief discussion, we decide our only option is to go out and actually *buy* food for tonight. It's hardly ideal. How can we claim to offer the best cakes for miles around if we can't even serve up our own baking on launch night?

I glance at my watch. 'I suppose there might be time to whip up some fairy cakes. Then we could cool them in the fridge and quickly ice them?'

Betty and Doreen agree this is a good compromise. So they leave me creaming butter and sugar at top speed while they head off to the supermarket to buy in other goodies.

Once the trays of fairy cakes are in the oven, I nip over to the treehouse but Betty and Doreen are nowhere to be seen.

They were just nipping to the local supermarket. They should be back by now. Where on earth are they?

I phone their mobiles but get no answer, so in the end, I go back to the house and flop down on the sofa, taking some deep breaths in an effort to quell the panic.

It's 5.15 p.m. We've got fifty people arriving in less than an hour. Betty and Doreen have gone AWOL, and I need to have a shower, get changed and prepare to welcome our guests with a glass of fizz.

Sighing, I trudge upstairs. After all the excitement and happy anticipation, this night is turning into a disaster.

I'm just about to turn on the shower when I hear a car pull up outside. Rushing to the window, I see Doreen getting out of Betty's little Fiesta and going to open the boot. Then Betty appears, before ducking into the back seat and emerging with a stack of about five Tupperware boxes, one on top of each other. I pull on my jeans again and run downstairs.

'Where have you been? I was worried,' I pant. 'What's all this?'

Doreen peers round the stack of cake tins she's carrying and beams at me. 'Baking from the WI ladies. I put in an emergency call to Molly Keene, the chairperson, and as soon as she heard it was you, she flew into action straight away, asking members if they could come to your aid by raiding their home-baking tins for donations.'

They plonk the tins and boxes on the bench in the kitchen and start taking off the lids to show me the spoils. There's a whole lemon cake, a large Bakewell tart and two big fruitcakes, plus an assortment of cupcakes with a range of colourful toppings. More than enough to please our guests.

'Betty and I went round and collected it all,' adds Doreen.

I shake my head in amazement. 'I think you're both amazing! And how kind are these women, coming to our aid like this? It all looks incredible.'

Betty smiles. 'I think the fact you stepped in and did their cake judging at such short notice probably helped a lot.'

I laugh out loud. 'I still can't believe it. Right, I need a shower then we're in business!' I bound up the stairs, full of renewed enthusiasm.

*****

It turns out to be a really successful night. Quite the opposite to the last time I opened a café!

The guests pour in soon after six, laughing and chattering, all eager to see for themselves the mysterious project in the garden of Honey Cottage finally unveiled. It helps that it's a beautiful, balmy evening, and that The Treehouse Café – the star of the night – looks like something from a magical Disney movie, exactly as it's meant to.

I'm so busy welcoming guests and making sure they have refreshments – and taking small groups up to look around the treehouse I barely have a chance to chat to Paloma or Jake. Or Theo. Apart from a quick hello.

But I'm aware of Theo all the time. He looks gorgeous tonight in a blue shirt the exact same shade as his eyes, and every time I catch him looking over at me, my heart skips a beat. As the night wears on and the Prosecco goes down, our glances become more frequent and lingering, until finally, Theo's face breaks into a big smile, which of course makes me smile, too. A huge smile of joy that he seems to feel the same. But it's achingly bittersweet because I know we can't be together.

A highlight of the night is when Rowena arrives, with a teenage girl who she introduces as Melanie. *Her daughter!*

I manage to grab Rowena alone, while Melanie is chatting to Paloma about becoming a graphic designer.

'I took your advice and plucked up the courage to phone her,' Rowena tells me, happiness shining from her eyes. 'And she was so happy to hear from me.'

'I knew she would be.' I give her arm a little squeeze.

Rowena laughs. 'Well, I didn't. And that was the problem. I thought she'd tell me to bugger off. But actually, I think she was relieved that I made the first move.'

'Of course she was. She couldn't stay angry forever with a mum like you!'

She smiles. 'Well, thank you, Twilight, for making me see sense. Melanie is thinking of coming to stay with me while she studies graphic design at the local college.'

'God, that's brilliant. A happy ending!'

When she goes off to find Melanie, I stare after her wistfully.

I'm so pleased for Rowena and her daughter, but the selfish part of me can't help wishing it could be *my* happy ending. I glance for the millionth time in Theo's direction, but he's chatting to someone and has his back to me.

My heart physically aches for him.

But I take a deep breath and prepare to speak to more guests just arriving.

The best chance of a happy ending for me is The Treehouse Café being a rip-roaring success. That would definitely be something to be glad about ...

After a while, I escape up into the treehouse on my own.

I pull up a chair and sit by a window, leaning on the sill

and looking out over the party, at the people mingling and chatting and laughing. It seems amazing that I created this. With Paloma's help. And Jake's, of course, and Betty's and Doreen's.

I smile to myself, thinking I could do a speech from up here, Oscars-style, thanking the world and his dog for all their help and support.

I look around for Paloma, but I can't see her. Funnily enough, I can't see Theo either. Or Jake. They can't have gone home, surely? Not without saying goodbye?

Suddenly, from my vantage point, I catch sight of Paloma hurrying up the garden from the direction of the house. As I watch, she very deliberately stops and adjusts the top of her strappy dress and shakes out her hair, before re-joining the throng.

I'm about to go down and join her when I suddenly clap eyes on Jake walking up from the house.

Aha! Caught you!

I'm now convinced there's something going on between Paloma and Jake. But why does she keep claiming she can't stand him?

He's scrubbed up extremely well tonight. The dark suit and white shirt show off his out-in-all-weathers tan and his longish auburn hair is pulled back in a ponytail, showing off his strong jaw and handsome features. He doesn't go over to Paloma, but he keeps casting the occasional glance in her direction.

I smile to myself. You can see everything from up here, in this magical space in the treetops.

Raking the crowd for Theo, I finally spot him, standing by the garden shed, chatting to a mate of his from the gym. I throw up silent thanks to the matchmaking gods that Olivia's not here tonight.

A wave of emotion suddenly surges through me. I'm so happy about the amazing turnout, but I wish with all my heart that Mum and Dad could be here to share it with me. Especially Dad. I'd love him to see what Jake has created from the wonderful treehouse he made for me all those years ago – and to hear all the lovely comments from the guests.

But obviously, he couldn't come. The hospital would never have allowed it. He's only just recovered from pneumonia ...

My eyes well up, thinking of my lovely, brave dad. The stoic way he gets on with the treatment and never complains. The North Star is winking in the sky and I find myself staring up at it and making a wish – that Mum and Dad will be back home again, happy and healthy, by Christmas.

Then I laugh at my foolishness. I'm clearly getting carried away by the magical aura of the treehouse ... imagining I'm living in a fairy tale where dreams really do come true!

And the Prosecco has obviously gone to my head big time, because just then I imagined I saw Mum in her best fuchsia pink dress, mingling with the crowd down there ...

Hang on!

My eyes widen in shock. I glance nervously at my glass then look down at the crowd again.

There's Dad! Talking to Paloma!

My eyes are not deceiving me. It really is him.

Mum and Dad are here!

Heart beating excitedly, I charge down the walkway, feeling it bounce energetically beneath my feet, trailing my fingers along the wooden handrail.

They spot me and their faces light up.

'Oh my God, you're here!' I squeak as the three of us huddle together. I hug Mum first then Dad more carefully, as if he's something extremely precious – which is just what he is. He looks a lot thinner – being tall accentuates the weight loss – and his normally tanned face is pale. But he's smiling and he's here, which is the main thing. 'How on earth did you manage it?'

Dad grins and squeezes my hand. 'We did a runner. Didn't tell the hospital otherwise they'd have forbidden me to travel. Germs, you know.'

Mum links his arm. 'There was no point in me objecting, of course. You know what he's like.'

'I do. Stubborn as a mule, eh, Dad?'

'Hey, you two. Stop ganging up on me.'

'Can you stay over?'

Mum nods. 'We'll need to get back first thing in the morning, and we won't stay out here long. We just wanted to be here for you, love.'

'The treehouse looks incredible,' says Dad, his eyes suspiciously misty. 'I'm so proud of you, Twilight.' He pulls me into his side and gives me a surprisingly fierce hug, and I allow myself a happy tear or two.

It was Dad's creation and he approves of what Jake has done with it.

What more could I ask?

Chapter 38

The next morning, I'm up early, baking scones for our first day.

Mum and Dad take a taxi to the station early, and I get ready and join Betty and Doreen in the The Treehouse Café to prepare for opening time. I have butterflies in my stomach the size of flying dinosaurs.

Even though we had assurances last night from so many people that they loved the treehouse and couldn't wait to come along for coffee, I can't help remembering that last horrendous first day, when hardly anyone came ...

But I needn't have worried.

By eleven o'clock, the café has been full three times over! Betty was right to suggest we bake a little extra of everything, just in case. Because of her foresight, there's a chance we might not actually run out of cake by three o'clock.

Stocks are running extremely low by closing time, and it's just as well there was some of the WI's fruitcake left from the previous night. We watch the last pair of customers descend the walkway, laughing and looking back for one last glimpse of the treehouse before they head for their car.

Then Betty sinks down on a chair, slips off her shoes and puts her feet up with a sigh. 'Well, girls, I think you could definitely call today a triumph.'

'I have a feeling totting up the takings will confirm it.' Doreen smiles gleefully at me. 'I reckon your mum and dad can shelve their idea of selling Honey Cottage. For today, at least.'

I take off my apron and, with a great big 'whoop', throw it up into the air. 'Today has been absolutely amazing. And it's all thanks to you two.'

'Well, I think we're *all* brilliant.' Betty smiles, reaching out and patting my arm.

Doreen nods, then says wistfully, 'Shame we won't see that lovely lad, Jake, any more, though.'

Betty winks at me. 'I think Doreen's in love.'

'No, I'm not. His age would be a problem.'

I laugh. 'Too young for you?'

'On the contrary. A bit too old. I fancy myself a toy boy,' Doreen says solemnly. Then she gives a wicked grin and waves a dismissive hand at Betty. 'Don't look so horrified. I was only joking.'

'Well, I'm not,' Betty retorts. 'Twilight, have you got his telephone number?'

I grin at their double act. It's going to be great fun working with them. And I have a feeling The Treehouse Café will brighten up their retirement even more than Jake ...

*****

Apart from the plentiful takings, there's another reason I'm delighted I was rushed off my feet today: I really haven't had time to think about anything except customers, coffees and cakes.

It's only when I finally climb into bed, after baking up a

storm in the kitchen ready for the following day, that thoughts of Theo start pouring into my head.

Today has been magical. I couldn't have hoped for a better first day at the café. But despite this, I can't shake the slightly hollow feeling inside that casts a shadow over the brilliance of the day. If only I hadn't fallen for Theo ...

The next morning, I'm feeling nervous all over again that we may not get the customers through the door. But if anything, we're kept even busier than the day before, which is exhausting and makes Doreen's bunions ache, but we wouldn't have it any other way. Several people mention that friends had recommended The Treehouse Café to them, which is all very exciting. If word of mouth continues, there may be no need for advertising.

Paloma rings me at six, knowing I'll have closed up. 'So how did it go today, Miss Businesswoman of the Year? Have you made your fortune yet?' She sounds in high spirits.

'Brilliant. We were even busier than yesterday.'

'Wow, that's fabulous,' she squeaks. 'I'm so proud of you!'

'Fancy a drink at The Three Blackbirds?' I ask, mentioning the pub at the end of the high street. I'm feeling in the mood to celebrate after the success of our first few days.

Paloma's tone changes. 'Oh, Twi, I'd love to, but I can't. Maybe tomorrow night?'

'Ooh, what are you up to, then?'

There's a slight pause, and I start to wish I hadn't asked.

Then she says, 'Actually, I'm meeting someone. A client. Yes, he's a potential new client and I'm hoping to hit him with a pint of real ale and my brilliance as a graphic designer.'

'A powerful combination,' I murmur, not convinced she's telling me the truth. I keep thinking about her disappearing off the other night and returning minus lipstick. And Jake following soon after.

'When's your drink?' I ask casually.

'Eight.'

'Right, well, have a great time! I mean, I hope it's a productive meeting.'

'Oh, it will be,' she says happily, which makes me even more curious. *Why won't she admit she's seeing Jake?*

There's nothing else for it.

I'm going to have to follow her tonight to the pub and witness their lovers' tryst for myself ...

Chapter 39

My plan is to finish off the baking then head down to The Three Blackbirds just before eight to catch Paloma and Jake in the act of going on a date.

I get all my baking equipment out, then I realise to my irritation that I've run out of plain flour for the scones the next day. Grabbing my purse, I dash out to catch the local mini supermarket before it closes.

It's been another humid day and once outside, I immediately sense a change in the air, as if a storm is brewing. I glance anxiously overhead, and sure enough, clouds are gathering, obscuring the sun. They're dark and threatening. I need to grab the flour and get straight home before the storm hits.

Coming out of the store, I'm focusing so hard on getting home fast that I practically mow down someone coming in.

Lucy.

'Oh, hi,' she says in her grating voice. 'I gather your launch went well, despite the little problem with the Pavlovas?'

I smile frostily. 'News travels fast. Yes, it was a huge success actually.'

'Well, good for you. I suppose you've heard the news about me and Jason? We're off to Paris next week to find a place to live.'

She looks so smug, I want to slap her. But I need to get home, away from the storm, and brawling with Lucy would hold me up.

So I smile sweetly. 'I hope you'll be very happy in Paris. With Jason. Must dash.'

Leaving her standing there, I glance up at the darkening sky and hurry for home.

What a piece of work Lucy is! Preening over getting back with Jason, when actually, it was probably her dad's offer of a job for Jason that swung it for her! And how the hell did the nosy cow find out about the Pavlovas?

I walk on, thinking about this. How *did* she find out? Betty, Doreen and I agreed we wouldn't tell anyone, so she must have spoken to someone from the Women's Institute.

Unless …

No, surely not.

My mind starts working overtime, mulling over something that seems totally unbelievable …

Could Lucy have switched off the fridge?

Now I think about it, there was a certain superior smile on her face when she mentioned our Pavlova disaster. Almost a triumphant look.

She told me there was a van outside the house and I hurried off to see who it was, leaving the café door unlocked. But there *was* no van! Oh my God, Lucy could easily have doubled back and sneaked in to do her dirty work with the fridge. I told Jason about the delicate Pavlovas in the fridge – he must have mentioned this innocently to Lucy and then she concocted her plan!

If it was anyone else, I'd think I was going mad even entertaining this theory.

But this is Lucy, so it's absolutely possible. Not only possible, but highly likely ...

I stop in my tracks, my head whirling with sheer incredulity. She must really hate me to go to such extreme lengths. But what have I ever done to her to deserve it?

I recall Jason saying there were things I didn't know about her. Things that, if I knew them, might make me understand her better.

But what things?

An urge to know suddenly grips me. I need to find out once and for all why she hates me so much!

A rumble of thunder in the distance turns my insides to water. But as I stand there, shocked to the core by Lucy's latest antics (and thoroughly dismayed at myself for not suspecting anything), I'm torn in two.

I want to race home to relative safety, out of the way of the storm. But something has reached boiling point deep within.

Glancing back, I spot Lucy coming out of the shop and heading in the opposite direction. Watching her jaunty, self-satisfied walk, I want to run after her and yell, 'Why, Lucy? Why am I the target of your breathtakingly spiteful behaviour?'

I hesitate.

She's not worth the bother. She's going to Paris soon and I won't have to worry about bumping into her in the street any more.

I should just go home.

But for some reason, I don't. I stay right where I am.

Lucy Slater is a bully. Pure and simple. And bullies are cowards. Face up to them and they're likely to back off.

I saw that in Lucy's eyes when she fell off the fence that

time. There was a split second before she fell into the trough when fear flashed across her face. She thought the worm had turned and she was shocked.

And scared ...

In a burst of clarity, I see that Lucy has lost her weird power over me. I'm seeing her clearly for the very first time. She's a sad, insecure person who needs to hit out to demonstrate her power over others.

I turn and start walking in the opposite direction, peering around pedestrians, searching for Lucy. Catching a fleeting glimpse of her up ahead, I quicken my step. I'm gaining on her but if I don't hurry, she'll reach her car and drive off, and then I'll have lost my opportunity.

I start to run as warm rain starts splashing down. 'Lucy!'

She half-glances behind her but keeps on walking, so I pick up speed, my heart pounding with the exertion and the sudden determination that's gripping me.

One last burst of speed and I catch up, running alongside her, shaking moisture from my hair. My face feels red and hot, despite the fat raindrops that are pattering down. Lucy looks at me, a mix of shock and bewilderment on her face.

Then her expression darkens. '*What?*'

'It was you who switched off the fridge, wasn't it?' I pant.

She shrugs and walks on.

'Just tell me what I've done to you,' I demand.

Her brow furrows as if she doesn't understand what I'm talking about.

'You said before that I'd done something to you that was best forgotten. What was it because I'm being honest here when I say I really haven't a clue how I can possibly have offended you.'

Her mouth is set in a firm line. She's refusing to look at me.

'Is it because of Jason? Because Jason and I happened years ago and I can tell you quite sincerely that there is nothing romantic going on between us. There hasn't been since we were eighteen and he broke up with me to be with you.'

Her look is sceptical, to say the least.

'Are you really jealous of me and Jason? Because there's absolutely no need to be.'

'Why would I believe that?' she demands.

I swallow. 'Easy. Because it's not Jason I'm in love with. I'm actually crazily, madly in love with someone else, okay? So you can stop your evil conniving and go torment someone else for a change!'

'You've got no idea!' She spits out the words.

I'm straining to hear her over the noise of the downpour. A bolt of lightning directly overhead sends a chill through me. 'What do you mean?'

She rounds on me, her eyes flashing with rage. 'I *mean*, I'm never ever going to forget what you and Jason did to me.'

I stare at her. 'What did we do to you?'

She says something else, but a giant rumble of thunder drowns out her words. She starts running towards her car.

'Lucy! What the hell did we do to you? Tell me! Because whatever you think we did, I can guarantee it didn't happen.'

'Oh, really?' she sneers, her eyes full of hatred. 'So you were there in the hospital on the night of the school leavers' ball, were you?'

A cold hand grips my insides. 'Hospital? What do you mean?'

She shakes her head and goes to get in her car, but I grab

hold of the handle before she does. 'Why were you in the hospital? I thought you were at home with a sprained ankle.'

'Let go!' she yells, scratching at my hand on the door handle.

'No! Not until you tell me what the hell you're talking about!'

'Get lost, you bitch! You ruined everything.'

The rain is pelting down furiously now. I glance up and as I do so, another huge fork of lightning splits the sky, illuminating everything around us, including Lucy's agonised, tear-stained face.

'Come on, then. How did I ruin things?' I shout.

'You think Jason is such a great guy, don't you? But you don't know him like I do.'

'What do you mean?'

'He wasn't faithful to you the whole time, you know. We slept together and you never found out. He was the first boy I had sex with. Six weeks before the school leavers' ball. And guess what? He told me that night that you and he were more or less over and that he was going to leave you for me.'

I stare at her. I don't believe it. She must be making it up. But my stomach feels curdled all the same.

'You don't believe me, do you? But he did say that. And then, guess what? The next day he told me he'd changed his mind and that you were the love of his life.'

I swallow hard, trying to take it in, as the deluge of raindrops continues to pepper my scalp, pouring over my already sodden hair. Water is running into my eyes and I flick it away.

I feel sick. I can't believe Jason kept all this a secret from me. I shake my head slowly, swallowing down the nausea. 'So he was unfaithful once. He wouldn't be the only guy in the world who made a mistake.'

'Yes, but you don't know the best bit,' she snarls, right in my face. 'After that night with Jason, I found out I was pregnant. And I was thrilled because I thought that if I had his baby, he would have to choose *me*. But guess what?'

'What?' A feeling of foreboding trickles through me.

'He made me get rid of it.'

'What?' I stare at her in horror. 'You're lying. Jason wouldn't do that. I know he wouldn't.'

She shrugs. 'Well, he didn't actually march me along to a doctor and demand he get me an appointment at the abortion clinic. But he made it very clear he thought it was a bad idea me having the baby.'

'You ... you *were* only sixteen.'

She sneers. 'I might have known you'd take his side.'

I shake my head. 'I'm not taking sides. It's just really sad.'

'Tell me about it!' she yells. 'The night you and Jason were having such a lovely time together at the school leavers' ball, I was in hospital having his baby surgically removed from my womb!'

My head is reeling with shock. We stare at each other, rain streaming down our faces.

It feels so surreal, having this conversation with Lucy while the storm rages around us. I know instinctively that she's telling the truth. I can see it in her face. And I feel such a fool for thinking of Jason in such glowing terms all these years. When I was a teenager, I thought he was Mr Perfect, and that never really changed, even when we went our separate ways. They say love makes you blind. Well, he certainly pulled the wool over my eyes about his involvement with Lucy.

I remember the time in the treehouse before the ball, telling Paloma I thought Jason was going off me. I'd been right in a way. He'd obviously had his fling with Lucy and was feeling really guilty about everything. Guilty over her. And guilty over me.

'Christ, I'm sorry, Lucy.' I feel genuinely bad for her. For the way she was treated by Jason, who obviously found himself torn between the two of us. He chose me and that must have crucified Lucy. I can almost understand why she must hate me. She probably blames me for losing her baby.

Yet she's forgiven Jason. She still loves him.

'If it weren't for you,' she yells, 'Jason would probably have stayed with me after I got pregnant. I'd have had the baby. *Our* baby. He would have been thirteen now. A teenager.'

'You knew it was a boy?'

Her shoulders slump. 'No. I just always feel it was a boy. A boy who looked just like Jason.'

My heart lurches at her agonised expression. 'You – you can have more babies.'

'Well, it hasn't happened so far, has it?' Her chin wobbles with emotion. 'Maybe that was my one and only chance to be a mother.'

I shake my head, feeling – against all the odds – incredibly sad for her.

Lucy says stiffly, 'Can I get in my car now, please?'

I let go of the handle.

We exchange a look. It's as if all the anger between us has burned itself out, leaving just an aching sadness.

Lucy's face suddenly crumples with emotion. She jerks open the car door, gets in and drives away, crashing the gears as she rounds a bend and disappears from view.

I walk home, shivering and drenched to the skin, my head whirling with everything she told me. So much grief and bitterness. And yet she still loves Jason. It's hard to understand, yet the conclusion I finally draw is that at least they have each other, for better or for worse ...

Back home, I stand under a hot shower for a long time, thinking about the past and how cruel people can be to each other. And marvelling at how I'd placed Jason on a pedestal, thinking of him as the perfect man, only to have the scales fall from my eyes so completely after what Lucy told me.

As I'm getting out of the shower, my mobile rings.

It's Mum and she can hardly get her words out. My heart starts beating fast. Is it bad news?

In the end, I say, 'Slow down, Mum. I can't hear what you're saying.'

'It's your dad.' Her voice sounds all breathy. 'We've just talked to the consultant and the tumour has shrunk.' She laughs. 'Can you believe it? The consultant, Mr Hobbs, never smiles. But he did today and that's how I knew it was good news, even before he said anything ...'

Mum chatters on and I stand there with no clothes on in the middle of my bedroom, listening to her in disbelief, with happy tears running down my face. Then I realise the curtains are open and the bedside lamp is on and Mrs Savage from over the road can probably see me in all my glory, so I dash to swish them shut.

After I've ended the call, I dance around the room, still entirely naked. My heart feels as if it's expanded to twice the size. I really need to see Paloma to tell her everything that's happened tonight! I'd decided not to bother crashing her meeting at the pub. But now, I can't wait to see her to tell her my great news ...

*****

I feel a bit silly lurking in the bushes round the back of The Three Blackbirds. But I'm actually burning with curiosity to see Paloma and Jake together.

It's five minutes to eight; she should be along any minute. Paloma is always punctual for business meetings – not that I believe she's meeting a client, despite what she told me.

I'm close to the pub's back entrance, which everyone tends to use, I guess because it leads straight from the car park. Paloma will be on foot, but old habits die hard. Also, Jake will have transport, having driven up from the south coast.

I hear a familiar laugh and Paloma appears round the corner of the building. She's on her phone and instead of walking straight into the pub, she lingers outside while she waits for the person on the other end of the phone to answer. I hold my breath. She's standing only ten yards from my hiding place.

The person takes his time answering. But eventually I hear her say, 'Hello, you! Are you on your way?' Her voice sounds seductive, intimate. The way you sound when you absolutely can't wait to see him.

The way you sound when you're newly in love, perhaps?

I've got a pesky tickle in my nose, but I rub it hard and it goes away.

Paloma gives a low chuckle and says, 'You're here already? Oh my God, can you actually believe what's happening to us? It fees unreal. My head is all over the place. I don't think I've ever felt so ... I don't know, *elated*! She laughs. 'It's lovely to know you feel the same.'

There's another pause, then: 'You mean you can't wait all of three seconds for me to join you in there?'

My heart beats faster. He's coming out. Jake is coming out!

A dark shape appears in the little porch, half-hidden from

view. Paloma smiles up at him and holds out her arms. And he walks right into them.

And a spasm of shock grips me. It's not Jake who's pulling her to him as if he'll never let her go.

It's Theo ...

I feel faint; it's just *so* not what I was expecting to see. Theo wrapped around *Paloma*? It can't be happening. I knew she *liked* Theo – but she never gave me any indication that she cared for him in that way!

I swallow on the lump of misery in my throat, watching them break apart and laugh, while still clinging to each other. Perhaps she's guessed how I feel about Theo myself, and that's why she's kept this meeting a secret.

My nose tickles – worse this time – and I rub it furiously.

But next second, an enormous sneeze surges out. In the silence of the night, it sounds deafening and they both swing round. Paloma flicks the light on her phone and then it's shining on my guilty face and they're both looking at me with startled expressions. As well they might.

Theo takes a step towards me.

'Twilight?' says Paloma, wonderingly. 'What on earth are you doing there?'

I glance miserably from her to Theo and back again. 'I was – er – looking for my purse.' I dig it out of my bag and hold it up. 'But now I've found it. Have a nice night!' And I flee from the pub car park, just wanting to escape their bemused and pitying looks. I hear Theo shouting after me, and a moment later, Paloma joins in. But I'm jogging along the high street by this time, heading for home, and I'm there in under a minute.

As I fumble to get the key in the lock, I reflect that at least I have one thing to be happy about. I've never been fitter!

All the better for running away from scenes that would break your heart into a million pieces ...

*****

I'm already hiding under the covers when the doorbell rings.

It shrills out three times with a pause in between. Then my mobile starts ringing. Quickly, I reach out a hand, fumble around for the offending object on the bedside table, and turn it off.

The last thing I want to do right now is have a discussion with Paloma and Theo *about* Paloma and Theo! I'm still trying to process the whole thing. I'd rather get over the shock and have time to practise my 'delighted-for-you' face so that neither of them ever knows that my heart has been unceremoniously ripped into pieces.

A single warm tear leaks out of my eye and is absorbed by the duvet that's wrapped tightly around me, in spite of the summer night's sticky heat.

*****

Somehow I manage to sleep, and when I wake next morning, it's to the sun blazing through the curtains and someone banging on the door.

When I turn on my phone, I've got twenty-six missed calls.

Paloma shouts through the letter slot. 'Twi, please let me in. I'm worried about you. We both are.'

A lump fills my throat at her casual mention of 'we'. They're obviously a couple already.

She tries again. 'I've got news I think you'd like to hear.'

I stare glumly through the chink in the curtains. I'd beg to differ, to be honest. But I suppose I have to face up to it at some point. I can't stay in bed for the rest of my life ...

Dragging myself up, I peer down onto the driveway. And Paloma chooses that moment to give up and turn away, so I have to bang on the window to attract her attention. Better get this over with. I've got a café to open in an hour.

I go to the door, plastering on a smile before I pull it open. 'Hi! Sorry about last night. Behaving so weirdly. I was overtired, I think.'

Can people behave like trainee psychopaths when they're overtired? I suppose it's possible.

'That's okay.' She takes my hand and leads me gently into the living room, as if I'm a five-year-old who's lost her favourite stuffed rabbit. I plop down on the sofa.

The smile is still in place. It's starting to ache a bit. 'So!' I say cheerily. 'You and Theo, eh? Wow, I'd never have guessed.'

She beams at me. 'I know. Me neither. It all happened so suddenly.'

I smile harder.

'One minute, I have no family at all,' she laughs. 'And the next, I have a gorgeous half-brother!'

Chapter 40

I stare blearily at her, feeling as if my brain has gone numb. Paloma's face is wreathed in smiles and tears of joy are pooling in her eyes.

'I'm sorry,' I say slowly, 'But I thought you just said *Theo's your half-brother*?'

She nods and the tears burst their banks. 'He is. I've been waiting for the results of the DNA test we did. And yesterday they arrived and it's true! Theo is my half-brother.'

Light is starting to glimmer through the darkness.

Theo is *related* to Paloma? No wonder they were so pleased to see each other last night.

'But – but *how*?' I stammer. 'I mean, how did you realise? *When* did you realise you might be related?' I shake my head. 'It's all so ... unbelievable!'

She slides along the sofa and grasps my hands. 'Isn't it? I'm so sorry I couldn't tell you. I just wanted to keep it to myself until I knew it was true.'

My head is spinning but I manage to mutter a coherent reply. 'Hey, don't apologise. I totally understand. You got your hopes up about your birth mum, then you found out she'd ...'

A flicker of sadness crosses her face. 'That's exactly why I was cautious this time,' she murmurs. 'Because that ... disappointment ... was horrendous.'

I squeeze her hands. 'It must have been.'

'I couldn't even talk about it to you; it was such a shock. She died in a house fire when she was only forty-two, along with her husband. She'd married by then, you see.'

'Oh God, how terrible.' My heart aches for her. *To have discovered where her birth mum lived and then to find out something so tragic ...*

She sits up, visibly brightening. 'What I didn't know at the time was that after she had me, my birth mum went on to have another child. I ran out on that woman, Sylvia, before she had a chance to tell me. But I went back later and had a proper chat about Mum. Sylvia knew a few people who remembered her. She was really kind. And she told me that when Mum got married, two years after having me adopted when she was sixteen, her surname changed to Steel and she and her husband had one son.'

My eyes widen in amazement.

'It was the day of the run when I had a breakthrough,' she rushes on excitedly. 'You remember when I had to gather in sponsorship forms for Lucy? Well, that's when I saw Theo's full name for the first time. Theo Steel. In black capital letters. I thought I was going to faint right there on the spot! So later, I plucked up courage to ask him some casual questions about his family and he said his parents died when he was young. And then Olivia asked him how he lost them both at the same time and he told us they died in a house fire when he was eighteen.' She beams at me. 'So then, of course, I knew it must be him!'

A memory dawns on me. 'I saw you that day, talking with

Theo and Olivia. I saw the expression on your face. You must have just stumbled on the truth. That Theo was your half-brother!'

She nods. 'That was when he told us about the fire, and I knew.' Tears are running down her face, and I pull her into a tight hug, my own throat choked with emotion for my lovely best friend, who deserves this so much after everything she's been through in her life.

I'm so wrapped up in her happiness, it's a few moments more before I realise what this means for me.

If Theo is Paloma's half-brother, Theo and I are always going to be connected. It's bittersweet, though, knowing we can never be together ...

I get Paloma a paper hanky and she mops her face. Then she sits back and smiles. 'So, enough about me. What about Jason?'

I grin. 'He's back with Lucy would you believe? But I really don't mind,' I add quickly, when her face falls. 'Honestly, I don't.'

It's probably time I told my best friend that the reason I don't mind is because I'm madly in love with her half-brother! God, what a mess!

Paloma nods firmly. 'He was never totally right for you anyway.' She grimaces. 'Actually, I've got something else to tell you.'

I stare at her. '*More* revelations?'

She nods, looking guilty. 'I know I keep saying I can't stand Jake, but it turns out there really must be a fine line between love and hate.'

'You *love* him?'

'No!' She laughs. 'At least, not yet. Give us time. But we *are* desperately in lust.'

'Why didn't you tell me?'

She shrugs. 'I wouldn't admit it to myself, never mind anyone else. I thought he was far too like Knob-Head Rufus – you know, arrogant artist, up his own arse – and I should give him a wide berth if I knew what was good for me. But when I was doing his website work, he sort of won me round.'

I burst out laughing and start singing, 'I knew it! I knew it!'

'Did you?'

'You were quite obviously snogging in the garden on launch night! You both looked so hilariously furtive coming back up to join everyone. *Separately*. I was watching from the tree-house.'

After we've laughed about that and I've told her the brilliant news about Dad, we go through to the kitchen to make coffee and she says, 'So that's my love life sorted. But what about you?'

I feel my face flushing. 'What about me? I'm fine on my own, thank you very much.' I turn my back on her and start spooning coffee into two mugs.

She peers at me. 'Twi? You've just put four spoons of coffee in there.'

'Oh, shit, have I?'

'Twi? Is there something you're not telling me? There is, isn't there? Oh my God, it's Theo, isn't it! That's why you were behaving so oddly last night, lurking in the bushes.'

My goofy smile says it all.

She throws back her head and appeals to the ceiling. 'Why on earth didn't I guess?'

Sitting forward, her eyes shining, she says, 'Theo is single. So what are you going to do about it?'

I shake my head miserably. 'He thinks he's jinxed.'

She frowns. 'Oh God, I know. He told me all about his fiancée and the baby. He's had so much sorrow in his personal relationships, he's afraid of getting involved again. But maybe you'd be the one to change his mind?'

'Hang on.' I stare at her. 'What did you say? There was a *baby*?'

She nods. 'Rachel died in hospital being treated for pre-eclampsia. The baby died, too.'

I'm too stunned to speak. Poor Theo. How much loss can one person bear?

She frowns. 'Actually, there's something else you need to know,' she says and I can tell from her face I'm not going to like it.

'Theo needs to go where the work is if he wants to pursue his career as a translator. He told me last night. He's moving to London.'

Chapter 41

When Paloma leaves, I head for bed, feeling as if the bottom has fallen out of my world.

So that's that, then. Theo is leaving for London, and any stupid dreams I might have had of us getting together have been well and truly crushed. Worse, I can't help the sneaking suspicion that I'm part of the reason he's leaving.

I trail through the day, trying to put on a brave face, reminding myself every time I'm on the verge of tears that Dad is getting better and The Treehouse Café is turning out to be an amazing success. After missing the reporter that time because I was judging cakes in the WI tent, she finally caught up with me the other day, and there's a story in today's local newspaper all about the new café, with gorgeous photos of the treehouse.

When we close up the café later, I try calling Paloma but she's either not there or on the phone already. I mooch around, watching a bit of TV and trying to eat something. Finally, at around seven, the doorbell goes and it's Paloma.

'Come on. We're going out for that drink,' she says bossily. 'Get out of those sloppy trackies.'

I groan and shake my head. 'I really don't feel like it. Look, come in and I'll open a bottle of wine and—'

'No! We're going out.' She smiles. 'Sorry. It's just I think it would do you good. We can talk about Theo.'

Tears fill my eyes. I'm too weak to argue.

Fifteen minutes later, we're in the pub and I'm swigging down wine like it's going out of fashion, wishing she'd stop going on about Theo and how lovely he is. I mean, I already know that. Obviously. So why is she being so insensitive?

Then I realise it's my fault for being too self-absorbed. Paloma's only just discovered Theo's her half-brother, for goodness' sake. She's perfectly entitled to chatter on and on about him, even if it is slowly driving me nuts.

The wine helps, though, making me more relaxed. And by the time we head home, more than three hours later, I'm actually feeling quite mellow.

Things will be fine. I'll concentrate on making The Treehouse Café an even bigger success. Betty was even talking about approaching bus tour operators to see if they'd like a unique treehouse coffee stop for their holiday-maker clients. I think it's a great idea ...

All the same, as I trail up the stairs to bed, my heart feels like a lead weight. It will be impossible to stop thoughts of Theo sneaking into my head day and night, taking me unawares when I'm trying to concentrate on the café. And it's not even as if I can banish him from my life and eventually get over him. As in out of sight, out of mind. Because as long as Paloma is my best friend, Theo is always going to be there.

My mobile goes. It's Paloma and I pick up.

'You've left a light on in the treehouse,' she says, without preamble.

'What?'

'You need to go and switch it off. It's a waste of electricity.'

I go to the window and peer out. 'There's no light on.'

'Yes, there is. Keep looking.'

I stare out into the darkness, wondering what on earth she's talking about because the treehouse is in pitch darkness.

And then the magic happens.

In the blink of an eye, The Treehouse Café is lit with hundreds of fairy lights, winking like stars against the black night sky.

I gasp. 'Oh my God. It's so beautiful. But how ... *who*? Did you organise this?'

She chuckles. 'It's a gift from someone special. We called Jake and he came round to set it up. I had to get you out of the house tonight for as long as I could, but he finished just in time. I'm surprised you didn't catch Jake's van driving off.'

My heart starts beating very fast. 'Where are you?'

'By your garden gate, but I'm going home now.'

I pause, swallowing hard, trying not to get my hopes up. 'Who's the someone special?'

'Go down and see. He's waiting for you, beside The Treehouse Café.' And she rings off.

With my legs feeling like jelly, I go downstairs and out through the back door, then I make my way slowly down the garden, heart beating crazily, hardly daring to hope ...

When I reach the treehouse, a man steps out of the shadows to meet me and my heart lurches.

Theo.

He's smiling at me with such warmth, my stomach flips over. 'You said you wanted lights. So now you've got lights. Do you like them?'

My heart is bumping crazily. Just hearing his gorgeous voice is enough to make my whole body quiver. 'I love them. They're ... just perfect.'

He bridges the gap between us, smoothing a lock of hair back from my face ever so gently, and a shiver of desire runs through me.

'I couldn't understand why I wasn't interested in getting to know Olivia better,' he murmurs. 'Then I realised it was because you were in my head and I couldn't even think of anyone else.'

I swallow hard. 'Really?' The single word comes out as a rather unattractive squeak but thankfully, he doesn't seem to be turned off. On the contrary, he pulls me against him and I collapse weakly on his chest, my head spinning at his glorious scent and his nearness.

'Are you going to work in London?' I manage to ask, pulling away slightly but still mesmerised by his beautiful mouth.

'Not any more.'

A feeling of utter relief courses through me. 'What made you change your mind?'

'Well, Paloma came to see me. My *half-sister*.' He chuckles, still clearly amazed at the discovery. 'She said I had a choice. I could either live in the past, dwelling on all the bad things that had happened to me and thinking I was cursed. Or I could do the sensible thing and be brave enough to walk into my future with hope.'

'And what did you decide to do?' I stop breathing, waiting for his reply.

He smiles and pulls me against him again, and my heart melts as he gazes into my eyes.

'I chose a hopeful future. With you. If you'll have me.'

My laugh is filled with joy and relief. 'I thought you'd never ask.'

Then his mouth comes down on mine and there's no more talking for quite some time ...

Two ex-friends. One Christmas to remember...

A funny, heartwarming read - the perfect book for fans of Jenny Colgan and Lucy Diamond.

Can Izzy sort the wheat from the chaff and the men from the boys?

When Izzy Fraser's long-term boyfriend walks out on her, she decides to take matters into her own hands...with unexpected consequences!

Lola Plumpton can't believe her luck. Until, of course, her luck runs out...

A warm and cosy festive tale you won't be able to put down.

Wedding season isn't always smooth sailing...

A funny, feel-good read about weddings gone wrong...